The Rose and the Crane

Clint Dohmen

ISBN: 0692930647
ISBN 13: 9780692930649
Library of Congress Control Number: 2017913570
Clint Dohmen, Torrance, CA

For Sakura.

(Thank you for all the breaks from pecking away at my keyboard with two fingers.)

Acknowledgements

It's like Mona Lisa Vito was speaking to me in the movie "My Cousin Vinny," when she said, "You can't even win a case by yourself, you're fuckin' useless." Well, I couldn't have gotten this novel to print without the extensive help of the following people: Jessica Hatch, my editor; Masayo Ozawa at abombinabull for her wonderful cover art; Simon Fellowes, history teacher extraordinaire from the land of the white rose; my brother Duncan Hobart Dohmen for checking my Japanese; Ms. Mizuho Bando at Osaka City University for checking my Japanese history; Prof. Hiroshi Niki, Prof. Nobutoshi Shimizu and Hideo Kawabata Sensei; and finally, Kevin Lang and Roxanne Lott who read all umpteen million of my drafts and managed to offer advice and encouragement after every one. I apologize for anyone I'm missing, but I have the memory of a gnat (a particularly memory-challenged one at that). It is not because I'm not grateful. Any historical "adjustments," are the product of my artistic license and not the fault of anyone above.

Chapter I

South of the Western Coast of Honshu, Japan, January, 1483

SIMON LANG DIDN'T think he had many days left as pilot of the Venetian carrack *Tigre*. Not that he was going to get fired, he'd be right hard to replace out here. Out here, being somewhere that was not China but was probably China-adjacent. Now, China-adjacent was fine if you were Chinese and knew your way around. Not so much if you were an English pilot who had never been to China, much less to China-adjacent. No, he thought his piloting days were numbered because he would probably be dead soon.

It wasn't all doom and gloom, though. Fortunately, the *Tigre* was blessed with a seaman who had been amongst Venice's shrewdest gamblers, known particularly for his talent at odds-making. This morning Simon had awoken to find that he had moved up two places, and was now rated as: third least likely to die. Only Neno, the ox of a first mate, and the odds-maker himself were better wagers to outlive Simon now. There were also two more pleasing trends on the odds board since the typhoon. First, everyone's life expectancy had increased by a few days. Second, the heavy favorite in cause of death had transitioned rapidly from dehydration, through drowning, and was now pegged at starvation. Simon thought starvation sounded a trifle more agreeable than the prior two favorites. Of course, both were a considerable improvement over "eaten," which had occasionally made an appearance at the top of the board. In giving it further consideration, he came to the conclusion that he'd have to keep his wits about him while he starved to death to ensure that "eaten" did not reappear on the board due to "starvation."

The shift to starvation as likeliest cause of death doubtless accounted for First Mate Neno Mocenigo's newfound status as most likely to live the longest. Neno could drop the weight of three people and still be as big as two. The colossal Venetian stood over six feet six inches and weighed in at a natural two hundred and seventy pounds. Taking size into consideration, it was a mystery to Simon why that same rationale hadn't given the ship's captain a commensurate jump in anticipated longevity. Sure, Captain Aldo Mitachionne's paunch had been reduced, but he was working from a not-insignificant head start. Perhaps the odds-maker held a grudge against the captain for some slight, and it was influencing his professionalism. *I think I'll bet the captain to outlive the odds-maker later this afternoon.* Simon smiled at the thought.

Giacomo Aversa would still be a Venetian bookmaker of note if it hadn't been for an unfortunate piece of betting luck. Prior to his jaunt on the *Tigre*, Giacomo had wagered correctly on the untimely demise of Pietro Barbo, more commonly known as Pope Paul II. Betting on papal appointments was a popular distraction for all levels of Venetian society, but for nearly a century, betting on their demise had been forbidden (and more lucrative). When news broke that the Venetian-born pontiff had died (a result of his gluttonous appetite for either food or altar boys, depending on whom you asked), Giacomo was briefly wealthy; very briefly. An anonymous tip (likely from his competition) led to the seizure of his assets, and after a brief stint in jail, bookmaker Aversa emerged as soon-to-become seaman Aversa. Slightly built, spry in the riggings, and sharp of mind, he had transitioned well to his new vocation.

It was seaman Aversa in the crow's nest who first spotted the squat, single-masted ship in the distance off the starboard bow. He rang the small bell attached to his perch and called out his unexpected discovery: "Ship, right ahead."

Yajuro Ueda stood stiff and unmoving as the wind-driven waves rocked his ship. Yajuro was not happy with his place in life. The taste of salt on his tongue, and the intermittent spray of seawater in his face, did not appeal to him. Yajuro liked his feet planted on solid ground. The men called him captain, but the title was empty. Yajuro was a glorified mule driver. His mule was a boat, and his cargo included grand treasures, but in his heart, Yajuro knew he was no better than a peasant mule driver.

Before losing an arm to the ignoble Hosokawa hirelings, Yajuro had been a samurai of regard. Now he lived as one to be pitied. And pity he had been shown with this mission. Were it not for his storied reputation on the battlefield, he would doubtless be a one-armed beggar at home in Yamaguchi. Yajuro was not ungrateful that the mighty Ouchi clan's leader had seen fit to give him this assignment, but it did little to restore his pride in himself.

Yajuro remonstrated against his own self-pitying. After all, the blow to his clan's pride at being forced from Kyoto was of far greater consequence than any of his trivial personal concerns. The Ouchi clan may have chosen the wrong side in the war for shogunal succession, but they had not been defeated on the field of battle. The loot that came aboard his ship after the sacking of Kyoto was only a minor token towards soothing the pain of that lost pride. It was a much-delayed final shipment from a war that had ended years earlier, but war cost money and this shipment was as valuable as all those that had preceded it.

The ship's hold also contained an unexpected bounty that Yajuro's lord was not yet aware of: two Hosokawa samurai who, based on their clothes, were clearly highborn. Given his daimyo's proclivity for beheading his enemies, Yajuro thought his little gift might help earn him a better detail in the next war. *And there would be a next war.* A weak shogun had been the initial cause of the civil war in Kyoto, and although that war was now over, very little was actually settled by it. The new shogun had no means of enforcing his will upon the country, and like the Ouchi, every clan of substance was armed to the teeth.

This was of course all speculation, and predicated on his safe return to Yamaguchi. In sizing up the huge, bizarrely crafted vessel bearing down on him now, he was not convinced that was a certainty. "What is that?" Yajuro shouted over the gusting wind to the samurai standing next to him.

"It is a ship," the samurai obediently replied.

Yajuro gave him an intense glare. "I know it is a ship, you simpleton. I want to know what *kind* of ship and, more importantly, *whose* ship?" *When you pound obedience into a man's skull, common sense often becomes collateral damage,* Yajuro lamented.

"*Sumimasen*," the samurai quickly apologized, "*shirimasen*." *I don't know.*

The approaching ship had a wide belly, raised deck structures both fore and aft, and three tall masts supporting larger sails than Yajuro had seen in his life. Yajuro had heard of monstrously sized Chinese ships, but none of those descriptions resembled what he was looking at. The samurai who stood on the upper deck with Yajuro were all as dumbstruck as their captain. Yajuro's vision was not what it used to be, and the crusted saltwater stinging his eyes did not help matters. "Can you see the flag?" Yajuro asked the same young samurai that he had previously queried.

"*Hai*," the samurai said promptly.

Yajuro glanced at the samurai and waited for more detail. It did not come. Scowling at the boy, who looked to be about seventeen, he exploded. "Well, what do you see?"

"A golden beast, perhaps a winged boar? It is holding a sword," the samurai replied hurriedly.

A winged boar? Who would put wings on a boar? I have never heard of any family crest with such markings, Yajuro thought. He studied the ship as it drew closer.

"What are those?" Yajuro asked, pointing his finger towards the vessel's side, though at this point he knew all his questions for the young samurai would be rhetorical. The ship seemed to have several round black barrels protruding through cutout sections in the deck's railing.

"*Wakarimasen.*" *I'm not sure,* the samurai replied, fully living up to Yajuro's expectations.

Yajuro, though, did have an idea what they were. He'd heard descriptions of the Chinese having black iron tubes that fired projectiles, and even though he'd never heard of them being used on ships before, he'd also never seen a ship that looked anything like this one. In an effort to hide the concern creeping into his own mind, Yajuro made a concentrated effort to deepen his voice as he shouted to his crew. "Make haste for the coast immediately!"

It was the only option he had. The hulking ship did not look like it could follow him into shallower waters. Yajuro set off to inspire the rowers.

"*Porca puttana*!" Captain Mitachionne yelled as the only ship they'd seen in weeks doubled its oar strokes and began to row north, away from them.

Simon was reasonably sure Aldo was referring to the ungainly looking ship they were trying to hail, but Aldo had been looking directly at him when he said it, and it was certainly plausible, based on Simon's past indiscretions, that the captain was referring to him. Simon cocked an eyebrow. "A whore, sure, but a pig-whore, really? I must protest."

"Not you, idiot Englishman," Aldo spat.

"I should say not."

"I would never demean a noble and intelligent animal in such a way. Unlike you, a pig has some redeeming characteristics."

Aldo looked his pilot over. Simon was twenty-five years old, tall at a shade over six feet, overly skinny (in Aldo's estimation), but with wide shoulders and a stout chest that even starvation hadn't diminished. An unruly, brownish-blond mop of cowlicks perched atop a scarred forehead, followed by high cheekbones, penetrating blue eyes, and a square jaw. As advertised, he had proven to be a superb pilot who had done a remarkable job of navigating uncharted waters all the way from the Red Sea. He was also a magnificent swordsman and an amusing drinking companion. *Well, maybe one or two redeeming characteristics,* Aldo thought, *but I'll never tell him that.*

Simon smiled for the second time that day. No small thing when starvation necessitated a concentrated effort just to move the muscles in his cheeks. His formerly portly, grand mustachioed captain-cum-business-partner was in fine form. This business venture of sailing to China to purchase silk and spice at its source may not have had a solid foundation in prudence, but it certainly had a solid foundation in companionability.

Aldo continued his rant. "They will not even pause briefly to see what grand bargains I can offer them? I'll give them armor to outfit their whole crew if they've got a barrel of wine aboard."

"I'll give them all the gaudy decorations in your cabin if they have two," Simon chimed in.

"I'd give them the wool equivalent of the sheep that have spent time in your bedroom for three."

"I'm English, not Welsh! Or God forbid, Scottish," Simon protested.

"Same thing, *Inglese*."

"Bloody well is not." But Aldo was closer to the mark than Simon liked to admit. Although the Lang family had ruled in Exeter for generations before the Yorkists killed his father, murdered his mother, and seized their lands, Simon well knew his mother's ancestry was Welsh. He'd spent far too many days of his youth in the cold, clammy castles of his aunts and uncles to forget that regrettable side of his lineage. Were he less conceited about his "Englishness," he might be thankful for the broad, powerful shoulders and thick chest that were a product of his Welsh blood.

"Kindly run those gentlemen down, and bring me close enough that I can have a word with their captain," Aldo ordered his pilot.

While their carrack was not the sleekest of ships, Simon could tell by the single bank of oars, wide, boxlike appearance, and lone, square-rigged mast that the other ship was not built for speed. With a comfortable wind blowing, they would have little difficulty overtaking it.

Yajuro was now disturbed. It was becoming clear that they wouldn't reach the coast before the strange ship reached them. And his ship carried treasures that needed protecting. With practiced mental discipline, Yajuro cleared all doubt and trepidation from his mind as he prepared for battle.

"Archers to the rail," he ordered. "Prepare to defend." Before Yajuro's eyes, his inept deck crew transformed from bumbling sailors into trained warriors. Arms and armor that had been unnecessary hindrances to their shipboard duties were equipped in a matter of minutes. Then, as one, his samurai moved smoothly to the port side of their *seki bune* fighting galley. Seconds later, they had all notched arrows into their bowstrings and stood at perfectly spaced intervals, awaiting their next command. *And this is why we pound obedience into their skulls,* Yajuro thought.

Simon and Aldo watched as brightly armored archers massed swiftly on the other ship's deck. The only consistent color seemed to be the small, rectangular, white and black flags protruding above the archers' backs.

"We are in poor shape for a fight," Aldo stated matter-of-factly.

"Yes, but the crew needs provisions." Simon shot a faux-worrisome look at Neno. "Thirst and hunger make men do irrational and primitive things. Without food, Neno may soon be eating the rest of us for dinner."

Aldo shuddered involuntarily as he remembered the screams of the ship's doctor that they had lost to cannibals. It had been the wrong Indian Sea island to search for fresh water. Not that he thought his loyal first mate would ever commit such an ungodly act... "Beat to quarters!"

Rat, tat, tat... tat, tat... tat, tat... tat... tat. A sailor rapped out a staccato beat on a snare drum. The sailor wasn't a drummer, so the beat was a tad slow and off-cadence, but everyone knew what he meant. The remaining twenty-four men, out of an original crew of a hundred and twenty, took up their positions for battle. The original drummer had been one of the other ninety-six.

The four iron-bore, twelve-pound cannons on each side of the boat had been Aldo's own clever modification. He had judged correctly that the *Tigre* had a low enough center of gravity at its waist to handle the large cannons, provided they were balanced evenly. Luca Magnani, the ageless ship's master carpenter, accomplished the feat before they left the Red Sea port of Al Quseir. After cutting openings for the cannons in the deck railing, Luca reinforced the remaining sections with iron bands. This enabled the railings to withstand the pull of the ropes as the cannons recoiled on their wheeled carriages. In addition to the large cannons, Luca had also equipped both the forecastle and the aftercastle with smaller hand cannons mounted on the railings. These modifications had proven to be one of the few well–thought-out ideas on the whole voyage.

"Cute little flags on their backs," Simon remarked.

"Hold, hold," Yajuro yelled. "Release!" His samurai archers with their long-shafted *daikyu* bows loosed their arrows with practiced skill. The instant their arrows cleared the daikyus' shafts; the samurai smoothly notched arrows again and let loose their second volley.

"Christ's bollocks," Simon said in shock while ducking behind the helm, arrows thudding into the awning above him. "I didn't think they'd have the range."

"Nor I," came Aldo's voice as he cringed behind an empty barrel. Being a good Catholic, he crossed himself at Simon's blasphemy. Like a true Venetian, Aldo was not opposed to the use of colorful language, but he abhorred Simon's near-constant inclusion of the savior in his maledictions.

Simon considered what he'd just witnessed. *An English or Welsh longbowman trained from infancy could equal the feat, but no one else in the world that I know of. Yet these people in strange armor, from an unknown island that is possibly China-adjacent, have just delivered an accurate volley at the limit of English longbow range.*

"Who are these people?" Aldo asked as he stood up and brushed himself down. But he quickly dove back behind the barrel as a second, third, fourth, and fifth volley peppered the *Tigre.*

"Thank Christ you Venetians put up these wooden awnings or we'd be skewered by now," Simon said, still amazed at what he was witnessing.

Aldo crossed himself again and scowled while remaining firmly planted behind his barrel. "You can thank the engineers at the Arsenal for the concept, and Luca for the execution. But there is no need to blaspheme."

The enemy arrows, which rained unceasingly from the sky, came at a flatter trajectory as the two ships drew closer. A howl from the forecastle announced to everyone that their meager manpower had just become that much scarcer. Aldo did not want to declare war on a country that Venice might have future trade relations with, but he also prized his own skin and that of his crew above his country's future diplomatic initiatives. Aldo looked down to the waist of the ship, where his sailors crouched tensely next to the starboard cannons. There were barely enough men left to serve the guns. "Fire!"

Chapter 2

A GREAT BOOMING sound traveled across the water, and Yajuro watched white wisps of smoke cough out of the black barrels that had initiated his sense of dread. Soon after his ears registered the sound, the air around him seemed to eddy as giant, cast-iron balls hissed past him, slamming into his ship and his men.

One well-aimed ball hit the *seki bune's* only mast, causing it to come crashing down onto the deck, crushing two samurai and trapping others beneath it. Another ball tore through the ranks of archers at chest level, blasting through the torso of the first man it came into contact with, ripping an arm from the man behind him, and knocking the head off a third. Still another cannonball skipped across the deck, severed a man's leg at the hip, and bounced up to smash another's face beyond recognition.

"Release arrows!" Yajuro roared.

"*Hai*!" the samurai warriors responded as one, smoothly re-notching their bows, oblivious to the cries of the wounded around them.

"Hard starboard," Aldo ordered.

"Aye, Captain," Simon said as he steered them closer to the fat, foreign galley. As the ships neared impact, the *Tigre's* crew put lit matches to the touchholes on the rail-mounted hand cannons. Tongues of fire erupted from the gun breeches, and rocks, glass, nails, and round shot swept across the enemy deck like an invisible scythe. Seaman Aversa picked off targets with a crossbow from his perch in the rigging.

"Place your scrotums against the bulwarks, gentlemen," Simon alerted the crew to brace for impact. The starboard side of the *Tigre* slammed into the port side of the smaller ship. Due to the grossly uneven weight difference, several samurai were tossed overboard, and the rest were thrown to the deck.

"Grappling hooks!" Aldo shouted needlessly to his skilled crew who, while considerably diminished in both strength and numbers, still knew their business. After all, they were Venetian, and Venice ruled the waves.

As if Kojiro Takeda's head didn't hurt badly enough, the disquiet in his stomach was overwhelming, forcing him to vomit into his mouth.

Two decks below Yajuro's samurai, the environment rolled rhythmically, loosening the remaining control Kojiro held over his temporomandibular joints, and the vomit spilled out of his mouth and onto his chest. His sense of smell regrettably chose that moment to return, and he inhaled the malodorous substance now covering what was left of his shredded *kimono*. Kojiro tried to focus his blurred vision, but he felt like a man with his eyes open underwater. Though he could see almost nothing, he could hear the sounds of creaking oak, and a man shouting orders.

As the nausea briefly subsided, Kojiro became aware of a searing pain in his abdomen. Since he could not see what was causing it, he attempted to use his hands to feel the injury, but discovered that his hands were bound behind him to a large, wooden pole. "*Ittai dokoya?*" he mumbled softly to himself. *Where the hell am I?*

Overwhelming the powerful stench of his vomit was another more fetid aroma: rotten flesh. A large, dead animal such as a pig, if left to rot in the summer sun, would smell similar, but there was only one type of meat that secreted these unique olfactory properties. As Kojiro heard the unmistakable sound of oars grating in their oarlocks above him, a misshapen round object rolled onto his lap. His vision focused momentarily, and in the dim light he was able to make out the head of a warrior monk. Shame and anger invaded his foggy brain in a rush as pieces of his memory returned.

The ship rolled again and the monk's head, with its accusatory eyes scorning him for being alive, skipped off his lap to find a new resting place against a dense form to his left. Kojiro initially guessed that the form may have been the rest of the monk, but as his hearing became more attuned to the environment, he realized that the form was straining to breathe.

"*Kikoeruka?*" *Can you hear me?* There was no answer, but Kojiro could still hear the raspy breaths. Someone was alive down here with him. Kojiro was roused from his speculation about the body by a familiar and loathsome shout on the deck above him. The cry of

"*Ouchi*" knifed through the sensory overload in his brain, pruning away all thoughts but one: vengeance.

Kojiro's entire body shuddered as the pole at his back jumped sideways. Pain shot through him, but the pole's movement loosened the ropes that bound his hands. He managed to work himself free, and he half-crawled, half-stumbled his way towards the source of the raspy breathing. Kojiro found his young friend Taro on his back, bound hand and foot, with an accumulation of monk heads resting against his body. Kojiro was unable to wake the severely injured samurai, but he removed Taro's restraints and scanned the dark, cramped quarters for a more comfortable place to lay him.

The space was bursting with treasure. It looked like the entirety of Kyoto's grand estates had been robbed and jammed into the hold of this boat. Also taking up space were crates of heads, at least one of which had spilled open during the voyage. Kojiro despised the Ouchi proclivity for taking trophy heads; it was devoid of honor. *Therefore making it well-suited to the Ouchi*, he thought. He reached under Taro's shoulders and pulled him towards a ladder, which, based on the light filtering down, led out of the hold.

After searching fruitlessly for weapons amongst the crates, barrels, sacks, and scrolls, he started up the ladder.

About halfway up, he was knocked viciously off the ladder as the entire ship jolted around him. Picking himself up, he looked at his hands and saw fresh blood. Kojiro swallowed and tasted the tang of copper. Blood ran down the back of his throat. "*Kuso.*" *Shit*, he muttered to himself, *broken nose*. With two deep exhalations, he blew snot and blood out of both nostrils, wiped his crooked nose on the sleeve of his ragged *kimono*, and started back up the ladder.

Dirty, sweating, nervous-looking peasants manned the deck above. They made no move to stand up or interfere with him, so he ignored them. He moved toward the stairs that led to the upper deck from where, like music to his ears, he heard screaming. Here, where the light was dim but not dark, he took the time to examine his abdomen, which pained him with every step. His skin was black, blue, and green, but he was not bleeding. *Broken ribs, I'll live long enough to kill somebody.*

Buddha smiled upon him as he approached the stairs, because an Ouchi samurai came tumbling down with a short, arrow-like projectile protruding from the back of his head. The man's dead hands still grasped his katana, a burden of which Kojiro relieved him. He stepped over the dead samurai, up the stairs, into daylight.

Yajuro took stock of his decimated crew. Most lay screaming and dying about him on the blood-slickened deck. "Form on me!" Yajuro shouted to his remaining men.

"*Hai*."

Six men joined him at the center of the deck, prepared to face whatever came off the enemy ship. He drew his katana with his one good arm and defiantly shouted the name of his clan: "Ouchi!" The six men who joined him echoed his deep-throated cry, as did the injured and dying who still had the strength and pride to shout for their captain and clan. Across the deck littered with splintered wood and mangled men, "Ouchi, Ouchi, Ouchi" reverberated. One man held his bowels inside his body with his left hand and tried to stand by bracing his sword on the deck with his right. Unsuccessful, he flopped back onto the deck but still managed to scream one last "Ouchi" before the blood gurgled from his mouth and he could speak no more.

Aldo fired his hand cannon, then moved next to Simon on the aftercastle deck where they observed the behavior on the enemy vessel. It was not encouraging. Their adversaries had just taken what looked to be upwards of eighty percent casualties, yet it appeared to have no impact whatsoever on their will to fight. *That just isn't normal,* Aldo thought. "What do you think they're all yelling?"

"Sounds to me like 'ouch,'" Simon said, "which, if true, would certainly go down as a monumental understatement."

Looking at the seven determined men on the enemy deck, and then looking back to his emaciated crew hauling feebly on the grappling lines, Aldo was not sure, even at three-to-one odds, that they would win this fight. It *was* certain, however, that any victory would come with losses they couldn't afford.

The same unspoken thought occurred to Simon as he watched an eighth man appear on the enemy deck. "I wonder how many more of the tough bastards there are below decks."

Kojiro emerged onto the deck, and although the sky was overcast, it took some time for his eyes to adjust to the increased brightness.

Hampering his ability to see clearly were thick clouds of white smoke that stung his eyes and smelled of rotten eggs. *What kind of devilment is this?* The high-octave screaming caused him no concern, but smoke without fire and the smell of hot springs in the middle of the ocean were disconcerting.

Squinting through the daylight and smoke, he could see over thirty crumpled and dying samurai, all with the Ouchi black, diamond-shaped marking on their *sashimono* flags. His gaze settled next on the towering ship that appeared to be the source of both the smoke and the Ouchis' misfortune. The strange ship was slowly pulling closer with grappling ropes, and it occurred to Kojiro that they might rob him of his vengeance completely.

The Ouchi samurai did not see him approach as they were entirely focused on the deadly, otherworldly enemy in front of them. Kojiro killed the first samurai with a forward thrust through his back and into his heart. He followed this with a roundhouse slash to the base of a second man's neck, which severed his head cleanly. *Tunnel vision kills,* Kojiro thought. He could tell from the outcome of his first two sword strokes that the previous owner of this newly acquired blade had taken pride in its upkeep.

The enemy captain turned towards him, and before he could give the command, two of his remaining samurai engaged.

The Ouchi samurai's katana came slicing down toward his head. Kojiro grabbed the man's wrist with his left hand and wrapped his right arm around the man's waist. Kojiro allowed the samurai's arm to continue its downward motion as he pivoted into the man. His hips shifted underneath the man's torso, and he assisted the man's momentum by pulling forward on the wrist and bucking up with his own hips. The man rose above Kojiro's back until his legs were perpendicular to the deck, at which point Kojiro stepped aside and pulled the man head first onto the boards, snapping his neck. Kojiro grabbed the man's falling katana with his left hand, and pivoted back on his rear foot to avoid a sword strike from his next attacker.

Kojiro had been born left-handed, much to the chagrin of his parents who, in keeping with Japanese society in general, prized conformity. From the moment he shifted the first pair of chopsticks into his left hand, his parents began forcing utensils and writing instruments back to his right. Eating was a wash, but in calligraphy, being right-handed was close to necessary. The over two thousand characters necessary to be fluent in Japanese were all written left to right, top to bottom. A left-hander making left to right brush-strokes had to cope with their hand covering their work, so Kojiro learned to use his right hand. Whenever his parents weren't looking, of course, he moved his chopsticks back to his left, not realizing that later in life, this ambidexterity would pay dividends.

Now holding swords in both of his hands, Kojiro swung them in a rearward, circular motion to gain momentum, then brought them down to bear on the shoulders of the attacker who had just missed him. Kojiro's blows sliced through the samurai's light shoulder armor near the neck, and cut through his trapezius muscles, causing him to release his own katana and drop to the deck in agony.

After watching his captive display his sword skills, Yajuro knew that with one arm, he had no chance to defeat him. *Even in my prime, I might not have been that good.* But to die at the hands of a skillful samurai was honorable. To fall to the white smoke magic that killed without skill or face-to-face contact was not. His stomach tensed. He turned his back on the ship that had destroyed his crew and lunged forward at the samurai with the crane marking on his tattered, stinking *kimono.*

Simon and Aldo stood in shock. They had never seen such a combination of dexterous movement and swordplay.

"He's got different markings on his clothing than the others, and no silly little flag on his back," Simon pointed out.

"Why, yes he does," Aldo countered. "Looks like some type of bird in a circle."

"I'd also venture to say that there are some hard feelings between him and those other fellows."

As they continued to watch, the man with the bird markings battered the one-armed enemy leader to the ground with rapid striking motions from the hilts of his swords. After the enemy leader fell, he proceeded to kill the remaining two warriors.

As the killings came to an end, there was complete silence on the *Tigre.* The Venetian crew stood transfixed. The spell was broken when Simon started slowly clapping. As the skill that he had just witnessed sank in further, Simon increased the speed and volume of his clapping until finally he shouted out to the swordsman.

"Well done, sir! I must say, very well done."

Kojiro paused after striking down the last man and looked at the deck around him. It was filled with men who had major body parts missing, flesh destroyed by small projectiles, or both. A few had been felled by small arrows similar to the one that bequeathed him his first Ouchi sword. He wondered if the same fate lay in store for him.

The ship dipped into the trough of a wave, and cold seawater mixed with blood rushed between his bare toes. Beating back human nature's tendency towards tunnel vision, Kojiro looked left, right, and behind, but no one rose to challenge him. A victory over a hated enemy, combined with the festering guilt of still being alive after so many of his friends had fallen, produced a guttural cry he could not contain. Part challenge, part exhaustion, part death wish, the deep explosion of his vocal cords echoed across the decks of both ships. Kojiro did not hear the clapping from the strange ship or the friendly shout. He did notice that the one-armed man he had knocked out with the hilts of his swords was coming around.

"What is your name?" Yajuro asked as he blinked into consciousness.

"I am Kojiro."

Surprise and understanding hit Yajuro all at once as he connected the name, the crane emblem, the stories he thought were children's fantasies, and what he'd just witnessed with his own eyes. He gasped.

"B... b... but you are dead. Everyone said you were dead!"

"*Shiteru.*" *I know,* Kojiro said with no emotion in his voice.

"That was ten years ago." Yajuro struggled for words. He never struggled for words. *Could this really be the man who held the Sanpo-in Temple gate for twelve hours?*

"How did you escape?" Yajuro stammered. "Where have you been for ten years?" Yajuro had never believed the legend of the minor clan samurai who killed hundreds of Ouchi at the temple gate, then disappeared just as the temple fell. He had always assumed it was an old soldier's tale invented to scare youngsters. Youngsters like the obedient dullard that now lay dead beside him.

Kojiro did not answer.

If Yajuro's opponent was indeed the man of legend, he knew he could expect no mercy from him. After all, the Ouchi had butchered all the monks at Sanpo-in and at every monastery they'd encountered since. But perhaps he could maintain his honor in death. After all, Yajuro, too, had once been a great samurai.

"I have heard of you, Kojiro-sama, and I ask that you let me die of my own accord."

"I could not care less how you die," Kojiro stated coldly as he tucked his new katanas into his belt.

Yajuro nodded his head slightly in thanks. Despite the harsh words, he was grateful for the concession. He felt around the blood-soaked deck and retrieved a short *tanto* dagger from the body of the young, dim samurai. He then pulled himself up to his knees and forcefully thrust the *tanto* into his lower abdomen. From there he pulled it horizontally across his stomach, then straight up and into his ribcage. The pain was immense, but as his life drained away, he was thankful. He had died with honor.

Well, now, that's something new, Simon thought. He had never seen anybody disembowel *himself* before. He'd seen people disemboweled in battle, and people disemboweled by torture, but this was the first time he'd seen it self-applied. *And this guy did it with one arm.* He thought about it again for a minute. He looked at Aldo. "Have you ever seen anything like that before?"

"No."

"It must be as painful as Christ's crucifixion."

Aldo crossed himself first, and then replied bluntly, "Yes."

"Why would anybody do something like that?"

"I have no idea."

"So now we go over there and meet the lone survivor?"

"You first," responded Aldo hastily.

"You're the language expert," Simon countered.

"I don't have your sword skills." Stroking Simon's ego had rarely failed Aldo.

"I can't argue with the truth," Simon conceded. He gestured at Neno to follow him. "Keep your mouth shut, eyes open, hands off your sword, and, most importantly, smile."

"*Si*," Neno replied, far louder than necessary, as was his habit.

I wonder if that's got anything to do with the fact that he hasn't had to address anyone on a face-to-face level since he was twelve, Simon thought.

Kojiro watched warily as two men, both with unsettlingly pale, white skin, jumped over to the Ouchi ship: one sprightly, the other not. Kojiro stood still with his heart pounding. He was not afraid of how large the two of them were, although they were both huge, one of them monstrously so. What troubled him was their color. They were the color of ghosts, and one had piercing blue eyes. Kojiro had never seen anybody with an eye color other than brown. It unnerved him.

Simon and Neno approached Kojiro wearing their best forced grins. As Simon approached, he could see that the mark on the man's clothing appeared to be a black crane encircled in blue. Simon took a quick glance behind him. He expected to see at least a dozen armed Venetian sailors clambering over the railing. There were none. He could see that Aldo was also playing it safe, observing from the aftercastle. Aldo did not lack for encouraging words, however.

"I think he must be tired by now. He has just killed six men in less than two minutes, and beaten another into a delirium so serious that he spilled out his own entrails. How much more energy could he have?"

Simon sized up the man with the extraordinary sword skills. He did not look tired. He looked a mess; shoeless, covered in other men's blood, clothing in tatters, but he was not breathing hard. In fact, it did not appear to Simon that he was breathing at all. He stood with a ramrod straight back, feet diagonally shoulder-width apart, a slight bend in the knees, and relaxed arms. It was not an intimidating pose, but one from which he could attack in a heartbeat. The man's eyes were very narrow, and Simon could not tell if that was a hereditary trait or if the man was a master squinter. The eyes were also very hard, and they conveyed nothing as they shifted slowly between himself and Neno.

Simon, moving slowly, opened his palms to show that he held no weapons. Then, still without haste, he made a sweeping bow, complete with gyrating hips and whirling arm movements.

"Marvelous! Marvelous!" cheered Aldo from the aftercastle. He had never seen such a refined gesture from the crude English pilot.

Kojiro thought about attacking the odd-looking giants before they did the same to him, but as he always did, he took the time to consider the situation before he acted rashly. They looked solid in form, so he doubted they were actually ghosts, and the smaller one seemed to have performed some type of comedic bow.

Another thought occurred to him. *Are they mocking me?* He looked into the eyes of the pseudo-ghosts. In spite of their idiotic grins, they didn't appear to be laughing at him. Kojiro returned what he believed to have been a bow. He placed his feet and legs together, palms against his legs, and bent slowly forward at the waist, hands sliding down to the front of his legs until they were just above the knees. After holding for a few seconds, he made the same movements in reverse. Normally, he would have held his bow longer to show more respect for new acquaintances, but he did not trust them yet and did not wish to remain in a vulnerable position for too long.

"Simon," the pilot said when Kojiro straightened, pointing to his chest.

Kojiro said, "Takeda," as he pointed to his nose.

"To-key-da," Simon said as best as he could.

The man stated his name again, but this time he said it a little more slowly. "Ta. Kay. Da."

Simon tried again. "Ta. Key. Da."

"Perfect!" Aldo bellowed from the safety of the *Tigre* in a tone that sounded a bit more sarcastic than Simon would have preferred. Simon got the feeling that perhaps Aldo was enjoying this a bit much.

Kojiro tried to pronounce the blue-eyed ghost's name. "Sai-mone."

Simon repeated, "Simon."

And Kojiro repeated, "Sai-mone."

"Simon."

"Sai-mone."

As good as it gets, Simon supposed.

Kojiro was satisfied that he was not likely to be attacked immediately, so his next thoughts were to secure the ship and aid his friend. He also did not wish to run off without explanation, so he pointed down and said, "*Tomodachi*." Not knowing what else to say, and knowing that time was crucial, he turned quickly and walked toward the stairs.

"Tomadaki?" Simon looked at Neno as the crane man walked away. Neno just shrugged. "Tomadaki?" Simon yelled inquiringly back at Aldo, a man with a skill for language the likes of which Simon begrudgingly had to admit, he had never seen.

"Sorry, I need more context," Aldo called. "There are too many things that may be in the direction he was pointing. He was pointing at the ship, but saying 'ship,' then running off would be odd. So I guess, as you *Inglese* say, I haven't the foggiest. If you go down with him and live, then perhaps you can report back with some more context, and I can translate '*tomodachi*' for you."

Aldo said the word exactly as the foreigner had said it, not as Simon had butchered it, which both impressed and annoyed Simon. The "if you live" condition was not lost on Simon either, but he wouldn't be in China-adjacent if curiosity didn't exercise an outsized influence on his behavior. Simon started walking towards the stairs, and Neno followed loyally.

"*Buona fortuna*," Aldo shouted as Neno and Simon descended into the galley's rowing deck.

The compartment under the top deck was dark and smelled of sweat, urine, and feces. Scores of men sat sober-faced, holding oars. Nobody stirred.

"Neno, how many men do you count?" Simon asked in a muffled voice.

Neno looked around. "There seems to be about fifteen oars per side. Three men are sitting on a bench pulling a single oar. That means," and here Neno paused a good while, "many."

Kojiro stood in front of the ninety seated men and began to scream something in his native tongue. Of course Simon didn't understand anything that was being said, but it was certainly being said with authority. After the outburst, Kojiro just stared at the rowers.

One emancipated peasant cautiously got to his feet and was just about to say something, when Kojiro stepped forward and beheaded the man.

Caught by surprise, Neno nonetheless had a loud sailor's expletive at the ready. "*Porca troia*!"

Simon was also taken aback, not just by the savagery of the act, but once again, by the speed of Takeda's blade. He had seen nothing but a momentary flash of steel followed by a man's head thumping onto the deck. In one smooth motion, Takeda had moved five feet, drawn his blade, cut a man's head off, replaced the blade in his belt, and moved back to his original position.

Takeda sounded infuriated when he started shouting at the rowers again, and his diatribe continued for quite some time. When he had finished, he paused, and the entire team of rowers answered as one. It sounded to Simon like they were saying "high." Afterwards, the rowers stared at their hands and bowed their heads as if they had done something in shame.

"Neno, are these rowers wearing chains or shackles?" Simon asked.

Neno squinted at the men in the dimly lit deck. "No."

Simon took some time to absorb what he was witnessing. "Why aren't they attacking? There are ninety of them and only three of us."

Neno had no answer, and they both watched as Kojiro walked a few steps and descended to a lower deck. The rowers remained unmoving and silent with their heads down. A short time later Kojiro reemerged with a body slung over his shoulder. He carried it past them and out onto the upper deck.

Simon and Neno followed, where they observed the crane-marked man named Takeda carefully lay the body down on a dry portion of the upper deck. They looked hard at the motionless man. His left arm was askew, and both his face and body were bruised and swollen. He also had stab wounds in at least four places on his body, and the crudely wrapped red dressings gave evidence that he had leaked a lot of blood.

"Did you notice the rope marks on Tee-ko-do's wrists?" Neno asked, speaking softly for only the second time that week and butchering the name even more badly than Simon had, much to Simon's gratification.

"Yes, his wrists are raw. I think we solved the mystery as to why this man killed all the others. He certainly wasn't a voluntary member of the crew." Simon studied the second man. He looked younger than their new friend, but how young was hard to tell. Takeda's facial expression did not change as he arranged his friend's body to make it more comfortable, but he did so with a gentleness that betrayed a compassion Simon wouldn't have expected from such a proficient killer.

Simon shouted back to the *Tigre*, "Ship secure."

Simon heard Aldo issue some commands, and ten men from the *Tigre*, along with Aldo, jumped aboard the foreign ship and began collecting weapons from both the living and the dead.

"Thanks for the backup," Simon said facetiously.

"As all mariners know, the *capitano* is the last man to leave his ship," Aldo replied indignantly.

Simon smiled for the third time that day and said, "Dear Aldo, please let me introduce you to *Tokayda*."

Aldo cringed at Simon's half-assed attempt at the poor fellow's name, for he had heard the initial introductions from afar and knew how to pronounce it properly. Aldo bowed deeply and gracefully, with perfect foot comportment and a sweeping removal of his hat. Even in the Doge's Palace, this bow would have stood out for its master artistry. "It is with the utmost pleasure that I make your acquaintance, Signor Takeda."

Kojiro stopped tending to Taro and stood. Judging by the garishness of his clothing compared to that of the other pale-skinned *gaijin* combing the deck, he guessed this was a man of rank on the barbarian boat, if not the captain himself. He had given the same ridiculous, ostentatious bow as the man named *Sai-mone* had, lending credence to Kojiro's judgment that this was their custom and not some way of mocking him. So, wishing to return respect where it was offered, he also bowed.

Aldo was a little disappointed that his grand gesture was returned with just a meager bending of the waist, but he took it as a symbol of the barbarian culture's backward ways and tried valiantly not to take offense.

The man then spoke. "*Watashi no namae wa Takeda, Kojiro desu.*"

Aldo recognized "Takeda" from the first introduction.

"His name is either Kojiro Takeda or Takeda Kojiro. I'm not sure which is the family name yet, nor do I know which we should use to address him. And I highly doubt it would be polite to address him by his name alone, as that is not common in any culture, but I know nothing of their honorifics yet," Aldo fretted.

"Do you think that's our most important concern right now?" Simon asked.

"Language is a tool, and the misuse of it can have consequences as dire as a misuse of the knife at a brit milah."

Simon gave Aldo a blank stare.

"It is the Jewish ceremony of circumcision." Aldo searched Simon's eyes for any sense of comprehension.

Simon continued to stare blankly.

"I apologize, I always forget what a startling lack of cultural variety you English have, unless of course, you count the sheep." Aldo continued quickly, not giving Simon a chance to interrupt. "When a baby is born into the religion of Judaism, they have the foreskin of their penis cut off with a knife, so you can understand why it is important not to misuse that tool."

Simon involuntarily reached for his groin area to check on things, feeling sympathy for Jewish babies everywhere. "The Jews were expelled from England almost two centuries ago. I did not know they had such customs."

"Well, they do, and much like that knife, the misuse of language can lead to very unpleasant outcomes. For example, what's the name of that 'gentleman' on the English throne that is *allegedly* trying to kill you?"

"He *is* trying to kill me."

"Yes, yes, I'm sure he is. Now what is his name?"

"King Edward the Fourth."

"Yes, King Edward the Fourth. Now imagine if I were a traveler from, say, this fellow's land, and I'm introduced to King Edward the Fourth on a ship, during inauspicious circumstances such as this. Do you think he would take kindly to me calling him Eddy? 'Hey Eddy, let's you and I talk business.' Wars have started for lesser insults."

"'Eddy,'" Simon mused. "I kind of like the sound of that. I'll have to use it if I ever get to meet the bastard. Best not to start a war over language, though, quite right." Simon then mumbled under his breath, "Maybe should've thought of that before you fired the cannons."

"Excuse me, I didn't catch that last part."

"I said maybe you should tell us what else he said before we leave him standing there any longer."

"Based on the pauses, intonation, and facial inflections, apart from his name being Takeda Kojiro or Kojiro Takeda, the remainder of the sentence correlates to 'my name is.' Of this, I am relatively certain."

Aldo continued. "If you look at his gentle handling of this person and his immediate need to get to him, I would say this is the '*tomodachi*' that he referred to when he pointed down before going below decks. Putting all of those pieces together, we can safely assume that '*tomodachi*' means friend, compatriot, crewmate, or something similar."

Kojiro heard the chubbier foreigner say *tomodachi*, and he pointed to Taro and repeated it. "*Tomodachi*."

Aldo straightened up, took a step forward, and while the sounds remained fresh in his mind, he repeated, "Atashi o nama wa Aldo Mitachionne."

Inwardly, Kojiro was shocked, but outwardly, he tried to remain expressionless. He wondered if this second *gaijin* with the ridiculously large mustache possibly spoke some of his language. *His language is not perfect, but his pronunciation and intonation are surprisingly good.*

Kojiro probed with a greeting. "*Hajimemashite*."

Aldo was pleased to see a trace of surprise on the man's stoic face, so he continued with the rhythm to which he always danced when encountering new languages. Much of Aldo's linguistic talent arose from his natural ability to mimic pronunciation and intonation. It didn't hurt that he had an excellent memory and a studious dispensation, but the less obvious source of his ability was his common sense. Common sense enabled him to observe another's behavior, and then *feeling* would guide him through the subtleties.

Aldo had been his parents' joy growing up. His mother's joy because after two helpings at every meal, he was the lone child amongst his five siblings who always asked for thirds. He was his father's joy because, like the truest of true Venetians, he was a merchant at heart and had the sea in his blood. In fact, he'd done nothing to disappoint his family until he turned thirty and decided to sail to China with a crazy Englishman. "Ha jee may ma she tay," Aldo tried.

Kojiro could see that the man was simply mimicking him, but still, he was good at it, and Kojiro appreciated the effort. Kojiro looked at Simon and said, "*Hajimemashite.*"

Simon tried to repeat, as Aldo had done, but he couldn't remember the order of the sounds, nor much of the sounds themselves for that matter.

"Jee gee may may see tay."

Aldo then pointed at Simon and said, "*Tomodachi,*" in spite of his embarrassment.

Kojiro nodded in understanding.

Aldo then pointed at Kojiro and asked. "*Tomodachi*?"

Kojiro responded, "*Hai*, tomodachi desu."

Chapter 3

SIMON WANTED TO help Kojiro's friend but he had no medical skill personally, and the *Tigre* had lost its doctor. For all Simon knew the natives were still eating him for leftovers.

Simon didn't really think his absence mattered terribly; the doctor never seemed to actually cure anybody of anything. He mixed potions and made solemn pronouncements about the will of God, but the live/die ratio of the sailors he had treated skewed dramatically in favor of "die." This, of course, was where God came into the picture, as in, "It was, unfortunately, the will of God that this poor sinner had to die." Conversely, in the rare situation where someone actually survived the doctor's bizarre treatments, it was invariably due largely to his own skills as a healer, with only a modicum of God's power assisting his skillful hands. Whatever the case, the *Tigre* had nothing to offer Kojiro for his friend. Their own crew were little more than sickly skeletons as it was. Simon tried to communicate their helplessness by opening his hands palms up and shaking his head. Kojiro seemed to discern his meaning as he went back to caring for his friend.

Aldo looked to Simon. "What now?"

"Well, there are two things I should tell you. First, the boat we have just commandeered has about ninety natives sitting below deck on rowing benches."

"Just sitting there?"

"Aye."

"And they outnumber us?"

"Roughly four to one."

"We must guard them immediately, no?"

"I don't think that will be necessary."

"*Perché no*? Why not?"

"Our new friend here seems to have that under control. You don't want to know how."

Aldo thought that perhaps he didn't.

"Second, this ship has so many valuables onboard, I'm almost more afraid of charging angry leprechauns than I am of the ninety rowers. It may be why they were quick to fire on us."

Aldo's eyes widened. "You mean trinkets of gold and the like?"

"Trinkets, silks, paintings, gems, and much more of 'the like,'" Simon answered.

"Well, I think we've earned them," Aldo pronounced. "Attacking us, a peaceful trading delegation from Venice, is in total violation of maritime law, not to mention common decency. It is only just compensation."

In spite of Simon's judgment, Aldo ordered five of his men with crossbows to guard the rowers while he sent the rest in search of treasure.

Aldo did not feel it was necessary for him to personally evaluate the ninety foreigners below them. "A good *capitano* should endeavor never to be away too long from the burden of his command, so I will return to the *Tigre* and supervise the transfer of cargo."

He did not fail to encourage his sailors before hopping back across to the *Tigre* twice as quickly as he had leapt off it: "If they look like they are going to overrun you, shout up to us so at least some of us have time to escape. I promise those who survive will pray for your souls." Aldo smiled warmly as he gave this encouragement, and his men smiled back at their captain's familiar gallows humor.

The men cheerfully set about picking the ship clean of its valuables, which proved to be a lot. Aldo and Simon watched, stunned, as their smiling crew brought up exquisite lacquerware, porcelain, gold-flecked paintings, elaborately designed silken robes, strange musical instruments, and countless trinkets in gold and silver.

"Stop smiling," Simon yelled out. "You ghouls are wasting away to nothingness, and we'll never get it all back to Venice." But his English pessimism fell on the deaf ears of a crew that knew good plunder when they found it. Even if they starved to death, at least they would do so as rich men.

Notably lacking in their spoils appeared to be food, causing Simon to assume the boat had not been off for a long voyage. That, of course, meant the owners of this treasure did not live too far from here, and that meant more of these fierce warriors might soon come looking for it. Based on the treasures they were "liberating," this seemed like the sort of boat that would be missed. It also meant that in spite of having visible land west of them, they were just as likely as not to land in the territory of the people they'd acquired this treasure from.

As the pallid Venetian ghouls continued to move down the ladder, up the ladder, across the deck, over to the *Tigre,* and back again, there was a certain treasure, near and dear to both their hearts, that they had yet to see emerge. Just when the captain and pilot had assumed their seizure was deficient, a three-foot high barrel emerged from the rowing deck on the shoulder of First Mate Neno. Aldo and Simon practically tripped over each other in their efforts to gain Neno's attention.

Kojiro watched as the ghostly barbarians took the treasures of Kyoto that the Ouchi had stolen and moved them to their own ship. Kojiro didn't care. He only cared about getting Taro help. Kojiro could tell that the barbarian ghost warriors were not healthy. They came on a ship that had incomparable strength, but the men themselves were weak. They had large frames, but those frames did not seem to be filled out, and many of them were hacking and coughing. He didn't know the physiology of people as white as these – he wasn't even completely sure they were human – but he knew sick. And they were sick. Much like Taro, they needed healing. By the contour of the islands north and west of them, he could tell that Honshu was to the north and Shikoku to the west. *We are close to Taro's village. Perhaps because they are sick, they will agree to travel there,* Kojiro thought.

Kojiro walked to the deck of the *Tigre* and was amazed at the size and strength of its design. He had come across Chinese and Korean boats with innovative features, but he had never seen a ship of war the likes of this one. He wanted to study the ship in detail, but for now he had to calculate how sign language and drawings might convince these sickly barbarians to sail to the friendly shores of Tosa. Simon and Aldo were staring at a barrel of *sake* on the deck of the *Tigre* when Kojiro approached. Kojiro pointed back to Taro, then he pointed south and west towards Shikoku.

"I think he wants us to take his man that way," Aldo said, "but do we trust him?"

"Trust him? I don't know. I think we can be sure, however, that he won't be taking us to the land of the owners of this ship."

"And we still need food." Aldo made a motion of bringing an invisible utensil to his mouth and chewing on imaginary food.

As Kojiro expected, the foreigners were malnourished, which gave him momentary pause to consider just how big the horse-sized man became when he was fully fed. Kojiro nodded at Aldo and used imaginary chopsticks to bring imaginary food to his mouth.

Since Aldo was on a roll, he pointed at the barrel he and Simon had been puzzling over. Aldo watched Kojiro's eyes scan the deck until something caught his eye. Kojiro retrieved a hammer, and with one blow, the planks on top of the barrel broke in. Kojiro then went hunting through the treasure already on board the *Tigre* and returned with three square, wooden, cup-shaped boxes and a ladle. Kojiro ladled the clear liquid in the barrel into the three boxes and raised his in the air. Simon and Aldo followed suit.

"*Kampai*," Kojiro said.

"*Kampai*," Aldo said.

"Come pee," Simon said mimicking the sound as closely as he was able, causing Aldo to nearly spill his beverage. They drained their boxes; the liquid was heavenly.

Chapter 4

"THAT'S AN AWFULLY narrow inlet, pilot." Everyone turned to look at the first mate who had joined them at the helm.

"That's what she said," Simon rejoined to no one's amusement. He snickered at his own wit anyway.

Neno had joined Aldo, Kojiro, and Simon at the rudder just as Simon steered the ship between two rocky outcroppings, each a hundred feet high. Kojiro, after a thorough study of the ship, had insisted the boat would not ground while entering the tiny bay beyond the outcroppings. The drawings and miming contortions Kojiro had gone through to convey this point had been no small source of entertainment for the crew.

I hope he's not grounding us for an ambush, Simon thought, still harboring some lingering doubt about the newcomer's motives. Aldo also seemed nervous, but as the sturdy carrack moved past the towering outcroppings, Aldo breathed a sigh of relief.

The scenery in the narrow cove was breathtaking. The water was a dark, clear blue that ended at a gently sloping beach of white sand. A small village of thatched-roof, A-frame houses started at the beach and ended in a patchwork of water-soaked rice fields. The village and fields were framed by lush green mountains of cedar, a tree easily identified by its perfume, which crept all the way down into the narrow bay. A wood also identifiable by the fits of sneezing that suddenly erupted from Neno.

"*Koko wa Kannoura, Taro no shushin,*" Kojiro said loudly over Neno's explosive fits.

During the short sailing trip, Aldo had already picked up a significant number of words and knew that "*koko*" meant "here" and "*wa*" seemed to be a particle denoting the subject. Based on that, he deduced that Kannoura was the name of the location where they had arrived. Aldo already knew that Taro was the name of Kojiro's friend, and "no" was a particle denoting ownership. "*Shushin*" he did not know, but because it was a village and Kojiro had given Taro ownership of it, he thought it might mean "home village."

Aldo responded in Kojiro's language, which he had learned was called *nihongo*, after the country they were in, which was called Nihon. Aldo suspected they were in the land of Cipangu that Marco Polo had written of, but for decorum, he would use the name that the people called themselves. "*Hai, wakarimasu. Koko wa Kannoura desu.*" Aldo had also learned that throwing "*desu*" onto the end of things seemed to make it more polite, and in trade as well as diplomacy, he had learned that polite was always better.

Kojiro was impressed. *The pudgy one is quite clever,* he thought to himself, *the giant not so much, and the yellow-haired one, perhaps somewhere in between.*

Once the boat was anchored safely in the sheltered bay, the crew assisted Kojiro in putting his gravely injured friend into a dinghy.

Simon and Aldo clambered into the boat, armed with their swords. Neno joined them with his poleaxe.

Neno was not born to vie for a professorship at the University of Bologna, but he was built like a stone house, had the strength of a horse, and was just plain terrifying in combat. Because of his reputation, he never had to give an order twice, making him an invaluable first mate. Neno's poleaxe consisted of a seven-foot pole with a hammerhead on one side, a spear tip at its end, and a triangular, six-inch dagger on the end opposite. The spearhead could unseat a rider, the hammerhead could batter him silly, and the dagger would execute a coup de grace. These were a weapon and a person you didn't want to tangle with.

Kojiro did not mention anything about their decision to take their weapons onto the boat.

By the time they pulled the dinghy onto the white sand, some of the villagers had come to investigate the towering ship and the strange, white apparitions getting off it. One of the villagers seemed to recognize Taro. The villager dropped to the sand and knelt, leaning forward at the waist in a bowing motion. The villager did not look up at them, despite what must have been agonizing curiosity. The other villagers who had made it to the beach soon followed suit.

"Clearly these people recognize greatness when they see it," Simon declared, referring to himself. "Do you think it's my breathtaking good looks or just my majestic aura?"

"If we've found a culture where vanity and pomposity are meritorious traits, you may want to stick around," Aldo replied, causing Simon to grin even wider.

It wasn't long before the villagers were scrambling at directions given by Kojiro, and four of them carried Taro into the village on a makeshift stretcher. As they walked into the village, Simon noticed the wide-eyed astonishment with which he and the Venetians were watched. The stupefaction in the villagers' faces appeared to transform into outright fear as Neno fell into a fit of thundering sneezes. That is, before the people bowed and lowered their heads upon catching sight of Taro.

In contrast to the multilevel A-framed houses, the largest residence in the village was a sprawling compound of single-story buildings with overlapping, slate gray, ceramic-tiled roofs. It was surrounded by a high, white wall. This is where the villagers brought Taro, but in order to get into the compound, they had to duck through a tiny door in the wall that looked to be no taller than four and a half feet high. Kojiro opened the door, and the villagers carrying Taro ducked through with practiced ease.

"Do we leave Neno here?" Simon asked, only half joking. But Neno was able to crouch and waddle through, much to Simon's amusement, and possibly Kojiro's as well, for Simon thought he saw the crease of a smile begin to form, although it ended so abruptly Simon couldn't be sure.

They emerged into a courtyard where intricately sculpted bushes and bright green mosses lined the gravel walking paths that meandered through the yard. "Exquisite," Aldo couldn't help but remark. He wanted to spend more time wandering the grounds, but they hustled after the peasants who bore Taro straight to the raised and covered wooden porch that surrounded the main house. It was neither tall, nor supported by ornate marble columns like a grand Venetian portico, but Aldo appreciated the functionality of the design. "It keeps you out of the muck, sheltered from the rain, and provides a satisfying view of this lovely garden," he said to no one in particular, knowing that neither Simon nor Neno had the slightest interest in such things.

"Did you say something?" Simon asked.

"No," Aldo replied.

Simon was surprised at how flimsy the walls to the house were as he watched Kojiro slide open a delicate wooden wall panel to allow Taro to be carried inside. "Wouldn't be hard to break into this place, now would it?"

"Perhaps, around here, they don't break into places as often as you English do."

"If I weren't so fond of plundering my neighbors' houses myself, I might argue with you," Simon answered with both his eyebrows raised to reinforce the irony of his words. Simon turned to follow Kojiro through the door when Aldo noticed that, in spite of the fact they had been rushing an injured person inside, everyone else had removed their footwear. Kojiro, who had none, made a considerable effort to wipe the sand and dirt off his feet with a strip of fabric torn from his *kimono.*

"Stop!" Aldo yelled.

Simon and Neno immediately took up defensive postures, with Neno lowering his poleaxe by forty-five degrees and Simon grabbing the hilt of his sword.

"No! No, no, no! Your shoes! Your shoes!"

Simon and Neno both looked at their shoes, then at each other, then at Aldo, then back to their shoes.

Aldo explained his observation, and after only a little resistance, Simon and Neno relented and removed their well-seasoned footwear. The aroma of old cheese that engulfed the portico — stemming from rotting foot fungus and other pedal distresses — caused Aldo to briefly consider whether he had made the right decision. Regardless, they all followed Kojiro into the home wearing only their torn, filthy, reeking, brown and black stockings.

The room they entered had scarcely more furnishings than the portico they entered from, which had none. "Brasidas would be proud," Aldo remarked.

Simon didn't ask about Brasidas, because he knew Aldo wanted him to ask.

Aldo explained anyway. "Brasidas was a Spartan general during the Peloponnesian War."

"I didn't ask."

Aldo continued on as if he hadn't heard Simon. "I reference him as an homage to the Spartan people's famous lack of interest in matters of decoration."

"Still not asking." Though he had never heard of Brasidas, Simon was not ignorant of the "Spartan" reference. Of course, Aldo had quite possibly chosen the most annoying way possible to express the sentiment.

Nonetheless, Simon had to agree with the substance of Aldo's conclusion. Aside from a small black shrine with smoking incense sticks resting in an alcove, there were no other objects whatsoever in the large room. The room was bordered by panels of wood and paper, with an open doorway leading to a wooden-floored hallway on the opposite side of the room. The floor consisted of equal-sized panels of yellow rice straw, which gave off a pleasant, distinctive smell reminiscent of wet autumn leaves.

The combined smells of incense and rice straw did nothing to mitigate the foul odor in the immediate vicinity of the door, but they did prevent that smell from traveling further into the house and overwhelming the whole room. The peasants carried Taro through the room and down the hallway, where they disappeared from view. Kojiro stayed with his companions just inside the entrance, waiting stiff-backed and silent. Thankfully, neither the incense nor the rice straw seemed to disturb Neno's delicate nasal passages, so they were all able to wait for what came next in silence.

What came next were two men, scurrying out from the hallway and across the large room. They came within three feet of the bedraggled group, bent at the waist, and presented their arms outstretched. Kojiro removed his swords from his belted waist and placed them into one of the men's hands. Aldo and Simon glanced at each other.

"In for a penny, in for a pound," Simon said as he surrendered his sword. Aldo followed suit, and upon a second trip necessitated by the size of the poleaxe, Neno did as well, although it required a substantial tug on the part of the servant.

Soon after they had relinquished their weapons, a short man wearing a lightweight, unadorned *yukata* emerged from the hallway where Taro had been taken. His graying hair was swept back from the sides into a ponytail, and the top of his head was completely shaven. As soon as he entered the room, his eyes grew big and his eyebrows jerked up at the sight of the foreigners, but he quickly brought them under control as he walked confidently across the room.

Aldo watched the greeting ritual carefully as Kojiro bowed before the short man in the same plain manner he had bowed to them, only he held his bow considerably longer than he had for Simon and Aldo. The short man returned Kojiro's bow, and when he straightened up, it appeared to be Kojiro's cue to do the same.

"*Arai Sama, gomen nasai,*" Kojiro spoke first.

Although it was always hard, at first, to recognize different facial traits in other races, Aldo was a master, and it was obvious to him that the older man was related to Taro. It did not require much further deduction on Aldo's part to understand that this was Taro's father. Aldo had already learned "*gomen nasai*" meant, "I'm sorry." In any culture, it could not be a good thing to bring a severely injured son home to his family, but what fault it was of Kojiro's, Aldo would have to inquire about in the future.

"*Iie, domou, arigatou gozai masu,*" Taro's father replied.

Here, too, Aldo already knew the words and had to assume the reason for their use. "*Iie*" meant "no," and the rest of the expression was "thank you very much." It seemed the father was thanking Kojiro for bringing his son home, in spite of his condition. This made ample sense, of course. Kojiro, though clearly a wreck himself, had brought Taro home alive. This also led Aldo to speculate that, although Kojiro apologized, perhaps Kojiro was not significantly to blame for Taro's condition. Either that, or this race of people was the very forgiving sort. *Maybe some combination of both?*

Kojiro then introduced them to Inotogo Arai, Taro's father and the head of the Arai clan. Aldo did not pick up on most of what Kojiro said to Taro's father, but he unmistakably heard the word "*tomodachi.*" *Friend.*

In spite of their visitors' shocking appearance and overwhelming body odor, the Arai household treated the European travelers with utmost respect. They were immediately given steaming hot baths, and Aldo was under no illusions as to why this was the first courtesy they received.

Later that night, having brought the crew off the ship, save for a rotating watch of two sailors, Simon and Aldo were led back into the main room of the Arai house by Kojiro. Two Venetians who had been wounded by Ouchi arrows were being looked after in the village, and the crew had all been scrubbed clean.

The clean but still gaunt crew members were in the main room when Aldo and Simon arrived. Neno had his recently washed hair tied back in a ponytail. In fact, the style was not dissimilar to that of the hard-looking, straight-faced group of locals also in the room, minus the shaved part on top. Of course, the similarities ended there, since Neno was inches away from hitting his head on the ceiling, and the locals were decidedly not. They stood rigid as rocks opposite the *Tigre's* crew over a long row of short tables. The tables had been laid end to end from one side of the room to the other, and there was room enough for forty people on each side, which is the approximate number of locals who were there.

Simon studied the silent, stern-looking group. Their plain clothing in subdued earthen colors did not differentiate them from the villagers they had already come across, but nonetheless, it was obvious from the set of their jaw and their unflinching gaze that they were a different sort. "Why do I get the feeling these are not peasants?" he asked Aldo.

"Because you are not a monkey. Though, perhaps, even a monkey could tell that these men are not peasants."

"Who are these men?" Simon asked Kojiro (annoyingly through Aldo's translation).

"*Samurai*," Kojiro responded, as if that explained everything.

Simon and Aldo were both pleased to see that the tables were practically sprouting small ceramic bottles. There seemed to be something missing from the room, though Simon couldn't quite put his finger on it. He was still puzzling it out when Inotogo Arai walked into the room and all the foreigners, including Kojiro, bowed deeply to him. Inotogo walked to the head of the tables and returned the bow to his followers. He then pointedly turned toward Simon, Kojiro, and the Venetians and bowed slowly at the waist. He held himself in the bowed position longer than he had for his countrymen.

Inotogo was dressed in a spotless gray *yukata*, and he was neatly groomed with the ponytail style of haircut common to the men of this land. He was thin and shorter than both Kojiro and his own son, but he moved with a grace and balance that told Simon he was not a man to be underestimated.

Aldo, realizing they had been shown respect by Inotogo Arai's long bow, returned the bow, this time in the same simple manner. Then Aldo politely requested his crew also bow.

They hesitated, so Aldo smiled and said bluntly, "If you whoremongering bastards don't bow nicely to the man, you will wish your mothers never opened their legs to the degenerate, drunken, illiterate thugs you all have for fathers." This statement, followed by a quick menacing glance at the crew by Neno, caused an eruption of ludicrous bowing that seemed to both puzzle and amuse their hosts. The crew of the *Tigre*, while brave and loyal to a man, were not the cream of Venetian society. Most of them had never been formally taught to bow, and some of them took it as a matter of pride that they had never bowed to anyone. Arms flew everywhere. One crewman bowed on his left side and bumped heads with the crewman next to him bowing on his right. Some of the men tried to cross their legs and nearly ended up falling onto the tables in front of them.

When the uncomfortable spectacle finally ended, Inotogo sat down and indicated that all of his guests should do the same. "*Minasan, suwatte kudasai.*"

Aldo informed his crew that they were being told to sit down.

That was when it registered with Simon.

"Aldo, there are no chairs."

"I don't need another Neno," Aldo responded. "I can see that there are no chairs. Just sit like they are sitting."

Simon glanced at Inotogo and Kojiro and saw that they were sitting cross-legged, with backs straighter than a Welsh arrow. He saw that the *samurai* were all kneeling and facing the table, also with noticeably straight backs. Simon attempted to sit like Kojiro and Inotogo, but his legs were not flexible enough to cross and lay flat, so he crossed his ankles and sat with his knees straight up. Simon was pleased to see that Aldo had not had much more luck in assuming that particular stance either, and had reverted to kneeling like the samurai across from them.

Simon initially held his back as straight as possible for king and country, which lasted all of about five minutes. Then the pain in his back forced him to wrap the crook of his arms around his knees as he began slouching. *What the hell, my king wants me dead anyway, I don't owe him anything,* Simon thought. He suffered some pangs of inadequacy when he saw that the *samurai* did not budge from their rigid composure.

When everyone was seated, in one fashion or another, Kojiro took up a *sake* bottle in two hands and proffered it to Inotogo. Inotogo held his cup out with both hands, and Kojiro filled it. Then, in the same manner, Inotogo poured for Kojiro. After Inotogo and Kojiro were done, all of the samurai poured *sake* for each other in the same way.

"Do you know what Saint Ambrose, the patron saint of Milan, said in the Year of Our Lord 387?" Aldo asked.

"Is there anything I could say that would prevent you from telling me?" Simon responded.

"'When in Rome, do what the Romans do,'" Aldo said, pouring *sake* into Simon's glass with two hands. The other Venetians followed the same ritual, until everyone had a full cup. Inotogo then raised his cup. All of the samurai followed, and with an indication from Aldo, so did the Venetians.

Inotogo shouted, "*Kampai*!"

All the Japanese echoed: "*Kampai*."

Aldo perfectly mimicked: "*Kampai*."

Simon, happy to begin consuming the *sake* yet less confident in his pronunciation, gave this toasting expression another try, mumbling it so as not to stand out: "Can pie." This caused Aldo to cough out loud in order to hide his mirth.

Then everybody drank, and the slow, two-handed ritual of pouring someone else's *sake* began again.

"Awfully inconvenient having to wait for someone else to pour. Do you think they'd be terribly offended if we started pouring our own?" Simon asked Aldo.

"We are unarmed and outnumbered. I believe it would be prudent to follow their customs as closely as possible until further notice."

Simon thought about the rower who lost his head for standing up and speaking to Kojiro. "Care for a refill?" he asked Aldo as he held out a bottle with both hands.

The drinking continued as food arrived from the kitchen. This is when Simon noticed another problem: no forks, no spoons, and no knives – just two long, thin, wooden sticks. The entire crew of the *Tigre* was mystified. They all watched as the locals deftly manipulated the sticks and attempted to replicate their maneuvering, but the results were comical. Eventually most of the Venetians were holding one stick in each hand and trapping the food between them. Some began eating with their hands, which visibly put off their hosts, so Aldo ordered a stop to it. Only Aldo was able to master the technique of the small eating sticks.

One dish came in a beautiful, small, covered porcelain box. When Simon opened it, he found a large, live shrimp crawling around inside. He looked over at Kojiro and saw that Kojiro had ripped the creature's head off, removed its shell, dipped it in sauce, and consumed it in one bite. Simon was not the squeamish type, as in fact he killed much of the food he ate, but he generally liked it to arrive at his table completely dead. Nevertheless, not wanting to offend his host, he followed Kojiro's example and devoured the poor little creature. It was the sweetest shrimp he had ever tasted.

In England, they would have boiled the creature for twenty minutes to make sure it was dead and free of all flavor before eating it. Simon wondered if any other boiled foods he ate in England would taste better if they were cooked less. But, then again, since England was the center of the world and at the forefront of modernity, he concluded it was not likely and didn't give it much further consideration.

After the live shrimp, they were treated to raw fish. Fish that, although dead, were still flopping on the plates in front of them, having just had their heads removed and lives extinguished. This caused the crew some consternation, and most of the men would not initially eat it. When Aldo looked at their host and saw that he was proud to be able to present this food to them, he made another pronouncement.

"Any gentleman who does not eat the fish in front of him will be disposed of in a manner very similar to the fish he is refusing to eat." When Neno reinforced this statement by glaring up and down the table, all of the fish were pronounced delicious and consumed.

Following the dilemma of the overly fresh fish, the spirits of the crew soared as the wonderful, savory smell of grilled beef came wafting into the room. After what seemed an eternity inhaling the aromatic smoke that only a grilled cow could produce, large platters of thinly sliced, fire-grilled beef emerged in the hands of the servants.

"Christ on the cross, this is the best beef I've ever tasted," exclaimed Simon after he wolfed down five slices.

"*Gloria Patri, et Filio, et Spiritui Sancto. Sicut erat in principio, et nunc, et semper, et in saecula saeculorum.* Amen." Aldo recited "Glory Be" for

Simon's soul, and then said, "I do believe that may be one of the few things you've been right about since I met you."

The meat was so tender, it melted in Aldo's mouth. There was no need to cut it, as it was brought to the table in edible sizes as every dish had been. "It's interesting that they don't cut anything at the table but bring it all out in manageable sizes. There aren't even any knives at the table. It could be that they prefer to keep weapons away from their dinner table."

"That might be a bloody wise thing to do," smirked Simon, as he remembered an experience from his youth. "As a young lad, I often snuck out of the castle and spent time in some of the seedier taverns in Exeter, the most wretched of all was called the Pig and Whistle. More often than not, the characters in this establishment ended the night in a drunken brawl. Table knives were the first weapons grabbed, but once I saw a wooden spoon used to scoop out an eyeball. The victim was a foul-mouthed bosun named Ben Bygporte. Before that unfortunate fracas, he had been known to his few friends, his very few friends, as 'Ben the Bosun.' To everybody else, he had been known as 'Ben the Belligerent Bastard.' The morning after, he became 'One-Eyed Ben.'"

Aldo was not the least bit surprised by this story. "No doubt a constant reminder of the danger in allowing English peasants access to dining utensils."

Simon laughed. "Indeed."

While the rest of the *Tigre's* crew continued to ravage the perfect slices of beef, Simon grew distracted. Out of the corner of his eye, he had spotted a grasshopper that had gained entry to the room and was cautiously sitting in the shadows near the sliding front door.

"I believe I'll stretch my legs," Simon said - a completely justified excuse as the case was.

He then walked to the door and scooped up the grasshopper. Catching a servant on her way from the kitchen with another tray of plates, he made a show of removing the lids and investigating the dishes. With a quick sleight of hand, he put the grasshopper into one of them. He then returned to the half-kneeling, half-sitting position that he had settled on, and looked around for someone to pour him more *sake*.

Since Aldo was deeply immersed in a multilingual conversation with Kojiro, Simon was forced to kick Giovanni under the table to get more *sake*. By this time he observed that the samurai were pouring bottles and holding their cups with one hand, although everybody who poured for Inotogo used two. His kick having served its purpose, he presented his cup to Giovanni with one hand, who, being one of the quicker studies amongst the crew, obliged him by also pouring with one.

As Simon drank and watched Aldo consume his dishes with perfect use of the two wooden sticks – "*ohashi*," as he learned they were called – he waited. Finally, Aldo opened the dish with the live grasshopper. Having been cooped up in a small box did not sit well with the creature, and the second that Aldo uncovered it, it leapt onto the table.

Inotogo was perplexed and very discomfited. How did his servants make such an embarrassing mistake? Kojiro too was astounded and wondered how a grasshopper had come to invade the dishes. Simon was immensely pleased with himself as he watched Aldo attempt to grab the grasshopper with his *ohashi*.

Aldo, consumed with fitting in with this new culture, did not take the time to consider that someone might be having fun at his expense. He assumed that, much like the shrimp, he was supposed to eat this live grasshopper. The roughly eight bottles of *sake* that he had drunk did not aid in his grasp of the situation, nor help in his efforts to catch the insect.

Inotogo, while initially mortified by the thought that his kitchen staff had made an incredible mistake, soon picked up on the true nature of the situation by observing Simon's behavior. The tall white man started with several snorting sounds that eventually transitioned into fits of uncontrollable laughter as he watched the shorter, darker white man chase the grasshopper. Inotogo smiled, and soon his samurai were also smiling as they came to understand the joke. The Venetians took a little longer to laugh because they lived in fear of Aldo's first mate. But when Neno himself laughed, the dam burst open.

Aldo finally realized that no one else had grasshoppers in their dishes. He turned immediately to the man he knew to be his tormentor and shot him the only look he could possibly give in such a situation. He smiled broadly at Simon and nodded in appreciation of his fine joke. If he were to react angrily, he knew it would only add to Simon's enjoyment and encourage him in the future. His revenge would have to come later, and it would be visited upon the Englishman Venetian style: with interest.

When Simon thought he could drink no more and knew he could eat no more, he downed what he thought would be his last cup of *sake*. Next to him, Aldo did the same. Kojiro, with a full cup in front of him that he had not touched recently, refilled their cups and ordered more bottles. Aldo and Simon, not wanting to waste alcohol, especially not one as smooth and flavorful as this one, downed their cups again. Kojiro and another of the samurai refilled them. Simon and Aldo drank them again. Now Simon really thought he had had enough, which was a feeling he rarely got. When Kojiro refilled their cups, he drank it again and turned his cup upside down on the table. Aldo did the same.

Kojiro was puzzled. The two barbarians could certainly hold their alcohol, and they apparently wanted more since they continued to drain their cups. Kojiro grabbed their cups, turned them right side up, and poured more *sake*.

"I can't refuse alcohol given freely, it's against my very nature," Simon slurred to Aldo. "But what do you think their plan is in all this?" It had taken Aldo some time to understand what was happening. He had not been modest in his *sake* consumption either.

"All the foreigners who stopped drinking have full cups."

"What?"

"They indicate that they are done drinking by leaving their cup full."

"You mean they waste it?"

"Perhaps that is why the cups are so small."

Contrary to the very nature of their beings, Simon and Aldo left full cups of alcohol in front of them. That is when they heard a rapid exchange of dialogue between Inotogo and a tall, slender woman who had entered the room unnoticed.

"What did they say?" Simon asked Aldo.

"I don't know, it was too quick for me," Aldo replied as he turned towards Kojiro. Kojiro told Aldo, who in turn, translated to

Simon, that the woman was the wife of Inotogo and that they had a disagreement over sleeping arrangements for the night. Kojiro then explained the disagreement honestly to Aldo.

"Inotogo-*sama* told his wife that he planned for you and your crew to spend the night either on your ship, or under guard in a village household. The Lady Arai then suggested that since you saved the life of their son, you two should spend the night in this house, and your crew should be quartered in the village, all without guard."

After Kojiro's explanation and Aldo's translation, Simon and Aldo focused on Inotogo and his wife again. They observed Lady Arai kneel and bow to her husband as she made a final remark. She then rose and gracefully strode from the room without having been introduced.

"What did she say?" Simon quickly inquired.

"She said that as always, her husband is wise and correct."

"Ah, just like England, a woman knows her place, though it would appear unfortunate for us in this case."

Kojiro spoke to Aldo, who continued translating for Simon. "What she meant was, 'This decision is far too important to be decided by a man, and you will follow my directions.'"

Simon looked bewildered. "How can you possibly interpret her remarks to have the complete opposite meaning?"

"It's obvious, isn't it?" Aldo answered. When he translated for Kojiro, the samurai could not understand how Simon could have missed the true meaning of the exchange. *Maybe he's not as smart as I thought.*

Simon frowned. "Well, it's not obvious to me. She said he was wise and correct."

"In front of others," Aldo translated, "she would not disagree with her husband. Who would? But the steel in her voice and the direct eye contact she made before walking out leave no question."

"Well, I'll tell you what, back in England we don't let our women make our decisions for us."

Kojiro responded evenly, through Aldo: "That would lead me to believe that in Japan, both the man and the woman know the nature of their relationships, whereas perhaps in England, only the women do?"

"That's absurd," Simon said without as much conviction as he would have wished.

Simon and Aldo spent that night and many more to come in the main house, unguarded.

Chapter 5

Three Months Later
The Hills above Kannoura

SIMON HAD NOT had any intention of staying on the far side of the world for so long, despite his comfortable surroundings. Memories of his mother's head dropping into the mud of Exeter Castle haunted his dreams every night, and he awoke every morning with a desire to return to England and exact revenge. She had been a woman who never missed an opportunity to say "I love you" to Simon, despite his father's complaints that it would make him soft. He had loved her back just as fiercely, and he regretted not having had the courage to risk his father's disapproval by returning those simple three words.

But Simon's vengeance was not the only consideration at hand. In addition to Taro Arai, who spent time convalescing from his Ouchi-bestowed wounds, most of the crew had suffered from joint weakness and physical malaise that would have made it impossible to sail on. Three months on the diet of the Nihon-jin, however, had strengthened the crew.

Now Simon was anxious to leave, but there was a mystery he needed to solve and he thought Taro was his best chance at solving it.

Once recovered from his injuries, Taro had proven to be a very pleasant companion. Eager to learn and more talkative than Kojiro, Taro had gradually introduced Simon to the surroundings of Kannoura. He found the young man sitting in the portico of an unwalled, wooden temple, nestled in the foothills overlooking the village. A few bald men nearby dragged long sticks across the ground, smoothing the gravel.

"You rake rocks?" Simon asked, settling in beside Taro.

"I don't rake rocks, the priests do," Taro answered. "I don't have the skill."

"It takes skill to rake rocks?"

"It takes skill to rake rocks properly."

"I bet the Irish would be good at it," Simon mused. "They rake rocks in Ireland; only they do it to get the rocks *out* of the soil."

"Ireland?" Taro asked curiously. While recovering from his injuries, he had studied the native languages of both Simon and Aldo. He wasn't picking them up as quickly as Kojiro was, but he was able to converse reasonably well.

"Dreadful little island, full of pirates, bogs, and rocks."

"What do they do with the rocks that they rake?"

"They build walls with them; lots of walls in Ireland. Now why on earth do you intentionally put all these small rocks *into* the soil, then rake them?" Simon stared curiously at the garden of rocks.

Taro pointed. "Do you see the four large, natural rocks in the sea of smaller white stones?"

"Of course."

"Those represent the four main islands of Japan: Honshu, Hokkaido, Kyushu, and the smallest is Shikoku. We are on Shikoku. What do you think the white stones represent?"

"The ocean," Simon answered confidently.

"Yes, you are correct, but also wrong. This is a Zen garden, and the rocks can represent many different things. Look at the pattern the priests have raked. Does anything else occur to you?"

Simon studied the rocks for another minute. "No."

"How about the mound of rocks in the corner?"

Simon hadn't noticed the three-foot-high mound of crushed white gravel. "Is it another island?"

"Yes and no. At night the moon will reflect off of it, and the ridges you see in the sea of gravel will look different."

Simon looked at the rectangular pattern of raked stone ridges and had some doubt as to how they could appear any different in moonlight or daylight, but he kept his opinion to himself. The breathtaking view of the village, harbor, and surrounding countryside was far more captivating to Simon, but a modicum of their hosts' politeness had rubbed off on him, so he feigned interest in the carefully raked rocks.

"Do you wish to practice Zazen?" Taro interrupted Simon's thoughts.

"What is Zazen?"

"It is a way to settle your mind and harness your energy. I would not ask Aldo. Though he seems open to our culture in many ways, he is very stubborn about his religion."

"Aye, that he is. I'm not going to have to sacrifice any living creatures, am I? Because even I draw the line there. I'm not a heathen Scot."

"I assure you, there is no sacrifice," Taro smiled.

The two of them walked into the temple where a priest was lighting incense. Taro sat on the *tatami* with his back straight and formed his hands into a circle over his lap. By this time the priest had finished and was walking about the room chanting in a soothing monotone. Somewhat alarmingly to Simon, the priest was also carrying a rod of thin, flexible bamboo. Simon had attained an improved level of flexibility over the past few months due to the unfortunate lack of chairs at meal times, so he did his best to imitate Taro's pose.

"What do I do now?"

"Think of nothing."

"Nothing?"

"And breathe."

"Of course I'll breathe, but how do I think of nothing?"

"Empty your mind of all thought."

"I believe Aldo would tell you that's the everyday state of my mind."

"Then the Way is close at hand, and you do not have to seek it from afar."

Simon cast a quick glance at Taro. *Is he having a go at me?* "It's not really the everyday state of my mind. Were Aldo to have said that, it would have been a joke."

"That's a shame?"

"Why is it a shame?"

"Because everyday mind is the Way, and if your mind is empty of all thought, you will more easily find enlightenment."

"Well, that's clear as mud."

"Clear as mud? But mud is not clear."

"Exactly." Simon thought he might be getting the hang of this Zen thing as he watched Taro ponder his own little Zen-ism for a moment. Even though it sounded quite impossible, out of respect for his host, Simon tried thinking of nothing again, but he found the more he tried not to have "thoughts," the more "thoughts" occurred to him. He looked over at Taro.

"Look down and look in front of you," Taro instructed him.

Simon tried to concentrate on a break in the *tatami* rectangles as thoughts continued to flood his mind. After what felt like hours, but was in fact about ten minutes, he began to feel sleepy and started to drift off.

Thwack! The sting from the priest's bamboo rod sent a tingle down Simon's spine. It was more than enough to wake him up, but probably not enough to leave a mark. His slumping shoulders shot back immediately, and his spine straightened. Out of the corner of his eye, he saw Taro interrupt his meditation to raise his palm towards the priest. The priest bowed to Taro, glared at Simon, then took up his rounds of chanting again. Over the next hour, which felt like days, Simon drifted off a couple more times, but he did not feel the sting of the priest's rod again. After an hour, the priest chimed a bell and Taro stood.

Simon tried to stand, but could not. His eyes searched the four-hundred-year-old temple while the blood began to circulate in his legs again. A calligraphy engraving on the wall caught his eye, which Taro noticed.

"It says 'Give and Take.'"

"What does it mean?"

"It means life is give and take."

"Give and take what?"

"What is not give and take?"

"Well, say, what if I only take?"

"Then someone only gives, and still, it is give and take."

"But that's not good."

"Good and bad are irrelevant, though one should strive for balance in give and take."

Simon could see this discussion quickly spiraling out of control, so he noted the expression for future use on Aldo and changed the subject to his mystery. No matter how many times he had prodded Kojiro over three months, he had failed to get an answer, but Taro was more talkative than most and Simon had built a relationship with him. "Who is Kojiro, and why did we find you on that ship?"

Taro knew that Kojiro had refused to answer this very question. Taro did not know Kojiro's reasons for his silence, but he suspected the two most likely causes were embarrassment and humility. Kojiro would certainly be too modest to describe his heroic exploits and was conversely embarrassed by his status as a *ronin.* In saving their lives, however, Taro judged that the foreigners had earned the right to hear their story.

"Kojiro is a samurai from a minor family. He shares his family name with a powerful clan, but he is not of that clan."

"What is a samurai?" Not wanting to appear stupid, Simon had not asked this question in front of others, but alone with Taro, he felt comfortable asking it.

"Above all, a samurai is a servant. The writing of the word itself means 'one who serves.' I believe the captain of your ship has mastered the writing of it."

Simon needed no reminders that Aldo was not only approaching fluency in speaking the foreign language, but he was also learning to read and write it as well; an accomplishment that Simon knew his destiny did not include. It required studying and patience, two of his weakest skill sets. "Go on."

"You have met the forty-four samurai who serve my father. They hold lands outside the village that you have seen, including the mountain we are on now."

"A hard-looking bunch."

"Hard-looking?"

"Tough."

"I see. Yes, they are tough. A samurai trains from the time they are born until the time they die. They learn the way of the spear, of the sword, and of the bow, which they start learning from horseback."

"That explains one thing."

"What thing?"

"How the Ouchi were able to wound two of my men, through ample defenses, from a moving platform at a great distance."

"Yes, to a samurai trained to shoot from horseback, the movement of the ocean would present little difficulty. I heard about your encounter. I must once again express my gratitude to you and your crew for saving my life."

Simon was not used to flattery, and he didn't know how to handle it. "No worries," he mumbled. "How about Kojiro?" he said to quickly change the subject.

"Yes, Kojiro. The family he served was assigned to protect the Sanpo-in Temple in Kyoto. Although the temple was indefensible and faced an Ouchi army one hundred times their size, the Hosokawa family had to send a token force. This token force would demonstrate their commitment to the warrior monks who were their allies. Kojiro's *daimyo* – I believe you say *liege lord* – came from a poor, unimportant region of Western Honshu, so he and his samurai were sent to be sacrificed.

"Bloody bastards those Hosokawas then, eh?"

"It was a logical move. The monks of that order control powerful temples in the mountains of Kyoto, and it was a small sacrifice to maintain the alliance. Also, you should know, my family owes nominal allegiance to the Hosokawa as well. They are the ruling family of southeastern Shikoku, though we rarely see more of them than their tax collector."

Simon thought it seemed awfully cold-hearted, but since Kojiro was still alive, he anticipated a good story was about to unfold and he kept his mouth shut.

"As it happens, all the samurai from that poor, unimportant village were cut down that day but one. One samurai stood at the gate of the temple and held it against all comers. He killed famed samurai by the dozens, and nameless samurai by the hundreds. It is said that this samurai wielded two katanas more skillfully than anyone had ever seen a person wield one. That samurai was Kojiro.

"Finally, as the sun set, and the cuts of a hundred swords began to wear him down, he was tackled to the ground by a giant from the Ouchi army. I can't imagine he was as big as your Neno, for I have never heard of a man that size, but the tales say it was a giant, at least by our Japanese standards. Kojiro broke the giant's neck, but the honorless Ouchi refused to let him get up and fight from his feet; at this point, they were probably too scared. As this unknown samurai from an unimportant village was pounded into submission on the ground, the master of the temple, in appreciation of Kojiro's heroic defense, dispatched his own personal squad of bodyguards to save Kojiro. These elite warrior monks, wielding their eight-foot-long *naginata*, fought their way through to Kojiro and carried him off to the mountains, leaving the master of the temple to the mercy of the Ouchi."

"What is a *naginata*?"

"A *naginata* is a long-shafted weapon that ends in a two-foot, curved blade that is sharpened on one side. In the hands of an expert, it will cut men down like a crop harvest. There are no better experts than the warrior monks."

"You keep putting the words 'warrior' and 'monk' together. Am I misunderstanding one or the other? Isn't a monk a religious person?"

"You are not misunderstanding. Not all monks are warriors. In fact, most aren't, but we have had many wars over religion, and the monks have had to adapt to protect themselves. As a result of their dedication, the warrior monks have become fearsome warriors, rivaling even the best samurai. I was in Kyoto studying both religion and the fighting styles of the monks when Kojiro was brought by the temple master's bodyguard to my temple at Tenryu-ji. Do your religions not have wars?"

"And how."

"Excuse me?"

"Yes."

"And are there not warrior monks?"

Simon thought deeply on the topic for a moment, and although thinking deeply was not a regular pastime for him, he stumbled upon a correlation. "We have Knights Templar, Knights Hospitaller, and the Teutonic Knights, I suppose you could call them 'warrior monks.' Those are at the top of the list, but there are probably dozens more than that. The 'Order of the Dragon' comes to mind as well, I've always wanted to find out what that was all about. If you ask me though, all the European 'warrior monks' I've met seem a bit 'touched.'"

"Touched?"

"Yea, barmy, potty, daft, cracked, one oar in the water types."

"I'm sorry, I still don't understand."

"Probably best. Please, continue with your story."

"Well, in their frustration at having sustained so many unanticipated losses in what should have been an easy victory, the Ouchi hanged the temple master, beheaded every monk they captured, and burned the temple to the ground. The story became a fairy tale throughout the Kansai region: the 'Legend of the Crane Warrior.'" I was there when the monks brought him into the temple, though, and I heard the story from the monks directly. They are not men given to exaggeration, quite the opposite, in fact, so I know it is no fairy tale."

"Kansai region?"

"We refer to the area near our capital of Kyoto as the 'Kansai' or 'Kinki' region. It is the western region of our main island, and in addition to Kyoto, it includes the major cities of Nara, Osaka, and Kobe."

"I'm sure Aldo would be thrilled to learn that. Did you say kinky region?"

"Yes, Kinki."

Simon giggled childishly. "Kinky region it is. Please go on."

Taro didn't understand the reason for Simon's laughter, which was uncharacteristically unmanly, but he continued. "Kojiro's lord was killed at the temple, and there is no greater dishonor to one who serves than to have no one to serve. A masterless samurai is called a '*ronin*,' and it is very shameful. He would have killed himself, but in honor of the temple master who sacrificed himself, he owed the monks his service. The monks insisted that he not go to war for them, but instead study the ways of peace, and for ten years, he did just that. He helped train me in the ways of the samurai while I received my spiritual training from the monks. He even came home to my village once, and that is how he knew to bring me, um, us, here."

"So how the hell did they ever catch him?" Simon asked. "And you?" he threw in as an afterthought.

"The Ouchi stormed Tenryu-ji. They brought over seventy thousand men, and as 'hard-looking' as the monks were, the thousand monks stood no chance. As the Ouchi bodies piled up around Kojiro and the monks, though, rumors of the resurrection of the Sanpo-in crane samurai began to take root in the Ouchi army. His two-sword fighting style is quite unique, and there were veterans from Sanpo-in who swore it was him. Of course, those rumors were true, except for the resurrection part. Seeing the fear in his army spread, the Ouchi general ordered a withdrawal to the perimeter where he torched the exterior buildings. The fire quickly spread. I was with Kojiro at this time, but I had been wounded and I could stand no longer. The last thing I remember was a wall crashing towards us and Kojiro covering me with his body. After that, I woke up here, although at night I have dreams of monk heads rolling across my body."

By God, these buggers are humble. Simon thought to himself that if the bodies in the temple had piled up around Kojiro, and Taro was standing next to Kojiro, then Taro must have had a big part in the killing himself, but he made no mention of it. *I'm going to have to teach them a thing or two about showmanship before I leave.* "Well, that's a bloody good story," he said aloud. "If even half of it's true, you chaps should be the stuff of books and song."

"I assure you, Kojiro is the stuff of Ouchi nightmares, but I see no need for people to *sing* about it."

Simon was apoplectic. "Then how on earth do you expect to get famous and be laid by many women?"

Taro blushed. "Fame is anathema to a devout and humble lifestyle, and why would one desire to have intercourse with *many* women? Is one not enough?"

"First of all, where did you learn the word anathema? I don't even know what it means."

"Aldo."

"Of course. And speak of the devil."

"I have cautioned you many times not to speak of the devil," Aldo huffed as his rotund, sweating form emerged from atop the last stair.

"Aldo, my good captain, we were just talking about you."

Aldo leaned over at the waist, and for a minute it appeared as though he might vomit. As opposed to the rest of the crew, whom the Japanese diet of fish, vegetables, and rice had made lean and fit,

Aldo had somehow eaten his way back to his portly, pre-voyage self. "By all means, continue then," he managed to wheeze out.

"Taro was just telling me the story of 'Kojiro and Taro,' and as a result, I discovered that he has a rather naïve view on consorting with the fairer sex. In short, he believes that one is enough."

Taro turned red. "First, it is the story of Kojiro, not the story of Kojiro and Taro, and second, when you find true love, is one woman not enough?" Taro looked to Aldo for help, but Aldo was still recovering his breath. Meanwhile, Simon was full of breath.

"My good man, it *is* the story of Taro and Kojiro. In spite of the fact that you nearly omitted yourself entirely from the narrative, I can read between the lines."

"Read between the lines?"

"I understand what happened in spite of the missing details in your story."

"In spite of?" Taro questioned.

"Never mind that, let's get back to true love. Are we on the magical island of Avalon? Is Excalibur going to emerge from the pond in your front garden?" Restraint began to lose its shaky hold on Simon's mouth. "Do leprechauns make gold in these forests?"

Taro's grasp of English was being overwhelmed. "Lepurakans?"

"Nasty little Irish faeries. Like I said before, and I'll say again, not much good comes out of Ireland. There's a reason they call it Bog Isle."

"Bogu Airu?"

Aldo, having nearly caught his breath, plopped down next to them on the portico and interrupted. "I know a bit about geography myself, and I'm pretty sure it's called the 'Emerald Isle.'"

"Not by anyone who has ever met the bogmen and bandits that inhabit the nasty place it isn't."

Lost in the excess of new vocabulary and uncomfortable discussing sex, Taro changed the subject. "With the death of the monks, Kojiro is *ronin* once again. I fear he may commit *seppuku* if we can't convince him that he now owes his service to you."

"Let me catch you up, Aldo," Simon said. He then proceeded to relay the story Taro had told him, which seemed all the more fantastical on the second telling.

"This is true, Taro?" Aldo asked, suspecting Simon had "added" a few details, as was his wont. Taro just nodded.

The wheels started turning in Simon's head, which happened occasionally. Simon could see a personally beneficial arrangement in his and Kojiro's future. Simon had no swords pledged to his name, and a long list of Yorkist arseholes to kill, beginning with one Percy Blythe. A warrior the likes of Kojiro would be an offer he couldn't refuse. "What is this alternative of service to me? You said *seppuku*? What is that?"

"It is a ritual form of suicide. One cuts the belly to spill one's insides, then continues to cut or stab oneself to death if he has no help. Usually the throat or heart are good places for follow-up thrusts. It is much better to have a friend, however, who will sever your head after the initial cut. I would be honored of course, were Kojiro to ask me to be his 'friend.'"

Taro watched as his words sank in. He knew the foreigners had watched an Ouchi captain perform the ritual without benefit of a second, and he trusted they didn't want to see it performed by Kojiro. He had no comprehension of the foreigners' lot in the world, but who would turn down the service of a legend?

Simon considered the concept of "give and take," to which he had just been introduced. For three months Kojiro had been teaching his fighting methods to Simon, perhaps he could return the favor by taking Kojiro into his service? *Although, that seems a little more akin to take and take,* Simon thought.

Chapter 6

Kannoura Village

"THE *GAIJIN* SEEM to be a stout and healthy breed despite their unnaturally pale skin," Kojiro began as he walked with Inotogo Arai through the paths of the vast family garden.

"Yes, they are strange, but…" Lord Arai tried to think of a suitable word.

"Likeable," Kojiro prompted.

"Yes, exactly," Lord Arai said with a smile. "Likeable, and at least two of them are very intelligent, one deceptively so, the other conspicuously so. The captain of the *gaijin* ship has picked up our language very quickly." Lord Arai paused. "And it is rumored that *you* have a gift for languages, too."

"*Iie*," Kojiro modestly denied this fact that they both knew to be true.

Inotogo got to his point. "There is a rumor. It is said that you are composing a death poem."

"Your household spies are good," Kojiro said, a little taken aback. "My daimyo and clan were killed at Sanpo-in. The monks who rescued me were slaughtered at Tenryu-ji. I would have already done the honorable thing, but I had an obligation to return your son to you. Selfishly, I also wished to live until I saw him regain his health, which he has now done. It seems my duty has been fulfilled and there is nothing left for me."

"You seem to be forgetting something," Inotogo said, beginning his part in the plot he had hatched with his son to preserve Kojiro's life.

"Am I?"

"From what I gather of the story, those 'likeable' *gaijin* saved the lives of you and Taro with their attack on the Ouchi ship."

"I would say that is accurate. Doubtless the Ouchi had a poor death planned for us."

"Then it would seem that your duties in this life are not yet fulfilled."

Kojiro was not following. "They aren't?"

"You owe the foreigners your service now."

"But… they are foreigners."

"Did your teachers at Tenryu-ji differentiate in their lessons as to whom the teachings of Buddha shall apply?"

"No, but…"

"But?"

"But they are foreigners."

"Your logic eludes me. Perhaps 'they are foreigners' is a Zen *koan* that I missed in my own studies?"

"It is not."

"You alone must decide your fate, but I believe you owe your service to the men who saved your life," Lord Arai continued. "And I hope you will forgive me, but I would put you doubly in their debt.

I cannot afford to allow my only son to leave again. With a weak emperor, our country will descend into war. Too many minor lords wish to expand their domains, and with no control from the capital in Kyoto, there is nothing to stop them. I must protect my people, and I need my son to help me do it."

After many long moments of reflection that went uninterrupted by Inotogo, Kojiro spoke. "I cannot answer at this point; I must observe them further. Indeed, they saved my life, but I cannot in good conscience serve a people who are unworthy, and being 'likeable' does not make one worthy. However, if I do decide to serve them, I will willingly serve long enough to repay your son's debt as well."

"I thank you for that. I've studied men for a long time. I think you may find these men worthy of your service, despite their barbarian nature."

The issue was postponed, however, when one of Lord Arai's *shinobi* ducked into the garden through the small servants' entrance, spotted Inotogo, and came running over.

The breathless spy, still dressed in the elegant, yellow silk robes of the Kono court, dove into a kneeling position before Lord Arai and Kojiro. "Arai Sama, Lord Kono marches on Kannoura," he blurted out as he handed Inotogo a slip of paper.

Lord Arai's features steeled.

He had known trouble would follow the unfinished business in Kyoto, but he was surprised that it had come so quickly. The fact that it was the Kono riding against him was disastrous, but not unexpected; it was why he had placed his best spy, the man kneeling before him, in that court.

"How much time do we have?"

"They are waiting for their more distant levies to arrive now. I'd say three days at the least, five at the most."

"Why did I not hear of this earlier?" Inotogo scolded his spy.

"*Honto ni, Gomen nasai*," the spy apologized. "Lord Kono sent me away on a trade mission while he gathered his host. It's possible he suspected me. I came straight here when I discovered his intentions."

"So be it." It was not within Inotogo's character to hold men responsible for events outside their control. "I have another mission for you."

"Anything, my lord." The spy was desperate to make up for a mistake that could be fatal to the entire clan.

"Ride to the castle at Kochi and ask the Hosokawa to fulfill the terms of our alliance. Explain the urgency. Take a fresh horse from the stable and leave yours."

"*Hai, wakarimasu.*" The spy hustled back through the short door.

"Why are you being attacked by the Kono clan?" Kojiro asked after the *shinobi* left.

Inotogo sighed. "The Kono have coveted my lands for generations," he explained as they increased their pace across the garden. "They have not dared to invade because we supplied swords to the Ashikaga Shogunate. It would seem the current weakness in both the shogunate and the Imperial Court has made them bold."

"What are their numbers?" Kojiro asked.

Inotogo unfolded the note that the spy had given him. "Six hundred samurai cavalry, and an estimated eight hundred peasants with spears."

Kojiro looked at Lord Arai. "I have met your household samurai. You have little more than forty. Do you hold the allegiance of more?"

"Some of their uncles and cousins, but no more than seventy, all told."

Kojiro thought back over what Inotogo had said. Gradually, the lord's words sank in. "*Six hundred cavalry*?" he asked incredulously.

"Yes, the Kono cavalry are notorious on Shikoku. I'm surprised word has not spread to Honshu. They are the only clan I'm aware of that fights primarily on horseback." He stiffened. "No clan on record has ever stood against the speed and brutality of a Kono cavalry charge."

"Over the last ten years of constant battle, I have seen all matter of fighting, but I have never seen the charge of that many cavalry. How do you defeat such a thing?"

"With our numbers, I don't know that we can. As you may be aware, we are known for the quality of our blades and the skill of our swordsmen, but unless we get the Kono off their horses, it will mean little."

"Sun Tzu says that when the few fight the many, the battlefield must be restricted."

Lord Arai knew the proverb. "I will flood the rice fields. It will limit the avenues of approach."

"Can you increase your numbers?"

"As you heard, I have sent for help from the Hosokawa, but I have low expectations there."

"Wise," Kojiro replied with more than a hint of bitterness.

"And I have peasants."

Kojiro was not encouraged by this last statement.

Chapter 7

Yuzuki Castle, Shikoku Island

THE MUSCULAR BLACK stallion pawed at the frost-covered dirt with his iron-shod hooves. He snorted his impatience, and the vapor in his breath cooled into visible white clouds in the late winter air. "*Kuro*," named unimaginatively for the color of his gorgeous coat, understood what was coming and hungered for it to begin. Selectively bred through generations of swift Mongol steeds and brute Korean warhorses, he could feel the excitement of an upcoming battle in every fiber of his body.

Kuro had maimed his first man before the age of two. A sadistic blacksmith had been too careless in his hoof-trimming duties, and a rearward kick to the head permanently ensured that Kuro would suffer no more indignities at the man's hands. He didn't really know what it meant to maim or kill, but he knew that his actions sometimes caused humans to move differently, or sometimes to stop moving entirely. Kuro had caused many enemies of his master to stop moving entirely.

Men had tried to break him, scared men. Kuro, like all horses, could sense and smell fear: a man's eyes might get wider as he approached; his voice might not be confident or sound overconfident; he might be too stiff in the saddle or not stiff enough. Kuro had many ways to tell, but the result had always been the same: the man dismounted either of his own accord or of Kuro's doing.

That is, until he met his master. His master had handled Kuro with unshakeable confidence from the first day they met. The man seemed to know instinctively what Kuro was going to do before he did it, and that had made him impossible to unsaddle. Eventually, Kuro learned to trust his master, and now Kuro would follow his human's commands without hesitation.

Lord Kono spent a great deal of time caring for his high-maintenance horse. It was unusual for a man of his stature to do work that was normally relegated to a lowly groom, but his horse rewarded this caring treatment tenfold. In battle, Kuro was utterly fearless and responded to Lord Kono's most subtle commands instantaneously. Kuro had struck, fractured, and trampled men to death; he feared nothing. Lord Kono knew that this time would be no different. The Arai clan would be brought to its knees, and their fertile land would finally belong to the superior Kono clan.

Kuro's heart raced as he saw the colorful standards raised throughout the assembly grounds. His spirits soared at the sounds of armored men marching and the issuing of harsh commands. He even allowed the lesser horses to assemble close to him. Kuro did not understand the idea of a "lesser" animal the way a human would, but he knew that all the other horses were slower and weaker than he.

Lord Kono surveyed the mounts of his men. In a Kono cavalry charge, the mettle of the mounts was as important as the mettle of his samurai. It would be the first battle for some of the horses.

Some of them would shy away from the enemy spears, and their riders would die. Other horses would panic in the chaos of battle, and their riders would die, too. However, through experience, he was confident that most horses would follow Kuro's lead and drive straight into the enemy; Kuro's brothers certainly would, for they had the same good breeding. Together, the Kono horses would shatter and break the Arai lines. Lord Kono strode to the nervous, fidgety groom holding his magnificent stallion.

Kuro's master approached him in full armor, as Kuro knew he would when the flags flew and the men gathered in formation. Amongst all the armored men, Kuro knew his rider by his unmistakably confident gait as much as by his yellow-lacquered chest plate and stag-antler helmet. Kuro heard his master shout in his deep, gravelly voice. It was followed by an answering cry from the gathered masses that never failed to fire the blood in his veins. Kuro then felt the light tap of his master's heels on his flank. Kuro restrained himself from leaping forward, instead willing himself to walk at a dignified pace, neck erect and head held high.

As Kuro moved forward between the columns of riders on either side of the parade grounds, the other horses fell in behind him in orderly rows. Kuro fought his instinct to jump to the front of the formation, but he did stay at least a neck's length ahead of any other horse. Even his master knew better than to try to prevent him from holding the lead, small though it might be.

They left the castle and parade grounds behind them, bright yellow *sashimono* flags rippling on the riders' backs in the stiff morning breeze. The winding wooded road to the coast unfolded before them as Kuro led his master's army to war.

Chapter 8

**Three Days Later,
Kannoura Village**

THE GRIM-LOOKING SAMURAI archers, with unstrung *daikyu* strapped to their backs, marched into the village in perfect formation. The archers' *sashimono*, also strapped to their backs, bore the *kamon* of the Hosokawa clan: eight circular stars surrounding one larger circular star. Unfortunately, as Inotogo observed, they were woefully few in number. As Inotogo walked to the center of the village to greet them, he estimated perhaps a hundred and ten men. Their leader, a young man named Tomohisa Okuda, bowed and apologized for the lack of resources that he brought.

Lord Arai returned the respectful bow of the Hosokawa leader and replied, "*Iie, domou arigatou gozaimasu.*" Inotogo thanked the man, both because it was customary and because he knew that the size of the contingent was not this man's fault.

He had *shinobi* in the Hosokawa court as well, and he knew Lord Hosokawa was scheming to expand his territory and influence near Kyoto. The Hosokawa family and their grand plans would give little thought to who controlled a minor seaside fiefdom on Japan's smallest main island. On the off chance that Inotogo was able to hold his territory, this small contingent of archers would be used as an excuse to demand his continued fealty. If, on the other hand, the Arai family fell to the Kono clan, the Hosokawa would merely be out a few archers.

Inotogo recognized it was the same logic that had consigned Kojiro's clan to its death at Sanpo-in. *I wonder what this Tomohisa Okuda did to earn himself a suicide mission,* Inotogo pondered.

Later that night, Lord Arai called a council of war. His spies and cavalry scouts reported that the Kono force had swelled at camp to comprise a final number of roughly eighteen hundred men. This included approximately a thousand peasants variously armed and armored, two hundred horse archers, and six hundred of their famous elite spear cavalry.

Lord Arai spoke.

"I, along with many of you at this table, have defended this village from bandits on land and pirates from the sea. We have fought in campaigns for our emperor and campaigns for our daimyo." Inotogo looked at Tomohisa here, not out of vindictiveness, but because if they survived this war, he wanted to communicate that the Arai clan would be asking the Hosokawa to answer for their meager support.

Tomohisa looked at the floor as Inotogo continued. "We have never fought against such numbers, and none of us has faced a Kono cavalry charge." The samurai around the room, battle-hardened though they were, exchanged brief but nervous glances.

In fact, only one person at the table had ever stood in the face of massed horses bearing down on him with lances leveled: Simon. Simon was surprised to find out that cavalry charges were not a regular thing for these warriors, so he wondered if he might not have something to contribute.

For now, he kept his mouth shut; it was something he was getting better and better at. Simon had fond feelings for the Nihon-jin, and they had nursed him and the *Tigre's* crew back to health. He wanted to help them, but he wanted to survive long enough to exact his revenge back in England as well. If it were just a matter of heart versus head, his heart would win out every time, but in this case it was heart versus heart: it would not be terribly grateful to pack up and run, but he *needed* to ensure that he'd be alive to cut off Percy Blythe's balls. It was a serious dilemma, but then again, Simon was a natural-born sucker for lost causes.

Lord Arai, followed by the man who appeared to be his oldest lieutenant, seemed to do most of the pointing and speaking. The language used was rudimentary, and with the aid of the map, even Simon was able to follow the discussion. The plan they came up with was simple, which as far as Simon was concerned, was the hallmark of any great plan. Given their limitations in terms of manpower, it was also sound.

The plan was to flood the rice fields around the village, which had already begun, and bottle up the cavalry on the one major and two minor roads leading into town. The steep, wooded mountains south of the town were impenetrable to cavalry, and the mountains north of town, where the temple was, were nearly so. They could be defended with a small contingent. Simon had an idea to further even out the numerical odds. As the discussion wound down, Simon looked at Aldo and shrugged.

Aldo saw Simon's shrug and knew what it meant. The *Inglese* had a talent for trivializing matters of importance through gesture, and it looked like he'd just made up his mind to stay and help the Nihon-jin. Aldo wanted to help them as well, but he couldn't see how chancing the deaths of any more of his crew or – bless the Lord for his mercy – even himself, could possibly improve his profits.

Aldo caught Simon's stare and forced himself to ponder their situation more deeply. Realistically, he knew the voyage would have ended in death without the villagers' help. He had seen the symptoms in his crew of a mysterious and deadly sailor's disease, one that only seemed to take hold on long voyages without fresh food: weakness, muscle pain, bleeding from the gums, and those symptoms had been exacerbated in his own crew by hunger. They would have started dying from that disease, and soon.

No, he still had a chance, albeit slim, to make some money on this voyage (and to return to Venice alive) and he owed it all to the people of Kannoura. A thought occurred to him. *If I fight alongside these people and we win, I may be able to create a monopoly trading for that enameled pottery or that wonderful sake.* Once the merchant side of his character reconciled itself with his innate desire to do the right thing, Aldo made up his mind: he would fight. He nodded back at Simon.

Simon looked at the table and spoke to make sure he understood the plan. He spoke in a mixture of English and Japanese, and both Aldo and Kojiro helped out when his Japanese failed him.

"You have assigned Taro to hold the northern ridge with a small contingent." Simon paused to make sure his Japanese was working. Seeing no confused faces, he continued on. "You are stationing the rest of your men in front of the village, from tree line to tree line, with heavy concentrations of spear-armed peasants on the three roads leading into town." He looked around again, and again his Japanese seemed adequate to the task. "This use of interior defensive lines will allow you to shift your resources where you are pressed most heavily. Behind the spears are your sword-armed samurai and behind them your archers."

"That is all correct," Inotogo responded.

"The range is too great for our ship's cannons to help you from the bay, so we will offload four cannons tonight and place them on your roads," Simon said, with consent from Aldo. "We will place two on the widest road, the one that leads straight into town, and one each on the northern and southern roads at the edges of the rice fields. We only have the manpower left to man four cannons, and we're going to need your spears and swords to protect them. A barricade across the roads will help disguise our weapons and also provide some additional protection to our sailors."

Lord Arai had heard of these "cannons" and the damage they had inflicted upon the Ouchi at sea. He did not hesitate to accept the help. He bowed to Simon and Aldo. "Domo, arigatou gozaimasu." Aldo left the house and called for his sailors, causing him to miss the furor that ensued shortly afterwards over a word that Simon didn't understand: *makibishi.*

Strangely, Lord Arai remained quiet while his heretofore-leading lieutenant debated loudly with a man that Simon had not really noticed was in the room. This other man had stood quietly behind Lord Arai's other lieutenants and not said a word up until this point. Now he was constantly bowing, and using Simon's go-to moves of throwing *'desu'* and *'kudasai'* around as much as possible. Although he was arguing with the utmost humility, he was clearly not backing down from his point of view.

It was then that Simon noticed how sun-darkened his face was, as well as his plain *kimono*. Another remarkable feature about the man was his height; next to Simon, he was the tallest man in the room. Simon had learned firsthand on the Ouchi ship that this nation took its caste system seriously, and nothing he'd seen in Kannoura had caused him to question this judgment. Nothing until now, that was. Taro moved next to Simon and pulled him out of the circle of men around the map.

"The man speaking now is Maeda. The name Maeda means 'in front of the rice field,' and he is first amongst our farmers."

"But he is a peasant!" Simon blurted out the obvious. In England a peasant's rank in the food chain was hardly different than it was here, and there were certainly no peasants who had ever spoken at *his* father's councils of war.

"I can see that your time spent with us has not been a complete waste," Taro smiled. "So you are shocked that a peasant speaks in our council of war." He said it as a statement, not a question.

"It's, uh, not what I would have expected." Simon surprised himself yet again by speaking diplomatically.

"It is very unusual, of course, but my father is not a usual man. We do not have enough samurai to defeat the Kono, even perhaps with the help of your 'cannon,' so our lives will depend on the performance of our farmers and fishermen. It is not an enviable position to be in, but nonetheless, that is where we are. Maeda is the backbone of the village during peacetime, and he will be the backbone of the villagers in battle. That is why my father invited him to this meeting. If he falls, the villagers will collapse and run. I don't need to tell you where that will leave us."

Simon thought about the stories he'd heard regarding the wholesale butchery of Lancastrians after the Battle of Towton, where his father died. "No, you don't. But what are they arguing about? What are *mackiebitches*?"

Taro smirked. "*Makibishi* are sharp iron spikes that are meant to injure an enemy's foot. In this case, my father's top advisor has proposed seeding the rice fields with them to stop enemy cavalry. Maeda-san has argued against it, citing the crippling injuries that the farmers will face once the battle is over."

"We call them caltrops, and they *are* damn effective against cavalry. I can see both sides. Also, you called him Maeda-*san*, but he is a peasant, I thought you only used *san* for your betters or your equals."

"He is a peasant, but he has earned my respect. I choose to call him *san*. You may address him as you wish."

"Does he have a first name?"

"No, he does not. Commoners are not entitled to a first name."

"So, no first name, but you call him '*san*.'"

"That is correct, but my father simply calls him Maeda. I respect that he is older than me as well as his work ethic, so I choose to use 'san.' No one will care what you call him."

"Because I'm a dumbass."

"Is that a question?" Taro smiled again.

Simon moved on from the Japanese titling conundrum. "So what is your father going to do?" The argument, if you could call it that, had finished and Maeda had returned to the outside of the circle with his head held down, his back still straight. Inotogo's first lieutenant stood with his back just as straight, but also with his head held high.

Inotogo spoke. "Diagram the rice fields and choose the ones that Kono cavalry are most likely to enter. Of course the fields next to the roads must be included. Then count the number of makibishi you put in each field and document the location as nearly as possible. Use a pattern so we will know where they lie in every field. After the battle, we will recover the makibishi. If we fail to find all the makibishi in a particular field, I trust the villagers will be cautioned to wear thick-soled footwear in that field." Inotogo then resummoned his stout farmer. "Maeda!"

"*Hai*!" Maeda made his way back to the interior of the circle with a face considerably less dour than it had been a minute earlier.

"Since the aftermath of this action will affect you the most, I task you with selecting a person to draw the diagrams."

"*Hai*, wakarimasu," Maeda answered enthusiastically.

"Ebitani," Inotogo addressed his top lieutenant, "since it is your idea, and you are the most experienced in battle, I entrust you with choosing the locations for the makibishi."

"*Hai*, wakarimasu," Ebitani answered obediently.

Taro explained the resolution to Simon. Simon came to the same conclusion as Ebitani and Maeda: *Inotogo Arai is a clever man.*

Simon headed towards the *Tigre* to prepare his armor. *I guess all that time spent learning the weak points in a samurai's armor from Kojiro may not go to waste after all.*

Chapter 9

The Following Morning
Lord Kono's Army

THE FOREST PARTED suddenly, offering a sweeping view of the village of Kannoura and the harbor beyond it. Lord Kono and his lead cavalry elements were struck silent by the sight of a colossal ship anchored in the tiny harbor.

"Whose ship is *that?*" Lord Kono spit the last word at his second in command, a grizzled old campaigner who had seen most of what war had to offer.

"Hosokawa?"

"My spies assured me they would send no reinforcements of significance."

"Maybe the spies were wrong."

"I know you have no use for spies, my good lieutenant, but they ferreted out the Arai spy in my court, and I see very few men and even fewer Hosokawa banners before us." Both men looked down at the village, and indeed, the Hosokawa sashimono were noticeable in their near absence. The Arai banner stood tall in the center and at both flanks of their lines, but the men below those banners looked to be less than half the Kono numbers. Nevertheless, the ship in the harbor troubled Lord Kono because it was unexpected. Unexpected was never good.

Lord Kono studied the terrain once again. He'd seen it for himself a year ago while disguised as a lowly merchant. The main road before them branched when it reached the western edge of the rice fields, and two lesser roads circumscribed the fields and led into town. The main road continued on as a raised levee straight into the center of the village. All three of the roads ended at a jumbled blockade of carts, barrels, and logs that appeared to be hastily thrown together by the Arai clan.

Lord Kono patted his horse's neck. "You'll make short work of that little obstruction, won't you?" His horse snorted twice, and by all appearances he seemed to be answering his master.

"Mountain column, forward!" Lord Kono barked. His trusted lieutenant's war fan flashed. His smallest column of horses left the road and began their climb through the woods onto the hilly ridge flanking the town's north side. Lord Kono did not have much hope that a flanking maneuver through the mountainous woods would be successful, but he had to explore the alternative. *And if there are men from that ship waiting to ambush us, those hills are the only place they could be hiding. We'll soon see,* he thought to himself.

"Do you see the glint from their iron and steel?"

"*Hai*," the old samurai lieutenant answered as he surveyed the village below. He could see that a line of spears covered the length of the rice fields' eastern border; thick at the three roads, much thinner in between. The grizzled old campaigner gripped his war fan in preparation for what was to come.

"It is too thin between the roads; they will die badly."

"But the fields are flooded, my lord."

"I will be on the center road, of course, but many of the men's mounts are sufficiently trained to maintain their charge through the muck."

The lieutenant was not convinced of this, since he did not know how long the fields had been flooded and how deep the mud would be under the water, but now was not the time to show any hesitation. To show anything but the utmost confidence in their plan could plant the seed of doubt in others' minds. Doubt was a killer in combat. "*Hai*!" he bellowed out with more sureness than he felt.

After giving his mountain column a twenty-minute head start, Lord Kono looked up at the noonday sun. It was time. "Advance," he said firmly. The old samurai, who had fought alongside his lord more often than either of them wanted to remember, waved his war fan.

Thump! Thump! Thump! Thump! The deep rumble of wooden mallets on stretched cowhide erupted behind the Kono lines and reverberated across the valley. The *taiko* drums beat out a marching pace, and Lord Kono tapped Kuro's flanks lightly. They moved down the hill at the head of the vast column of horses: Lord Kono always led from the front.

Kuro loved the drums, and the drums walked forward with the column, beating out their pace: *Boom!* two, three, four, five, *Boom!* two, three, four, five. Kuro knew the drum commands: a slow five-second beat for walking, an increase to three seconds for a trot, and finally a trio of three-beat sequences for a charge. He could assemble, rally, or retreat with drumbeat commands alone, though he had yet to experience retreat. Kuro pranced to the beat, raising his knees up high in an exaggerated motion to keep time with the drums. His master patted him on the shoulder and spoke softly to him.

"Only the best pears for you as we feast our victory tonight."

The sound of his master's voice always put him at ease, but he wasn't nervous. He was excited.

The formidable army advanced slowly toward the village. At the western edge of the rice fields, where the road split into three, Lord Kono gave his commands. "Column right! Column left!" his deep voice growled. "Center column to me!"

The war fan fluttered, the taiko drums pounded, and the columns of horses flowed like three streams onto their designated roads. Lord Kono directed his strongest horses and most experienced samurai onto the hard dirt levee that led straight into the center of town. The column paused briefly and drew up to five horses abreast – the maximum that the levee's width allowed.

When the left and right columns had done the same on their perimeter roads, Lord Kono ordered the advance. "Walking pace!" The columns moved along their respective roads to the sound of the drums: *Boom!* two, three, four, five, *Boom!* two, three, four, five.

"Move to trot," Lord Kono ordered, as they continued to move along the levee unmolested.

Boom! two, three, *Boom!* two, three, the drums beat out the pattern.

Lord Kono glanced to his right and then his left. The other two columns of horsemen skirted the edges of the rice fields, all headed east toward the village. With the drumbeats unifying their movements, all three columns moved as one. The meagerly armed peasants occupied little of Lord Kono's thought or consideration as they trailed behind his awe-inducing host, breathing in the dust kicked up by the horses. *We won't be needing the peasants today,* Lord Kono judged as he looked at the half-assed barricade thrown across the road.

At three hundred yards, the arrows began to fall: high, arching, unaimed arrows that would have done little damage except that the column was so densely packed due to the constraints of the road. Horses and men began to fall behind him.

"Steady," Lord Kono said as Kuro strained at the bit.

"Patience, Kuro, patience," he whispered into his horse's ear. "I know you have the energy for a charge at full gallop from this distance, but other horses do not."

The arrows peppered the air again, and more horses dropped. At two hundred yards, Lord Kono first took notice of the two large, open iron tubes pointed at him, but they did not register as a threat. "Charge!" he roared, and the war fan waved. The drummers responded in turn.

Boom! Boom! Boom!

Boom! Boom! Boom!

Boom! Boom! Boom!

Lord Kono dug his heels into Kuro's flanks, and the steed broke instantly into a gallop. Lord Kono dropped his lance next to the right side of Kuro's neck, and held on as Kuro broke away from the column.

"Kono!" Lord Kono bellowed.

"Kono!" his men echoed behind him, and the answering cry came from the roads on the right and left.

Breathtaking, Kojiro thought as he watched the Kono horses thundering toward him. B*eautiful animals, colorful riders, and naked steel; if they weren't coming to kill me, I would cheer.*

Kuro worked his leg muscles like no other horse in the army could, pulling his rider far in front of the rest of the column. His master did not try to slow him down. At this stage, he never did. Arrows whistled past his ear, but Kuro paid them no mind.

Then suddenly, Kuro's world erupted. A belch of fire issued from the round tube in front of him, and a swirling rush of wind passed next to his left ear. Kuro reared up and turned in time to see horses and men behind him disintegrate into shattered bones and horseflesh. Then another tube erupted at the second low point he had spotted in the barricade, and an eddy of air passed to his right this time. He had never heard such screams, cries, and whinnies of pain and distress, but the weight of his master was still in the saddle, and his master's lance still rested by his neck, right where it should be. Kuro pinned his ears back and made straight for the fire-breathing iron tubes.

Kojiro observed carefully as Neno ran the two gun crews at the center barricade. The guns had jumped high and shot backwards with such force on their improvised carriage wheels that Kojiro was surprised the restraining ropes tied to the barricade stopped their rearward trajectories. And there was that smell; it was the smell of hot springs, accompanied by thick clouds of white smoke that stung his eyes. Kojiro moved away from the acrid smoke, but the stink of sulfur wouldn't leave his nostrils.

"Get it swabbed, *pezzo di merda*, or those barbarians are going to spit you on their pretty little lances like a lamb at Easter!" Neno yelled at his sailors.

Kojiro heard the big *gaijin* shouting, but to him it appeared the foreign sailors didn't need the motivation. Their teamwork was impeccable.

"Solid shot, load."

"*Si*," came the reply of his men. In a swift, practiced motion, one sailor shoved a wet mop into the barrel of the cannon, a second crewmember followed with a powder charge, then a third crewman loaded a cannonball, after which he jumped sprightly to the side.

"Wad."

"*Si*," another sailor shouted as he rammed wadding into the muzzle to prevent the ball from rolling out.

"*Muoviti, muoviti più veloce*!" Neno yelled at his crew to move faster, although the whole procedure was accomplished in under a minute.

"Give fire."

The whole crew stepped aside as the gunner touched a lit match to the gunpowder in the touchhole. The cannon roared and jumped again, and for a third time the approaching column of horses rippled in a dervish of death and destruction.

Kojiro saw that the man at the head of the column still came on towards their position with barely a pause. Based on the magnificent horse that the man sat astride and his stag-antler *wakidate*, Kojiro guessed that man was Lord Kono himself. "At least we do not fight cowards," Kojiro observed aloud to no one in particular.

Simon, standing nearby, heard the comment.

"I would prefer to fight cowards."

"Invincibility lies in one's self," Kojiro responded calmly.

"Easy for you to say."

"I did not say it. Sun Tzu said it."

Simon didn't ask, and unlike Aldo would have done, Kojiro did not elaborate.

"I must find out more about this Sun Tzu," Aldo chimed in as he leveled his crossbow and fired across the barricade into a horse's chest.

Kojiro watched Aldo and another member of the *Tigre's* crew, whose name he had learned was Giovanni, manipulate their crossbows with deadly effect. *That weapon is slow to reload but immensely powerful,* he thought as he watched horse and rider tumble forward after being struck by Aldo's shot.

"Reload, *imbecilli*!" Neno yelled.

Before Neno's gun crews could get off another salvo, many of the Kono cavalrymen moved off the raised levee and into the muddy, water-filled rice fields. The cannons on the left and right flanks were having a similar influence on the Kono cavalry who poured into the rice fields, where they discovered a nasty surprise. The makibishi served their purpose, bringing horses to their knees and making their riders easy prey for the sparse but skilled Hosokawa archers.

As the riders continued to approach, enemy horse archers behind the charging cavalry began to loose their own arrows into the thin formations of Arai spearmen who were bracing for the cavalry charge's impact. Simon again marveled at the archery skills of these samurai warriors, whose arrows shot true even while the archers galloped on horseback. Unfortunately, Simon's admiration was tempered by the realization that the peasant spearmen, their best line of defense for charging cavalry, were becoming disheartened. As spearmen fell to arrows, and the fearsome drum-propelled Kono cavalry charge came relentlessly onward in spite of their losses, some of the villagers began to shuffle backwards.

A loud call rang out from the tall peasant who had been at the war council: "*Banzai*!" This cry, repeated up and down the line, halted the villagers' backward slide, but their spears were neither steady nor strongly held.

"*Banzai*? Isn't that the miniature pruned trees?" Simon asked Aldo. "Why are they screaming for shrubbery at a time like this?"

"That's '*bonsai*,' not '*banzai*.' The former are those amazing, little creations, one of which I must obtain before we leave. The latter is clearly a rallying cry. Can you not hear the distinct difference in pronunciation?"

Simon listened as the last echoes of the word died out. "Nope."

Chapter 10

NENO SAW THE giant black horse coming toward him. The cannon fire had not slowed this animal in the least, and it was bearing down on him and the gun crews. They would not get another shot off. Neno had seen cavalry amongst unarmored gun crews, and the results were not pretty. He would not rely solely on others to protect his men.

Kuro's head was spinning with adrenaline; his nostrils flared, and he sailed across the levee toward the humans straight ahead. Another horse followed closely behind him, and behind them, more horses had rallied from the shock of the cannon. The iron tubes had not erupted again, and Kuro knew he would reach his destination. Kuro leapt clear over the iron tube, kicking a human in the head as he did so. The rush of horses behind him broke apart the barricade, and the Kono charge struck home.

After clearing the barricade, Lord Kono pressed his left knee into Kuro's ribs; Kuro wheeled left and surged forward. The lord ran his lance through the eye of a peasant holding a spear. Then, even as more horses surged through the gap behind him, Lord Kono found himself surrounded by men with spears. His steed, sensing danger, kicked with his rear legs, then raised himself up in the air and came crashing down with his forelegs onto an Arai spearman.

The terrifying facemask and kabuto of Lord Kono, the brutality of his giant steed, and the swiftness of his deadly blows with both the point and butt of his lance spread fear amongst the peasants. They gave ground, and every yard they gave was quickly filled with more lethal Kono samurai on horseback. *That fire-tube was an unexpected obstacle, but now we will win this day like we have won every other,* Lord Kono thought. *And I will have those tubes to use myself in the next battle.*

Simon could not take full advantage of his sword skills amongst the crowd of spears, swords, and horses near the barricade. He moved off the main road toward the edge of the rice fields. Here, he had room to maneuver amongst a sparser formation of samurai and peasants holding the line between the center road and the left flank. *Bloody marvelous charge,* he thought, as the Kono samurai who had moved off the road advanced toward him through the rice fields. Most of them were on foot since their mounts had either been shot out from under them or hit makibishi. The mud was slowing their advance considerably, and the archers were doing their work. *Perhaps like Agincourt in 1415, the mud will save an Englishman again today.*

The enemy peasants also moved through the rice fields, having fled the road in terror of the cannons. Although the cannons were silent now, the peasants did not go back to the road.

The first dismounted Kono cavalryman reached Simon just as Kojiro joined him in line. Simon roared a primeval cry and bashed the Kono samurai's head with his shield. He then cleaved downward with his flat-bladed, double-edged sword using all the muscle in his powerful six-foot-three frame. His blade did not penetrate the man's shoulder armor, but the force of both his blows sent the man crashing to the ground. Before the man had time to recover, Simon stabbed his blade into the gap between his armored mask and cuirass, pushing through the man's neck and into his spine.

"Very ugly," Kojiro remarked at Simon's brutish tactics. Kojiro then swung his two blades in his trademark circular motion through the air, parried an attack on his left, and drove his other blade into the abdomen of a lightly armored peasant on his right. He removed that sword from the peasant and chopped the hand off the samurai on his left. Kojiro swung his blades in that same windmill motion again and went to work on his next two opponents.

"Flashy, I'll give you that," Simon barked out from inside his fully encapsulated helmet.

"Remember where to strike," Kojiro reminded him.

Prior to the engagement, Kojiro had been kind enough to instruct Simon in vulnerable points in the samurai armor, and Simon had paid close attention. Simon himself was armored from head to toe with custom-made German plate armor. Not only were there few vulnerable places in this armor, the enemy had no idea where those few places were. Although the armor was heavy, Simon moved adroitly enough, and he used his shield as both an offensive and defensive weapon. The Japanese were not used to fighting against a shield, and Simon's use of the shield, accomplished swordplay, and deft movements began to build a body count.

"Invincibility lies in one's self," Kojiro reminded Simon as he gave an almost imperceptibly approving nod to Simon's kills.

Simon still had no idea what he was talking about, but he recognized the complimentary nod. The Arai samurai who fought beside them were better than the dismounted Kono swordsmen they faced, but the Arai line was being pushed back by the sheer weight of numbers arrayed against them.

The samurai to Simon's left fell, and his victorious opponent turned and swung his katana at full strength into Simon's back. It did not penetrate the armor, but it did dent the metal. If Simon lived through this battle, he knew he would feel that one in the morning. Simon used the ten-inch advantage of his combined sword and arm length to shove the Kono over the three-foot drop into the rice field. In the pause that followed, he brought the hilt of his sword crashing down on the head of another Kono samurai approaching from his right.

The Kono samurai was briefly stunned. Simon swung his sword in a wide arcing motion, bringing the blade through the back of the Kono samurai's left knee, where it found another gap in the armor. With Simon's power, his blade cleaved the lower half of the samurai's leg clear off. He dropped onto the stub of his leg, blood surging from open arteries. Simon reset with a high guard to take on the samurai he had pushed into the ditch, but Kojiro killed the man before he got the chance.

Chapter 11

The process of aging had slowly snuck up on Inotogo Arai. It had begun with a subtle graying of the hair, an odd wrinkle or two around the eyes, and an increased soreness in the joints. The stamina, strength, and speed of his youth had waned, replaced by experience and wisdom, but this was a trade he would go back on right now if he could. Aging was a curse for all, but much more so for a man who lives and dies by the sword.

Lord Arai sat astride his warhorse, surveying the developing bloodbath. He looked detached, breathing deeply, as screams of pain, fear, death, and rage filled his ears. There was something else that filled the battlefield's air: a stench. It was the foul odor of blood, excrement, and fear. To any unbiased observer, however, Lord Arai showed no sign of being disturbed by any of this.

When he had battled at a younger age he had sliced through his enemies with power and speed. As he got older, he had had to adapt to his *new* body. He learned long ago that developing precision, not power, would suit an older man. His swordsmanship now, at least as told by witnesses, bordered on magical. With a flick of the wrist, his razor-sharp, Arai-forged blade would find a chink in his enemy's armor that no one else had seen, and a light slash across an inner forearm would open a major artery and kill an opponent half his age. No need for theatrics, no need for an excess of power. Timing and precision were the keys to his skill. *Let the blade do the work* was his mantra.

Now, as the Kono cavalry spearhead edged closer and closer to his archers and the battle turned against him, he took measured breaths and thought of an old proverb. *If you know the art of breathing, you have the strength, wisdom, and courage of ten tigers.*

Lord Arai turned to his retainers, grouped tightly around him. "We will charge the center. Notify the Hosokawa archers to clear a path."

The retainer blinked. "But lord, it might be better to wait." The retainer was worried, and he was right to be.

If you fall, we all fall. The men's morale will crumble. We need to stay here, he thought.

Lord Arai wore his distinctive silver and charcoal armor, and on the front of his *kabuto* the *maedate* was a horizontal crescent moon. At the side of his *kabuto*, his *wakidate* were golden falcon wings. These symbols were unmistakable; he would be a magnet for the arrows, spears, and swords of the Kono, and his loyal bodyguards knew it. They did not want him to die. And Lord Arai was not as young as the last time he had led them into battle. The retainer hesitated and humbly said, "It would be very difficult for us to protect you if you should decide to go forward."

The lord turned slowly to him. "I thank you for your concern, and I understand your intentions, but we will engage." Lord Arai knew it was a risk, a huge risk, but if the Kono reached his archers, they would massacre them. The center would fall. If the center fell, the battle would be over whether he lived or not.

He gave his familiar counsel to his bodyguard as he strung his bow: "Take arrows in your forehead, but never in your back."

Lord Arai then signaled his entry into the battle by drawing an arrow and sending it hurtling twenty yards into the neck of a Kono rider. As the rider tumbled from his mount, Lord Arai drew his katana and shouted, "Arai!"

His fifteen-man bodyguard drew their weapons and shouted "Arai!" as one.

Pointing his sword forward, Lord Arai charged through the parted archers and straight into the lead Kono cavalry elements. His bodyguard, as ever, raced into the battle right beside him.

Chapter 12

SIMON AND KOJIRO did not initially notice Lord Arai's entry into battle. They were too busy fighting for their lives. Simon tried to remain vertical, but his armor was being pummeled from all angles and directions, and he was being battered mercilessly with strikes so swift he could barely see them. Luckily, the enemy had yet to draw his blood.

Although Simon had played his advantages to the hilt – height, reach, strength, the enemy's unfamiliarity with his shield and armor – he was reaching the point of total exhaustion. What had started as a chilly morning and pleasant noon had turned into a hot afternoon with neither water nor shade for relief. *And this is how the Teutonic Knights met their doom at the hands of the Lithuanians and Poles at Grunwald in 1410: heat exhaustion. Why do I think of shite at times like this? Goddamn Aldo!*

Simon finished off a Kono samurai with a thrust to the eye, then quickly turned as he heard a bone-chilling scream. His visor restricted his vision, but he could see an Arai samurai being hacked to death by two Kono peasants. They stood over the helpless man whose helmet had been knocked off, and they were striking his bare head. One spear tip came down hard on the fallen Arai samurai, slicing through the jaw and getting stuck there. The peasant twisted the blade violently and kicked the man hard under the chin to free his weapon. The spear was retrieved when the jawbone broke in two. The Arai samurai was still alive, and the Kono peasant hacked down again.

Simon reacted angrily; he had shared *sake* with the man on the ground. In spite of his exhausted and battered body, Simon moved with surprising agility. The two peasants didn't see the knight in his full armor approach, but they heard the rattle. It was too late. Simon smashed the edge of his metal shield into the skull of the first Kono peasant, sending him crashing to the ground. The second peasant turned and swung his spear, which hit the top of Simon's helmet and sailed harmlessly off. If it weren't for the helmet, the stroke would have taken off a piece of Simon's scalp. He thrust his sword powerfully into the peasant's unarmored groin, sending the peasant backwards, mortally wounded.

Simon walked past the two writhing Kono peasants and looked at his dying drinking mate. *Poor bugger.* Dark red blood disguised the deep gashes beneath the young face; his unblinking eyes stared wildly into space. It was a disturbing sight. Simon had seen such things before; they often came back to him on sleepless nights. He looked too long. Now this was another face he'd have to drink away into sleep.

Neno did not like to lose crewmen unless it was by his own hand. He was halfway around the world and had lost enough already. Sure, for the most part they were good-for-nothing, whoring drunkards, but then, so was Neno, and only he had the right to remove them from the ranks of the living.

But the first Kono rider on the giant black stallion had infringed on his rights. He'd clobbered the head of one of his sailors before Neno had had time to react. Poleaxe in hand, Neno had tried to fight his way toward that rider, but a wave of enemy cavalry prevented it. Alongside Aldo and Giovanni, who had abandoned their crossbows for swords, he'd had to fight like a madman to protect the rest of his unarmored gun crews. With his unnatural strength, uncommon skill with a poleaxe, and plain old meanness, he and several of the stouter spear-wielding Arai peasants had carved a semicircle around the guns that the Kono cavalrymen could not penetrate.

As Neno protected his sailors, a Kono cavalryman decided to try his luck. Neno used the hammer side of his poleaxe to trap the rider's lance at the spearhead and pull it out of the man's hands. He then reversed his grip on his weapon and swung the triangular dagger with all his might straight into the man's face, killing him instantly.

The Arai peasants near Neno had seen their share of skilled practitioners at killing, but they marveled at Neno's use of his poleaxe. He wasn't just killing cavalrymen; he seemed to have the advantage over the men on horses and not the other way around. Neno's below-average ability to pick up their language and clumsiness around the village had not prepared them for the way he comported himself in battle. Inspired to be fighting alongside such a brute, two peasants moved in next to Neno and killed the next samurai that Neno unhorsed. This symbiotic relationship kept the gun crews safe for the moment.

Chapter 13

TARO HAD BEEN placed in charge of the critical mountain flank. If the mountain ridge fell, Kono riders would descend on the right flank of the Arai line and roll it up with little effort. Thus far, Taro had effectively directed his spear-wielding peasants and small cavalry contingent into positions where they had beaten back the Kono riders, including a critical stand around the temple, where the monks had joined in its defense.

Now, Taro had a decision to make. The Kono had not come for over half an hour, and his scouts reported only a few horse tracks retreating back east on the mountain ridge. Either he was being lured into abandoning the flank, or the Kono had not sent a strong attack along the ridge. *If I stay here and the Kono use most of their men to attack below, my father will be vastly outnumbered and eventually fall. But if I abandon my control of the mountain and the Kono are waiting for me to leave, we will all be massacred when the Kono come pouring out of the mountains behind me.* Ultimately, he decided he had to trust the skill of his scouts. They had tracked deer and bear in these woods since infancy, and he would rely on their reports.

Taro willed his voice not to crack. The weariness of combat helped calm his nerves, but he knew that all the men around him might have doubts about his next decision. He looked in their eyes with an expression that he hoped would convey confidence. "We go to our daimyo!" Taro shouted to his samurai cavalry and the sword and spear-wielding peasants alike. "Arai!" he shouted, in a close likeness to the deep baritone his father had in his youth.

The warriors returned the battle cry. "Arai!"

Taro turned his mount and started toward the valley floor, hoping he had made the right decision.

The first Kono cavalryman that Lord Arai reached was trying to extract his lance from the rib cage of a Hosokawa archer when Lord Arai cleaved open the back of his skull. His next opponent stabbed purposefully at Lord Arai's midsection, which Inotogo deftly dodged. He then moved in tight to the other rider and slashed three times quickly across the man's face.

The man reached for his face in agony and wheeled his horse to escape the onslaught. This left the back of his neck exposed, so Lord Arai sliced quickly across it, severing his spine and causing his head to flop forward. Lord Arai spurred his horse towards another Kono samurai, but by then his bodyguard had surged past him to cut a bloody swath through the spearhead of the enemy cavalry.

Near the cannons, Lord Kono fought like a possessed demon; his horse equaled him in intensity. The Arai soldiers tried to torment the black beast and bring it to its knees as they stabbed or slashed, to no avail. Lord Kono wielded his spear like a virtuoso, and the Arai soldiers fell as so many had fallen before them.

Kuro and his master no longer fought alone. Kuro's charge through the center of the enemy line, coupled with the silencing of the enemy cannon in the center, had opened the floodgates. The remainder of the bodyguard had rejoined his master, and Kuro fought next to familiar horses.

Kuro dodged left and swung his hips into an enemy from behind, knocking him to the ground where Kuro stomped into his ribs. Kuro did not see a long, scythelike *naginata* swing at him, but he shifted right based on the subtle foot commands of his master, which saved him from taking the *naginata* across the backs of his rear legs. His master punished the foot soldier who had the audacity to attack his horse by chopping his hand off at the wrist.

As Lord Arai and his bodyguard crashed into the Kono cavalry, a shout went up across the Arai lines announcing that their leader had joined the battle, injecting renewed energy into samurai and peasants alike. Simon heard the unified cry out of the mouths of the Arai samurai and did not know what it meant, but he watched the tired, injured, and outnumbered Arai near him redouble their efforts and actually push the enemy back to the edge of the rice fields. Simon joined in their surge, battering an enemy peasant into unconsciousness with the hilt of his sword.

Kojiro knew that if Lord Arai fell, the battle would be lost. It would turn into a massacre; a circumstance he was all too familiar with. He hesitated to leave Simon's side, but from all appearances, Simon could more than care for himself. Kojiro struck out towards Inotogo Arai.

Lord Arai's initial charge had blunted the Kono surge, but now his bodyguard was enveloped, and he was fighting for his life. His blade danced back and forth, unhorsing and killing enemy samurai less than half his age, but still the enemy came. Around him, his skilled but outnumbered bodyguard fought and died bravely.

"You twatting, sniveling, pissing gits!" Simon shouted at his attackers who continued to multiply. More and more Kono peasants were catching up to the Kono samurai and joining them in battle.

As the numbers became overwhelming, a mounted Kono samurai singled Simon out. His blade came down swiftly and Simon raised his own English battle sword to deflect it; Simon's sword shattered. *Well, that's never happened before. Bollocks.* As his world turned into a slow-motion nightmare, Simon briefly contemplated his own mortality.

Battling his way towards the father of his friend, Kojiro whirled his two swords in flurries so swift they were invisible to the naked eye. The only thing visible was the result; a grim path of dead and dying Kono warriors behind him.

Lord Kono looked out upon the sea of his samurai, some still mounted, some not, and saw an opening of daylight where an enemy samurai was cutting a swath of carnage through his men. Only the man did not wear the Arai *kamon*, instead his armor bore the mark of a black on blue crane.

I would never have thought Lord Arai would enlist mercenary help, Lord Kono thought to himself. *The fool has always been blinded by ideals. No matter, this black crane will pay for hiring to the wrong side in this fight.* Lord Kono lowered his lance and spurred his great horse towards the oncoming threat.

Maeda speared the Kono rider in the neck, halting Simon's review of all the misdeeds in his life. *Boy, was I a little gobshite,* he silently summarized his findings. *No time to dwell on the past now, but I sure do owe a few apologies if ever I get the chance.*

Simon wheeled around searching for a weapon, any weapon. While he combed the ground and spider-crawled his fingers over dead bodies, Maeda held the enemy at bay with skilled and aggressive use of his long spear.

Then, as Simon's gauntlet-clad fingers finally grasped the hilt of one of the peculiar, single-edged foreign swords, the unthinkable happened. An enemy samurai wielding a long-bladed, two-handed sword ducked underneath Maeda's occupied spear and drove his blade into Maeda's chest. Maeda fell to the ground, and Simon watched as the peasant line collapsed. Maeda had been their leader in spirit as well as in might, and being neither born nor trained to fight, the villagers' instincts took over: they ran. Simon regained his feet, wielding his new weapon, but he had little time to marvel at its light weight and balance as he, like the remaining Arai samurai holding the line without the villagers, became an island in a sea of Kono attackers.

Without warning, Simon's island grew. A tall, lean boy, with a hard-set grimace that belied his tender age, appeared from nowhere and lifted the spear from Maeda's dying grasp. With the butt end of the spear, he effortlessly deflected a blow from the long sword that had killed Maeda, and followed that with a stunning blow to the attacking samurai's chin.

While the Kono samurai stumbled backwards, momentarily stunned, the boy drove his spear into the warrior's side, under his chest plate. The boy impaled the samurai who had killed Maeda and raised him a good five feet off the ground. Then, in a booming voice that rose above the maelstrom of battle, the boy declared his proud heritage, "Maeda!" Without a glance at Simon, the boy took up the position in line that his fallen father had held. Though untrained, the Arai peasants were hardworking men of stout heart, and when the son of their village leader returned to battle, so did they.

Taro and his cavalry contingent streamed from the woods and headed straight for the rear of the Kono left cavalry wing, which had begun rolling up the Arai right flank.

The enemy didn't see him coming. As Taro's small detachment hit the enemy's rear, the element of surprise and the Arai samurais' superior sword skills stopped the Kono flanking force in its tracks.

Kojiro, tied up with a mounted rider on his left, and an unhorsed samurai on his right, did not see the charging horse until it was too late. Lord Kono's lance tip only missed its mark due to pure luck. Another Kono horse's rear bumped into him at the last second, and Lord Kono's lance had glanced off the top of his shoulder armor. Kojiro killed the unhorsed samurai, killed the man on the horse who had probably saved his life, and turned to face Lord Kono himself.

Simon, with Maeda's son, a small remnant of the peasants, and even fewer remaining samurai, were being pushed back into the village.

It was clear the fight was nearly over. Since he had witnessed these barbarians kill *themselves* over poor performances and other such trivialities, they did not strike Simon as the kind of people who would have an overabundance of mercy were he to attempt surrender. He would die in a rice field in a country that wasn't even on the map.

Neno did not know if the crewman who had been kicked in the head would live or die, but he was determined to hold the offender accountable. With the Arai peasants still holding firm around his gun crews, Neno saw an opportunity to approach his nemesis on the black horse.

Kojiro had nearly cut his way through to the rider, and most of the Kono samurai were focused on this threat, including the rider himself.

The rider's charge at Kojiro, though, had left him just outside Neno's circle of spears. Neno took two giant strides outside the protection of the spear wall and chopped down savagely with the dagger blade of his poleaxe, burying it squarely into the rider's collarbone. He then used the purchase that his stuck blade offered him to pull the rider off his mount. Once the rider fell to the ground, Neno, in a practiced motion, removed the dagger side of the poleaxe from the rider's collarbone, adjusted his grip, and raised the poleaxe straight up, perpendicular to the ground. Then, with all of his ridiculous strength, he plunged the spear tip of the poleaxe through the rider's leather throat armor. The blade traveled through Lord Kono's windpipe and into the ground beneath his head.

Neno did not know that he had killed Lord Kono, because Neno did not know who Lord Kono was, but the Kono samurai around them certainly did. A cry of anguish swept the Kono line and spread quickly across the entire battlefield. Although they still held superior numbers, the fight quickly drained from the host.

Simon knew something big had happened because the enemy soldiers paused their fearsome onslaught. And whatever happened seemed to have encouraged the indefatigable Arai samurai, because all around him they went on the attack; once again beating the Kono all the way back into the mud and water of the rice fields.

After surprising the enemy from the rear, Taro was battling forward towards his father when he heard the cry erupt along the Kono lines. Lord Kono was dead. The enemy fought on valiantly, but they were no match for the Arai swords once their morale was sapped. He and his small contingent rolled the Kono left flank and sent them reeling across the rice fields. By the time he reached his father, all the Kono were dead, dying, or fleeing.

The Kono samurai fought to reclaim the body of their leader, but the demoralized samurai could not force the combination of Neno and Kojiro to budge. The Kono peasants had already dropped their weapons and fled.

Simon, so exhausted that he had to lean on his newly acquired Japanese sword, turned to see Aldo brandishing his crossbow and cheering wildly along with the victorious samurai. *No doubt the future holds many stories of Aldo's prowess on this battlefield, one or two of which may actually be true*, Simon thought.

He noticed that, next to him, Maeda's son did not lean on his spear, but instead stood erect and focused on the retreating Kono army. *Bloody showoff; I could stand like that, too, if I wanted to*, he lied to himself.

Only one member of the Kono clan still stood firm and unbowed: the jet-black horse. He could not be settled and would not leave the side of his dead master. Three men had already been hurt trying to grab his bridle, and now an uneasy stalemate had been reached. The horse stood next to his master, while everyone else gave the horse a twenty-foot berth.

Neno approached the nervous circle that surrounded the black horse, which included several of his sailors. Giacomo Aversa, a normally fearless man who leapt about a ship's rigging with the agility of a monkey, warned Neno by looking at the horse, crossing himself, and saying "*Il diavolo*" in a hushed voice.

"*Idiota*," Neno replied as he strode straight up to the horse, grabbed its bridle, and looked into the horse's eyes. "If you defy me, I will butcher you and eat you raw, which I understand is quite a delicacy here. And you seem quite the well-cared-for beauty; I bet you'd taste extra special."

Kuro felt something he had never felt before as he stared into the eyes of the tremendously sized, pale-skinned murderer: a twinge of doubt. His master had never even been unhorsed, but this man had not only done that, he'd killed him in the blink of an eye. Now the human was talking to him; he did not like the menace in the man's voice.

Neno meant his threat full well, and he was pretty sure the horse understood him. In any event, the horse came willingly as Neno pulled it forcefully by the reins. He led it into a corral on the western edge of the village where the Arai clan kept their mounts. Before removing the horse's bridle, he pointed his blood-stained poleaxe straight at the horse's eye and cautioned it once again. "If I hear of any trouble from you, I'll come back and remove those pretty black eyes of yours."

Kuro decided not to test the large human.

Kojiro walked slowly through the rice fields. Scattered around him was the detritus of war: cleaved helmets, broken swords, horse carcasses, discarded flags, thousands of scattered arrows and bodies, hundreds dead. Samurai and peasants, friendly and hostile, lay side by side. Many of the dead were floating in the waterlogged rice fields. Others lay contorted in odd shapes on the footpaths and road.

Wading through the knee-high, muddy water, fatigued and suffering from his own wounds, Kojiro could smell dead flesh baking in the sun. A sudden movement caught his attention; a soldier was trying to drag his body out of the swampy fields. Kojiro moved to him quickly, planted his feet firmly in the soft mud, and heaved the soldier onto the bank.

The samurai was barely human. He was covered in mud, blood, and his own entrails. Kojiro took his eyes off the ashen face and looked around. The villagers had begun to venture into the fields to look for their loved ones.

"Come here!" Kojiro shouted. Four nervous-looking villagers came rushing over to the samurai and bowed. "Take him to the village immediately."

"But he is a Kono," one man said, pointing to the family crest on the armor. "And he will die soon anyway."

"He is samurai. And he will not die in the mud. Now, take him carefully," Kojiro commanded.

The villagers picked up the lame, dying soldier. Sweating and heaving with exertion, the men carried him back to the village.

Kojiro scanned the field again. He recognized the corpse of an Arai samurai with a snapped-off spear protruding from his stomach. He moved towards it. Hovering over the dead man, Kojiro recited the samurai maxim. "Integrity, respect, courage, honor, compassion, honesty."

He bowed deeply, paused, and said the last. "Duty." He picked up the sword near the dead body, cleaned it with a strip of his clothing, and stuck it in his belt. "Your sword will be safe," he said to the dead man. "It will be returned to your family." As he walked, he collected the swords of more men he knew, more *souls*.

Simon observed Kojiro and asked what he was doing, which Kojiro politely explained. "Do you have anything similar in your culture?"

"The Northmen bury their dead with their weapons, we English try to pass them on to our descendants. Apparently mine had been passed on one too many times."

"Northmen?"

"You don't want to know. They're almost worse than the Irish."

Kojiro didn't inquire further. The battle was over, but its impact had just begun. It would take days to bury the dead, weeks for the warriors to recover from their wounds, months to restore the rice fields, and generations to rebuild the population. But for tonight, that would all be forgotten. Warriors did what came naturally to them after battle: they got blind drunk.

In the weeks following the battle, the famous Arai forges were unduly busy with requests for their quality arms coming from Hosokawa aligned clans throughout the islands. One spring morning, however, nobody went to work, instead, they joined Kojiro for a short trek to a grove of trees for something Kojiro called "*hanami*."

"Bless the good lord!" Aldo said upon arrival.

"Jesus sodding Christ!" Simon said.

"*Sakura*," Kojiro informed them with a pleased look. "Cherry blossoms."

When Simon had seen this grove of trees weeks ago, the branches had been barren; now they were awash in delicate, bright pink flowers. Simon had never seen so much pink in his life. In fact, he didn't know this much pink could exist in one location. It was breathtaking. While he and Aldo gaped in amazement, the villagers laid out blankets under the trees, put casks of *sake* into the mountain stream, and began grilling vegetables and seafood.

The party lasted until early evening when Inotogo clapped his hands and spoke in his soothing but commanding tone.

He began his speech by commending his samurai, one by one, for their bravery in the battle against the Kono, and followed that by thanking his tradesmen for their technical skills in producing the weapons that aided in their victory. Inotogo moved on to his farmers and fishermen, whom he commended both for their hard labor since the battle, despite the loss of so many, and also for their bravery in the fight. Inotogo also thanked the foreigners profusely for their support and martial skills, making particular note of Neno's slaying of the Kono Daimyo. Finally, he singled out one boy and asked him to rise. Simon recognized the boy and hoped he wasn't in any trouble, since that boy's father had saved his life.

As it turned out, the boy wasn't in trouble. "Mina-san, *kore kara, Maeda wa, Arai no samurai desu*!"

"Is that possible?" Simon asked Kojiro in astonishment.

"Rare, but possible, as you can see, it just happened." Kojiro informed him in a tone that, if Simon hadn't known better, he would have thought a tad patronizing.

Kojiro continued, "In one action, Arai Sama has strengthened the loyalty of his peasants who lost much in the battle, and he has added a valiant retainer after losing many. Maeda's father was stout also, and his father before him, so I believe his blood will make an honorable samurai family. Inotogo took all of this into his thinking, of course; he is a wise leader."

Simon nodded, impressed. "Does the poor bugger get a first name now, or do I have to keep calling him 'in front of the rice field guy?'"

"Yes and no."

"Why do you answer so many of my questions with 'yes and no?'"

"He will get a family name now, and it will be Maeda."

"What?"

"Maeda was his first and only name, now he has earned it as his family name, but he will also be called something else."

"And that something else will be a first name?"

"Yes."

"What will it be, and who will decide?"

"It will likely come from one of his characteristics, and he may decide, or Lord Arai may decide, or the samurai may choose his name. 'Taro' means firstborn, and Maeda is also firstborn, but he will not take the same name as the daimyo's son. He is tall, thin, and brave; his name may also come from one of those characteristics."

"When will we find out?"

"Sometime."

Simon's head was spinning so he inquired no further. After the cheers for Maeda died down, the congratulatory *sake* pours began. Maeda poured with the utmost courtesy; first for Inotogo, then for all the samurai whose ranks he had just entered and whose societal class his entire family had just risen into. After that, in a show that the remaining Arai warriors supported their daimyo's class-jumping decision, the samurai poured for Maeda, one-handed of course.

Chapter 14

KURO WAS WARY of the large man who had killed his master. He did not like to let him out of his eyesight when he came near the stable. When the human walked around the corral where Kuro grazed, Kuro never turned his back on him. Kuro craved exercise and missed the long rides and training he used to do with his master, but his master was gone and he had found a rider he would tolerate. That rider was not the big man. Like his master, this rider too was neither afraid of him nor cruel to him. His commands were different, but the human who sometimes wore black armor with a blue crane insignia was also a masterful rider.

Neno knew they would be leaving soon so he accompanied Kojiro to the corral one last time. Neno did not like horses, especially the big, black one he had captured. He didn't like that they had a mind of their own and he didn't like that you had to feed them and take care of them. Luckily, Kojiro had volunteered to do both, and it seemed to Neno like a good match.

It also made him uneasy that this horse seemed to follow him with its gaze no matter where he stood. He had seen the damage this horse could do in battle and counted himself lucky that he had emerged from his battle with the beast unscathed.

When they arrived at the corral Neno pointed at the horse, looked at Kojiro, and said, "Yours."

The horse was rightfully Neno's to give since Neno had killed the previous owner, but Kojiro couldn't accept such a marvelous gift. "No, it is yours."

"I hate horses. Especially that one," Neno replied, pointing his gigantic index finger straight between Kuro's eyes.

"I could not take it," Kojiro repeated.

"Then I will eat it for my last dinner here," Neno said, well aware of the reaction he would get from Kojiro. The *Nihon-jin* were not the only ones who could achieve their desired results through indirect communication.

Kuro did not know what the big man and the crane man were talking about, but he didn't like the tone of their discussion, or the big man's finger pointing at him.

"But he is a supreme war horse!" Kojiro protested.

"Do they taste better?" Neno asked, feigning stupidity.

"In fact, they taste worse," Kojiro informed Neno from experience. "Too much muscle; I will accept your gift, for this horse cannot be eaten." As astute as Kojiro was in the study of man, he still had difficulty comprehending the *gaijins'* use of sarcasm, and could not yet tell when they were serious and when they weren't.

Kuro didn't know why, but as the humans walked off, he felt a great sense of relief.

Later that night, Kojiro decided that his destiny would lie in service to his new friends. Not only had they proven quick of mind and stout in battle, they had shown generosity and nobility in their hearts. He was still conflicted over the idea of serving a foreigner, but he reasoned that the option of seppuku would never be further away than the swords at his waist, should his decision prove to be a foolish one. Although they had saved his life, that, in and of itself, did not make them worthy of his service. He would continue to monitor the foreigners' behavior and judge for himself.

When Kojiro announced this news the next morning it was difficult to pin down who was *most* pleased by the news. Morale soared amongst the *Tigre's* crew, who welcomed such a boost to their combined martial prowess. Simon and Aldo couldn't have been more pleased to have kept their friend, and both Inotogo and Taro Arai shared satisfied glances that their machinations had had the desired effect. The only disappointed party was the villagers at Kannoura who did not like the thought of losing such a great protector with the clouds of war rolling across their island.

Chapter 15

MESSENGERS ARRIVED IN the village daily with news of alliances made or broken, and battles won or lost in the weeks following their *hanami* outing. Simon had grown attached to the *Nihon-jin*, but he had his own war to fight, and, with Aldo's crew as healthy as it was ever going to get, he was prepared to leave. On the day that they finally and regretfully left Kannoura, Lord Arai brought his entire village to the beach to bid them farewell.

As the profuse bowing drew to a close, Taro approached Simon and handed him a sword in a scabbard. Simon looked at Kojiro, not knowing if he was meant to look at it now, or just to take it. The *Nihon-jin* were quite tied up in their etiquette, and he did not want to violate yet another rule just as he was leaving. Aldo already had enough stories of his faux-pas to use against him for two lifetimes as it was.

Kojiro met Simon's eyes, nodded at him, and said, "*Douzo.*"

Simon drew the blade from its scabbard. Instead of the single-edged blade of the *Nihon-jin*, it appeared to be an exact replica of the English blade that he had broken; only it wasn't. Simon had never wielded a blade with such balance, flexibility, and strength. The edges were polished to razor sharpness along both cutting edges, and carved into the blade, just above the hilt, was a beautifully detailed red rose.

Kojiro spoke. "The best swordsmith in Kannoura said there was nothing wrong with the design of your sword, and it was my observation that you are used to fighting with it, no? All have said you fought with it effectively, so I asked him to honor the original design. This blade, however, has forty thousand layers of steel hammered together at temperatures regulated by the master swordsmith himself. Each thin layer joins together to form an edge that is the sharpest in all of *Nihon*, yet strong and flexible enough to never break. In your stories you told me that you serve a family of the rose. A master engraver, different from the swordsmith himself, carved the rose. The black lacquer handle was done by a master of his trade separate from the swordsmith or the engraver. The Arai family and I commissioned the seventeen best craftsmen in Tosa to create this humble token as a symbol of our gratitude."

For not more than the third time in his life, Simon was speechless. He could only bow, and he did not give his flourishing European style bow. Instead, he put his arms at his sides and bent slowly at the waist in the way of the people he had received this gift from. He held the position as he had seen done when a great deal of respect was called for, then he slowly rose again.

Taro then turned to a nearby cart and picked up what appeared to be a long pole wrapped in a blanket. He walked over to Neno and handed it to him, which he followed with a short bow. Neno unwrapped the blanket to reveal a weapon that none assembled, neither *gaijin* nor *Nihon-jin*, had ever seen before. It was a combination of Neno's deadly halberd and the *naginata.* An eight-foot pole ended in a two-foot, curved scythe, while a triangular eight-inch dagger protruded from the reverse side of the blade just where the shaft met it. It was a weapon meant to be wielded by a large man, and meant to inflict gruesome damage.

Neno swung the weapon in a circle around his body, then brought it down in a chopping motion. "It is so light," he said, trying to sound grateful but doubting how such a light weapon could possibly be strong enough.

Kojiro understood the question implicit in the compliment. "It was forged just as the Simon's sword was. The blade will not break, and the force from the increased speed of your wielding will make up for the loss in weight."

Neno, not convinced, but aware of the honor of such a gift spoke again, "*È incredibile. Grazie.*"

"It is not a horse, but it's the best I could do," Kojiro responded.

"I don't like the horse, and with this I can kill many horses," Neno smiled.

Lord Arai, his retainers, and Taro all bowed. It was a hard farewell. Fighting next to a man created a bond like no other, and the hospitality of these people towards peculiar looking strangers from across the ocean was almost inconceivable. They left the four cannons behind, and God willing, Simon thought, the village and the Arai clan would survive.

As the crew rowed out to the *Tigre,* Simon looked at Aldo, "It seems you are not to receive a gift. Unlucky!" He smiled grandly at this.

Aldo smiled back and said, "My dear Simon, I have a gift that you will be offering me your sword for within a fortnight."

And with that, Simon knew immediately what gift Aldo had received. "They gave you *sake*, didn't they?"

"Barrels of that wonderful *Tosatsuru,* my dear friend; enough to fill a quarter of the hold. You were sleeping when they loaded it aboard."

That was not my only gift, sempre sia lodato! Aldo thought to himself. He had enough loot aboard, were they to make it back to Venice, for him to turn a healthy profit and still offer reasonable compensation to the families of the sailors who had died. But Aldo had not sailed to China to make a *healthy* profit, he had sailed to China to become wealthy.

And thus, the reason for a temporary addition to their crew. Inotogo had told Aldo that the tattooed pilot on the dinghy with them could lead them to the wealthy Ryukyu trading kingdom. Aldo hoped that in that kingdom, he might find a clue to the location of the fabled Spice Islands.

Simon looked at his sword and hoped they weren't blown off course again. As he cradled the sword in his hands, his mind drifted to his mother's flaxen hair, that he would smell as often as possible when he was a child. From there, he was helpless to stop his mind from remembering Lord Percy Blythe yanking at her beautiful hair, to free his mother's head from the mud and hold it up for display.

Chapter 16

Rougemont Castle, Exeter, Southwest England

"In God's name, what is that confounded noise?"

The naked woman with long golden locks and generous tits turned to face Lord Percy Blythe. "I don't know, my lord, but it must be something important."

The commotion outside could have been less important than the temperature of the guards' oatmeal, but Maureen didn't give a damn. She'd already been awake for half an hour contemplating how to separate her skin from the foul-smelling rolls of pale stomach fat that were glued to her back by a combination of dried sweat and bodily fluids. The brief spate of yelling outside the window came as a godsend.

Must be some village idiot horsing around, Lord Blythe presumed. *This village seems overly blessed with that sort.* He studied the woman's face. He didn't know her name, nor did he want to. She was nothing more than lowborn rubbish he had picked up slumming in a village alehouse. *But you know what, as long as she's here, maybe I'll do her another favor before I send her off.*

Lord Blythe strode over to the window and looked into the courtyard, then towards the red walls that gave the stout castle its name. His bed companion heard the sound of urine splashing into the pisspot. *Nothing seems out of the ordinary*, Blythe thought. "Do you know where I was educated?" he asked pompously.

"No," she said massaging her temple to relieve her pounding headache. *He may be lord of the manor, but he barely lasted sixty seconds, and his member is no longer than an inchworm. I better lay off the mead for a while.*

"It was at Winchester College," the lord said bombastically, "one of the oldest and best schools in all of England."

Shut up, you pompous ass, the peasant girl thought to herself. *I can't believe I washed for this twat.*

"And do you know our school motto?"

Who gives a toss, she thought.

"Manners makyth man." Blythe let out a loud morning fart. His right hand held his George Thomas firmly while his left fanned his ass. He was about to say something more marvelous about himself to the local strumpet, but a loud rapping on his door preempted the remark. *I guess I'll find out what this bothersome ruckus is about.*

Lord Blythe turned from the window, walked to his clothes, and started to dress. After putting on his leggings and tunic, he adjusted his oversized codpiece, buckled his belt, and walked towards the door. "Keep your delicate little buttocks beneath the sheets. I shan't be long." Blythe paused and stroked the thin black wisps of hair emanating from his chin as if they were a grand lion's mane.

This forced Lord Blythe's bed companion to consider another factor that the demon of fermented barley had disguised from her the night before. *Jaisus, there's not a spot of difference between the hairs on his face and those between his legs.*

Percy continued. "And there will be a couple more pennies and a penis coming your way," he said with a lecherous grin.

The tavern girl threw up in her mouth.

"I told you not to bother me when I'm providing enjoyment to the female of the species," Lord Blythe scolded his Captain of the Guard as he opened the door.

"I'm most regretful for the interruption sir, but I've got some Frenchie here demanding to see you." The captain glanced in the direction of Blythe's bed, where he saw a woman with a look on her face that he did not interpret as enjoyment.

"What's his name?"

"He calls himself John Paul the Belly, though I can't make out why that is. Thin as a straw of barley."

"Jean-Paul de Bailly," Lord Percy corrected. "Send him in immediately and have the kitchen bring some wine."

A slender, well-dressed man entered the room. Subtle creases in his forehead hinted that he was older than his otherwise youthful appearance and healthy physique would suggest. His deep-set green eyes were carved into a perpetual squint.

Lord Percy waved in a servant bearing a crystal decanter and two silver goblets. The decanter contained a thin, purplish-pink liquid that his guest glanced at disapprovingly. Lord Blythe noticed the look. "I assure you it's decent. Chianti from a vineyard nestled in a small valley in the Hampshire countryside."

Jean-Paul looked from his employer to the naked woman in the bed. "Perhaps we should talk somewhere more private?" he asked in modestly accented English.

"She has no concern for worldly matters, Jean-Paul. Her thoughts extend as far as where her next coin is coming from and nothing more. Is he dead?"

The professional spymaster was not convinced it was wise to discuss important matters in front of uninvolved parties, but Lord Blythe was paying his wages, and generous wages they were. "In London he escaped the four men that I hired from the establishment *you* recommended." Jean-Paul stressed the word "you" ever so slightly; just enough to make a point.

"Escaped?"

"Did I say escaped? I meant killed. He filleted all four of them like they were flounder. He was drunk and leaving the Red Lion Pub with a very pretty young lady, but according to the *jolie femme*, less than a minute after his sword left its scabbard, he was the only one standing. I saw the results of his sword work the next day."

"He was up against amateur London river rats, but I didn't know he had such skill with a blade."

"I have nothing but the testimony of the woman and four dead bodies to support that conclusion, but I would hazard to guess that he took his young knightly training seriously. And he did have the Lancastrian veterans in this castle to learn from."

"Yes, yes, but surely you were able to take care of him?"

"Is there a reason the life of this minor noble causes you such distress?"

Percy Blythe gulped down his second glass of wine and ruminated for a moment, then, perhaps inopportunely, decided there wasn't any harm in sharing more information with the hired killer. This was after he'd poured himself another full goblet and cast a pointed glare toward de Bailly who hadn't touched his wine.

"Apparently he's a distant second cousin, twice removed or something like that, of someone with royal blood. It's all too confusing these days. The red rose of the House of Lancaster, the white rose of the House of York, I need a bloody guidebook to remember what family falls on which side of the shrub. And that's not to count the families that may, at any given point in time, be playing both sides of the family tree.

"I just know King Edward doesn't want any complications when it's time for his young sons to succeed him. I can't imagine Simon Lang having any claim to the throne, though. I mean, he's half Welsh for Chrissakes. Far be it from me to second-guess our good king, of course, and the Langs' misfortune has proven to be my rather good fortune." With that remark, Lord Blythe gestured to indicate the castle around him. "Rooting out these Lancastrian sympathizers has been no easy task, mind you; they're more common than lice around these parts. My public beheading of the Lady Lang has kept them on their best behavior for the time being, but I still desire to crush their spirits further."

Not wishing to offend his host and benefactor, but against his better judgment, Jean-Paul took a sip of wine from his goblet. He immediately regretted it; overly sweet, it had fruit characteristics suitable for jam. *So the English king himself wants this man dead. That could make it worth more money.* "I employed a crossbowman at Calais, but Madame Luck seems to favor Monsieur Lang. He was seen entering the house of yet another pretty woman, this one married apparently, but my man never saw him leave and never saw him in Calais again."

"Perhaps the husband killed him?" Lord Blythe asked hopefully.

"Unfortunately, *non.* I think it's most likely that after London, he realized his danger and started taking precautions. Perhaps he made one of the ruffians in London talk before slicing him open? I had the impression that the witness was quite charmed by this Simon Lang, so perhaps she left that detail out of the story she told me."

Lord Blythe was becoming exasperated. "But finally you killed him, right?"

"Not as such."

"What the devil does that mean?"

"Eventually I tracked him to Venice, but he was gone by the time I arrived."

"Gone where?"

"To his death, I'm relatively sure. Venice was buzzing with the news that he was part of some ridiculous adventure to sail to China. The last I heard of him was that he'd started up the Nile River from Alexandria. That was over six months ago."

Lord Blythe sighed deeply. It was not the information he was hoping for, but at least the young Lang was not hiding in Brittany, scheming to take his castle back.

"I wish for you to remain in my employ until you can confirm Simon Lang's fate. It seems I won't be getting any satisfaction this morning."

"Amen," mumbled the servant girl, as she skipped from the bed.

Chapter 17

Gloucestershire, England

THE HORSES BORE their riders south from Warwick Castle, following the Avon River down to a small market town. The galloping turned into a trot as the band of men entered the village of crooked shops, pubs, and houses decorated in the favored style of blackened oak beams and white walls. The group continued past the Old Black Bear Inn to the nearby abbey.

Tewkesbury Abbey stood on elevated ground overlooking the market town. The magnificent Norman abbey with its pristine surroundings was a world apart from the squalid town below it. Like most medieval settlements, the roads were covered with mud, horseshit, and the contents of pisspots. Filth and disease were plentiful. Castles and abbeys were located on higher ground not just for defensive reasons but sanitation. The shit always washed downhill.

The horses came to a halt in front of a cream-yellow stone structure. Jurassic limestone imported from France made up the walls of the Romanesque church. It was the same stone that had been used to build the Tower of London and Canterbury Cathedral. The abbey was serene and beautiful, but the peace of the night was quickly broken as two soldiers dismounted and shouted at a passing monk.

"You! Over here! Now!"

The Benedictine monk was startled as the soldiers moved to confront him. One drew his sword and pointed it at his throat while the other roughly frisked his black habit.

"All clear," they announced back to the lone figure still mounted on his horse. The monk was not used to being treated this way. After all, he had the power to condemn a man's soul to eternal damnation. *What mortal man has the temerity to treat me this way?* wondered the monk.

Richard, the Duke of Gloucester and brother to King Edward IV, feared no man or monk. His feet landed in the mud as he dismounted and walked quickly towards the abbey entrance.

"Stay here," Richard gruffly ordered his men. "Do not let anybody in." Richard looked tired and sounded edgy.

The monk recognized the Duke of Gloucester by his handsome facial features and slightly stooped back. "Thank you, sire, for coming to our humble monastery," the monk said nervously as Richard strode purposefully past him. 'Humble' wasn't the word to describe the Benedictine monastery. It was one of the richest monasteries in all England.

"Is this your first time to the Abbey?" the monk asked as he stared. The king's brother's shoulders were not level due to a malformed spine, and he appeared to be unusually slender. In fact, the monk thought he had an almost feminine build, but he nonetheless moved with power and authority.

"No, you know damn well it's not. Take me to the vault."

The monk smiled, but his mind was racing. He was most uneasy. The monk certainly did know about Richard and his history with the abbey. It took a month to reconsecrate it after all the blood he and his brother spilled inside.

As they entered the doorway, the monk's eyes unconsciously shot to the sacristy door. Behind it was a large vaulted chamber full of treasure. The door itself was reinforced with steel from the armor and swords of Lancastrian knights who had been slaughtered on these very grounds. After the Yorkist victory at the Battle of Tewkesbury in 1471, a number of Lancastrian knights and their squires had sought sanctuary in the abbey. The henchmen of Richard and his brother King Edward had viciously dragged the men out, violating the law of sanctuary, and butchered them.

"Beautiful," Richard remarked. The silent, dark, and cold atmosphere comforted his restless mind. As the two walked towards the high altar, Richard admired the sculpted nave, high vaulted ceilings, and great Norman columns. He looked approvingly at the stained glass depicting knights in full armor as well as King Solomon and King David.

"The vault is just behind the marble altar near the Beauchamp Chapel," the monk said in a low tone.

"I'm aware," Richard replied dismissively. The doors leading to the vault were open, and the two carefully descended the stone stairs. Five candles lit the small room. Richard walked towards an elaborately decorated tomb.

"Thank you, you may leave," Richard said quietly but firmly.

"If you require my assistance, I will be waiting in the chapter house." The monk bowed gracefully and ascended the stone stairs, grateful to leave a company that was welcome to neither party.

Richard knelt and crossed himself in front of the vault. He ran his hand slowly across the stone effigy. Richard waited until he heard the footsteps of the monk disappear. He was desperate to speak and clear his conscience. "I am sorry, brother. I should have saved you," Richard whispered. "I betrayed you."

He turned suddenly; he thought he heard a noise. *Is somebody trying to sneak up on me?* There was no one. He turned back to the tomb where the bones of his brother George, the Duke of Clarence, lay.

Richard's voice became erratic. "I can no longer trust anybody, not even my own family. Is it your ghost seeking revenge? I think Edward wants to kill me, too. I need to be careful. He is cunning, and I no longer believe he is of our father's blood. He probably wants me dead." His breathing was quick and shallow. "People are speaking behind my back. I think Edward is spreading rumors. Even those filthy peasants say, 'Bentback Dick is a paranoid prick.' They don't think I know it, but I know it." Richard again looked around to see if he had been followed. "It will not be tolerated much longer."

"Is he agitated?" the elderly abbot asked, as the monk entered the chapter house.

The head abbot knew Richard. He had witnessed the duke's ruthless streak after the battle of Tewkesbury.

"I am not sure."

The abbot looked at the young monk. "You know about his brother George, don't you?"

"I have heard rumors."

The abbot shut the oak door as quietly as he could. "When George's body came to the Abbey to be buried, it smelled of wine from head to foot."

"So, it is true. He drowned in a barrel of wine, like the stories say."

"He drowned in a barrel of wine or *was* drowned in a barrel of wine, I cannot say. As you know, King Edward ordered him executed for high treason, but whether he was executed quietly or actually drowned of his own accord we will never know." The abbot looked around. "But Edward was a bastard. George, being older than Richard, was the rightful heir to the throne."

"A bastard?" the monk said, sounding stunned, although he had heard the rumor before.

"In France, they call Edward the Bastard of Rouen. They say he's the product of a stout English longbowman, hence his six-foot-four frame, taller than any of his forbears. From a source I shall not disclose, Edward's purported father, Richard Plantagenet, was nowhere near his mother Cecily Neville nine months prior to Edward's birth. I cannot confirm the story of the longbowman."

The monk could not hide his shock. "Richard sided with Edward, knowing George was his only full-blooded brother."

"Yes, though I don't know if he was aware that Edward planned to have George killed."

"It's a wonder he hasn't gone insane with guilt."

Chapter 18

The Pig and Whistle Pub, Exeter

"Where is that damnable bar maid?" Maurice, the long-bearded, grizzled proprietor of the Pig and Whistle bellowed out to no one in particular.

"Sod off, you old git," Maureen spat as she walked in from the street, smoothing out her hair and fastening on her apron.

"I expect my employees to be here on time, woman, and you're at least two hours late."

"Well, you know what I say about expectations."

"Expectations lead to disappointment?"

"Indeed. A circumstance your wife is no doubt intimately familiar with."

Maurice spluttered for a moment. "She bore me three strapping sons, she did."

"Aye, strapping they are, smart they're not." Maureen cocked an eyebrow as she began polishing goblets and pints. "It's a shame they don't take after the missus more."

"So who were you shagging that kept it up this late into the morning?"

"Not that it's any of your business, but I spent the night being properly wined and dined in the castle by his lordship," Maureen blatantly mischaracterized her romp with a straight face. "I stole a good bit of breakfast before I left this morning, too. Nothing like the shite we eat around here."

"You cook the food we eat around here."

"Like I said."

"Well," Maurice persisted, "your shagging of Yorkist swan scoffers is interfering with my business. The traveler at the end of the bar has been waiting an hour for food."

"I wasn't just shagging any Yorkist swan scoffer," Maureen said. "I was shagging the *head* Yorkist swan scoffer around these parts, and it brought me more coin than you pay me in a month. Maybe if you paid me what I'm worth, I wouldn't have to go around swallowing inchworms to earn a living."

She had a valid point, but they both knew he couldn't afford to pay her more money. The disastrous loss of nearly thirty thousand men in the Lancastrian defeat at Towton had reduced the male population of the surrounding countryside by fully eighty percent, and the punishing taxes levied by Lord Percy Blythe kept the remaining twenty percent of the original population at home. Most of the pub's customers were Yorkist leeches who had come at Blythe's solicitation, and the rest were soldiers from the castle garrison. Maurice, himself one of the rare survivors of the massacre at Towton, despised serving his new masters, but unlike the dead, he still had to provide for his family. Occasionally, travelers would pass through and stop for a meal, as was the case today.

"Go see to our customer and shut your gob," he said.

"You keep bellyaching, and I won't tell you what I heard in the castle."

Maurice noticed the middle-aged traveler perk up, though whether it was due to Maureen's remark or the fact that he was finally going to get some service, Maurice couldn't tell.

"It sounds like you're not a fan of the lord of the manor," the traveler responded as Maurice moved closer.

"I'm not. Neither him nor any of the land-thieving scum he brought with him, and I'm too old to care who hears me say it."

"Well, in that case, my name is Jasper, though I'd appreciate it if you kept that between us. I go by John in unfriendly territory, and by unfriendly, I mean anywhere ruled by Yorkists."

"Well you're in friendly enough company at the moment, good sir. I don't get many in here that I like to serve. Let me buy you an ale."

"I have coin enough and some extra to boot if your waitress wouldn't mind sharing her story with me, too."

"If you have coin, she'll likely want to share more with you than her information."

Maureen reappeared from the kitchen in time to hear this remark. "He's not wrong. I'm an easy fuck. How about it?"

"Tempting as your offer is, madam," Jasper said, "I should like to stick with hearing what you learned in the castle today. I'll pay well for good information. It's somewhat the purpose of my travels."

"All right, then. It seems Lord Little Pecker has hired people to kill the young Lord Lang, but he's still alive."

"Young Lord Lang?" Jasper inquired.

Maurice answered. "Aye, Simon Lang, he's the rightful heir to the castle. I watched his father fall at Towton. Bravest man I've ever seen."

"You were at Towton?" Jasper Tudor, Earl of Pembroke and guardian uncle to Henry Tudor, aspirant to the Crown of England, seemed genuinely surprised. He hadn't fought at Towton, but he knew very few Lancastrians had survived the unchivalrous post-battle slaughter. He himself had personally experienced Yorkist chivalry when they beheaded his father after the Battle of Mortimer's Cross.

"Aye, Palm Sunday, 1461, I was in that freezing meadow in North Yorkshire."

"Oh, don't let him get started, he'll never stop," Maureen cut in.

"This one lost her man that day." Maurice directed a glance at his tavern maid. "Stout lad Timmy was, watched my back all day." Maurice crossed himself here, and Jasper thought he could see moisture building in Maureen's eyes, which she quickly wiped away.

"Fat lot of good it did him." Maureen wanted to head back to the kitchen, but like nightmares that she couldn't leave until she woke up, she could never escape the draw of hearing about her husband. She knew he'd had no choice but to go and fight. You didn't refuse your lord's call to arms, but she couldn't help blaming him for dying. It wasn't the degrading shambles her life had become after his death that bothered her. She was more or less numb to that. It was the loss of his love. He had loved her, and she him, and without that love, she was hollow inside.

Maurice continued, and Jasper showed no signs of cutting him off. "Eighty thousand Englishmen out to kill each other that day.

Couldn't see a thing through the snow, but somehow their archers found the mark and ours didn't. It rained arrows until the gentility could stand it no longer. When they find a weak spot in the armor, bodkin-tipped arrows don't discriminate knight from plebe. No doubt the growing losses amongst the peerage inspired our attack. We left our hill and charged up theirs in whiteout conditions. Whatever my thoughts about the high and mighty" — Maurice paused here – "excuse my bluntness, sir, as I can see from the cut of your thread, that you are one of my betters."

"I value bluntness, good man, please continue."

"Well, as I was saying, Simon's father was not chastising us from behind. He led from the front. A true knight he was. After eight hours of fighting we had nearly pushed those bastards all the way back up their hill. Timmy's axe was drenched in Yorkist blood, and my spear had done its fair share of work, too." Maurice remembered this moment of lost glory with a mixture of pride and sadness at what could have been. "Then I saw that flag: three golden lions on a crimson background. The Duke of Norfolk and thousands of his fresh troops arrived just in time to save their arses. We were drained from fighting all day, and we didn't have a chance. All around his lordship, the men dropped their weapons and ran, but he just kept fighting. It was then that I lost good Tim. They couldn't take him down in hand-to-hand combat, so they felled him with an arrow. He died right away, though, no pain, which was a mercy after what happened next."

Maureen let a tear fall as emotion exerted a rare controlling influence over her. She could smell the black pudding starting to cook on the grill, so she left to tend to it. She knew the rest of the story anyway.

"Lord Lang stood at the crest of the hill, outlined against the sky like a painting. His armor was battered and he was beset on all sides, but he refused to give an inch. Finally, a mallet blow knocked him down from behind. Then the Yorkist peasants descended upon him. They mutilated his body and robbed his corpse till he lay naked in the mud and the snow."

Maurice spat on the floor in disgust. "They did the same to all who couldn't escape that day. The Yorkists hunted and slaughtered everyone they could find, regardless of rank. By the end of the day, the creeks were choked with bodies, and the rivers were dirty shades of brown and crimson. I'm not ashamed to say that I hid under dead bodies until I escaped in the dark. I couldn't afford a noble last stand. I've got three boys working down at the docks, and a wife who deserves better than me. But that Simon, he's got genuine heroic blood running through his veins. Mark my words, he'll come calling one day, and there will be hell to pay for both his father and mother."

Maureen returned with a cup of ale for the traveler and a fragrant plate of grilled blood pudding that Jasper immediately set into. "It's sad what they did to his mother. She was always good to the poor. And to make the boy watch her head being lopped off was just cruel."

"That would be your bedmate from last night, you shameless whore."

"All the virtue in the world doesn't put food in my mouth or a roof over my head. Speaking of which," she looked at Jasper, "you said something about coin."

"Did you hear anything else?" Jasper asked.

"I heard that that Simon sailed off on some foolish venture to someplace called *Cheena* from which he is not expected to return, though they'll be waiting for him if he does. I also heard that Lord Blythe is planning further mischief to bring Exeter to heel, although what more he could possibly do, I can't imagine."

Maurice cut in. "Natural-born sailor, that boy. Used to run away down to the docks where he learned the trade. His mother would nearly skin him alive, but then after she was executed, there was no one to stop him. The boy could take some rough treatment, too, I'll tell you that. Being an orphaned noble boy didn't do him any favors on the docks or on the ships, but it didn't take long before he was giving better than he got. Eventually, when you combined the weapons training he got on account of being a noble, with the toughness he picked up down on the docks, no one but out-of-towners who didn't know any better would mess with him."

Jasper thought this Simon Lang sounded like the interesting sort. *Perhaps if he returns he may be helpful in gaining this region's support.* Jasper put two gold coins on the table and slid one to Maureen. "Thank you for the information, and thank you for your husband's sacrifice." Then he slid one to Maurice. "Thank you for your service to the red rose."

Chapter 19

Off the Ryukyu Islands,
South of Kyushu, Japan, East of China

THE HULL OF the *Tigre* cut cleanly through the aquamarine sea. Barracuda, box jellyfish, manta rays, moray eels, hammerhead sharks, and a plethora of colorful fish swam amongst the coral on both sides of the ship.

Simon should have been calm, but he wasn't. He stared at the craggy-faced foreigner steering the carrack through the coral reefs. It was Simon's job to steer the ship, and he didn't trust the old man who was covered from arsehole to earlobe in brightly colored tattoos. But Lord Arai had told them that this pirate could be trusted to get them to the capital of the Ryukyu Islands, and Simon trusted Lord Arai's advice. Nonetheless, he did not like the thought of a pirate steering his ship, so he kept both eyes focused on the old man.

The old man for his part was nervous as well. Aside from the fact that he was piloting a ship the size and shape of which he'd never seen before, there was a large, pale white devil that kept staring at him and a laconic samurai never far away, whom he suspected would like nothing better than to cut his head off.

Kojiro stood relaxed but alert with his hand poised close to the hilt of his sword. He would cut the pirate in half at the first sign of treachery, or maybe even without it. The pilot was a *Wako*: a sea bandit, and Kojiro did not like bandits. The notorious *Wako* terrorized the coastal fishing villages of Japan, China, Korea, and Southeast Asia: killing, kidnapping, plundering, and pillaging.

Recently, the sea bandits had begun traveling further afield, raiding more deeply into China, which had proven lucrative. However, due to these forays, their original coastal bases in the outlying Japanese islands had become too distant. The Ryukyu Islands had proven to be the perfect waypoint for their pirating depredations.

The Ryukyus were midway between Japan and the coastline of southeast China, with dangerous reefs to discourage unfamiliar sailors. Additionally, the Ryukyu Kingdom offered established trade markets where the pirates could sell their wares. A shady arrangement between the *Wakos* and the king of the Ryukyu Islands had been struck: the king turned a blind eye to the *Wako* piracy and gave them a safe haven to rest and trade. They, in return, did not attack any of the treasure-laden Ryukyu trading ships.

These men have no honor, Kojiro thought. *They fight for nothing more than treasure and sell out to the highest bidder. But Lord Arai uses this man to sell his wares to the Ryukyu Kingdom, so I will not kill him today.*

"This man, so he is a pirate?" Simon double-checked if he had heard right.

Aldo answered. "Kojiro called him a *Wako*, which he described as a sort of a sea bandit, which I feel comfortable translating as 'pirate.'

Something like the Moor pirates that infest the Mediterranean Sea, I should imagine. They sail around the coast of Asia and raid for whatever there is of value. They will also take the pretty girls and strong boys. I imagine it could also be strong girls and pretty boys for that matter. The strong ones are sold for farm labor, and well, you can imagine what the pretty ones are sold for. The slave trade seems to be just as lucrative here as it is everywhere else in the world."

Aldo looked at Simon; he thought of a relevant religious fact that this would be an opportune time to introduce. Aldo knew Simon would do well to learn more religious facts and saw it as his God-given duty to present them, bidden or not. "Do you know that the beloved Saint Patrick, the patron saint of Ireland, isn't actually Irish?"

"Huh," Simon said, not caring what Aldo was on about.

"He was a slave. When he was sixteen, he was captured by Irish raiders and taken to Ireland from northern England."

Now this was actually a bit of information Simon thought he could use for future entertainment. *I will inform the Irish at Ye Olde Cheshire Cheese in London, on their St. Patrick's Day, that the famous patron saint of Ireland is actually English.* Simon thought about it and grinned widely. *That should start some fun.* In answer to Aldo, though, he just grunted. *Mustn't encourage him to share any other religious information with me.*

Simon's thoughts drifted back to the marauder at the helm. "The *Wako* sound a bit like the Norsemen."

"Oh, the Vikings, you mean," Aldo replied. "Fortunately, they never raided as far as Venice, but I've traded with Norsemen. They do seem to be a bit unpleasant."

"They're actually a bit more than unpleasant. They plundered my hometown of Exeter on numerous occasions, the bastards. In

1003, they razed our only church. The Vikings seem to have been particularly fond of raiding churches and monasteries. I'll give them this; it must be hard to resist all that money that the Church leaches from the people." Simon smiled, anticipating the effect his last comment would have on Aldo.

Aldo did not take the bait. "Pagans" was all he replied.

A bit disappointed at Aldo's muted reaction, Simon tried again. "But I suppose burning the church was a good thing."

This time he got a reaction. Aldo shot Simon a look that would have killed a lesser man and said, "I know that you are not an especially devout follower of our Lord, but to commend the destruction of a church is beyond blasphemy."

"Upon the grounds of the razed church, Exeter Cathedral was built, which is one of the finest churches in the world. That's what I was going to say if you had let me continue."

Aldo's eyes narrowed. "Well, yes, of course. The Lord works in mysterious ways."

Simon thought it time to change the subject. He'd had enough religious discussion for the day, perhaps even for the year. "So what is this mysterious harbor we are sailing to?"

"According to Lord Arai, it is called Naha," Aldo answered, "and by the looks of it, we are about to arrive."

In the distance, Simon saw what looked to be a colossal, winding, stone-walled fortification on a hill above a harbor. As they got closer, he could see more detail in the grand castle that dominated the landscape around it. It was a commanding structure, protected naturally by the island's hills as well its own multilayered fortifications. *I would not want to try to take that by force*, he thought.

Speaking in a strange dialect of Japanese that required Kojiro's translation, the pirate said, "That is *Shuri-jo Castle*. The King of Ryukyu lives there."

The *Wako* pirate said nothing else as he steered the *Tigre* skillfully into the bustling port. Simon marveled at the vast array of sea vessels moored in the harbor; flat-bottomed Chinese junks with brightly colored flags, Javanese sailing vessels, Arab *dhows*, and a multitude of other seafaring craft.

The *Wako* looked anxiously at the foreboding samurai as the ship's dinghy was lowered into the water. He knew that as a general rule, samurai killed bandits on sight, and this one's disposition throughout the voyage had not been encouraging. When the samurai approached him, he hoped he would still have a head left to bury into a nice pair of breasts this evening.

"*Ike*!" was all the samurai said to him. A bit rude and abrupt to be told just 'go' after bringing them safely here, but he was not going to dwell on the insult. He scrambled down the ladder to the dinghy.

"Shall we?" Aldo asked.

"Indeed we shall," Simon replied coolly.

In fact, Simon was quite excited about visiting this exotic port. Once ashore, Simon was struck by the variety of people: bearded Arabs wearing white turbans and flowing white *thobes*; Chinese in brightly colored, elegant silk *hanfu;* Indians wearing knee-length cotton shirts; Javanese wearing colorful sarongs; and a host of other nationalities all jostling to trade. Although he and Aldo were the only white people in the market, they were not so dissimilar from lighter skinned Arabs, so they did not attract an undue amount of attention.

The smell coming from the market had Aldo enchanted from the minute they stepped off the dinghy, and he headed towards it while Simon and Kojiro decided to look for something resembling a drinking establishment. Aldo soon discovered the enticing smells were a combination of frankincense, myrrh, nutmeg, ginger, cloves, and cinnamon. In addition to the spices, the market appeared to hold everything imaginable for sale; ivory, gold, gems, animal skins, silks, silver, slaves, weapons, lacquerware, glass, and thousands of other assorted items. Because it was a port city, Aldo had expected a market but not this big, not this wonderful. He stood and smiled. *There is money to be made here.*

When Simon returned to the dinghy a few hours after the sun sank, he was feeling quite refreshed. He and Kojiro had managed to sample alcohol from at least six different countries, and he had liked everything but the Chinese *sake.* To his mind, that had tasted like beef stock. When he arrived back at the dock, he was surprised to see that half the Ouchi booty and many of their original Venetian wares were being carted off by people he had learned were called Javanese.

Aldo walked down the dock and greeted Simon with a smile that was wider than usual. "My friend, I have made an excellent trade," he said, fishing through the top pocket of his shirt. Then, with a grand flourish, he pulled out an egg-shaped seed about three centimeters in length.

"Do you know what this is?" Aldo asked beaming.

"A rat penis?" Simon replied, worried where this was heading.

"Nutmeg, my friend." Aldo seemed delirious with delight. "Some people believe it wards off the plague, and others are convinced that it causes self-abortions, all of which is, of course, total nonsense, but people will pay outrageous prices for this back in Europe. Nutmeg means money. We, my friend, are rich."

Simon perked up a bit. He liked the sound of 'rich,' particularly when it was attached to the pronouns 'we,' 'me,' and 'I.' "So, how many barrels or boxes of these nutmegs did we get?"

"Just this one."

Aldo still looked pleased in spite of that revelation. Simon carefully inspected the seed. "That must be one hell of a good nutmeg."

Aldo tapped the side of his nose. "I have the directions to an island of spices; full of cloves and nutmeg. I paid for the directions, not the 'rat penis.'"

Simon looked forlornly at the woodblock paintings from Kyoto being offloaded at the dock. He had wanted to return to England with at least a few of them, but Aldo was a Venetian and Venetians knew trade. *Don't they? Maybe I found a defective one. Well, what's done is done.* "Where is the map?"

"There is no map. The exact direction was discreetly revealed to me, but the seller refused to write it down; the information is too valuable." Aldo paused, looked around, and gently whispered into Simon's ear, "South, my friend."

Simon looked at Aldo as if he were a simpleton. "South is a direction, not a map."

Aldo leaned closer, cupping his hand around Simon's ear this time. "South; sail as straight as the crow flies. Not south-southwest and not south-southeast, just straight south. The journey may take weeks because we will be against a current that sweeps north, but we must persevere south."

Simon turned and started walking back into Naha.

"Where are you going?" Aldo shouted.

"East. Not northeast or north-northeast, just east," Simon said. "There's a drinking establishment there, and if I'm lucky, perhaps a lady or two of dubious moral character. And since '*south*' is the secret direction to our riches, I don't need to be sober tomorrow; even Neno can steer a ship in one direction."

Chapter 20

Anchored off the Molucca Islands

"Just swords. No armor and definitely no shields," Aldo said. "And Neno, you can leave your new weapon aboard. You are frightening enough without it."

"*Si, Capitano,*" Neno said obediently.

Aldo was huddled with a small group of people at the stern of the *Tigre*. Kojiro, Simon, Neno, and four sailors were listening intently to Captain Mitacchione. "We are here to trade, and we don't want the natives getting any wrong ideas." He turned to the four sailors. "When we reach land, smile, look friendly, and keep your wits about you."

Aldo narrowed his eyes and studied the four dopey and toothless faces. "Second thought, don't smile and forget what I said about wits, just try to look friendly."

"*Si, Capitano,*" they all replied.

Simon had his doubts about the 'lightly armed' policy, but Aldo had been right about getting here in the first place and Simon wasn't going to second-guess him in front of the crew.

Aldo looked towards the lush, green volcanic island. "Man the dinghy."

The *Tigre* was anchored only five hundred yards offshore, and the experienced sailors cut through the serene, azure waters quickly.

"Ease up," Aldo said as the boat began to glide towards the black sandy beach.

"Si," the sailors responded.

"Way enough," Aldo shouted. The crew responded to his order and stopped rowing, raising the oars out of the water and straight up into the air. Standing on the beach were several darkly tanned farm workers waiting to greet the newcomers.

"They're all smiling, that's a good sign," Simon said.

"They should be used to traders coming here, just as I anticipated. That is why I did not want us to come ashore fully armed and looking like a raiding party. I'm sure they've been following the progress of our dinghy from the treetops."

After the crew pulled the boat up onto dry sand, Aldo observed what appeared to be a house and a barn about a mile inland. He pointed at it and then realized that he didn't know what to say. He looked at Simon and chuckled. Obviously the islanders wouldn't speak his heathen tongue. Then he looked at Kojiro, who shrugged his shoulders. *It's really annoying that he keeps picking up body language from Simon,* Aldo thought to himself. But Aldo needn't have worried about language. The islanders knew what to do and soon had them ambling along a hard dirt trail towards the house. Aldo ordered the four sailors to stay by the dinghy, much to their relief.

"I should have brought Kuro," Kojiro observed. "He needs to walk around."

"If all goes well, you can exercise him while we load our treasure," Aldo grinned.

The weather was warm, the humidity oppressive, and an overpowering smell invaded their nostrils, not unpleasant, but overwhelming nonetheless. "Ah, the smell of cloves," Aldo said as they sweated and trudged their way up the trail. "It is the smell of money."

The cloves seemed to be a part of the air itself. Simon felt as though every breeze would drown him in aroma. The forty- foot-tall clove trees lined the side of the path; workers could be seen picking the bright red flower buds and placing them in baskets. The workers in the trees cast wide-eyed glances at the visitors but continued with their work. The crew of the *Tigre* eventually came to a low-walled, roughly cut timber house. The area in front of the house was hard, cleared red dirt, and the fragrant clove buds laid out drying on it in the sun.

Behind the house was a stable, also made from crudely hewn, unpainted logs. One of their escorting farmworkers pounded on the front door to the house, and with a last smile, he and the other islanders disappeared back down the cart trail.

The door opened, and a tall, slender Arab with a long, immaculately groomed beard emerged. He wore a loose fitting cotton tunic.

"*As-salaamu alaykum*," Aldo greeted the man. He had dealt with Arab traders on many occasions, so his Arabic was passable.

"*Wa alaykum salaam*," the Arab returned his greeting.

"*Isme Aldo.*"

"*Isme Ismail ibn Umar*," the man replied. He gestured for the group to come inside.

They entered a cool, dim room, with one door on the east wall leading further into the house and another door on the north wall leading to the stable in back. Like everywhere else on the island, the smell of cloves drowned out the smell of anything else. Ismail ibn Umar opened his hand and pointed at the reddish-colored hardwood chairs that surrounded a table in the center of the room. The smooth-topped table was made from the same beautifully colored wood as the chairs. Unlike the crudely finished logs that made up the structure of the house, the table and chairs were finely constructed, as were the other furnishings in the room.

Ismail disappeared through the east door and reemerged after a slight absence with five white porcelain cups on an ornately designed silver platter. He placed the cups in front of his guests and indicated that they should drink.

Simon didn't know what the steaming hot blackish liquid was, but it smelled wonderful. Simon looked at Aldo, but Aldo didn't know either. Simon looked at Kojiro who responded to his inquisitive glance with "*shirimasen*," meaning he didn't know either.

Aldo spoke with Ismail in a mixture of Italian and Arabic and announced that the liquid was called "*qahwah*." After Simon had consumed two cups of the bitter, flavorful liquid he felt strangely energized. It was similar to when he drank alcohol, except his senses seemed more acute, instead of less. Simon asked for a third cup, and the man seemed happy to oblige.

"So when do we discuss business?" Simon asked Aldo, oddly feeling an urgent need to defecate.

"Patience, my ill-mannered friend, unlike the English, the Arabs like to behave with some civility towards their guests before they go straight to business." Without giving Simon a chance to respond, Aldo turned back to Ismail and continued talking and laughing.

Simon fidgeted and shifted in his seat while Kojiro sat patiently, not saying a word. Neno, not sure he trusted their host at all, watched the doors nervously. At the end of their wide-ranging conversation, Aldo stood. "Ismail will check the quality of our woolen goods, glassware, and Italian armor, and will trade cloves for them if they meet his standards. He says that nutmeg grows on a different group of islands, so he has none to offer us." Aldo was disappointed by the last piece of information but knew he could still make a great deal of money from the cloves.

Neno stood up quickly, happy that they would soon be leaving the building where they could be so easily trapped. Before he reached the door, an unmistakable sound shook the house. *Boom*!

They all heard the single cannon's report coming from the direction of the *Tigre*. Simon looked at Ismail's face for any reactions that would indicate treachery, but the man was clearly as alarmed by the cannon's report as they were. Neno was already out the door and staring down the cart path as Aldo spoke hastily to Ismail. Simon waited to hear what Ismail had to say while Kojiro took up a defensive position at the door.

Aldo translated his conversation for them. "It could either be Turks or indigenous tribes from another island, but the Turks aren't due to collect taxes for another month. This region is host to several tribes that survive partly through piracy and theft. As an added bonus, most of them are headhunters, and some of them are cannibals."

"You know, that's funny because you didn't say anything about headhunting cannibals when you showed me that seed you were so proud of," Simon said.

"You didn't ask."

"Why is this funny?" Kojiro asked seriously. "It does not seem funny that Aldo would not tell you such an important detail."

"It's not funny, Kojiro, that is the 'sarcasm' I have been teaching you about. You say something that is the opposite of what you mean."

"Why do you do that again?" Kojiro asked.

"To antagonize the people I know."

"Antagonize?"

Aldo translated for Kojiro. "*Ijime suru.*"

"Okay, I understand what you do, but still not why."

"Because he's a giant asshole," Aldo explained.

"Okay, now I understand why," Kojiro said.

Simon nodded in agreement with Aldo, then redirected the conversation. "Is there anything else I should know?"

"Well, getting caught by them isn't pleasant," Aldo said as he nervously played with his fingers. "Unlike the European peasants of the Great Famine of 1315 who ate human flesh to survive, these tribes eat human flesh for pleasure. Ismail tells me that it is part of their culture to hang the victims' heads over wood fires and slowly smoke them. The flesh of the chin and cheeks are apparently considered a delicacy."

"Well, how does Ismail normally protect himself from these flesh eaters?" Simon asked.

Aldo spoke with Ismail again then translated. "There is a contingent of Arab cavalry normally stationed here, but they left three days ago to put down an uprising on another island. He and the other traders on this island are knights, so the headhunting tribes usually give them a wide berth. It's unusual for them to strike at anything other than unarmed merchant vessels or weaker Melanesian tribes."

Kojiro spoke. "If this man's warriors are on another island, perhaps they were tricked into leaving for an attack here?"

Aldo received a short response from Ismail. "He says it's possible. The martial technology of the islanders is inferior, but they are clever in war."

"Okay, well, I'm not hearing any more cannon fire, so I'm guessing the *Tigre* is not tangling with an Ottoman galley. That means it was a warning shot. How do these headhunters usually travel, and is there anything else we should know?"

Aldo spoke with Ismail again. "They travel from island to island by canoe. They're fleet-footed, use crude bows and arrows, sometimes poisoned, and prefer to hack their opponents to death with thick-bladed, three-foot-long knives. They wear no armor and in fact, fight half naked, but they're nearly fearless."

After the last exchange with Aldo, Ismail said something briefly and disappeared into the house. Simon looked quizzically at Aldo.

"He's going to prepare," Aldo said.

"To leave?" Simon wondered.

"I don't know," Aldo admitted.

Simon, Aldo, and Kojiro walked outside where they met up with Neno. What they saw and heard were not encouraging. The workers from the fields streamed past them with looks of terror in their eyes. Bloodcurdling screams filled the air from those not lucky enough to escape whatever terror was chasing them.

"Sure wish I had my armor," Simon said. "I don't much care for the sound of poisoned arrows."

"I wish I had my halberd," Neno said.

"And I wish I were sitting in a trattoria in Venice right now, but I'm not," Aldo said. "Sorry I recommended arming ourselves lightly, it was the trader in me. That appears to have been a mistake on my part."

"Well, we all make mistakes," Simon said. "No sense dwelling on it now."

Although Aldo appreciated Simon's insouciant attitude, he was pretty sure that 'not dwelling on it now' meant there would be ample time spent dwelling on it in the future. *If we live to do so, that is.*

"*Fukusui bon ni kaerazu,*" Kojiro said with his eyes fixed in the direction of the screaming.

"I'm sorry, what was that?" Simon asked.

"Once the water spills from a bowl, it does not go back in."

"Huh, we have a similar expression about milk, though God knows why it's milk and not whisky. I've yet to see a single soul cry over spilled milk, but I've seen some pretty hard blokes cry over spilled whisky."

They didn't have to wait long to see it was not Turks. The dark forms moved through the clove trees like a wave, driving their prey in front of them. As they gave chase, they roared an angry, high-pitched battle cry that mingled with the shrieks of the farmers they caught, whose skin they stripped alive.

"Quite an impressive show of terror, I'd say," Simon remarked, eyes wide. "It's driving all the farm workers headlong towards the other side of the plantation. So these are the herders, where are the catchers?"

"*Soukana*," Kojiro said his thoughts out loud. *Simon is right, they are driving the farm workers into a trap.*

And then the enemy was upon them.

The attacking tribesmen were indeed headhunters, as could be evidenced by the sacks tied to the loincloths at their waists, some of which already contained the severed, bloody heads of farm workers. The skin of the attackers was dark brown, almost black, and they had wild, curly black hair. The only clothing on their body was the loincloth, and they were barefoot. The three headhunters who emerged from the trees nearby were wearing necklaces of teeth that appeared to be of human origin.

Upon seeing that the four companions were not running like everybody else, they began to howl and scream in a lupine manner. This was only a subtle change from their previous vocal emanations, but it attracted other headhunters into the clearing around the house. When the headhunters did scream, their open mouths revealed teeth that had been sharpened into canine points.

"You could eat human flesh with those teeth," Aldo remarked.

Kojiro did not know if these savage-looking men really ate other humans, as the olive-skinned man had suggested, but if they did, he would make sure he was dead before they got a chance to sink their teeth into him. And if he were destined to die on this fragrant island of spice, he would not die alone.

Kojiro drew both the katana and *wakizashi* from his belt simultaneously, twirled them 360 degrees around his sides to feel their balance, and thrust them both forward. The katana in his right hand drove cleanly through the skin, ribs, heart, and muscle and out the back of a headhunter rushing forward on his right. The *wakizashi* in his left drove through the tattooed stomach of a squat, potbellied tribesman on his left.

The man on Kojiro's right died instantly, and as Kojiro withdrew the bloody Arai blade, the headhunter simply slumped to the ground. The man on the left did not die instantly, so Kojiro stepped into the man until the cloth of his blue *yukata* touched the skin of the man's potbelly. Once there, he drove the blade downwards, clean through the man's groin causing his intestines and bowels to spill out between his legs. Without a pause, or even a look, Kojiro thrust his katana at head level and put the blade through the mouth of another wolf-toothed attacker who had raced at them from the trees before any of the Europeans had even seen him.

The whole episode had taken a matter of seconds. To Simon's eye, it looked more like a gracefully choreographed ballet than a gruesome life-and-death struggle. "Do you twirl the swords just to show off? It all seems a tad flashy."

"*Nihon-jin* do not 'show off,'" Kojiro replied.

"Really? Because that sure did look an awful lot like showing off to me."

"Checking balance."

"Huh, okay, if you say so," Simon said insincerely. He then had to sidestep a blow from something that looked like a gigantic, ornamented butcher knife. Simon drew his sword, thought about attempting to twirl it in a circle, then decided this wasn't the most opportune time to try something new.

The headhunter stumbled forward after Simon's sidestep gave his knife nothing but air, and Simon sliced off the arm that had been holding the knife. The beautiful Arai sword cut through the man's muscle and sinew like butter. Simon paused to marvel at the blade before he thrust it through the man's torso just below the rib cage. The sword's sharpness was almost surreal.

Neno, meanwhile, turned his back to the other three and faced off against two headhunters who had initially passed them on the right, but had come back when they heard their companions' wild howls of anger turn into piercing screams of pain. The light Italian long sword practically flew as he put his monstrous strength behind it. The two men quickly went down, shredded to ribbons.

"I thought he needed a poled weapon to fight," Simon remarked.

"Oh no, he's quite handy with a sword as well," Aldo informed Simon unnecessarily.

Then the drumbeats started. *Thonk, pat, pat. Thonk, pat, pat. Thonk, pat, pat.*

The sounds were coming from the opposite side of the island from whence the initial headhunters had come. The effect was definitely unnerving, especially when it came shortly after the appearance of the wild-looking, canine-toothed, wolf-howling tribesmen.

"I guess that's the second part of the trap," said Simon as he disemboweled a very large headhunter who had come screaming out of the trees.

"Yes, so it would seem," said Aldo as he ducked, dodged, and cut a man's leg off at the knee. Simon finished the man by slicing his throat as he lay on the ground.

The four companions had formed a rough circle about fifty feet from the house and were fighting off random attacks from all sides. The headhunters came screeching like banshees from out of the trees in ones and twos, but never gathered together to form a coordinated assault.

"I wonder what's become of that nice Arab merchant," Simon mused.

"Either headless or hiding, I suspect," said Aldo.

The drums got closer. Then they stopped altogether, and the second wave came into view. There were at least two hundred cannibals, and they looked terrifying. They had been marching abreast, spread out across the plantation, just like the first group had been, but from the opposite direction. Their bags were bulging with the heads of the farm workers who had fallen into their trap. When one of them noticed Simon, Kojiro, Aldo, and Neno surrounded by their dead compatriots, he gave out the highest-pitched, loudest, longest scream they had heard yet. The call echoed up and down their line ending in a crescendo, at which point all the headhunters started running towards their little group.

"Huh, I'm thinking run," said Simon. "We'll swim for the boat."

"I'm not sure I disagree," said Aldo.

"Go," said Neno. "I can't outrun them."

"Yes, the terror momentarily made me forget about our sizeable friend here," said Simon, worriedly chewing his lip.

The natives were forty yards away and closing quickly.

"I stay," said Kojiro.

The tribesmen were thirty yards away.

"Then again, there are few activities in this world that I despise more than running," said Simon. Simon glanced briefly at Kojiro who returned his look. *Why do I get the odd feeling this fellow is judging me?* he thought.

"Well, if the cowardly English don't run, how on earth could a respected man of Venice do so?" Aldo remarked.

"I don't know. Have you seen one we could ask?" inquired Simon.

The headhunters drew to within twenty yards and showed no sign of slowing down. Simon, Kojiro, Aldo, and Neno braced for the impact, but with no shields or armor, they would not last long. The mass of humanity would just overwhelm them.

Then, from behind the plantation house, a blindingly bright form emerged astride a brilliantly armored gray Arabian charger. It was Ismail ibn Umar. A painstakingly polished coat of mail started underneath his conical helmet and hung like a dress below his knees. Underneath his mail he wore thickly padded leather armor. Brightly polished steel greaves and plate armor boots emerged from below the hem of the mail. Equally polished gauntlets with spiked knuckles held the reins of the horse in one hand and an impressive looking fifteen-foot lance in the other. His helmet had hinged earpieces, an arrow-shaped nosepiece, and a five-inch spike crested the helmet.

Ismail rounded the corner of the house and headed straight towards the mass of headhunters at a full gallop. The sun's rays reflecting off the Arab knight's armor caused the entire column of headhunters to pause and stare. Kojiro did not hesitate. He charged forward, katana and *wakizashi* flashing, and decapitated the two men who seemed to be leading the headhunters' column. Then, Kojiro pushed into the massed column, swords ablaze.

"Shall we?" asked Simon.

"Si," replied Aldo. Neno had already joined Kojiro.

Ismail charged straight into the middle of the column at a full gallop. His lance impaled one of the headhunters, and with the impaled man in tow, Ismail galloped straight through the column, knocking men over, while his horse trampled the ones unlucky enough to fall underfoot. When he emerged on the far side, he pulled his lance from the torso of the dead headhunter, galloped thirty yards further, wheeled his horse, and drove straight back into the crowd, lance leveled.

Neno pushed, kicked, cut, stabbed, and sliced his way forward, throwing the fearsome-looking but much smaller attackers about like they were nothing more than small children.

The headhunters were not used to their plans falling apart. They were also not used to fighting warriors with a lifetime of martial training, as they usually took great care in their advanced planning stages to avoid them at all cost. In this case, their ruse had failed them. There was supposed to be a lone Arab knight left on the island, but for some reason four more trained fighters were on hand. They had no back-up plan, so all the fighters could do was resort to the tactics they had employed for decades: man to man, brute force combat. Although the numerical odds still favored the headhunters, this style of combat decidedly did not.

Kojiro stabbed, spun, and struck again. He parried a blow from one of the native knives with his katana and stabbed the man through the heart with his *wakizashi*.

Simon was greatly enjoying his new sword. He would cut left and open a man's bowels, cut right and sever a man's arm, then stab forward and puncture a man's chest cavity. He had truly found a tool that he was growing fond of. The blacksmith who had forged his sword had folded, quenched, tempered, and sharpened the sword to faultlessness. The sword was perfect in every way.

This sword is worthy of a name, Simon thought. He knew a Hampshire knight who harped on endlessly about his marvelous sword: The Brainbiter. At the time, Simon had laughed at the absurdity of naming an inanimate object, and he had ridiculed the Hampshire knight just shy of causing a duel. But now, this sword made him wonder if he had been wrong.

The headhunters were communicating their strikes through exaggerated body movements, and Aldo was having no difficulty dodging or parrying their chopping attacks and making the untrained warriors pay with their lives, but there were so many of them pressing in on him.

Ismail's charging cavalry attacks had had the desired effect of stopping the column's forward momentum, but eventually he had been surrounded and was now hacking downwards with his curved scimitar. The natives had been caught off guard, but they were brave and ruthless, and not used to losing.

Then the crew of the *Tigre* arrived.

Skilled Venetian sailors, adapting to warfare throughout their sprawling trade routes, had learned to use both the recurve bow and the crossbow. On this occasion, the crew of the *Tigre* had brought both. First, they fired the crossbows, whose powerful bolts flew clear through some of the half-naked headhunters, then, they switched to the rapidly reloadable recurve bows and unleashed Armageddon.

An hour earlier, Giacomo Aversa had spotted the dugout canoes from his usual perch in the crow's nest. He could see the light reflecting off of metal blades and had advised Luca Magnani, who had been placed in charge of the ship with the captain and first mate gone. Luca ordered the crew to fire a cannon in warning to the shore party. It would have been useless to try to hit the small, fast, maneuverable canoes. Gambling that the ship would be too intimidating to attack, he left only two crewmen to watch it and headed ashore with the remainder. Upon approaching the sound of clashing blades he didn't need to give any orders, the men knew their business, but he did anyway. "Shoot the *baldracche,* and if you hit the *capitano*, I will skin you alive!" Magnani shouted.

The arrows, being directly fired from cover, proved to be too much for the headhunters. Thanks to the skill of the Venetians, every arrow seemed to find its mark. They came at a rate of fifteen per minute. Like a wave breaking, the headhunters scattered into the trees and fled towards their canoes.

Simon and his group were just grateful to see them go, but Ismail apparently was not. His horse galloped after them, and his scimitar slashed down again and again as he made the natives pay for having dared attack his plantation. Lone combatants, unarmored, on foot, and fleeing were easy prey to even the least trained of cavalrymen, and Ismail was *not* the least trained of cavalrymen. Simon was not sure how many of the headhunters would make it back to their boats, but he did not think it would be many.

"Well, that was a wee bit of excitement, now, wasn't it?" Simon remarked. "Thank you, master carpenter!" he called out as he saw

Magnani emerge from the trees. Magnani gave Simon a flourishing bow.

Aldo spoke. "The poor cannibals should be grateful they did not win. For, had they won, I think they may have regretted their actions once they got the taste of an Englishman in their bellies. That is, of course, if your flesh tastes anything like the overcooked flavorless cuisine that you English eat."

"Quite right, quite right. No doubt you Italians are the tastier lot. A fact that I would have been more than happy to point out had they started lighting fires under giant cooking cauldrons."

"*Futari mo oishikunai, kamoshirenai. Ofuro ni hairanai to kusai.*" Kojiro did not smile as he said this.

Aldo laughed. "He just said that it's likely neither one of us would taste good since we both stink due to our infrequent bathing."

Simon lifted an eyebrow. "I think he's starting to like us."

Kojiro found a well and some cotton cloth on the property and began cleaning his blades. Aldo ordered Neno and his crew back to the ship, just in case the natives thought to attack it. That is, if Ismail had left any of them alive.

The farm workers slowly emerged from their hiding places. They looked bewildered but grateful as they grabbed a hold of their rescuers' arms and pumped them up and down. This continued until Ismail returned with his scimitar drenched in blood. He was no longer blindingly bright, as his armor and that of his horse were covered in crimson. Some of the blood was fresh enough or thickly pooled enough to still be dripping, while other spots had already dried to a rusty hue under the sun's hot rays. Ismail removed his helmet and the mail hood underneath it.

"I am in your debt, my friends. Without your assistance, my workers would be on their way to someone's belly, and I would be on my way to Allah. If you have a few days to spare, you will be my guests, and I will send for nutmeg and mace from the isles where the nutmeg tree grows. I'm afraid that as grateful as I am, I am still not allowed to disclose the location of those islands, but we will negotiate a fair trade."

And so it was that after four days of enjoying Ismail's lavish hospitality, including many cups of the remarkable beverage *qahwah*, the *Tigre* sailed for Egypt, with a fortune's worth of clove, nutmeg, and mace.

Chapter 21

Tower of London, Summer, 1483

The Tower of London was not in fact a single tower at all, but a series of towers, buildings, and walls that served as both palace and fortress for the royal family of England. The White Tower, the keep, was completed in 1100 by William the Conqueror, and at ninety feet tall, it was still the tallest building in London.

But the White Tower was not the only tower within the inner wall of the castle. The Garden Tower, pleasantly named due to its proximity to the Constable's garden, also contained living quarters, and this summer, those quarters were all the more pleasant since they were filled with the sounds of children's laughter. The two precocious youths housed in the Garden Tower could easily have spent their days moping about and wallowing in self-pity, but these two were made of sterner stuff.

After all, their father was King Edward the Fourth.

In addition to having a father who was a great champion in battle, their mother, Elizabeth Woodville, was no wilting violet either. Elizabeth had not been born into nobility, but she had been born with a sharp mind, a strong will, and remarkable beauty. Her strength and character played no small part in her husband's successful reign. So with parents like these, thirteen-year-old Edward V and his ten-year-old brother, Richard Shrewsbury, Duke of York, did not dwell on the recent death of their father, or the semi-captivity forced upon them by their uncle, Richard of Gloucester. Instead, they played.

"You have offended the honor of my lady, Edward, and you shall pay with your life." With those words, the slender ten year old brought his wooden sword down squarely onto the wooden shield held high by his thirteen-year-old brother.

"I am your king, and your lady has plotted against me. You will not live to see her again." Edward then struck swiftly with his own wooden sword, taking care not to actually strike the cherubic younger brother that he loved with all his heart.

Richard laughed at his brother's quick retort. Edward would make a good king someday. He was smart, strong, polite, and generous to a fault. The fact that their uncle and erstwhile protector had temporarily usurped the throne and was calling himself King Richard III did not concern him. They were the sons of the great King Edward IV, and someday they would claim their birthright. Meanwhile, there was the honor of imaginary ladies to protect and traitorous Lancastrian villains to dispose of. Neither brother gave it any thought when the captain of the guard entered the room and strode purposefully towards them. The captain of the guard was a renowned knight who had always been a loyal servant to their father.

Edward spoke while parrying a strike aimed straight for his heart. "Captain, it is a pleasure to see you. Perhaps you have come to give my brother some tips? His footwork seems to leave him off-balance too often." And with that statement, Edward slipped to his brother's right, pushed his brother in the back with his shield, and tripped him with his foot. Before his brother hit the decorative red carpet though, Edward grabbed the back of his doublet and gave a sharp pull upwards to lessen the force of his brother's fall.

Chagrined, Richard stood up and brushed himself off, bowing to his brother. "You win again, my king. I guess I shall not live to see my lady again." Richard then turned to the recently arrived knight and addressed him. "Captain, you have fought many battles; do you have any secrets that will help me beat my brother just once?"

The captain of the guard was a big, bald man in his mid-forties, whose body and face bore innumerable battle scars. He had been standard-bearer to King Edward IV, where he had earned most of those scars, and now he was part of Richard III's personal bodyguard. There was a reason he had been given those prominent martial positions for two different kings; his loyalty to the Yorkist cause was without question, as a lot of Lancastrian souls could attest to. It was not unusual for him to visit the two princes in the tower.

The captain thought he liked the princes. They seemed healthy, they took their military training seriously, and they always treated him with respect. He knew for certain he liked their father. King Edward IV had been a steadfast leader, putting the sword to Lancastrian and Scot alike, oftentimes through the use of his brother Richard, whom the captain now served. So the chances were good that Edward IV's sons would be children that he should like.

Only, he didn't know for sure because his mind didn't process emotions properly. He had known that he was different from a young age, but he was smart and he quickly learned to model other people's behavior. He smiled when other people smiled and laughed when other people laughed, but it was all a show. He didn't feel sad or happy and didn't understand why people cared when things died. Whether it was a horse, an ant, or his own mother, he never shed a tear and couldn't understand why other people did. So with Richard III's orders clear in his head, when the young prince asked him to teach a lesson in swordplay, he proceeded without hesitation. "Certainly," said the captain.

Richard watched in horror as his older brother's chest exploded, to allow the captain of the guard's sword through it. Richard did not think of himself at this time, but felt only grief for his beloved brother even as the captain's sword swung again and the blade entered his own torso. As he watched his intestines spill out onto the beautifully embroidered rug, and the life drained out of his ten-year-old body, Richard looked questioningly up at his murderer, but he did not see any answers in the captain's face.

When he was sure both boys were dead, the captain wrapped them up in the carpet he had slain them on, leaving no bloodstains on the floor for people to question. He had been prepared to do some scrubbing, but as it turned out, it wasn't necessary. It was not difficult for him to carry the boys down the stairs and out to his waiting cart as they weighed no more than a combined one hundred seventy-five pounds. Once he had loaded them onto the back of his cart, it was an hour-long trip to his estate outside of London where a pen of starving hogs waited to polish off all evidence that the princes had ever existed.

The captain of the guard crossed himself as he hacked apart the small bodies and tossed them to the pigs. He did so not out of remorse, because he didn't feel remorse, but because he knew that was what you were supposed to do in such situations.

He really had borne them no ill will.

Richard III was pleased with how the summer was wrapping up. After he beheaded Edward IV's in-laws and servants without trial, all of London, and indeed the whole countryside, seemed to be coming around to his way of thinking. Now, he had just gotten word that everything had gone as planned in the Garden Tower.

*Magnificent, h*e thought. He didn't have anything personal against his nephews, but sooner or later someone was bound to have supported one or the other's claim to the throne, and he did not want that hanging over his head. He would reward the captain of the guard richly for both his service and his silence.

The only thorn left in my side now is that damned Lancastrian Henry that isn't really a Lancastrian at all, but a Tudor, he thought, as he dismissed the captain. *The last true Lancastrian was that nutter Henry VI. If only that whoremongering John of Gaunt could have kept his trouser snake in his trousers, I wouldn't have the great-great-grandson of a bastard claiming he has a right to the throne.*

Richard shook his head in dismay. *And to add insult to injury, he's half Welsh! It's so absurd as to be almost unbelievable. But the Lancastrians are nothing if not predictable. They would follow a cow into battle if its great-great-grandmother once gave milk to King Henry V. That's why I'd like that last Lang of Exeter killed as well.*

Chapter 22

Venice

THE PROSPEROUS VOYAGE had been very good for Aldo. He made enough money to open his own merchant house. Now he traded and commissioned ships to carry his goods from the comfort of his own home, an expansive three-story warehouse and residence situated on the Grand Canal. The magnificent structure sported a whitewashed façade with a majestic row of Gothic columns and arches both street-side and canal-side. The main entryway led into a giant, open-air courtyard where goods could be shuffled to and from the storehouses nearby. The second floor contained Aldo's spacious residence, and the third floor housed apartments and offices for the merchants, traders, and accountants that he employed.

The lavish second floor suite had a wide, covered portico that overlooked the canal. It was here that Aldo frequently entertained guests with his tales of adventure and heroism. Alas, the view of the canal had its good and bad days. Bad days were those in the hot summer when the air didn't move and the smells of sewage drifted up from the canal. Although Venice was at the forefront of modernity with its *gatoli* system of indoor plumbing, there was no avoiding the fact that all the waste transported through the gatoli pipe systems eventually ended up in the canals. On the bad days, Aldo entertained inside.

The prosperous voyage had been good to Simon, too. He had accumulated enough wealth to hire and equip mercenaries to assist him in reclaiming his ancestral lands. That is, if the chance ever arose. He also had gained the inestimable value of Kojiro's services. The unintended negative consequence, of which he was not yet aware, was that the notoriety of the voyage had attracted Yorkist attention.

Aldo had been generous enough to offer Simon and Kojiro their own apartments on the third floor of his sweeping residence while Simon plotted his uncertain future. The trio liked to spend the late afternoons drinking wine, conversing, and watching the boat traffic on the canal. Kojiro did not converse as much as Aldo and Simon, but he seemed to smile at least once a conversation, which was a considerable improvement from the first time they had met.

During the day, Kojiro and Simon practiced sword fighting in the courtyard along the canal. Kojiro was surprised to discover that Western plate armor was not that much heavier than his own samurai armor had been. He learned to maneuver quite well with it.

Simon was not equal to Kojiro's speed and agility, but he compensated with his size, strength, and superior reach. Nevertheless, he didn't care to speculate as to who would win a duel to the death. They sparred for hours every day. Simon taught Kojiro the vulnerable points in western armor, just as Kojiro had done for Simon before the battle at Kannoura. Kojiro relentlessly drilled Simon in his own sword, wrestling, and takedown techniques, while Simon shared European fighting styles in return. Aldo watched and sipped wine.

On one particularly suffocating afternoon in the courtyard, Aldo, after consuming four glasses of a very light and slightly sweet pinkish wine from the Champagne region, could no longer hold his peace. "Enough! Please, enough! There is not a sane person in the city drilling on a day like today. Neither the Genoese nor the Turks are at the gates! Relinquish your weapons; less training and more fun! Cede to my command, or I shall evict you from my house!"

It was an empty threat, but Simon and Kojiro were sweltering in their armor. As partial payment for Kojiro's service, Simon had ordered the samurai a custom suit of armor designed by the finest craftsmen in Venice. He even paid extra to have Kojiro's blue crest of the crane engraved on both shoulder plates of the black steel armor.

"Because you insist, we will desist." Simon grinned at his clever word play.

Aldo rolled his eyes.

Kojiro, not understanding Simon, nonetheless gauged from Aldo's reaction that the Englishman had once again said something that only he found amusing. Kojiro looked at Aldo and rolled his eyes to show comprehension.

Aldo clapped. "Precisely, Kojiro, precisely."

Simon pretended to feel hurt as he sheathed his sword and walked over to Aldo. "And what is this fine-looking potion that you have been sipping on?"

Aldo poured the flat, pink liquid into two Venetian glass goblets and handed them to Kojiro and Aldo. "I acquired some barrels of this at a bargain since the Champenois are not particularly known for their winemaking skills. I was going to trade it to some Hungarians for furs, but I find it quite refreshing so I'm thinking now that I may hold onto it. It goes down well on a hot afternoon, no?"

Kojiro, who had developed a taste for Western wines, took a sip and nodded his head in appreciation.

Simon agreed. "Wonderful wine, but it isn't doing your waistline any favors. You must be buying your clothes at that establishment that panders to the well-proportioned people these days. I think the shop is called The Fat Venetian?"

Aldo patted his belly and smiled. "Yes, I'm afraid this is my just reward for prosperity, and a tribute to the fine food and drink of Venice. I can't understand why you two insist on all this training business. It's embarrassing, really. I tell my friends that you're both 'touched by the Lord.' They believe me without hesitation."

"Doubtless, your equally rotund friends will find themselves on a Turkish spit roasting over a fire one day and wonder how it possibly came to pass. But enough talk of obese merchants. What did you have in mind for this afternoon?"

"Why, I thought a relaxing stroll along the piazza would be nice. Perhaps I shall purchase some more paintings for my living quarters, or perhaps we shall just enjoy wine and some female companionship? Of course, I won't be bringing either of you until you've bathed."

Aldo knew Kojiro would have bathed anyway. He always did after training. Kojiro was the most hygienic man Aldo had ever met. He was certainly no barbarian. Simon, on the other hand, gave no thought to offending others with his body odor. "It doesn't offend me," he would grin and say. *And Simon was English nobility! The Lord be blessed, but the English were a dirty people.* However, Simon did like voluptuous Venetian women and those who did not charge for their services would pay him no attention when he smelled like a wet dog. "Yes, yes, I'll have a bath, but none of that *aqua mirabilis* crap you Italian pretty boys cover yourselves with."

Within an hour, the three of them were strolling along the Piazza San Marco. Aldo wore a fancy, red- and gold-striped silk tunic with a white ruffled collar, red sheer leggings, and a wide-brimmed black hat that had an ostentatious white ostrich feather protruding from its showy gold band. His tunic swelled at the waist, where his ample belly gave evidence that he was a man of wealth, and from his belt hung a medium length, emerald-hilted broadsword, proving that he was a man due respect in this prosperous city-state.

Kojiro wore the *bashofu kasuri yukata* he had picked up in the Ryukyu Kingdom. This was a light but stiff *kimono* made from the fibers of banana plants. Kojiro's *yukata* was dyed in various shades of blue, creating an intentionally blurry pattern of swallows. The *yukata* was perfect for the heat and humidity of the swamp city. On his feet he wore thonged, straw *zori* sandals, also very comfortable in the heat.

Simon was envious. Kojiro not only looked comfortable in his clothing, but he walked gracefully, never seemed to sweat, and looked to the entire world as if he weren't wretchedly hot. "Kojiro, would you kindly try to act a little more miserable for me, please? People will think me a sniveler if I'm the only one who gripes about the heat."

Kojiro still had trouble with irony and did not know the proper response to Simon's comment. "Yes, I will try" was all he could manage.

Although he was a foreigner, Kojiro was allowed to carry his katana and *wakizashi* on the streets of Venice. He was a member of a noble class, albeit a noble class the Venetians had never heard of, other than possibly Marco Polo's references to the mysterious island of 'Cipangu.' Venice was the hub of fifteenth century world trade, and as such, Venetians were used to seeing strangely dressed foreigners. In order to foster good relations with other nations and thus improve trade possibilities, the Venetians paid proper respect to the nobility of all countries. So while the sight of Kojiro's simple dress, ponytail, and dual swords drew curious glances, he otherwise went about his business undisturbed. In fact, Simon drew far more attention when he traveled the city without bathing.

Traveling with the three companions were Aldo's giant Neapolitan Mastiffs: Augustus and Nero. Both animals were two hundred and fifty-pound, muscular monsters with gigantic heads and even larger jowls. They were devoted to their owner, who could not resist feeding them table scraps at nearly every meal. The spoiled gray dogs ate better than many of the citizens in Venice. In looks, they were difficult to tell apart, but in personality, they couldn't have been more different. Nero, like his namesake, was a neurotic, high-strung basketcase; whereas Augustus, also like his namesake, was majestic, deliberate, and calm. Nero was never seen without at least six inches of drool hanging from his jowls, but Augustus, quite unusually for the breed, rarely drooled. It was almost as if he knew himself to be above such a crude trait, and he willed it not to happen.

The Piazza San Marco, as it opened up before them, was a wonder to behold. At the eastern end of the piazza stood the grand Basilica Cattedrale Patriacale di San Marco, with its Gothic archways, ornate religious carvings, gold inlaid domes, and marble statuary. The statues of four Greek horses, stolen during the Venetian-inspired Fourth Crusade's sack of Constantinople, stood vigilant guard in front of the grand cathedral, daring anyone to challenge the might of Venice. South of the cathedral stood the Doge's Palace, its narrow gothic columns and biblical carvings matching those of its neighbor. The Doge's Palace continued south, where it opened up onto the lagoon which surrounded the island.

Across from the cathedral stood the magnificent campanile, a three hundred-foot-tall lookout tower with a dominating view of the city and all its surroundings. The two-story Byzantine columned buildings that made up the north, south, and west edges of the piazza housed government officials, clergy, and businesses. The businesses ranged from trading houses and banks, to bars and inns. It was towards one of these particular bars that Aldo, Kojiro, Simon, and Augustus strode. Nero didn't really stride. He sort of loped.

"Do you see that painter whose works I liked last week?" Aldo asked.

"No, but I particularly like this one," Simon said. He was looking over a painting of a partially clothed buxom woman. "I didn't know Christian folk were allowed to paint such things," Simon said as he studied the painting's 'details' carefully. "But why do all the women in these paintings have fat asses?"

"Simon, these dear ladies have ample asses. Some might even say voluptuous or sensuous. I personally find small asses quite unattractive."

While Simon, Aldo, and Kojiro discussed the merits of various paintings, Augustus sat stiffly upright in the dignified manner befitting a descendent of Alexander the Great's mighty Molossus war dogs. Nero, on the other hand, took to chasing pigeons around the piazza. It was a fair match. The pigeons were slow and stupid, but Nero, although surprisingly agile for a dog of his size, could not decide which pigeon he wanted to chase and wound up chasing one after another until his master called for him.

Aldo, Simon, and Kojiro took up their usual seats at an outdoor table at their favorite *osteria*. Aldo ordered Nero to lie down next to Augustus who lay upright on his elbows and haunches, head erect, ready to respond to a command at a moment's notice. Nero protested this forced constraint immediately and then again every few minutes with a high-pitched whine. This was uncharacteristic of such a large animal, but Aldo held firm. After about fifteen minutes, Nero gave up. He let out a huge sigh, flopped over on his side, and used his eyes in an attempt to communicate to all passing patrons that he was the most mistreated dog in all of Italy.

Jean-Paul de Bailly had worked at the small wine bar off the piazza for a month, as he studied the behavior of the Lancastrian noble and his friends. It hadn't been hard to get the job at Simon's favorite spot; Venice was a merit-based society and Jean-Paul knew his wine. He helped the owner select his wines at the market, and his selections had been popular with the bar's customers. So much so that it was now the most fashionable place on the piazza to quaff the latest imports from France, Spain, and the Italian mainland.

But Jean-Paul was not there to earn a living as a sommelier. He was being paid handsomely to complete a different job entirely, and to do it in a manner that would not create an international incident. He'd surveilled his target, he'd been patient, and he was not going to fail. In fact, as a professional assassin he was a little bit disappointed that it was going to be this easy. The Englishman and his friends drank too much, and that would be their downfall.

"You have shaved and bathed, Simon, but you sweat like a pig. I can't tell if I smell the swamp or you. Why can't you be more like this fellow?" Aldo said, pointing at Kojiro. "I don't believe I've ever seen the man perspire." Aldo began the evening's verbal jousting while he ordered another bottle of Burgundy.

"Well, aside from Kojiro here, a man who works, sweats. But then I can see how you would know nothing about that, my pudgy, pig-bellied friend."

The wine came, delivered by the French waiter who seemed to have a talent for always recommending the right wine. He and Aldo had engaged in more than one long conversation about the effects of temperature, growing season, and irrigation on any number of varietals from all over the world. These conversations bored Simon to tears, but he listened patiently because the Frenchman inevitably served them a delicious libation at their conclusion.

Jean-Paul had chosen the wine that he was going to poison them with carefully. Aldo was a superb wine taster who always sniffed the bouquet before he sampled a wine so he had chosen a wine that he was sure Aldo would never have sampled before. This would ensure Aldo would be unaware of the flavor profiles that the wine was supposed to have. No one other than the Champenois themselves ever consumed the unremarkable wine that they produced.

"Here you are, *messieurs*. I think you will like this one."

Aldo recognized the pale pink color of the wine that Jean-Paul poured into his goblet. "Ah, Jean-Paul, good choice! I believe I was consuming this very same product from Champagne this afternoon. We likely got them from the same shipment."

Kojiro noticed what appeared to be a momentary look of surprise or panic, or both, in the waiter's narrow green eyes after Aldo's comment. *But why would that be?* he wondered to himself. Being immersed in a world of unfamiliar languages, Kojiro had become adept at discerning meaning from body language and facial expressions, and the waiter's current facial expression concerned him.

Aldo raised the glass, brought it to his nose, and inhaled deeply like he always did.

Jean-Paul watched for a brief instant, bowed, and began making his way to the rear of the bar. Successful or not, he did not want to wait around for the consequences. *Damn that man and his voracious appetite for wine!* The back of the bar opened out onto a walkway that bordered the lagoon, and Jean-Paul walked hurriedly towards one of the many docks.

In addition to the waiter's unusual facial expression, Kojiro noticed that Jean-Paul did not stay at the table for his usual conversation with Aldo after the first taste. Kojiro stood and watched as the waiter walked all the way out the back door. Then he looked at Aldo and the glass of wine.

Aldo shook his head and pinched his nose in disgust. "Not as good as the one I chose, that's for sure. Odd that they aren't from the same batch. I wouldn't think many shipments of this stuff come in. But we are paying for it, so it will be drunk!"

Aldo poured some for Simon and Kojiro and was about to toss his glass back when Kojiro knocked the glass from his hands. It shattered on the cobblestones of the courtyard. Nero, awakened by the crashing sound of glass, ran to the spilled liquid and was about to lick it off the ground when Kojiro kicked him squarely in the head. Nero let out a yelp, not from the pain—because Kojiro's sandals had little effect on his immense cranium—but from his hurt feelings. These humans never kicked him!

Aldo and Simon were bewildered by Kojiro's behavior.

"Grab the bottle of wine, pour out your glasses away from this greedy dog, and follow me," Kojiro ordered in a calm, no-nonsense tone. He then walked rapidly through the bar and out the back. Simon and Aldo looked at each other with questioning glances, but they obediently poured out their glasses, grabbed the bottle off the table, and followed Kojiro with Augustus and Nero in tow.

Initially Jean-Paul walked at a brisk pace towards the gondola he had waiting for him near the Doge's Palace. He knew that running would draw attention to himself, and he had learned not to run unless *absolutely* necessary. He did not hear the pursuit behind him, but after all the time he'd spent in the game, he could feel it. Eventually, he ceased worrying about drawing attention to himself and took off at a run.

Aldo and Simon quickly put together the facts of the situation and realized why Kojiro was chasing the waiter.

"Pounce!" Aldo ordered his dogs. Nero, neurotic though he was, responded to his master's guard commands with a single-minded determination that was belied by his daily behavior. Augustus reacted just as quickly as Nero, but of course that was to be expected of Augustus.

Simon watched the two dogs spring forward like they had been shot from a crossbow, shoulder muscles rippling, thigh muscles bulging, and jowls flapping as they tore after the fleeing waiter.

Jean-Paul cursed his bad luck, but he knew he would get another chance. His boat was twenty yards away; the slant-eyed foreigner, while faster than Jean-Paul himself, would not catch him in time. His next attempt could not be as subtle. He would not be able to get as close to the Lancastrian again, but he would make it work. His professional reputation and the second half of his fee depended on it.

Jean-Paul leaned forward in anticipation of releasing the rope that moored his gondola, when he found himself face down on the dock with an enormous weight on top of him. Jean-Paul pushed up with his hands, but the weight did not move. Then the snout of one of those ugly, dirty dogs that the Venetian merchant kept appeared in front of his face. The nasty animal opened its mouth in a warning snarl that revealed a huge jaw stocked full of healthy white teeth.

Kojiro almost laughed out loud when two hundred and fifty pounds of muscular dog sent the one hundred and thirty pound waiter flying onto his face. He was surprised to see that it had been Nero who got there first. The two dogs worked well as a team, though, because no sooner had Nero knocked the man down then Augustus went straight for the man's face. He was too well trained to bite without being ordered to do so, but it wasn't necessary. The waiter was scared stiff.

By the time Simon and Aldo caught up with Kojiro and the dogs, Aldo was out of breath.

"Get your filthy beast off of me!" Jean-Paul blurted out, but Aldo was too winded to give the dogs commands.

Simon saved him the trouble by pushing Nero off and sitting Jean-Paul up. "I believe this is the wine you recommended?" Simon offered the bottle to Jean-Paul. Jean-Paul shook his head.

"I will tell you who hired me, if you let me live," Jean-Paul said with resignation. He had no desire to be a martyr for some English cause.

"Well, unfortunately for you, I'm already pretty sure that the King of England wants me dead, so I don't see how you have anything to offer me," Simon responded.

"But I can tell you the name of the man who hired me," Jean-Paul protested desperately.

"Go ahead."

"I need your word that I will not be harmed."

"I swear on the blood of our Savior, the Lord Jesus Christ. May I go to hell and be tortured by Lucifer himself and a thousand demons for all eternity if I break my vow," Simon swore his oath.

Aldo raised his eyebrows.

Jean-Paul had not expected a vow nearly that unbreakable, and relieved, gave the information readily. "His name is Lord Blythe. He said he was acting on the orders of the late King Edward himself."

"The late?" Simon asked, genuinely shocked.

"King Edward died April ninth of this year. His brother Richard of Gloucester was appointed Lord Protector of Edward's young children until the eldest son can be crowned. Richard will be running things until then."

"Don't see how anything could go wrong with that plan," Simon said in his very best sarcastic tone (not knowing something had indeed already gone drastically wrong for the princes). Simon was not surprised to find out that King Edward would commission the man who had taken his lands to also take his life. It made perfect sense in fact, because no one had more to lose than Lord Blythe if Simon ever returned to England. *Thank God for Aldo and his wine tasting, and Kojiro and his instincts. This Jean-Paul character is a true professional.* Jean-Paul had really crossed the line, though; he had forced Simon to be wary of the alcohol that he consumed.

Simon removed the slender blade from his belt and thrust it up through the back of Jean-Paul's neck at a forty-five-degree angle. Jean-Paul let out a high-pitched scream as the Venetian stiletto worked its way slowly up through the brain. Within seconds, his body went limp. Simon then worked the knife back and forth during the withdrawal, scrambling the brain.

Aldo was not totally surprised; he had already begun crossing himself in anticipation. "Did you really have to swear all of that?"

"Sure. If I had given my word as a knight and a gentleman I might not have been able to kill him. But the way I understand it with this whole Christian thing, I can repent for all my sins when I'm about to die and I'm forgiven. Isn't that the deal?"

"I believe that's a very generous reading of the teachings of the Church."

"Well, it looks to be a beautiful sunset tonight. Back for another bottle of wine?" Simon asked as he kicked Jean-Paul's body into the lagoon. The four of them sauntered back to the bar. Nero began a hopeless chase of seagulls.

Chapter 23

Venice, One Year Later

A COMBINATION OF the evening tide and underground river flows worked in harmony to flush the gatoli system's canal deposits and their accompanying smells out to sea, making Aldo's open porch a pleasant location for treasonous plotting. "You'll need transportation and some men," Aldo told Simon.

"Thank you, King Obvious," Simon responded. From the trading ships that passed through Venice, they had learned that the exiled Henry Tudor was in Brittany recruiting all and sundry to overthrow King Richard III. Although he hated to admit it, the gaudy Venetians had grown on Simon over the last year, but he couldn't dodge Yorkist assassins for the rest of his life and Henry Tudor presented his best, and perhaps last, opportunity to avenge his mother.

"With an attitude like that, I might not volunteer my ship for transport."

"Now why in hades would you even consider removing your fat ass from these plush surroundings to transport me to France?"

"Bah, I'm bored. There are only so many ways I can tell the story of how I saved you and my entire crew from those cannibals."

"Oh, I don't know, I think the last version where the petrified King of the Cannibals fell to his knees and begged you for mercy still has some legs on it."

"True, true, or the one where I heroically saved a scantily clad beauty from the cannibals' pot while you were cowering in a bush somewhere; that still gets a hearty round of applause from the crowd."

Simon waggled his eyebrows. "Yes, that's definitely one of *my* favorites."

Aldo sighed and looked out over the canal. "In all seriousness, though, I need more stories, and I have a feeling that a voyage with you will produce some. Besides, when I travel, I trade, and when I trade, I make money, so what is there to lose?"

"Well," Simon squinted, "your head for one thing. I've got to tell you, the odds are this story may not end well; check with Seaman Aversa for exact numbers. I hear he's back to operating an underground betting parlor again."

"No, not *my* head. I cannot afford to involve the nation of Venice in your internal English politics; it would be bad for business. But I will happily transport you so that you may lose your own head bedside your fellow Englishmen."

"No matter, I should think I won't need much more than Kojiro here and a few others."

Kojiro looked squarely into Simon's eyes and spoke without emotion. "I'm sorry, I cannot."

"Huh," Simon said, surprised. "That is actually a very wise decision but not exactly what I was expecting."

"I did not make that decision, of course. I already pledged my service to you. I spoke with what I believe you call *irony*?"

Aldo spit the wine he had just ingested out his nose. Burgundy and mucus sprayed the railing of his porch, and he choked on the liquid still caught in his throat.

Kojiro jumped from his chair, startled by Aldo's sudden difficulties. He moved quickly to Aldo's side, and his face broke into a look of genuine concern. Simon's face did not.

"I do not understand. Is he okay?" Kojiro asked.

"Yes, he's just fine," Simon answered. "He's just a little overly amused by your jest, and I have to say I'm quite impressed myself."

"Did I make a mistake?" Kojiro asked as water ran from Aldo's eyes. He was trying to learn the ways of these foreigners and he wished to join in their joking, but it was difficult to translate humor.

"No, you did not make a mistake. In fact, the total lack of emotion in your voice seems a bit *too* well suited to irony," Simon conceded. "Have you quite finished?" he then asked Aldo.

"Nearly," Aldo managed to utter.

"Okay, so I have transportation and one follower. I should like to see what Neno has been up to lately."

Chapter 24

SIMON WALKED UP to the door of a particularly sketchy bordello in the red light district of Castelletto, where Neno was known to semi-permanently reside. After knocking on the peeling green painted door, he was greeted with, "*Mi dica*?" the tone of which conveyed anything but 'May I help you?'

"Neno," Simon replied. The door opened and a small, dirty, rat-faced man gave him a look of vague recognition. The pimp jerked his thumb at the stairs then sat down in an entryway chair and went back to picking at a large scab on his nose.

Simon made his way up a dark, narrow staircase that stank of mildew until he reached the third floor, where he knocked on the door of Neno's regular room. His repeated knocks were not answered, so he hollered at the door in his unmistakable deep voice.

"Good morning, Neno, I wondered if I might be able to engage your services once again." He heard the thump of a large object falling from a considerable height. The thump was followed by very rapid cursing in Venetian and shortly afterwards, the door opened.

"Come in, please." Along with those words from Neno, Simon was treated to an odor of vomit, red wine, and only God knew what else coming from the behemoth-sized first mate's unshaven face. Simon looked around the room to see a poorly furnished, cramped space with tattered red and gold wall hangings depicting famous Venetian personalities and battlefield triumphs.

Times had not been good for Neno. He had received a fair portion of the spoils from the voyage, but he had a problem. In fact, Neno had several problems. One was that he liked women, a lot, and Venice catered to his needs. The City of Masks offered gambling dens, alcohol from all parts of the world, and of course, Neno's favorite spot in the city: the "Bridge of Tits," which just happened to be 'on the way' to nearly everywhere Neno went in the city.

The giant proceeded to sit on a stool next to the bed and dunk his head in a bucket of water. Simon looked at the high clearance of the bed and assumed that Neno falling out of it was the likely cause of the thump he had heard.

"So you are going on another trading voyage?" Neno asked.

"No, I'm going back to England to either take back my land or lose my head. The latter, unfortunately, is a much likelier outcome than the former."

Neno did not have much to think about. "But there will be money?"

"Yes. Aldo will pay you as first mate while we sail, and if you will fight for me, I will pay you the rate of a mercenary captain."

"I will fight."

Chapter 25

Tower Hill, London, England

THE SCREAMS ECHOED across the bloodstained ground. Four horses made the initial pull on the four separate limbs of an unlucky servant of Edward IV, one who *claimed* to have switched allegiances to the new king.

"My lord, what about the drawing and hanging part of his decreed punishment? Doesn't that usually come first?" Lord Percy Blythe asked.

Lord Percy was thoroughly enjoying his first trip to the capital since Richard had become king. During the war against the Scots, he had served Richard personally, and they had struck up a nominal friendship during the campaign. Thus it was that Percy had maintained his fiefdom and privileges upon the change in regents. On this occasion, the king had summoned him to obtain an update on intelligence in the west country.

"But I've always like the quartering best," Richard replied, "and I want to make sure he's *alive* for this part. As you know, when they're pulled through the streets behind a horse, one bad bump to the head, and *poof*! Fun over. Likewise, when the hangman is having a bad day then the hanging kills him and the quartering becomes a moot point. Even when they survive those trials there is usually very little fight left in them, and the sport is practically taken out of the quartering."

"Oh, quite so, quite so, I never thought about it that way. This is much more entertaining," Blythe replied as the handler of the horses cracked his whip. The horses stretched the victim's body further apart, accompanied by much snapping and popping from his joints.

"See? You can barely hear the cracking over his screaming, which would never have been possible if he'd been drawn and hung first. The human body is fascinating." Soon after this remark, both of the prisoner's arms wrenched free from his body with a tremendous ripping sound. This freed the tension on the horses tied to his legs, and they took off at a gallop across the courtyard dragging the mercifully unconscious man behind them until he bled out.

"We can hang him now if you'd like, my friend," Richard joked.

Lord Percy Blythe laughed. His king had nothing if not a brilliant sense of humor. "Do you think he was actually disloyal?"

"I doubt it, but with that damn Tudor plotting against me again, it's better to be safe than sorry. And by the way, is my wife dead yet?"

"Very shortly, according to her physicians. They're spreading the word that it's tuberculosis."

"That should suffice. I can't believe I had to poison her personally, but she insists on having her food tested unless it comes directly from me; paranoid shrew."

"Well regardless, the poison is taking hold now and your niece, Elizabeth of York, will make the perfect second wife. She is still hesitant because she believes the rumors that you murdered her two brothers, the princes, but she will come around. I told her that she should stop listening to the gossip of servants and peasants. We do need to go forward with the wedding as soon as possible, though. It is rumored that Henry Tudor wishes to marry her and join the House of Lancaster to the House of York. That rumor is causing unrest in my region, but even more so in Wales, as some people see it as a way to end these wars."

"They will see an end to these wars after I have Henry Tudor's head on a spike on London Bridge! And why can we not just kill *all* the Welsh and be done with it? They are nothing but a blemish on this beautiful island."

Percy frowned sympathetically. "I wish we could, but I can't hold the western border without the Welsh chieftains that are loyal to you, and the rest are too damned hard to root out of the godforsaken hills in that country."

"I know, I know," Richard waved a dismissive hand. "The question was rhetorical, I'm not daft. So when is Henry expected to come, and how many men will he be bringing with him?"

"Our spies are working on it now, my king."

"Well, then I certainly hope our spies are better than our assassins. I understand that even little Lord Lang is still alive."

Chapter 26

Le Marais, Paris, France, Autumn, 1484

"Harry, my boy, how are you on this bright and beautiful morning?" boomed Jasper Tudor, Henry Tudor's perpetually cheerful uncle.

Jasper, born, raised, and having fought his way across nearly every inch of Wales, called Henry by his Welsh name. And Jasper was the one man who could call the Earl of Richmond and potential king-to-be, anything he wanted. Jasper had raised the boy after his mother, Margaret Beaufort, great-granddaughter of John of Gaunt, was taken away by Edward IV. Jasper had also rescued Harry from his birthplace (and Jasper's former property) of Pembroke Castle, Wales, and smuggled him to safety in Brittany. From there, Jasper became more of a father than an uncle and raised the boy to manhood. Henry's real father, Jasper's brother Edmund, had died in Yorkist captivity before Henry was born.

"I'm well, uncle, I'm well, and you?" Henry truly loved his uncle and counted on him almost exclusively for advice. Since a channel storm had doomed their attempted revolt in October, 1483, the relatives had spent many an evening developing the strategy that had led them to today. The clever political machinations of King Richard III had forced them to flee Brittany, but in France, they found opportunity.

"Oh, couldn't be better. I love a good jousting tournament, and with the King of France putting up the prize money, we've got knights from all over Europe camped on the tournament field. And it must be said, the King of France was generous enough to let us use these lavish accommodations," Jasper said with a smile.

Henry Tudor looked around the bleak, cold, and empty room. "At least it keeps the rain off our heads." He remarked in his typical undauntable fashion. Their room in the large monastic complex had some peculiar stone engravings on the walls that Henry had been meaning to ask about. "I'm curious about that symbol on the beam over my bed. What are the two knights on one horse?" Henry asked as he looked toward the high vaulted ceiling.

"Ah, that is the symbol of the Poor Knights of the Temple of King Solomon, better known as the Knights Templar," Jasper said as he looked in the direction Henry was pointing.

Henry had heard of the Knights Templar and their famous Crusade battles, as every child had, but he knew few details beyond that.

Jasper looked carefully at the Templar's Latin inscription and read it out loud. "*Sigillum Militum Xristi*, the Seal of the Soldiers of Christ. Two knights riding a horse together symbolized the Templar's vow to poverty. Unfortunately for them, it was also used by the King of France as conclusive proof that the Knights Templar dabbled in homosexuality, which in turn, helped he and the pope to disband the order. This conveniently freed the good king from all his debts to the order."

"Fortuitous."

"Indeed. This monastery we are quartered in was once called Le Temple. It was their headquarters." Jasper looked out from one of the tower's windows and pointed to the lush fields below. "Those fields where the tournament is being held were once marshland. The Knights Templar spent a small fortune draining the marsh to create the fields and farmlands you see now."

"When you say they were disbanded, what exactly do you mean?"

"Well, the French King burned some of them alive, but most of them simply joined other orders, moved to friendlier countries, or renounced their Templar vows and retired. The common belief is that they were all tortured and killed, but I find that propaganda unlikely; many of them were highly intelligent men with no small amount of martial experience. If you look on the fields below, however, you will see that their legacy lives on."

Henry gave his uncle a quizzical look. "You mean other than the fields themselves?"

"Yes, look at the tents of the men who have come here to compete. Notice the flags and pennants with red crosses that end in wide footings? Those are Templar crosses, and as you can see, they're part of the design of many flags."

"There are a lot of them."

"There were tens of thousands of Templars, and they controlled banking from Europe to the Middle East. You can't erase that sort of legacy by kingly proclamation or papal decree."

"I suppose not. So, some of the men who fight may be descendants of the Templars?"

"Without doubt; certainly some of the knights from Portugal, Leon, and Switzerland will have Templar blood in their veins. It is rumored a high percentage of the Templars fled to those countries."

"I do appreciate a good historical story, uncle, and it seems you never fail to oblige. Unfortunately, I'm afraid our men will have to miss the opportunity to test their mettle against that warrior blood."

Now it was Jasper's turn to look quizzically at Henry.

Henry knew he was taking a chance here, but it was a calculated decision. "Our men will be forbidden to fight in the tournament."

Jasper looked at Henry as if he'd lost his mind. "They'll ignore that order."

"They'll try, but I'm going to send the Brandons and Sir John Cheyne to oversee the registrations."

"It will be terrible for morale."

"Understood, but we're too close to returning to England, and we only have, what, five hundred Englishmen loyal to the House of Lancaster here with us?"

"Yes, give or take," Jasper answered.

"They must be given orders that they are to watch only. We can't afford to have any of them hurt."

"I understand your reasoning and I admire your foresight, but it's not going to make you popular. As you can imagine, the French will be ceaseless in their accusations of cowardice when no Englishmen partake in the games. You may lose in morale more than you gain in the health of the men."

Henry sighed. "Yes, it's a valid point, and it's one that I have considered, but we are too few. I trust that the men who have put their titles under attainder and their heads on the chopping block to join me here will not be dissuaded by a singular event of sport. Additionally, we desperately need French help if I'm to have any chance of gaining the crown, and I don't want a tournament to spawn any personal grudges between our men and the French. Please find William Brandon and have him spread the word."

"I will do as you command, nephew." *That boy has a sharp mind; sharper than mine for sure. I hope he lives long enough to become king,* Jasper thought as he headed towards the tent of William Brandon, one of Henry's fiercest knights.

Chapter 27

IF KURO NEVER saw another boat again for the rest of his life it would be too soon. He hadn't gotten nearly the exercise he'd desired on the crowded streets of Venice, and the walk across the French countryside, while pleasant, could hardly be considered taxing exercise.

Now, as his human coaxed him forward, he liked what he saw. The plains outside the walls of Paris were overflowing with tents, each sporting its own brilliantly colored flags and banners. Men wearing armor and brightly colored surcoats strode about the makeshift encampment leading horses in matching caparisons. Men and horses enveloped in this much color could only mean one thing: battle, and Kuro longed for a fight.

The large man who'd killed his first master still accompanied them. This was a minor irritation, but the large man had ignored him and he returned the favor. Kuro was surprised to see a number of horses nearly matching his own size in the camp, but it did not overly concern him. He knew he was without equal on the battlefield. Kuro snorted in the direction of a large bay horse that eyed him as he pranced by.

Simon guided his horse, a fine, tall, light gray Andalusian stallion towards a crowded tent at the edge of the combat arenas. He let Kojiro lead the way, of course, because Kuro got fidgety when he wasn't in the lead. Simon sometimes wondered if the big black charger wasn't part human. It had taken longer than Simon hoped to get to Paris: Aldo had insisted on waiting three months for his large, new ship to be finished. *Probably over-compensating for something,* Simon thought.

As he suspected, the tent was for registration, and he moved to sign them up for three-person combat. They had heard of the tournament upon landing in France, and he thought it would be the perfect opportunity for Kojiro to practice fighting against European knights without getting killed in the process. And just as importantly, he hoped the tournament could serve as an opening to meet his distant Lancastrian relative, Henry Tudor.

Simon gave his name to the registrar and was surprised that he did not write anything down. Instead, the registrar turned quickly to a rough-looking, armored nobleman behind him. This nobleman was, in turn, flanked by a nearly identical man on his left and a freakishly large man on his right.

"Are you English?" the first rough-looking noble inquired of Simon.

"I am."

"I don't recognize you, but Lord Henry has forbidden his men to participate in this tournament."

"Oh?" Simon uttered, surprised to hear this information. "And why is that?"

"You know damn well why it is. You're not one of those thick-os are you?"

"Well, that would depend on who you ask. My good friend Aldo here would swear that is the truth of it."

Aldo nodded once in agreement.

"But based on the assumption that I am a 'thick-o,' can you please tell me?"

William Brandon was perplexed that someone hadn't gotten word that the English were not to fight. He had posted notices in all the English quarters; there had been no end to the griping about it. "What's your name and where are you from?"

"I am Simon Lang of Exeter. My father fell at Towton fighting for Henry VI, the rightful King of England. Well, formerly of Exeter, we are now the Langs of Nowhere in Particular. And did I say we? I meant me. The Yorkists executed my mother in front of me and I'm all that's left of 'the Langs.'"

A look of recognition crossed the face of the behemoth on the right. He spoke up.

"I know your family. Your father fought well at Towton. I was for King Edward."

The giant had just announced that he fought against King Henry at Towton, but Simon detected neither malice nor gloating in his voice. Simon nonetheless could not prevent the anger from entering his voice.

"My father died at Towton, and the Yorkist pigs butchered his body."

With this statement the two noble Englishmen accompanying the giant put hands to sword hilts. Simon unconsciously did the same.

Kojiro did not react at all while standing next to Simon, but Simon had learned that a lack of motion on the part of Kojiro did not indicate a lack of preparation. In fact, the more settled he became, the more likely he was to strike. Aldo touched his sword hilt as well, and Neno bulled his way forward until he too stood next to Simon. Neno, giant though he was, did not equal the height of the man who just announced he had fought for the Yorkist cause at Towton. Though he did outweigh the bruiser by a good three stones.

The tension subsided nearly as quickly as it had begun. The giant behind the table darted out to stay the hands of his compatriots. He bowed his head towards Simon. "You are correct. The Yorkist actions after the battle were shameful. It is one of the reasons I fight for Henry now."

Simon recognized the peace offering and forced his mind to overrule his emotions, something Kojiro had been tutoring him on largely unsuccessfully up to this point. "Thank you for the kind words about my father," Simon managed to say without heat in his voice.

Kojiro shot Simon a look. It was not a look that anyone else would have noticed, but Simon felt the weight of the millisecond, millimeter shift in Kojiro's eyes and knew he was receiving a *sensei's* approval for his restraint. Between the presently related history and the man's colossal size, Simon knew who the man was. There were not many six-foot-nine-inch knights who had fought for the Yorkist King Edward IV then switched to the Lancastrian cause.

"I suppose that would make you Sir John Cheyne."

Cheyne nodded his head slightly in confirmation. "Though your father was a Lancastrian of renown, you have not fought for the red rose in any battle that I am aware of," Sir Cheyne more asked than stated.

"That is correct; I have not. To honor my father, I have sought to not have his family name end in a pauper's jail. I first seek to provide for my own. Only after that could I give thought to kings and thrones."

"Yet you are here," the noble next to Cheyne commented.

"I am here because assassins chase me across all four corners of the Earth, and were they successful, it would severely hamper my ability to continue the family name."

"Allow me to introduce you," Cheyne interjected quickly to forestall the ill will that appeared to be creeping back into the conversation. "This is William Brandon, and next to him is his brother Thomas. Their family has ever been servant to the Lancastrian cause."

Both Brandon brothers eyed Simon and his odd compatriots with a mixture of suspicion and curiosity, but they bowed their heads in greeting, knowing that Cheyne the Giant did not force introductions lightly.

Before Simon had a chance to respond to the introduction, William Brandon spoke again. "Richard III has sent men to kill *you*?" he asked with a hint of disbelief in his voice.

"I'm afraid so," Simon replied. "It's got something to do with my great-uncles or great-great-uncles, or first aunts twice removed. I don't really know the entire lineage, but I seem to be very unimportant to everybody but Dick and his brother Eddy before him."

William Brandon liked the terms 'Dick and Eddy,' the use of which was terribly amusing and would soon join his own vocabulary, but as a lifelong warrior for the Lancastrian cause, he found it hard to believe that the person standing in front of him, whom he'd never met before, had enough royal blood to interest the Yorkists. Of course it wasn't outside the realm of possibility since Dick's paranoia made Eddy's paranoia seem perfectly reasonable. The man did not appear addled in any way, and William, like Cheyne, had heard of his father. He was startled out of his contemplation by the interesting newcomer.

"So, can you write my name down please?" Simon asked again. "I am not a part of Henry's complement as you can tell."

The registrar again looked at William Brandon who shrugged his shoulders. "I suppose so. He's not one of our men."

"Simon Lang of Exeter, though I use that title in a very liberal sense at the moment, plus two for the sword competition."

The registrar looked back at William Brandon again because he had been given very strict instructions by the queen regent to obey the Englishmen in regards to their own kind.

"Fair enough," William Brandon replied. He switched his casual gaze at the registrar to an intense gaze at Simon. "Be forewarned, though, as the only Englishman in this tournament you will be carrying the hopes of five hundred or so of your drunken countrymen. They will support you loudly of course, but I would not want to be the cause of their disappointment. Make a good showing of it, Lang." And with that, William Brandon bowed politely.

"I shall endeavor to persevere to the utmost of my capabilities, sir," Simon replied and smiled. He then verified that his name had been recorded properly, and he, Aldo, Kojiro, and Neno led their horses back to see which of Aldo's delectable Venetian culinary treats had survived the voyage. Kojiro was allowed to lead Kuro in front, of course.

After Simon rode off, William Brandon turned to his brother Thomas and Sir John Cheyne. "I think we should tell Lord Henry about our new acquaintance."

Kuro was not happy at all. He could *hear* fighting, he could *smell* fighting, and he could even *see* fighting when his master took him riding, but he wasn't *doing* any fighting. It was frustrating, and he let his master know.

Before the tournament started, Kojiro had asked Simon if he wished to use Kuro for the jousting tournament, but Simon had politely declined saying, "First, I don't think Kuro would allow anybody but you to ride him, and second, I'm not here for the showy personal glory that comes from jousting. I'm here to show Henry Tudor that our services would be valuable to him on the battlefield."

That conversation had sealed Kuro's fate. They initially put him in a camp corral that had been purposefully built for the tournament, but by the second day of the tournament Kuro had bitten three other horses and Simon had been forced to pay for a stall inside the walls of Paris. This reduced the exercise Kuro was getting since Kojiro had to walk all the way into Paris to exercise him, but it was financially necessary because Kojiro was no longer paying damages to aggrieved knights.

Chapter 28

THE SHIELDS WERE hung for the first round of the three-person foot combat. Colorful coats of arms were nailed to posts by squires and pages, although this pageantry went largely unwatched due to the much more popular jousting taking place next door. The nearby sound of cheers and pounding horses' hooves would have drowned out all sound on the sparsely attended combat arena but for the volume put forth by the few Englishmen who had gathered to watch their only countryman in the competition. The English fans' audible contribution lent an air of excitement to the normally spectator-dearth competition.

In addition to the English fans, most of the other spectators for the team sword fighting were French peasants. Overjoyed to be granted time off from their mundane, labor-intensive, painful, dirty, degrading, thankless lives, they sprawled out on the open field on the south side of the staked-out combat arena. It was not that the peasants were anxious to see the sword fighting, it was more the fact that they had no access to the jousting and they'd take what they could get. Across the combat arena from the peasant field, raised, covered viewing stands had been erected for the upper classes and nobility.

Though the stands were less than a quarter full, this was still a major accomplishment, since the event was taking place at the same time as the jousting. Aldo and the English knights sat in the stands while the common English men-at-arms and archers milled about the field with the peasants. Henry and Jasper sat in the box seats reserved for royalty in the middle of the stands with Henry's bodyguard John Cheyne. No other royalty joined them as the rest of the royalty were all preoccupied with the jousting. A few French nobles—friends of the French knights who would compete with the Englishmen in the first round—sat on the benches as far away from the English knights as they could get. It did not save them from the odd bit of partially consumed foodstuffs that occasionally flew at them from the English side.

On the east side of the arena, three stout, five-foot-high wooden poles held the blue shields, decorated with golden fleur-de-lis, of the French competitors. The French knights stood next to their shields in shining head-to-toe plate armor, waiting for their opponents.

Simon walked to one of the poles on the west side of the arena and, no longer needing to hide his identity amongst his fellow Englishmen, hung the shield bearing the Lang coat of arms. The shield had been magnificently crafted by the finest armorer in all of Venice, and at no small expense. The Lang coat of arms was divided into four quadrants by the red cross of St. George, denoting the family's loyalty to England. In the upper left and lower right quadrant, the red, arrow-tongued dragon of Wales on a green background paid homage to the family's Welsh ancestry. The upper right and lower left quadrants were decorated with the red rose of Lancaster.

As Simon hung his shield, the overwhelmingly English crowd roared their approval, causing the French knights to look around in mild dismay. Next to Simon, Neno hung a shield with the Venetian coat of arms; a winged golden lion on a red background.

Lastly, Kojiro hung the shield that Aldo had gifted him in Venice: a blue winged crane on a black background. Kojiro did not intend to ever use the shield in combat, but he had to admit, it was an eye-pleasing decoration. Once the preliminary rituals were out of the way, all six combatants stepped forward into the arena.

Kojiro did not like the blunt longswords that he had to wield for the competition, but they would have to suffice. As much as Simon tried to convert him to the use of sword and shield, he steadfastly refused, insisting on the use of two swords, clumsy, dull, and unbalanced though they were. As they approached the Frenchmen in the center of the arena, Kojiro singled out the biggest one directly across from him and moved in. Kojiro spun his two swords at his sides in a 360-degree windmill as was his ritual and stepped forward.

"What the devil?" Henry jumped up from his seat in the viewing box as the man in jet-black armor darted forward with two blades flashing.

"I do believe he's using two swords and no shield," Jasper commented.

"Well, he won't last long that way," Henry opined.

Immediately after stepping forward, Kojiro used his left sword to fend off a powerful overhead blow from the Frenchman. Then, in one swift movement, he stepped to the left side of his opponent and swept his right sword backwards into the back of the man's right knee. The Frenchman had been about to step forward onto that leg, and the force of the blow caused the Frenchman's right leg to swing forward into the air. The French knight landed with a huge clanking of armor squarely on his back. Kojiro rested the tips of both his swords on the man's neck, and his battle was over.

"Well, he's bloody good with them, isn't he? I stand corrected," Henry remarked to Jasper as the largest of the Frenchmen went down to uproarious applause from the heavily partisan crowd.

Neno's French opponent barely had the speed to fend off the relentless blows that Neno brought down about his shoulders and head. The Frenchman was taken completely by surprise at the speed of the blows coming from such a large man.

More important than the speed, however, was the fact that the Frenchman was severely overmatched in strength. As Neno backed the man up nearly to the French shields at the eastern end of the combat arena, Neno dropped his shield, moved that hand to form a double grip on his sword, and brought a thundering blow down squarely on the man's head, knocking the man unconscious and bringing another round of resounding cheers from the gallery. The English crowd had no care for the Republic of Venice, but if this man was fighting alongside an Englishman and they were beating Frenchmen, that was all that mattered.

Simon maneuvered to a position where he could see his teammates and grinned inside the fully enclosed armet that covered his entire head and face as he watched Neno's opponent crumple to the ground. He had already seen Kojiro make short work of his opponent, but Simon had toyed with the clearly inferior swordsman he was facing until he knew it was his show alone.

After Neno's opponent fell, Simon dodged a clumsy lunge from his own opponent and cracked the man on his head with the hilt of his sword. The stunned man moved backwards, and Simon proceeded to land sword strikes all about his torso. The Frenchman was unable to respond quickly enough to defend himself. Simon backed the man all the way up to the viewing stands, and when he stood squarely in front of Henry Tudor, Simon thrust his sword forward into the Frenchman's armored neckpiece and pinned him against the wooden wall of the viewing stands.

Simon opened the cheek piece of his armet, clearing half his mouth to open air, and asked politely, "Do you yield?"

The dejected Frenchman muttered a sullen *oui*, and the contest was over.

The English crowd in the stands jumped to their feet and cheered. Opposite them, on the other side of the combat grounds, the English yeoman archers and men-at-arms yelled so loudly that spectators from the jousting grounds came over to ask what had happened.

"Who did you say this man was again?" Henry asked Sir Cheyne.

"He's a noble from Exeter. His father served the Lancastrian cause and died valiantly at Towton. I personally witnessed his father fall. He was one of the few that did not turn and try to run. His father took some killing."

"What do you know of him, Jasper?" Henry turned towards his uncle after receiving this information from his bodyguard.

"I heard the same about his father from a stout docker at a pub in Exeter. I have investigated, and his family actually has royal blood, though severely diluted. They have no claim that would cause any concern to you, and they've always been loyal to the Lancastrian cause. Their lands were taken by Edward and given to Lord Percy Blythe, a minor Yorkist noble. Simon's mother had her head chopped off in front of the young Lang on the orders of Blythe. He's got Welsh lineage much like you, but I don't think he's spent much time in Wales personally. Apparently he's a skilled ship's navigator, like many of the men from Exeter, and has been traipsing about the world for the last few years, including an outlandish story about him traveling to the far eastern lands discovered by Marco Polo."

Jasper finished his speech and settled back against his chair.

"You seem to know quite a bit, then, don't you?" Henry winked at his uncle. "He is clearly good with a sword, as are his teammates. What do you know about them?"

"The big fellow from Venice is apparently just a ship's officer, but as you know, Venetian sailors are also soldiers by necessity. I don't have any idea who the knight with the blue crane insignia is. They say he has the looks of an Eastern barbarian, yet doesn't quite look like any Easterner that anyone has ever seen before. The whole camp whispers about him."

"Find out what you can. And make sure we are available to watch his future competitions."

"Of course, my lord," Jasper replied.

Chapter 29

SIMON AND HIS retinue did not have to buy any drinks at the feasting that night, nor for the next four nights as they made short work of opponents from across the continent. Huge knights from Germany barely removed from their barbarian ancestors; agile swordsmen from Aragon; blond-haired, blue-eyed Nordic warriors from Denmark; and a staggering number of Frenchmen all fell victim to the trio's swords. And with each day's display of swordsmanship, the crowds got bigger and their reputation more outlandish, until finally, on the last day of the tournament, the jousting competition was scheduled for a later time to ensure it would still have spectators.

On the fifth and final day of the tournament, extra stands were erected on the east and west sides of the arena to accommodate all the noble spectators who came from throughout France to see the dual sword-wielding wonder, the brute from Venice, and the English lord of no land. The peasants crammed into the field that they had been allotted, jostling with English yeoman soldiers for viewing space.

Henry and Jasper sat in their box seats while Sir Cheyne along with the Brandon brothers ensured the drunken English knights and soldiers did not start fights with their French hosts. On this day, however, Henry was not alone in the box seats. The thirteen-year-old French boy-king Charles VIII and his older sister and regent Anne of Beaujeu were also in attendance, as were the most privileged members of their court.

The regent spoke with Henry. "*Bonjour, Lord Henry, comment allez-vous?*"

"*Très bien, Madame Beaujeu, merci.*"

"It seems your English knight has been putting on quite a show. It's being talked about at all the parties. I thought I'd come see it for myself," the regent of France switched to English.

"We are honored by your presence, Madame, and of course by that of his Majesty." At the mention of his name, the young king glanced briefly at Henry, smiled, and then turned his gaze expectantly back towards the arena where the combatants were placing their shields. "Unfortunately he is not my knight at the moment, although I do hope to remedy that situation."

"But his shield bears the Lancastrian red rose."

"Indeed, and his family has a history of loyalty to the cause. It seems this Simon fellow, however, has been out adventuring. As much as my sources have been able to determine, that fellow with the blue crane on his armor comes from somewhere east of Marco Polo's voyages."

Anne of Beaujeu had not maintained her regency by happenstance. Although she was Charles' sister and due the honor, there had never been a shortage of powerful men eager to usurp her position and rule France. But "Madame la Grande," as she was known, combined common sense, intelligence, and practicality with an unmatched adroitness in political machinations to maintain her preeminence in all matters related to France. "How very captivating! Now, since the final contest will be against three men in my service, you must humor me with a wager," she said with a trace of mischief in her voice.

Henry was quite aware of the regent's guile, but also completely at the mercy of his hostess. "I live by the courtesy of your generosity, Madame; though I don't know what I could possibly offer against your vast riches."

"If my French knights prevail, you will assist me in the annexation of Brittany."

"That is a steep price, Madame. Francis II, the Duke of Brittany, has always treated me well."

"Yet he would have sent you to England to be beheaded. And I understand dear Richard is doing far worse than simple beheadings these days."

"I believe that was purely the doing of his ministers. I bear Francis no ill will."

"That may be, dear Henry, but he allies himself with the House of York at the moment, so he is your enemy regardless of your personal feelings."

Henry sighed because he knew that Anne was right, but he really didn't want to see Francis come to harm. Francis had sheltered him and supported his cause for years, and he could not forget that kindness, regardless of his current diplomatic leanings. "And if I win?"

"I will support another expedition for you to take the throne."

Henry jolted straight upright in his seat. *She knows damn well I can't attack Richard with my five hundred men alone. She also knows I don't have the money to hire enough mercenaries to complete the task. But with the help of France, that could all change.* He had no choice. "I accept your bet, Madame." Then he turned to watch the competition with a sense of uneasiness. The throne of England could be decided in one contest of arms.

Chapter 30

Simon looked across the field at their final opponents. In addition to two gold and blue shields, a third shield bearing the white, X-shaped cross of St Andrew on a blue background hung on the middle pole: one of the French King's elite Garde Écossaise: The Scottish Guard.

With the mutual enmity of England in common, France and Scotland had always been loosely allied. But what started out as the occasional band of Scotsmen crossing the channel to aid France in her wars with England gradually evolved into Scotsmen making up regular companies in the French army. The best and fiercest warriors from these companies were selected for the Scottish Guard. In addition to being a feared unit on the battlefield, the Scottish Guard served as the French King's immediate bodyguard. It looked as though Simon was going to find out how elite "elite" was in France.

As had become customary in the tournament, Kojiro picked out his opponent first and moved in for the 'kill.' This time, after his traditional two-armed windmill, Kojiro brought both swords down overhead onto the knight who stood on the left.

The French knight deflected one blow with his shield and the other with his sword. Kojiro spun to his left and struck horizontally backwards at what he thought would be his opponent's back, but instead he struck the shield of the towering Scotsman who had initially been in the center. The Scot had closed ranks and stepped to his teammate's right. Kojiro did not think this was honorable behavior; a man should fight his own battles.

Kojiro looked at his new opponent and stabbed forward below the man's shield with his left sword while swinging horizontally towards his first opponent with his right. The Scotsman brought his shield down with a tremendous grunt, nearly knocking the sword out of Kojiro's left hand, while his first opponent parried his right sword stroke with his own longsword.

Charles VIII clapped with delight as the captain of his personal bodyguard displayed his prowess for all to see. Anne de Beaujeu smiled and winked at Henry while the French in the crowd erupted in cheers.

Henry's palms began to sweat. Until now, no one had yet survived the crane warrior's initial onslaught.

Neno attacked the knight on the right with pounding overhead blows as he always did. However, he quickly learned that he could not just bully this Frenchman like he had all his previous opponents. The man was not nearly his equal in strength, but he made up for it with the speed and skill of his sword strokes. And to make matters worse, the enemy defended each other when one of them *did* get outmaneuvered. In frustration, Neno slammed the other man's shield with his own and received a rap across the back of his shoulders from the second Frenchman's sword for his efforts.

Kojiro did not think his opponents fought honorably, but he had to admit that they fought well. Individually, he knew he could take any of them—save perhaps the large Scotsman, that would be a contest—but since the enemy worked seamlessly together, he could not find an opening. In fact, he himself had been pressed hard as his opponents effectively used their shields as a weapon, punching at Kojiro's face and torso then always stepping back to stand together with their teammates.

The Scotsman fought with consummate skill, and Simon found himself fighting to the best of his ability for the first time in the tournament. Even fighting at his best, however, Simon could not break through the giant Celt's defense. Inside Simon's armet, the sweat poured down his forehead like rain.

Anne de Beaujeu was in a win-win situation. She had intended to finance and equip another expedition for Henry anyway, but if she won the bet, she could also use Henry and his knights to help bring Brittany into the nation of France. She had never seen the captain of the Garde Écossaise lose a fight. Ever. And in spite of the skill of the foreign warriors, she did not think he would do so today.

Henry studied the teamwork of the French and found he liked it. They formed like an old-fashioned Saxon shield wall when on defense, and their teamwork was impeccable. But he *had* to win this bet. He desperately hoped his distant relative from Exeter had some kind of plan.

Simon could not break their shield wall. All the usual tactics, stabbing low, crushing overhead blows, physically pushing them backwards, were all countered by the skilled French knights and their powerful Scottish ally. It was getting tiresome.

The only upside to their opponents' defensive teamwork was that they did not stray far enough from their teammates to mount any sustained attacks of their own. Simon guessed that their tactic was to wait until their opponents' sword strokes became weaker and slower, at which point they would leave their defensive formation and attack. Simon looked at Kojiro and Neno and thought that with Neno's aggressive pounding blows, he would be reaching that point soon.

Neno's arms were getting tired. The French and the Scotsman countered all of his blows, and their conservative defensive movements left them quite a bit fresher. But Neno had fought Turks, pirates, and Genoese for days on end; he could fight through sore arms. While the contest ebbed and flowed, the crowd cheered and screamed insults at the combatants. Most of these insults were based entirely upon the nationality of the insulter and the insulted, but all were truly enjoying the spectacular demonstration of swordplay.

In the arena, a conversation began as well. "You know Ai'll be wearing your head for a hat now, doncha?" the Scotsman offered to Simon.

"Why do Scottish farmers herd their cattle to the edge of the cliffs?" Simon returned as he swatted away a powerful overhead blow.

"I'm sure ye'll tell me."

"They push back harder." Simon delivered the punch line along with a stabbing thrust that the Scot blocked with his shield. The Scotsman roared with a deep laugh that echoed from the inside of his close helm, then he stabbed back.

Kojiro, like Simon, deduced that the French were waiting for them to tire, and since Kojiro was the most active person in the arena, he guessed that they might assume he would be the first to wear down. He encouraged them in this assumption by striking a flurry of blows that brought the crowd to its feet, then by subtly reducing the strength of his blows as they progressed.

He did not think these skilled opponents would fall for anything less than his best deception. Up until now in the competition, there had been no competition, but now Kojiro was finding out that there were western knights in addition to Simon, Neno, and Aldo that had real combat skills. As the strength and duration of Kojiro's blows diminished, all three of their opponents began to conserve less energy and counterattack more forcefully when they got a shot at him.

"I'm afraid the smaller one seems to be losing some of his flair," Anne said to Henry. She had seen the Guard captain wear out his enemies before, but she'd never seen it take this long. After a few of his powerful blows, his enemies usually folded. This Englishman and his men were certainly knights to be reckoned with. She would be glad if Henry could persuade them into his service, and thereby *hers*.

"Yes, I'm afraid you may be right," Henry replied dejectedly, because he certainly had never seen a man who could fight as long and as energetically as the Crane warrior had, yet he did appear to be tiring and the captain of the Scots Guard was not yielding an inch.

Neno was forced to take a step backwards when the Scotsman struck at him from the side; his sore arms could not fully deflect the tremendously strong blow. Unwittingly though, he assisted Kojiro with his plan, and that was enough. Seeing Neno's momentary loss of balance from the Scotsman's blow, the Frenchman across from Neno began to batter him backwards the way Neno himself had done to so many opponents before. Neno was able to deflect most of the blows, but the Frenchman ably countered his return strikes and continued to drive him back towards his own shield on the pole.

Their opponents had broken the shield wall.

The Scotsman, not entirely convinced by Kojiro's performance, nor Neno's apparent loss of strength, yelled at his teammate to come back, but it was too late. As soon as the Frenchman vacated his position in the shield wall, Kojiro stepped into it so quickly the move was impossible to counter. From his position on the Scot's flank, Kojiro stabbed his sword up and below the plate neck guard that made up the lower portion of the Scot's close helm. The sword was a tight fit in that small space, but it was a killing thrust. Kojiro held his blade motionless in that position.

The Scot captain admired the control it took for the man to have thrust so quickly at such a small opening yet to have stopped short of injuring him.

"I yield, ye little bastard!" the Scotsman bellowed out goodheartedly. "Kindly ramove that thing from me head, if you will."

Kojiro quickly withdrew his blade and bowed to the man.

"Polite wee bastard, isn't he?" the giant Scot mumbled, then removed his helmet, revealing a wide grin. Sir Walter Scott had not lost a tournament battle since he was a child, but far from being bitter, he was pleased to have met such worthy competition.

Without help from his colleagues, Simon's Frenchman was no match for Simon's sword skills. He was quickly battered into submission. The Frenchman who had taken off after Neno soon discovered that Neno was not as tired as he had suspected. Using a technique that he had learned from Kojiro, Neno grabbed his opponent's sword arm and pulled it forward in the direction it was initially headed. He then turned into his opponent so they were both facing in the direction of his opponent's momentum and planted his right leg in front of his opponent's right leg. The movement had its desired result, and the Frenchman flipped over his leg and onto his back. Neno pressed his sword to the eye opening in the man's visor, and the match was over.

As the English in the crowd screamed their approval, Henry took a deep, relieved breath. He then looked at the King and the King's regent sister and saw that they did not seem overly displeased, which was just as important as winning the bet since a bet was just words; a regent lived within the boundaries of behavior set by themselves.

Anne looked into Henry's studying eyes and laughed. "I'll have Brittany without your help, Henry. I never counted on it anyway. I just thought a wager might add some excitement to our match today, and based on your reaction to the fight, I was successful. Fantastic entertainment! I've never seen Sir Walter Scott lose at anything before. I don't even want to know how drunk he's going to be tonight or how many fights he's going to start.

And yes, I will supply you with troops and money. If that bastard Richard wants to keep supporting French rebels, I will give him a reason to pay closer attention to his own damn country. No offense intended."

"None taken, Madame, I cannot express my gratitude enough." Henry was going back to England, and he was going to do it with French support.

The king, the regent, and their entourage walked to the dais to present the awards. The dais had been built at the lowest end of the box seats, just behind the wooden palisade that separated the noble spectators from the arena. The king, since he was the sponsor of the tournament, stood on the dais and waited while the winning team approached.

Simon, Neno, and Kojiro bowed to the king then knelt in front of him with one knee bent and one on the ground.

"Rise, skilled knights, your performance was magnificent!"

The trio rose, and Simon eyed the very large and very heavy looking bag in the king's hand. He had to consciously force his eyes away from it.

The king spoke again. "Based on the demonstration of swordsmanship I witnessed today, it is my pleasure to have sponsored the contest at which it could be viewed." The English soldiers and lords cheered the French king loudly at his magnanimous pronouncement. He then used both hands and extended the bag over the palisade.

Simon forced himself to walk, not run, towards the bag of gold coins. Upon receiving his prize, he bowed deeply before returning to his teammates. He could not control the smile on his face.

"Why, that's a curious bow." Henry remarked to Jasper as they watched the man in the crane armor look at the French boy-king and bend at the waist with his hands at his sides.

"That it is, Harry, that it is. I'm looking forward to learning more about that interesting gentleman."

Chapter 31

THE FEASTING THAT night was the most spectacular yet. Simon and his entourage sat at the head of the English table inside one of the great feasting tents. The air smelled of roast mutton and the wine, mead, and cider flowed freely. Neno worked on a gigantic leg of lamb while Simon and Aldo discussed the merits of a peppery Bordeaux.

Kojiro sat next to Simon and ate quietly, marveling at the barbarism of Western eating habits. The food was brought (sometimes by hand) in large portions to the table where the guests used knives and their hands to cut or break off bite-sized portions.

Knives at the table! Kojiro did not understand why weapons would be used as utensils at the table. The civilized thing to do of course was to have the portions cut in the kitchen, then served in the proper sizes at the table.

In order not to offend, Kojiro forced himself to eat pieces of meat that other men had touched with their filthy hands, which would have been unappetizing enough had he not known how infrequently the English washed themselves. Kojiro's thoughts about what the men had been doing with their hands before dinner were thankfully interrupted when Henry Tudor entered the tent with Jasper Tudor and John Cheyne in tow. The entire tent went silent as the men bowed to Henry. Two men, whose sense of balance had long since disappeared into their cups of mead, fell over as they attempted to bow.

Henry spoke. "Carry on, men. Enjoy the feast. England had but one entrant into the contest, and he won it. I think that is cause for celebration!" The Englishmen toasted and cheered their king and their victorious countryman and, as Henry showed no signs of wishing to speak further, they returned to their commitment to inebriation.

Simon stood as Henry made his way towards him and offered the wooden stool upon which he had been sitting. Henry took the seat and gestured for Simon, Neno, Kojiro, and Jasper to sit with him. Aldo, not having taken part in the competition, and not wanting to distract from his friends' moment of glory, bowed politely to Henry and left in search of better wine. When Kojiro stood to do the same, Henry gestured that he should stay.

"I wanted a look at this mysterious foreigner from a faraway land who fights like a whirlwind. I also want to meet this distant relative of mine who has managed to keep himself free of what some are now calling the Wars of the Roses."

Simon answered. "I'm afraid any relation between us is extremely remote, Your Majesty, and even under penalty of torture, I would not be able to tell you what it was. Genealogy was never a favorite subject of mine."

"An Englishman that does not brag about his distinguished heritage? Well, you're a bit of an oddity, aren't you?" The question was serious.

"Quite so, I believe. My mother tried to force that knowledge into my head, but I'm afraid I was ever a poor pupil. It can be difficult to force things into this thick head of mine."

"Apparently that did not apply to your sword lessons from what I've observed, nor your navigational training from what I've heard of your reputation."

"You flatter me, Your Majesty, but I suppose if I had spent less time sailing, and more time listening to my mother, I would know how I was related to you."

"My uncle assures me you're distant enough that you pose no threat to me and that is as far as I care." Henry smiled warmly. "I gather dear Richard, however, has not come to the same conclusion?"

"You are correct, Majesty. Both Richard and Edward before him seem bothered by the fact that some bastard fifth cousin of mine, three times removed, used to be the great-great-great-great-granddaughter of the butler of a King Edward or a King John or a King Henry or something like that. And because of that, they've tried to kill me."

"That was roughly Jasper here's assessment of your claim to the throne as well." Henry smiled again. "Then you've come here to join me and end these attempts on your life?" he asked.

It was the very opening Simon had hoped joining the tournament would give him. "I have, Your Majesty, if you will have me."

"If I will have you?" Henry laughed softly as he spoke the words slowly. "I plan to take London and kill Richard, yet I have very few men with which to do it. Richard is a renowned warrior and a skilled campaigner whereas I have no experience whatsoever. In fact, it appears I will be relying a great deal on the French to take back the throne of England. If that's not a bitter irony, I don't know what is. And you present me with the option of obtaining the services of a man who has just bested the best swords in all of Europe. I'm afraid for your sake that I shall have to say 'yes.' I will most certainly welcome you to follow me into my folly."

Folly was something that had never factored much into the decisions Simon made. "I pledge my fealty to you, Majesty."

"I accept. Might I ask what the Venetian and this horribly fascinating yet unnervingly quiet *warrior of the crane* may do?" Henry used the term that the camp finally seemed to have settled on when referring to Kojiro. Kojiro had overheard conversations describing him thusly, and since it was far from insulting, he'd made no effort to introduce himself with his true name.

"I will ask them, Your Majesty, but it is my sincere hope that they will join me," Simon said as he winked at Kojiro and Neno.

Then Jasper spoke for the first time. "Your crest bears the red dragon of Cadwaladr ap Cadwallon, from the line of pre-Saxon Briton kings. Henry himself bears this crest due to his Welsh lineage. Do you know what part of Wales your ancestors hail from?"

"As a child, I practiced my seafaring skills by sailing from Devon to South Wales. I often sailed to the small port town of Kidwelly where my mother was born. I would visit relatives with my mother east of Kidwelly in the hamlet of Ystradgynlais, south to Llanelli, and north to Aberystwyth. The family on my mother's side are all from this region, which I seem to remember is known as Carmarthenshire. Thank God my mother was born in Kidwelly though, because I can barely pronounce those other bloody villages."

Henry smiled at Simon's straightforward language as he paused for thought. He remembered the small, sturdy castle in Kidwelly because it was only a few hours' sail from the castle where he was born: Pembroke Castle. Henry also remembered the night he had to escape from Pembroke Castle through the natural limestone cavern below it. It was not a pleasant memory. *I will have my revenge on the Yorkists for expelling me from my own bloody birthplace.*

Jasper interrupted his thoughts. "The king needs the help of the Welsh. We cannot beat Richard without recruits from Wales. The French regent has promised us two thousand men, we have barely five hundred Englishmen with us at the moment, and Richard will have at least ten thousand men. Double that, if he has time to assemble his northern armies. We plan to return to England via Wales, and God willing, Harry's Welsh ancestry will bring us recruits. If it does not, we are condemned men. If you've noticed, the Welsh dragon flies on our standard below the cross of St George. It is not an accident."

He took a sip of cider and continued. "This brings us back to you. You and your compatriots appear to be the equal of ten swords apiece, but even that is not enough. War is as much a numbers game as it is a skills game, and we need more of both. Without substantial support from the Welsh, we are on a fool's errand. Are you aware that the men from Carmarthenshire are probably the best archers in all of Christendom?"

Jasper was of course quite familiar with the area of Carmarthenshire outlined by Simon and even more familiar with the skill of their archers. They were the best in Wales, which possibly made them the best in the world. *If this Simon fellow can recruit men from Carmarthenshire, it really will be a stroke of luck*, Jasper thought to himself. "More importantly, do you think you could recruit the archers of Carmarthenshire to the cause of Henry Tudor?"

Simon answered bluntly. "Purely to serve me or purely to serve you, Your Majesty, I doubt it. No offense intended."

"None taken, I desire honesty," Henry replied.

"But if you pay them, you will have little trouble recruiting 'loyal' followers. At least they will be loyal as long as the money lasts. The Welsh are a mercenary lot."

Henry and Jasper talked amongst themselves for a couple of minutes before Henry spoke again. "The French will be giving us money. Can I trust you to hire good men and meet up with me as I march from Pembroke?"

"You can trust me to do my best, Your Majesty. And if I am successful, all that I ask is the return of my family's estates in Exeter if you are successful."

"I will return the title of your family's property, Lang. Jasper has told me that your family has always remained loyal to the House of Lancaster, but you will have to evict the current Yorkist lord yourself."

"That part would be my pleasure, Your Majesty."

And with that, Henry, Jasper, and Sir Cheyne left, but not before Sir Cheyne stared hard at the men in the tent and gave a booming warning to all of the revelers. "You will not, I repeat *WILL NOT* start fights with any Frenchmen tonight. If any man disobeys me, I will see that they are beheaded by a blind, feeble, old executioner with a dull axe!" There were no fights between the English and the French that night.

Months passed while Henry's army gathered strength, and some of that strength came from an unexpected quarter. Yorkists, who had been loyal to King Edward but were disgusted by the usurpation of the throne by Richard, arrived daily.

After years abroad, Simon was anxious to return to England, but he served Henry now, and Henry would not become king if his invasion was premature. Finally, on a hot summer day in 1485, Jasper delivered the order for Simon to begin recruiting in Wales.

Chapter 32

Carmarthen Bay, Coast of Southern Wales

ALDO'S NEWEST AND grandest boat, the one he had insisted on waiting for, was named the *Triarii.* The *Triarii,* was named after the traditional ancient Roman third line of battle. The *Triarii* were the wealthier, well-armored citizens who would not be committed to battle until the less wealthy and less well-armored had died in front of them. Aldo's *Triarii* was likely the grandest boat anyone in Kidwelly had ever seen, and the shore of Carmarthen Bay was lined with gawkers.

"I like the flag," Simon said, smirking as he looked at the small English courtesy flag Aldo was having flown on the foremast. It was a red cross on a white background: the Cross of Saint George, the flag of London and England.

"I will be more than happy to burn that flag when I leave these waters," Aldo said through a clenched smile.

"Do you know why you *Inglese* fly that abhorrent flag?" Aldo asked.

"Because it is the flag of England and St. George, of course," Simon replied with full confidence.

"It is in fact the Cross of St. George, of that you are correct."

Simon knew there was more coming, so he began to walk quickly towards the dinghy.

Aldo followed without missing a beat. "But it was not first the flag of England, it was the flag of Genoa before that." Aldo spat as he mouthed the name of the Venetians' bitter rivals.

Kojiro, also headed towards the dinghy, moved closer to the pair, and asked, "Then how did it become the flag of England?"

Simon shot Kojiro a glance, but Kojiro's face betrayed no hint as to his motivation in asking the question. *Wait, did he smile? No, couldn't be,* Simon thought to himself.

Kojiro got the glance from Simon that he had hoped for. He had observed that Simon hated Aldo's lectures, so he had purposefully prompted Aldo into speaking more.

"That is an insightful question, Kojiro-san." Aldo had taken to calling Kojiro Kojiro-san, even when they were not conversing in Japanese because it let others *around* them know about Aldo's mastery of foreign languages.

Aldo continued. "You English sought protection from the Genoese navy when you entered the Mediterranean, so for a fee, the Genoese allowed you to fly their flag." Aldo, in fact, had heard this as a rumor, and was not completely confident in its veracity, but there was no reason to share this minor detail with Simon.

"And now, I allow you to fly the flag of England and St. George to protect you in the Bay of Carmarthen. A fair trade, I would say."

Kojiro looked around the bay and saw nothing but small sail boats, fishing boats, and assorted dinghies. If they all stormed the *Triarii* at once, they would have no hope of success. *So Simon says it is a fair trade when it is clearly not.* Kojiro looked at Simon's face and saw his usual wide grin. *And he finds this funny. An English phrase where the intended meaning is opposite to that presented by the words themselves amuses the English. Aldo does not seem amused. Perhaps it does not amuse Venetians?*

"We fought four wars against the Genoese whoremongers. It is not a fair trade." Aldo could not help but say this, even as he knew Simon was toying with him.

"Whoremongers, too? I think I'm starting to like these Genoese, because if there's anything an Englishman likes more than a fellow whoremonger, I can't think what it might be."

"Bah, you English have no manners and no education. Why do I bother trying to teach you anything?

"Surely you should stop," Simon agreed.

"Why do we not sail to the dock forthwith?" Kojiro interrupted as he eyed the wooden wharves protruding from the shore.

"I'm afraid, Kojiro, that I don't know what kind of reception I'm due for here," Simon said. "The land belongs to my relatives, or at least it did last time I came here, but they are Welsh and I am English."

"It makes a difference even though you are family?" Kojiro asked, surprised.

"It might. A lot depends on the mood of the Welsh at any given time. And for more fun unpredictability, I'm a rebel in my own country."

Kojiro did not understand why Simon used the word *fun* to describe this situation. *Perhaps I misunderstand 'unpredictability.'*

Simon continued his evaluation of the circumstances as they took their places in the dinghy. "I do not wish to endanger Aldo's ship by making it vulnerable to boarders from the docks. That is why I recommend the distant anchoring. Out here in the bay, it is in little danger."

"No danger," Aldo announced confidently before he gave a litany of detailed instructions to Magnani who would remain aboard the ship. Aldo had spared no expense on his latest ship. It was a carrack with three masts, two topsails, thirty guns on each side, and two cannon fore and aft, a practically unrivaled ship of war that also contained a tremendously large hold for storage. *If I had had this much room in the Tigre for spices, I would have bribed my way into being the Doge of Venice by now,* Aldo thought to himself.

"It doesn't look like much," Aldo remarked as the disembarkation party surveyed the houses, cottages, huts, hovels, shacks, sheds, dumps, rattraps, and various other structures that defied qualification crammed up against the coast.

"*Soo desu nee*," Kojiro agreed.

"Well, as much as I know you'd like me to argue with you gents, I can't dispute your conclusion. It's a pisspot," Simon concurred.

It took some careful rowing to keep them all dry as the skilled Venetian sailors maneuvered their way through the breakers and onto shore.

As Simon hopped over the gunwale of the dinghy and onto the wet, gray sand, he thought he recognized the Welshman who approached his small landing party. As the man came closer, Simon knew exactly who he was. It was the second cousin that he vaguely remembered stealing gingerbread and sugared almonds from as a child.

Simon recognized his cousin even after all the years due to his unmistakable shock of bright orange hair and the wide, thick nose that heredity doomed all his Welsh relatives to. Funnily enough, though, age had been kind to his cousin. The rest of his features: sharp, deep-set green eyes, a strong jaw, high cheekbones, evenly set white teeth—a rarity in England, much less Wales—and ears proportional to the size of his head, more than made up for the nose. His cousin, four years Simon's junior, had actually grown into a handsome man, albeit one with an overly prominent nose.

Simon greeted his relative. "Cousin! It's been far too long. What, twenty years? Ah, I've missed the clean air and fine winds of your fair," and here Simon choked a bit and enunciated the word rather quietly, "city."

Simon's cousin smiled broadly, showing off his uncannily straight teeth. "And you would be the boy who stole my treats, moped about my father's castle, and asked your mum at least every hour when you were going to leave this godforsaken devil's torture chamber of boredom, if I'm not mistaken?"

Simon was taken aback. The boy had matured into a straight-talking, likeable man. "Ah, yes, I'm ashamed to say. That little knave was indeed me. Your memory is sharp."

"Well, don't let it bother you. I was a snot-nosed, whiny little tattletale, as much as my mother tries to convince me otherwise. I would much rather have memories of being the arrogant, bullying relative from out of town, if truth be told."

Aldo burst into an uncontrollable fit of laughter. "You were an arrogant bully as a child? You? You who must be tortured to admit that you have royal heritage? Acting all this time as though you were not pretentious. Now I hear from the voice of your own kin that you really *are* a typical English peacock! You should be ashamed of yourself, playing the modesty game this whole time to fool dear Aldo!"

Simon was chagrined, but he took his lumps in stride. "Yes, Aldo, I've been perpetrating an elaborate hoax for the sole purpose of one day ridiculing you for misjudging my character."

"I am Duncan Bevan," Simon's cousin said, "son of Thomas Bevan." And with the introduction he bowed modestly.

Simon remembered that the name Bevan was an Anglicized version of the Welsh "ap or ab Evan," meaning son of Evan. Most Welshmen did not have true surnames, simply known as "son of," but his uncle, Sir Thomas Bevan had changed that, preferring the English system of a true last name.

"Introduce me to your friends, cousin, then we'll go to meet my father. I daresay he was shocked when he got word that your banner had been seen disembarking from that magnificent ship anchoring in the bay." Duncan full well realized that one of the men with Simon was likely the captain of the ship, and he also knew that flattery was always a good way to start new relationships. In this case, he meant it sincerely; the carrack anchoring off of Kidwelly did look truly magnificent.

Aldo liked Simon's relative immediately. The boy was stout, witty, seemed to have Simon's jovial personality, and clearly had both expansive knowledge of, and fine taste in, sailing vessels.

"I am *Capitano* Aldo Mitachionne and this is my first mate Neno," Aldo introduced himself with a flourishing bow. Neno bowed and grunted.

"And the quiet one?" Duncan asked.

"This is Kojiro," Simon said as Kojiro bowed in his traditional, reserved Japanese style.

As Duncan looked at Kojiro more closely he couldn't help but stare. Kojiro was dressed in typical, loose-fitting sailor's garb, but his eyes and facial features were like none he'd ever seen before.

Simon noticed his cousin staring. "He's not from around here."

Duncan did not wish to be rude, so he inquired no more and led the small party away from the beach. As they walked towards the castle, Duncan spoke frankly. "I'm afraid you're walking into a rather sticky situation."

"Oh?" Simon asked.

"Well it's a bad news-good news sort of thing, and I'd be remiss if I didn't give you the bad news first."

"By all means," Simon replied.

"You may be hanged when we get to my father's castle."

"Well, that is a bit of bad news, I daresay. And the good news?"

"Your friends likely won't be. I see that the vessel you arrived on flies the flag of Venice in addition to that of St. George, and there is not a faction in England or Wales that doesn't drool over the possible wealth creation that trade with Venice could engender."

Aldo clapped Simon on the back. "Well, it's good to be appreciated somewhere. For immediate purposes, I extend full Venetian citizenship on Kojiro here, with all the rights and privileges not to be hanged that go along with it."

"I will die happily with Simon, if you please," Kojiro stated in his standard monotone.

Aldo did not know if he was offended or not. He had just offered to vouch for Kojiro's Venetian citizenship, and Kojiro had volunteered for death instead.

Simon beamed. "Now that's the spirit, Kojiro! I wish I had more friends like you." He stared accusingly at Aldo. "So, pray tell, why might I be hanged?"

"Well, obviously my father wouldn't hang you, since you are family after all and your mother was always his favorite cousin. But Rhys Ap Thomas, the most powerful warlord in Wales, stays at the castle now to recruit Carmarthen bowmen."

"And for whom does he recruit them?" Simon asked.

"Officially he recruits them for King Richard. They say that he has sworn to Richard and that if Henry arrives on the coast of Wales, Henry will proceed only over his belly."

"And unofficially?"

Duncan shrugged. "Unofficially, who knows? He hasn't survived this long as a powerful Welshman in an English world by being foolish. If Henry can gather a big enough army to make a go of it, chances are, he'll side with Henry. Rhys is a survivor, but he's a true Welsh patriot at heart. Wales is likely to gain much more autonomy with Henry on the throne of England than Richard. Richard hates the Welsh."

"So I've heard," Simon responded.

Duncan continued to speak as Kidwelly Castle drew nearer. "So Rhys may hang you as a public show of loyalty to Richard, or he may not. As Rhys goes, though, so likely goes most of Wales, so you're best off being in his favor. Though I know you do not hold the Welsh in the highest regard—no offense by the way, few English do—you should know that we are a people that you would prefer to fight 'with' rather than 'against.'"

Simon knew this last part to be the truth. For hundreds of years English monarchs had struggled to control the fierce, combative

Welsh tribes, and even after the defeat and beheading of Llywelyn ap Gruffydd by Edward I at the Battle of Orewin Bridge in 1282, which officially brought Wales under English subjugation, the Welsh had never been an easy people to control. And the skill of Welsh longbowmen struck fear into the hearts of brave soldiers throughout Europe. Merely peasants, but raised from birth to pull the six-foot-tall longbows that had terrorized France for the last century, Welsh archers were a prized commodity on any battlefield.

"Dear cousin," Simon grinned, "though I never stayed long in this dung heap that people who draw maps refer to as 'Wales,' rest assured, I have heard that some of you know how to use a bow." And by the time Simon ended his sentence, they were walking beneath the raised portcullis at the gate of the castle. A wave of unpleasant nostalgia washed over Simon as he remembered the courtyard where he had spent some of the most tedious days of his youth.

Kojiro looked around the castle. Situated on a ridge with steep slopes on either side, the stone castle was small, but its towers were tall and the walls sturdy. Kojiro thought he could hold the place with a hundred men against thousands.

Waiting in the courtyard, and by all appearances somewhat nervously, was Lord Sir Thomas Bevan. Simon could see that Lord Bevan had aged gracefully and looked to be a fit sixty-five year old with the same unfortunate nose that he had given his son, but also with the same otherwise handsome features.

Lord Bevan was indeed nervous. He did not fear harm to himself, though. He was a fearless veteran of many campaigns for Welsh freedom, and had faced death many times, but he was afraid that he may not be able to protect his own family. Oh, he would die to prevent any harm coming to his favorite cousin's child, English though he may be, but he feared that even his death and that of his household knights and archers would not be enough to save the poor bastard. He was a man who held familial bonds higher in honor than anything else.

Simon bowed to his mother's cousin, who was flanked on either side by his household guard; five knights, all grim-faced and all carrying scars of battle on one part of their body or another. Most recognizable was the forty-year-old man who stood directly to Lord Bevan's right, for one of his scars extended from the left corner of his mouth all the way up to his ear, giving the impression that he was permanently half-smiling even though the rest of his demeanor indicated anything but.

Lord Bevan's standard of a brown, diving hunting hawk with legs extended, grasping a quiver of black arrows on a white background, stood flapping in the breeze behind the Lord himself. This coat-of-arms also decorated the tunics of his household guard. Lord Bevan bowed back to his first cousin once removed, a boy he really considered to be his nephew. "I cannot be happier to see my dear cousin's child after all these years, nephew. Alas, I will tell you now, you were a fool to come here."

I have been called a lot worse, Simon thought.

"We may all die within the walls of my castle tonight, but rest assured, myself and my men will die with you." In spite of that rather ominous statement, not one of the men flanking Lord Bevan even blinked.

Simon noticed the lack of reaction and thought, *That type of loyalty is earned neither quickly nor lightly.*

His uncle carried on. "Just so we are clear, and I instructed my son to tell you this, Sir Rhys Ap Thomas and two hundred of his men also enjoy my hospitality at the moment. You may have noticed the three-bird decoration that a heavy majority of the men-at-arms walking my castle grounds sport on their tunics. That is his coat of arms.

"As for myself, you see the only five knights that my overtaxed lands can afford standing next to me, and other than my son, I have nothing but the peasant levy to support me. They would be no match for Thomas' professional soldiers."

Simon understood his uncle's meaning full well. They had no hope of battling their way out.

Then his uncle smiled. "But, be it our last day before joining the Lord in his grace or not, I'll be damned if you don't get the full hospitality that I offered you as a child."

Simon did not think the Lord Bevan appreciated the irony in that statement.

Sir Thomas Bevan and his knights began to lead them across the open castle grounds towards what Simon remembered to be the dining hall, but they were stopped halfway across the courtyard by a tall, dark-haired, muscular man who sported a tremendous mustache. The man was accompanied by ten retainers; all outfitted with the same three-bird tunics that the tall man wore.

"Sir Bevan," the man's voice boomed. "Who do we have here now?"

"Rhys Ap Thomas, this is my dear cousin's boy, Simon Lang."

"Ah, then that would have been your father that died at Towton, would it not?"

"It would," Simon answered, as politely as he could.

"And I can see from your shield that you proudly display the red rose of Lancaster beside my beloved dragon of Wales, which clearly means you must have a giant set of balls."

Simon said nothing in reply but looked Rhys up and down, deciding where he would strike.

Kojiro looked at the ten men with the three-bird heraldry decorating their Western armor, working out how he would kill them. He knew Simon would manage their leader and he figured Aldo was good for one or two, Neno for three or four, so that only left somewhere between four and six.

Rhys' voice boomed again. "You land in a nation ruled by King Richard, and yet you have the red rose of Lancaster on your shield. Did you get lost? Brittany and France are well south of here. And I hear you're English to boot, so the red dragon on your surcoat is a lie."

"Me? Lost?" Simon chuckled. "Hardly. These are the lands of my family. It seems you are lost. I've heard of you, too. In fact I've heard that you yourself fought for the red rose in the past."

"Yes, the past," Rhys swiftly interrupted.

Simon continued. "And you've been exiled to Brittany as well for your troubles. I've also heard that since you refused to join the rebellion of 1483, you've been given titles and money by Richard. Well, if King Richard doesn't like me being here, he should send someone capable of doing something about it. And I can tell you now, some country bumpkin who has been bribed to betray his own country is not that person."

Insolent bastard, Rhys thought.

"Oh, and you're a lot shorter than the stories make you out to be." Simon made this remark in spite of the fact that Rhys was actually slightly taller than he had thought from the stories and a good few inches taller than Simon himself. Simon smiled widely after his comments and bowed while Rhys' retinue all reached for their swords.

Rhys motioned for his men to leave their weapons sheathed as he looked Simon up and down, wondering what type of man this was who clearly did not fear him. He sneered. "By all rights I should hang you. You are doubtless a minion of Henry Tudor." And at the mention of hanging their lord's favorite nephew, Sir Thomas Bevan's five retainers all reached for their sword hilts, outnumbered though they were.

Sir Bevan motioned for his men to still their blades. "You enjoy my hospitality, Rhys, and you ask for my archers. I will not have you hang my cousin's child."

"He talks big, Sir Bevan, yet I've heard nothing of his exploits in the wars. Is there any justification for this bravado that I'm hearing now from the whippersnapper?"

Simon did not give Sir Bevan a chance to answer. "I have no exploits to speak of," Simon lied, "but neither do I feel the need to share my stories with an over-famous Welsh sheep shagger."

"You insolent English twat!" Rhys exclaimed, breaking out with an extremely deep and hearty laugh, catching everyone off-guard. "No respect for your ancestry, I see. A common fault among you English pricks." There was a pause. "I have an idea."

"Wonderful," Simon said with a hint of sarcasm, "the Welsh are widely known for their *ideas*."

"Show me some of your Welsh heritage, and I won't hang you."

Rhys called to one of the hundred or so of his men who had by now surrounded the group, and in short order, a Welsh longbow appeared in his hand. "I want to see you hit that," Rhys said as he pointed to a straw dummy at least a hundred yards across the castle grounds.

Simon considered carefully. He didn't know if Rhys truly intended to hang him or not, which of course would never happen. He'd die fighting. Unfortunately, based on what he'd seen and heard from his dear uncle and his retinue, his friends and relatives would die fighting, too.

"To hang me, you presuppose that I would not cut off your nuts first, but if you wish to see a display of archery, I will happily grant you one."

Of course the game was fixed. There wasn't a chance in hell that Simon could hit the designated target. Simon was immensely strong, but pulling a longbow required a special kind of strength. To even pull a Welsh longbow to its full extension took years of practice, training, and an almost unnatural strengthening of the shoulder muscles.

Simon thought he probably had the strength to pull it fully once, but there was a significant chance his arrow would sail clean over the castle wall or skip across the ground. As for actually getting near the target, it wasn't going to happen. He and Rhys both knew it.

Rhys smiled a genuinely pleasant smile. Not the smile of a man that was about to hang him, but then again, you never knew. Simon had met people who didn't feel any emotions at all, people who faked emotions to get along in life, but who could run their sword through the belly of a pregnant woman or split open the head of an infant with an axe without blinking an eye. Perhaps Rhys was one of those people.

Simon thought quickly. "I am an English knight and lord, and your test is too easy for me. And besides being too easy, it is the job of a peasant or a farmer to pull a bowstring. But, as I said, if you wish to see a display of archery, I will show you one. I will have my smallest, weakest servant hit your target, and afterwards, if you still desire to make empty threats, I will happily slice you from arsehole to earlobe."

Rhys laughed again. He was starting to like this Englishman. He looked over at the most pitiful-looking man in Simon's retinue, a man with strange, small eyes who was dressed like a sailor but didn't stand like one. That man was clearly the lowly peasant that Simon referred to, and there was no way he hid enough muscle underneath his loose-fitting shirt to *pull* a longbow, much less hit the target. "Give the bow to the wee little man. Are you sure you wouldn't rather have your knight give it a try? He looks a stout fellow," Rhys asked as he pointed the hilt of his sword at Neno.

Knight? I quite like the sound of that, Neno thought to himself as he unconsciously looked around him, feeling awkward at being identified above his station.

"No. That wouldn't be fair to you; much too easy for him as well."

Rhys gave the dark-skinned man a second, more thorough look. He had the uneasy feeling he was falling into a trap, but for the life of him, he couldn't figure out what it might be. The peasant was a foreigner without question, but that just made it *less* likely he could shoot a longbow. Everyone in the world knew you had to grow up with a longbow to know how to shoot one, and only the English and Welsh did that. Regardless, he had no option now. "Let's see what he can do then."

"It's far, can I have four tries?" Kojiro asked.

Rhys nearly bent over in laughter. Simon kept a straight face, but his asshole puckered tightly. Simon had seen Japanese archery skills, *but maybe it was not a talent of Kojiro's?*

Rhys knew the game was his now. Either you could shoot a longbow or you couldn't. There would be no 'beginner's luck' on a target at a hundred yards. And if you couldn't hit it the first time, you wouldn't be able to hit it on the fourth try either.

"Sure, give him four tries. If he can't hit the target in four tries, your servant hangs beside you. You must introduce me to this other well-dressed man with you; I understand his ship flies the flag of Venice?"

"It does indeed, and he is a merchant among merchants. If I don't have to kill you, I will be pleased to make the introductions," Simon offered. Then all attention turned to Kojiro who was fumbling as he tried to fit an arrow to the string of a Welsh longbow.

Simon could not control the lump that formed in his throat. Rhys' men began to join their leader in his good humor.

All at once, though, the laughter stopped. It didn't slowly trail off; it just stopped, as if everyone in the courtyard had their tongues removed at once. Not even breathing could be heard as Kojiro drew the enormous Welsh bow fully back to his ear with what appeared to be no more effort than if he were plucking a harp string. When he released the first arrow, the entire gathering, Simon included, snapped their heads at once in the direction of the target.

The arrow buried itself into the head of the dummy. Everyone turned to watch Kojiro load his second arrow, but by the time they turned their heads, his second arrow was already sailing downrange. The second arrow pierced the heart of the dummy.

Now half the crowd looked at Kojiro and half the crowd looked at the target. None of them ever saw the full process from arrow fitting to target penetration because it was just too fast. The half of Rhys' men-at-arms and knights who had been watching Kojiro and not the target jerked their heads immediately as they heard an audible groan from the crowd that had been watching the target. Kojiro had sent his third arrow right into the location on the target, had it been a real human being, that would have been occupied by his balls.

When the fourth arrow did not immediately follow the third, all eyes turned quickly to Kojiro to see what the problem was. The gaiety amongst Rhys Ap Thomas' men subsided as everyone saw that the fourth arrow was pulled fully to Kojiro's ear and aimed directly at Rhys's face. At a distance of no more than five feet, the plate armor-piercing, bodkin-tipped arrow would likely enter the front of Rhys's face and exit the back of his skull, and there wasn't anything anybody could do about it. After all, the only thing Kojiro had to do was *stop* holding the pressure of two hundred pounds of pull weight, and Rhys would cease to breathe air.

Rhys' men were loyal men, experienced in battle, and to a man they drew swords and fit arrows. They did know better, however, after the demonstration that they had just witnessed, to do any more than that.

"I'm afraid I've been cheated, Lang," Rhys opined.

"You have indeed been cheated, Rhys. I'm an Englishman. My word is not my bond. My word is only but a tool, much like a sword or an, ahem, arrow, that I use for my purposes. This man is a warrior the like of which I've never seen, and he will put that arrow straight through your eye and likely clear through your brain if I ask him to."

Rhys swallowed and turned his head from the tip of the arrow towards Simon. "You know that I have always been friendly towards Lancastrians."

"Really?" Simon queried.

"The Yorkists razed my family's castle of Carreg Cennen when I was a child, and my grandfather was killed at the battle of Mortimer's Cross fighting for the Lancastrians."

"So you will fight for Henry?" Simon asked.

"My loyalty has always been with the Welsh, not the monarch in London," Rhys said cryptically.

"What about the land Richard gave you?"

"I accepted title, money, and land because I would be mad not to. I pledged my allegiance to Richard because it was the only way to stop him from holding my son hostage in London."

"And the oath?" Simon said carefully, looking into the unblinking eyes of Rhys.

How the hell does he know about that? Rhys wondered.

"Ah, the oath. I did pledge that any invasion of Wales by Henry would have to take place over my body."

"It seems we have a problem, then, if you are a man of your oath."

"I am a man of my oath," Rhys said soberly. He paused. "But I will find a way to resolve this delicate problem."

Simon studied him suspiciously. The Welsh were a clever folk; savage and rustic, but clever. He gave a nod, and Kojiro lowered the bow. Rhys' men heaved a collective sigh of relief.

Rhys smiled. "I think a drink is in order. What say you?"

"Do they still serve disgusting Welsh ale around here?" Simon asked.

"Indeed they do. I'd love to hear more of this *peasant* servant of yours over a drink."

Chapter 33

GRATEFUL THAT HIS favorite cousin's son was not going to be hanged, at least not yet, Sir Thomas Bevan had a feast the likes of which were not normally seen outside of Christmas or Easter. Pigs and sheep were roasted over spits, quail and pheasant baked in his wood-fired kitchen ovens along with fresh bread. The vegetables from his tenant farms were boiled in giant pots until all the taste was leeched out of them and they reached mushy English perfection.

Sir Thomas Bevan was not yet convinced his nephew was safe, though, and it being his feasting hall where he was lord, his five armed knights stood behind him at the head of the table. Sober, grim-faced, armed, and armored, they did not partake in any of the festivities. Though they were far overmatched by the two hundred of Rhys's men feasting in the hall, the point was not lost.

Rhys recognized that Lord Bevan was first and foremost loyal to his familial bonds, and he liked that. *Not only do the best archers in Wales come from this area,* he thought to himself, *but they are loyal and stubborn against all odds, as every Welshman should be.* Rhys, two of his men, and Simon sat next to Lord Bevan at the head of the U in the table, and Duncan, Aldo, and Kojiro sat next to them. On the two sides of the U, the remainder of Rhys' men, Neno, some of the *Triarii*'s crew, and some local Welsh chieftains sat.

"Sir Bevan, I am sad that your knights are not able to join in this glorious feasting that you have prepared for us," Rhys stated, knowing full well that Lord Bevan meant to demonstrate through their presence that he and he alone ruled in his lands.

"Alas, I wish I could allow them to join us, Rhys, but unfortunately, they must later patrol the grounds to ensure there are no English spies among us," Sir Bevan blatantly lied.

"A righteous and necessary undertaking no doubt," Rhys grinned at the explanation. "So, Mr. Lord, Sir Simon Lang," Rhys exaggerated the importance of Simon's heritage, "what brings you to the service of our dear Henry?"

Simon was well aware by now that Rhys Ap Thomas must have been in some communication with Henry but was likely still playing the field with his loyalty. He decided to skip the hogwash with this man who was clearly capable of producing his own copious amounts of bullshit. "Bent-Back Dick keeps trying to kill me." Simon had never met Richard in person and had no personal knowledge of his rumored spinal deformity, but that was no reason to hold back on the disparaging remarks.

"Really?" Rhys roared, honestly surprised. "Well I'll be damned. I knew he was a paranoid prick, but I had no idea his assassination list ran so low!" With this little bit of humor, Rhys laughed heartily. "So you're some type of pre-invasion scouting force or something like that?"

"Something like that," Simon replied, not quite ready to give up any more information, but also knowing that Rhys probably had all the same knowledge that he did.

"And Henry is going to land in Pembroke with boatloads of frog eaters sometime in the near future? No need to answer, no need to answer, I already know," Rhys announced then drained a very large cup of mead in one swig. "I'm quite aware of Henry's plans. He's not going to take Richard with just a few boatloads of Frenchmen, mind you. In fact, I've been communicating with him regularly, and he fully anticipates my support."

"And will he have it?" Simon asked pointedly.

"Well, I'd say the odds are about sixty forty in his favor at the moment, but you never know, things could change," Rhys answered honestly. "The way I stand on this issue will have a great deal of impact on how my nation is treated by yours for the foreseeable future. It behooves me to decide wisely, but as I said, I'm leaning in Henry's favor."

"I don't suppose I could offer you any incentive that may tip those odds, could I?" Simon asked.

"So you've got French gold, have you?" Rhys intuited from the remark.

"I do," Simon returned Rhys's directness.

"Well, how much are we talking?"

And with that Simon quoted a figure equivalent to half the French gold Henry had entrusted him with. It was a substantial amount, and it now sat in the hold of the *Triarii.*

"Well that would put me squarely at sixty-five thirty-five, without a doubt," Rhys grinned.

Simon and Rhys then went back and forth for a couple minutes until Simon finally offered nearly three-quarters of what he had been given. "Well, I'll tell you this," Rhys said, "you've got me up to a solid seventy-five twenty-five in Henry's favor, but I'll need to see the gold."

"I will not only let you *see half* the money, I'll *give* you *half* the money. The rest you can have when you bring Welsh troops to join Henry. And just so we're clear, I haven't seen a Welsh boat, or fleet for that matter, capable of 'pirating' the money from my dear friend Aldo's boat."

"I admire a man who knows how to bargain, Lord Lang!" Rhys cried. "When I bring all of South Wales to meet Henry, you can bring me the remainder of my gold. For now, we drink," he said as he drained yet another goblet of mead all at once.

Simon noticed that the wording "I'll bring all of South Wales to meet Henry" left a lot to be desired in terms of clarification. He didn't think he would get much better from the crafty Welshman though, so he toasted Rhys and their new odds. "Here's to seventy-five twenty-five."

After the toast, Rhys summoned one of his retainers. "Send messengers to all who owe fealty to me, as well as those who wish to kill Englishmen and get paid for it. They are to raise their levies and meet me in a week's time."

The retainer bowed and walked swiftly out of the room.

Chapter 34

IT DID NOT take long for word to cross the Welsh countryside. Pikes flashed by the light of the moon as the fiercely patriotic Welsh crowded onto the forest paths, mountain trails, and riverside roads.

Peasant farmer Dai Evans was out in his fields when he saw the messenger on horseback tear past his cottage and up towards the manor house. "I wonder what that's all about," he wondered out loud since messengers on horseback came rarely to his lord's humble manor and *never* at high speed.

"Nothing good, I'm sure," his wife Gwen retorted.

Dai wasn't the only one to notice. His friend Howel, who lived in the cottage next door, walked out into the lane and remarked exactly as Dai had, "I wonder what that's all about."

It wasn't long before they both knew. Shortly after the horse messenger galloped back away from the manor, Lord Fellowes' personal servant came jogging down from the manor house where he stopped to talk to Dai. "The levy is raised. You are to report in the morning." And almost as an afterthought, the servant smiled and said, "We are going to march on London."

Dai and Howel shared a look, their faces grim. Only half of the men in the village had returned home from the last march to war, and both of their wives were expecting. Dai went back inside his cottage to break the news to his wife.

"I know," Gwen said as she fought through tears. "You need to come back alive no matter what."

"I don't want to leave you," Dai said, "but I am duty-bound."

Gwen knew this was the lot of poor peasants, and her husband had no choice. She choked back her tears to try to be strong for him. "I will tell our child that you died for Wales if I must; do your duty."

Dai hugged his wife until he thought he would squeeze the life out of her.

The next morning Dai stood with his pike on his shoulder next to Howel and their other neighbors, while Lord Fellowes reviewed them from his horse. Lord Fellowes was dressed in well-worn mail that had protected him on many occasions. His coat of arms, a brown and green oak tree on a white background, adorned his tunic and the tunics of his men.

Lord Fellowes stopped in front of Dai. "It's Dai Evans, if I am not mistaken?"

"Yes, Lord."

"You stood until there were none left standing beside you the last time we fought, did you not?"

"I did, Lord," Dai answered humbly, but honestly.

"Then you shall be in the front and center of the pikes when we go to battle."

Lord Fellowes was a practical man with a good memory and a good head on his shoulders, which he dearly hoped he could keep there. He remembered that this stout lad had fought like the devil himself in their last border squabble with the English. Lord Fellowes didn't care that others were senior to Dai in age or status; it was Fellowes who stood to lose his head if they lost to Richard. And if the rumors he had heard about Richard were true, losing his head might be the best possible outcome.

"I am honored, my lord," Dai answered. And indeed, he was. Dai had seen his first battle when he was fifteen, and from the start, he'd had the ability to keep his head when all turned to chaos around him. He got a congratulatory clap on the shoulder from Howel and a quick glance around at his fellow pikemen revealed that Lord Fellowes' decision was a popular one.

When Lord Fellowes finished reviewing his peasant pikemen and the semiprofessional men-at-arms from his household, he spoke a few words. "We will not all return from this journey, that is reality. But the soil of Wales and the pride of your ancestors run thick in your blood. I would not want to be the Englishman standing across from you." With that, his standard bearer unfurled a pennant emblazoned with the Fellowes' family oak tree, and the column marched west.

Gwen cried as she watched her husband leave. She called out as he passed, "*Da bochi chi.*" Gwen said her Welsh goodbye as the tears streamed down her cheeks, and she prayed that she would not be raising their child alone.

Carmarthen, Wales

Simon heard the clang of armor before he saw the men. He was standing on a hill near the coast on a cold, damp Welsh afternoon with Duncan and Kojiro. They stood and watched as a column of a hundred or so grim-faced men wearing the livery of a brown oak tree marched past them. There was no joking or bantering amongst the group; they marched with discipline. These were veterans.

The Welshmen marched on towards a giant encampment near the coast of southwest Wales that was exploding in size by the hour. Duncan looked at Simon. "The dragon in the west is awakened, dear cousin. I suggest you pray for England."

Chapter 35

Mill Bay, Pembrokeshire, August 7, 1485

"So, Harry, it appears as though Rhys has prepared a welcome for us," Jasper commented from the deck of the French ship *Margaret.*

"So it would seem." Henry scanned the panoply of colors and standards on the bluffs above Mill Bay. The purple three-bird standard of Rhys Ap Thomas flew prominently above all the others.

"Do you think he keeps his word to Richard or to me?" Henry asked.

"His grandfather died beside me at the Battle of Mortimer's Cross, so I hope that counts for something," Jasper replied. "But God only knows what runs through his mind. He did not support our attempt two years ago, and was rewarded by Richard for that. What do you think, Sir John?"

Sir John de Vere, the thirteenth Earl of Oxford, had joined Henry's company in France after escaping Richard's captivity. As a renowned military commander, Henry had immediately and wisely taken him on as a close advisor. The Earl of Oxford was both a cunning military strategist and an able battlefield tactician, and Henry, though inexperienced in warfare himself, was good at utilizing the talents of others.

"If he's going to make a move against us, it will likely come after he's had time to gather more support from the countryside and he's lured us more deeply into Wales," Oxford answered.

"You give me great comfort, Oxford. So who's coming with me to find out?" Henry grinned as he stepped towards the dinghy that would bring him ashore.

They had been receiving updates on the ships' location from spies along the coast, and when it was reported that the ships had been spotted of the coast of Pembrokeshire, Rhys knew it was the place where Henry would land.

"This is his uncle's home ground. It is where I would have landed, too," he said to his small retinue, which included Simon. "He's a clever bastard, I'll give him that," Rhys said as a dinghy grounded onto the shore of Mill Bay with pennants waving. Along with the cross of St. George, Henry's flag was emblazoned with the red dragon of Cadwaladr on a white over green background: the flag of Wales. "The men will certainly appreciate that."

"So have you decided for Henry?" Simon asked.

"Of course I have," Rhys said with no conviction whatsoever. "By chance, would you mind getting out of this hot sun with me?"

Simon looked at the overcast Welsh sky then puzzlingly at Rhys. In spite of his bewilderment however, he spurred his Andalusian stallion after him.

"Ah, Mullock Bridge," Rhys said as they came to a rather unremarkable bridge that led inland from the coast. "Let's take our horses under there and shade ourselves from the sun."

Simon looked up again at the gray Welsh sky and kept his mouth shut even as Henry and his entourage passed overhead. *Perhaps he's a bit daft?* Simon wondered.

After the sound of hooves receded, Rhys spoke again. "Well, that should about do it. I think I have protected my skin sufficiently." Then Rhys, with Simon in tow, trotted away to meet Henry.

Henry addressed the Welsh warlord as if he had no doubts of his loyalty. "Rhys, it is good to see you, my friend."

Henry was pleased to see a friendly face riding alongside his ambiguous ally. "And Lord Lang, a pleasure to see you again as well. I trust your sword master from afar and your giant are well?"

"They are, thank you, my lord," Simon replied.

"And Rhys, I hear you have begun to raise the countryside, but I see naught but pennants. Where are the men?"

"They are assembling as we speak," Rhys said without answering the question.

"A more important question, of course, is do you raise them for me or for Richard?"

"Why, for you, of course, my king," Rhys stated very matter-of-factly, convincing exactly no one of the truthfulness in his statement. "I am happy to see Jasper, and you as well, Oxford. No doubt your presence will help sway many to Lord Henry's cause."

"We are counting on dear Oxford to buttress our support in England, without question, but we need you and Wales behind us, Rhys," Henry stated directly.

"Forgive my forwardness, milord, but that will be much easier to accomplish if your men behave themselves. You bring an army of French and English to march across Wales. Any, shall we say, misbehavior, will cost you."

Henry took advantage of the opening on an issue that he knew he needed to address. "Let me introduce you to Philibert de Chandee," Henry said as he introduced a man wearing a tunic decorated with golden fleur-de-lis on a blue background. "He is in command of our French allies and has personally assured me that his men will not become a 'problem' for us."

"This is true, monsieur," Philibert spoke up. "You have my word on it. And that of my captain, Sir Walter Scott."

Simon had recognized the large Scot immediately from their tournament encounter, but had not wanted to interrupt the formal introduction process.

"The King of France has sent his Scottish Guard to join you?" Rhys asked. He was somewhat surprised because he had not been sure how committed France actually was to Henry's cause. The presence of the Scot's Guard was evidence that the King of France was in deep. He knew the reputation of the elite warriors, and he knew that French kings, in general, liked to keep them close to their person.

"A hoindred of us, saarr," Walter Scott added in his deep, booming voice. "And it's a pleasure to see ye again, Lord Lang. I shall be pleased to fight beside ye this time."

Rhys's head moved as if on a swivel. He looked at Simon, then back at Sir Walter Scott. Then he looked back at Simon with a newfound respect. Captains in the Garde Écossaise were not known for giving compliments, especially not to Englishmen. A hundred Scottish Guards would provide an immovable anchor on the battlefield. He was beginning to like Henry's chances more and more.

"So what is your plan?" he asked the would-be king.

"We march separately across Wales, recruiting as many to our banner as we can. I will march north along the coast then east. You can march from 'wherever' you are," Henry paused here to see if Rhys would volunteer his position. He did not so Henry continued, "through the center of Wales to meet with me at Welshpool. From there we will cross into England and march on London together."

Rhys was quite sure he could attract more support with a march through the right districts, but would their final numbers be enough to confront the King of England and his royal army? He didn't know, but he thought he might as well play along for now. "I will meet you at Welshpool then," Rhys agreed.

After spending some time bantering with Sir Walter Scott, Simon set off back to Carmarthen with Rhys and his retinue, where he met with Kojiro, Neno, and Aldo. "We're marching with Rhys across Wales, gentlemen, and there's little in this world I can think of that I would like to do less."

"Ah, let me correct you," Aldo told Simon. "*You're* marching across Wales with the rest of these poor wretches. I'm sailing in a London-y type direction in the comfort of my quarters on the *Triarii* to await the inevitable news of your demise."

"Why would you want to do that? You'll miss all the fun," Simon teased. In fact, Simon did not want Aldo and his Venetian sailors taking part in a land war in England. Henry was bringing enough foreigners into this battle as it was. Except for Neno, of course. Simon had already hired Neno.

"Really?" Aldo said with a grin.

"When was the last time you trudged through peat bogs and thorn bushes carrying heavy loads, sleeping on muddy ground, eating slop, suffering from fatigue, and being surrounded by men who don't bathe?"

"Don't forget the sheep shit," Aldo reminded Simon. "I've seen an awful lot of sheep droppings since I came ashore. I can't imagine there's anyplace to camp in this country where it wouldn't be smelling distance to sheep excrement."

"It builds character," Simon said grinning. "And Aldo, we'll see you in London or in hell."

"The Good Lord rewards his loyal servants, my misguided friend. He will send me to my just reward, and as part of that reward, perhaps he will allow me to send you water as you roast in the fires of eternal damnation."

What on earth are they talking about? Kojiro wondered.

Chapter 36

Nottingham, England

OFFA'S DYKE WAS a wide, deep ditch built by King Offa in the eighth century between Wales and England to protect the Mercian farmers from marauding Welsh bandits. Watling Street ran parallel to a portion of the dyke, an ancient Roman road that snaked along the Welsh border then arced east towards the Midlands of England.

In spite of the dangers presented by the decaying road at night, as well as the Welsh bandits that still existed centuries later, two riders spurred their perspiring mounts along the ancient route towards Nottingham. By morning, the horses had reached Nottingham Castle, nearly dead from exhaustion.

Nottingham Castle was built on a hundred and thirty-foot cliff and therefore was practically unassailable. Richard had chosen to reside at Nottingham for the summer both for the strength of its fortifications and for its location near the center of England. He did not yet know where Henry would land. The riders changed mounts at the castle, then took off northwards at a gallop; the Royal Hunting Lodge in Sherwood Forest was their destination.

As they entered the sweetly scented forest the riders passed the men of green, the men who enforced the draconian forest law. The beasts of the forest: red deer, hare, fox, pheasant, quail, wild boar, and wolf were all protected. Only the king was permitted to hunt them.

If a peasant was caught poaching, the punishment was severe: hanging, castration, or the possibility of being ripped apart by hunting dogs. Yet starving peasants occasionally took their chances. The two spies who had ridden nonstop all the way from South Wales drew near to a group of mounted men surrounding a pack of wolfhounds. The hounds were hungrily devouring the entrails of a dead hart.

The exhausted spies delivered their news.

"He landed when?" Richard shrieked.

"Four days ago," the messenger answered meekly. "At Mill Bay in Pembrokeshire."

I should have known it would be Wales, Richard thought smugly. "And I'm only finding out now?"

"The Welsh lookouts were slow to report, Majesty. And it seems Rhys Ap Thomas and a number of Welshmen have joined him, making it difficult for us to get through. Rhys controls all the roads in Wales."

"Well, of course a number of the bloody Welsh have joined him. *You* should have accounted for that."

The spy glanced nervously at his compatriot, well aware that the king was known to be less than kind to bearers of bad news. Fortunately for the messengers, Richard seemed to be suffering from one of his increasingly rarer bouts of sanity, so he did not dwell on the late notice.

"The Welsh are the most untrustworthy race of creatures in God's world, aside from possibly the Scottish. How many men does he have with him?"

"With him, he has four or five hundred Englishmen, including, most importantly, the Earl of Oxford. John Savage and Rhys Ap Thomas have been seen raising recruits. I think you would have to assume it is for Henry."

"Since he's a Welshman, I knew I was in danger of losing Rhys, but he has always been a man of his word. I had hoped that when he swore an invader would have to walk across his belly before landing in my kingdom, he might stick to his word," Richard said, staring at the dead beast before him. "No matter, I think I can find horses strong enough to quarter the great Welsh rube when this is all over. Savage is a bigger concern, however, since he is Thomas Stanley's nephew. That gives me less reason to trust Thomas Stanley; less even than the fact that Henry Tudor is his stepson. I want John Savage branded a traitor immediately, and I want Lord Strange, Thomas Stanley's son, seized as an 'added incentive' for Thomas to do the right thing. What other forces have you seen?"

"Henry has somewhere near two thousand French mercenaries at best count, but no more."

"How many Welsh does Rhys appear capable of raising?"

"Based on the musters across Wales that our spies have reported, I would say no more than three thousand."

"That won't be enough to save the upstart, illegitimate Welsh sheep shagger from the blade of my sword." Richard glared at the spies. "And have any other English lords defected?"

"Only Gilbert Talbot looks likely to turn at the moment, Highness, but the guardian lords at the border of Wales, though they have not joined him, have not formed against him either."

"Spineless pricks; I'll have their heads impaled on spikes. Send messengers to Norfolk, Surrey, Nottingham, Lovell, both Stanleys, and Brackenbury. Have them meet me at Leicester immediately. And send word around the country, first to the north where at least I know I can rely on their loyalty; order the levies raised and have them join me without delay. Mark carefully any lords that do not appear to assemble with haste. After I have crushed this pretender, I will need to hire extra executioners for all the heads that are going to roll on Tower Hill. And that damned French bitch Anne and her thumb-sucking, frog-eating, pants-pissing little brother will pay for their interference, too, God help me."

"Yes, Your Highness." The spies turned and rode away even more quickly than they had come, grateful to still have their heads attached to their bodies.

Chapter 37

August 20, 1485, Blue Boar Inn, Leicester
Richard III's Headquarters

"Are you informing me that Lord Stanley is unable to attend this delightful gathering because he is under the weather?" Richard sarcastically queried his herald.

Richard had suspected the Stanleys of treachery all along. Or at minimum he knew they would weigh their options until the last second, as they always did. He'd already declared William Stanley, Lord Stanley's younger brother, a traitor since William's diplomacy had helped get Henry's invading force across the Welsh border and into England without a fight.

With thirteen thousand men to Henry's approximate six thousand, based on the latest information from his agents, Richard did not need the Stanleys, but their help would have turned the upcoming battle into a massacre instead of just a trouncing.

"But the scoundrel is still well enough to march this way with two thousand men?" Richard asked, again rhetorically. The herald was reporting to a counsel of war made up of the king; Henry Percy, the fourth Earl of Northumberland; Sir Robert Brackenbury, the Constable of the Tower; Sir Robert Percy, the king's childhood friend; Sir Percival Thirwell, the king's standard bearer; Sir Richard Ratcliffe, Sir William Catesby, and Baron Francis Lovell, the king's three most trusted advisors; and John Howard, the Duke of Norfolk.

"Yes, Your Majesty, and his brother brings closer to four thousand. They are wealthy, after all," the herald added unnecessarily.

"Really, you are so insightful. And how can I delicately put it? A bit too forthcoming," Richard hissed, with a shark-eyed stare. "Do you think I am stupid? Does everybody in England think I am bloody stupid?"

"I am sorry if I have caused offence," the herald said very, very nervously.

When Richard was upset, he tugged on the rings of his fingers. He was now tugging. The herald froze.

Richard was seething inside.

I'm in trouble, the herald thought, trembling.

Rumors were circulating about Richard's mental health. He was spending much of his time alone in churches. He was always agitated, irritable, and on edge.

"I have Lord Thomas Stanley's whore-bred son, Lord Strange, don't I? That brazen family is tricky. I know Stanley isn't here now, but he and his brother will both go as the fight goes. They always do. Neither of them is a lost cause yet, and if Lord Stanley doesn't see reason when we meet Henry on the battlefield, I will send him his firstborn son's head on a pike. I'm not going to worry about them for now. We can beat Henry without them."

Richard looked around the room. He saw the terrified herald's lips quivering. *Was that a smile?*

"Did you just smirk?" Richard asked with a quiet menace.

"No, sire," the herald stuttered.

Richard's lips tensed and thinned. His eyes flashed, and his fist hit the table. "I don't care for your insolence or your unbecoming face," he roared. "Guards, restrain that vile plebian."

Two of Richard's bodyguards seized the herald and held him firm.

Richard gingerly removed his three rings from his right hand. He placed them discreetly on an oak table. He daintily picked up a loaded crossbow and walked up to the herald so that he could stare into his terrified eyes. Richard's gaze was chilling as he just stared, contemplating. He then raised the crossbow.

"Doctor Foster went to Gloucester,
In a shower of rain.
He stepped in a piddle,
Right up to his middle—"

At the word, 'middle' a bolt made of hazel flew from the crossbow. The herald's right eye exploded. The bolt exited through the back of his skull, and he fell limp onto the cold stone floor. Richard finished the rhyme: *"and never went there again."*

"Get that man out of my sight," Richard ordered as if nothing of any consequence had just happened. He then continued with his battlefield deployment instructions.

Chapter 38

August 20, 1485
Merevale Abbey, near Atherstone, Warwickshire
Henry's Headquarters

KOJIRO HAD TROUBLE remembering *gaijin* names and as the war council assembled, he asked Simon for a reminder.

"You know who Henry is; I should hope that I don't have to remind you of that. Next to him is his uncle, Jasper Tudor. Going around the room, you have the Earl of Oxford, who is an experienced campaigner and likely to plan much of the strategy; Gilbert Talbot, an English lord and a tough bastard with a sword in his hand; Philibert de Chandee, who leads the French troops; Rhys Ap Thomas, whom I'm sure you can't forget; and John Savage, another English lord."

"Henry, Jasper, Oxford, Phil, Gil, Tom, and John," Kojiro neatly summarized.

"That's it."

'Gil' spoke first. "The local sheriff tells us that an old Roman road called Fenn Lane leads straight east across the marsh. There's a bridge over the creek in the marsh, and we would only be able to get men five abreast on the bridge. It would be a great place for Richard to bottle us up and shoot us to pieces with his cannons."

Talbot, although only a recent addition to the cause, was proving invaluable. An Englishman, and a man well known for his steadfastness in battle, he was able to utilize assets in the English countryside much as Rhys Ap Thomas had done in Wales.

"What's your recommendation, Oxford?" Henry deferred to the veteran soldier.

Out of courtesy, Lord Oxford had waited to be asked, and was pleased to see that the young king hopeful had the good sense to ask him. "I believe they have to cover the road since it's the most direct route past their flank and on to London. That, however, may give us a chance to even out the odds a little."

"How so?" Henry asked.

"They'll want us on that road and at the marsh before they strike, so it's too late for us to withdraw. I am fairly sure that's why Talbot's intelligence tells us that Lord Northumberland waits out of sight, east of the marsh. He doesn't want to come upon us too quickly and ruin his chances of trapping us on the narrow road. If we can freeze Northumberland where he sits with a feint towards that bridge, and we can wheel quickly left around the marsh, we may be able to attack the remainder of Richard's forces and carry the day before Northumberland is able to support."

Oxford frowned at the map. "We will still be outnumbered without the aid of the Stanleys, but we should have a fighting chance, and our right flank will be secured by the marsh. Northumberland would have to push his troops over that same narrow bridge in order to outflank us to the right, and I know the man; he puts caution in the word 'cautious.' Furthermore, if Northumberland moved to our right, it would expose his left flank to the Stanleys who are sitting pretty up on those hills. I don't think Richard has any better idea than we do what those dawdling Stanleys have in mind."

"What if Richard decides to station his whole army east of the marshes and wait for us?" Henry asked.

Lord Oxford liked the question; it showed that Henry had at least a rudimentary grasp of tactics, and knew how to think for himself. "He could do so, but he's coming from Nottingham in the northeast, and he'd be passing a considerable amount of high ground, including a particularly large hill called Ambion, in order to do so.

"If he were to move his entire army east of the marshes, we would be able to maneuver left and take the high ground north of him. That would create the threat of bypassing his army entirely to the north and marching on London, something he could not allow. Given those circumstances, he would have to attack us on the high ground, giving us the ability to utilize interior defensive lines which might offset our inferiority in numbers."

Oxford looked at the faces around him. "Whatever else may be said of Richard, he has a very good military mind. He did not attain his current status through birthright alone. I expect him to keep the majority of his forces between us and that high ground to the northeast."

"Then why wouldn't he just block the road with his left flank and wait for us on the high ground?" Henry inquired. "Then he would have superior numbers *and* the interior lines you talked about."

"Well, he might. And we shall have to be prepared for that as well. But there are two factors that lead me to believe that he will not. First, the hilltop at Ambion is not wide, and if he were to line the hilltop it would have to be in a compact formation. A compact formation would negate the flanking advantage that his numbers give him. I fully expect him to spread his forces out in a long line, and thereby seek to envelop our flank or perhaps even both flanks."

"Well, that doesn't sound promising," Henry said, but before pursuing that train of thought, he asked, "And the second reason?"

"Tradition, my lord, tradition; if there's anything we English care for more than tradition, I don't know what it is. And traditionally, opposing armies line up across from each other on a wide field and beat the hell out of each other until one side gives in. That field is here." Lord Oxford stabbed his index finger onto a point on the map labeled 'Redmor Plain.' "This field is north of the marsh and south of the hills. It would allow Richard to block any attempt for us to reach the hills, use his superior numbers to outflank us, and it would follow 'tradition.'"

"Okay, I can see your logic, so how do we avoid the flanking you mentioned?"

"We're fighting at least double our number," Oxford said, "so I don't think we can avoid the fact that if they deploy in an extended line, they will be able to flank us. What we can do is plant our right flank at the edge of this marsh, which should secure it, then deploy in thick column formations and hope we can break through their extended lines before they completely turn our left flank. We'll need to harass their flanking movements on our left with cavalry while we try to punch through."

Henry was intelligent enough to see Oxford's plan as their best option, but he had another old warrior to consult. "Uncle Jasper, what do you think?"

"I think it's a sound plan. Just be aware, nephew, that you must be prepared to adapt your plans quickly as battlefield conditions change."

"So everyone has told me." Henry smiled at his uncle as he said this. "Oxford, you will lead the vanguard, and I give you the authority to adjust the deployment of your command as you see fit."

"Yes, my Lord," Oxford replied and bowed dutifully.

"Savage, your cavalry and my exiles will hold Oxford's left flank. Be prepared to set a pike wall if the cavalry does not hold."

"Yes, my lord," John Savage answered as he also bowed.

"Lang, I trust that you have no objection to fighting alongside your fellow Englishmen with Savage on the far left flank?"

"I will be honored to do so," Simon replied.

"Philibert, you will be at the center of the vanguard, and Rhys, you and Talbot will hold the right. But Rhys, I will need your Welsh cavalry to support the far left, and with your permission, I will assign them to Savage."

"Of course, my lord," Rhys replied. Simon noticed that Rhys exhibited none of the rebellious swagger that he had on their initial meeting. *I suppose that's because his head is on the line here, too,* he mused.

"*Bon*" was all that Philibert said, but he gave a grand bow to go with his answer.

Lord Oxford spoke again. "Crossbows, longbows, and handgunners to the front, pikes to support them. If we have time we'll bring the French cannons to bear. The English have likely already set their own artillery pieces, so we may not have the time. Swords and axes will move behind the pikes and break out when the opportunity presents itself. Longbows will start in front and withdraw to the rear. Most of us here have done this before. Are there any questions about the tactics to be used, gentlemen?"

Jasper Tudor, Gilbert Talbot, John Savage, Philibert de Chandee and Rhys Ap Thomas were all experienced campaigners and Lord Oxford's plan for battle gave pause to none of them. But it did give pause to one person in the room.

Kojiro did not feel that he had the standing to address the meeting directly, merely being the servant of a minor noble at the war council, but he forced his fingers strongly into a pressure point in Simon's shoulder, causing the broad-shouldered knight to flinch.

As the brief yet excruciating pain came and went, Simon knew Kojiro had a thought worthy of his attention. Simon just wished for the sake of his shoulder that his friend was a little less shy about public speech.

Henry noticed the champion of the Paris tournament flinch. "You have a thought, Simon? I would hear your thoughts."

Oxford, Talbot, and Savage seemed annoyed by the delay, but Rhys and Jasper looked intently at Simon. He hesitated, not only because of his company, but because Kojiro had yet to tell him what the hell he thought.

Philibert de Chandee gave Simon additional prodding. "This man is held in the highest regard by the captain of the Garde

Écossaise, I too would hear his thoughts." With this endorsement, Oxford, Talbot, and Savage appeared to become slightly less annoyed.

Kojiro spoke softly in Japanese to Simon, and Simon pointed out the small detail that Kojiro had suggested.

Lord Oxford no longer seemed annoyed. "I agree. It would be prudent to post pikemen there." Oxford looked up from the map at the strange foreigner who attended Lord Lang and thought to himself, *There's a lot below the surface of that impassive face, isn't there?*

Chapter 39

August 21, 1485
Outside Lord Thomas Stanley's camp at the village of Dadlington

"SO, LITTLE BROTHER, the king has already deemed you a traitor," Lord Stanley stated as he poured a glass of claret for his brother and himself.

There were no servants to pour their wine in the forest clearing because, officially, Lord Stanley and his brother were on opposing sides, and Lord Stanley knew that servants could not keep their mouths shut. Both Stanleys had brought a handful of loyal men to the meeting, just enough to keep from getting ambushed while traveling away from their respective camps.

And both brothers had *very* loyal men. Their men were loyal because their leaders did not join conflicts overly hastily. Every man in England and Wales knew that the Stanley family always picked the winning side, and if no winning side obviously presented itself, the Stanleys were not opposed to having their men sit out an entire battle. So, if you fought for the Stanleys, you either won your battles and were richly rewarded, or you didn't fight at all and preserved your hide. That created great loyalty amongst the Stanley battle hosts.

"So I've heard, big brother, so I've heard."

"Of course, if you were to come in on Richard's side at just the right moment, I'm guessing your status as a traitor would be revoked and you would be justly rewarded."

William Stanley laughed. "I could then make the case that I aided Henry in order to lure him into a trap."

Lord Stanley grinned back. "Quite so, and if you were to set up just south of Henry's right flank, north of the village of Stoke Golding, you could roll Henry's flank after he engages Richard."

"I could indeed, brother, and what of you?"

"I plan to set up on the hills north of Dadlington off Richard's left flank. Maybe a half-mile east of you?"

"So you will join Richard?"

"I don't know."

"He has your son as a hostage."

"Yes, but I'm married to Henry's dear mother and things could go poorly at home if I were to help kill my own stepson. I might never have intercourse again."

"And people think we have it so easy with our armies and our wealth. All I hear about is how wonderful it must be to have the power to choose your own side. They never consider the fallout that we have to deal with, up to and including retribution in the boudoir itself." Sir William drained his cup. "Tasty. Where did that come from?"

"An area known as Graves in the Bordeaux region of France. I'm addicted to the stuff at the moment. It is from an archbishop owned estate called Château Pape Clément."

"The priests are making decent wine these days, and the monks seem to brew a fair ale. Maybe the clergy aren't useless pricks after all." William took another sip. "Well, brother, have we decided what we're going to do tomorrow?"

"Dear William, why on earth would we make such a momentous decision before the battle even starts?" Both had a good laugh at that one, and after a brotherly embrace, they rode back to their camps.

Chapter 40

August 22, 0600 Hours, Fenn Lane
Henry's Army

THE DAWN LIGHT broke as the long column of men moved east along the ancient Roman road. Sunlight flickered off the keenly polished armor of the mounted nobles. Behind their respective lords, the brightly colored tunics of the foot soldiers advertised their factions. It was a peculiar hodgepodge: France, Wales, Scotland, England, and countless nobles' individual familial coats of arms were mixed in with the muted earthen tones of the yeoman archer ranks.

Simon, Neno, Duncan, and Kojiro all rode their horses near the front. They rode beneath Simon's rose and dragon banner that hung limply in the still, humid August morning air, which smelled of musty grass and sweat. Duncan's Carmarthen archers walked in loose formation behind them.

Neno, although he had been briefed once before, asked for a review of the battle plan. "And can you make it simple, *per cortesia*?"

Simon obliged because he did not think it would hurt to remind everyone of the current situation.

"We are marching east on this road until we come to a marsh. King Richard and his army are east of said marsh. We believe King Richard has placed Lord Northumberland and his army directly east of it.

"There is a bridge on this road that crosses a stream in the marsh. We are not going to cross that bridge, but thanks to Kojiro's suggestion in the war council, we are going to leave a contingent of pikemen at that bridge, in case King Richard wants to use it to get around our flank.

"Lord Thomas Stanley and Sir William Stanley are both sitting with their armies on separate hills to the south of us. We don't know whose side they're on. I don't know if they know whose side they are on. It will behoove us to start out winning quickly, though, because they like winners.

"With Northumberland directly east of the marsh, it is likely the Earl of Norfolk will be to his right, which would place him north and east of the marsh. Sir Robert Brackenbury has brought the artillery from the Tower of London to the battlefield, and we assume he has placed it also east of the marsh, where they expect us to attack. We are not going to attack across this road through the marsh. Instead, we are going to break left and circle north of the marsh where there is a great plain."

"The plain where Norfolk is likely deploying at the front of Richard's main force," Duncan helpfully added.

"Yes, *that* plain." Simon glared at his cousin, who just shrugged. "As I was saying, we will circle north of the marsh and meet Richard on the plain, hopefully leaving Northumberland out of the fight. Lord Oxford will lead the vanguard, John Savage will hold the left, Philibert and the French will be in the center, and Rhys Ap Thomas and Talbot will hold the right. We here will fight under Savage on the left.

"So if we turn north at the marsh, the Stanleys will be behind us?" Neno asked.

"Yes."

"I hope they join our side."

"Me too," Simon admitted.

0630 Hours
Ambion Hill
South of the village of Market Bosworth

"Henry's marching on the Roman road towards our left flank, where Lord Northumberland waits. Keep riders ready to bring Northumberland forward as soon as half of Henry's men cross the marsh bridge," Richard ordered.

He hadn't slept a wink all night. He was tired and pale as a ghost, but he was comfortable leading men into battle and so he shouted orders with confidence. "When he's within range, start your cannon, Brackenbury. When he's committed to the crossing or if he gives up on it, you'll hook around the marshes, Norfolk, and smash him on his left flank. Do you both understand?" he asked with purpose.

"I do, Your Majesty," the Duke of Norfolk and Sir Robert Brackenbury answered in unison.

"I don't want a single Lancastrian, Welsh sheep shagger, or French frog, to emerge alive from that swamp," Richard warned as he dismissed his trusted captains to do his bidding.

0700 Hours
The hills north of Dadlington Village

"Lord Stanley, King Richard orders you to attack as soon as Henry's vanguard is halfway across the bridge," a herald from King Richard informed Lord Thomas Stanley.

"Thank you, kind messenger, please inform the king that we wait for his command."

Didn't I just give you that command? the herald thought. But it was not his place to question lords, so he rode back to his king.

0715 Hours
The hills north of the Village of Stoke Golding, half a mile west of Dadlington, south of the Roman road

"Sir William Stanley, King Henry asks you to support his right flank as he maneuvers north around the swamp to confront Richard," a herald from Henry Tudor announced.

"Thank you, trusted messenger. Please inform the king that we will support him on his command," Sir William Stanley answered.

That's not much of an answer, the herald thought. Nevertheless, he pulled back on the left rein. His horse turned, and he rode swiftly back to Henry Tudor.

0730 Hours
Southwest of Ambion Hill

The Duke of Norfolk ordered his troops from column formation into line formation as they approached the field north of the marsh from the east. Peasants carrying their clumsy hand cannons made their way slowly past the front rank of billmen and halberdiers, well aware that they would die first. Filling in behind the ranks of peasant billmen and halberdiers were the professional men-at-arms, and behind them, actual knights. The longbowmen deposited their bundles of arrows on the ground and strung their tremendous yew bows before also making their way forward.

Behind the Duke of Norfolk's vanguard, King Richard's men formed ranks, proudly flying the standard of the King of England: gold fleur-de-lis on a blue background and England's golden lions on a red background. King Richard and his bodyguard cantered below his personal standard of the white boar while the king personally organized his formations and encouraged his men.

"Make no mistake, men; this is an invasion by France. This is not a civil war. You fight today for your king and for England!"

Boom!

A cannon opened fire, and Richard's horse jumped, startled by the sudden explosion. The Battle of Bosworth had begun.

0800 Hours
Roman road, west of the marsh
King Henry's Army

The first cannonball ripped a hole through the Lancastrian column. It struck about forty yards behind Duncan's archers, always an independent lot, who had peeled off the road unbidden. Ten men who had fought battles in England and followed Henry through Brittany, France, and now back to England again would never see their dream of a Lancastrian England. Those not killed outright were maimed badly enough that they would be dead within the hour.

Maybe Kojiro was right; maybe fighting with gunpowder is devoid of honor, Simon thought as he looked back at the men he had broken bread with in France.

"Get those bloody corpses to the side. Ranks close up," a nasty-looking sergeant-at-arms bellowed at his troops.

"Unlucky bastards," one soldier mumbled as the bodies were carried off the road.

In fact, it *had* been a lucky shot. The serpentine cannons were firing from across the marsh, and between the inherent inaccuracy of the weapons themselves and the distance, few cannonballs were finding their mark. Unfortunately, those that did find their mark in the tightly packed columns had an outsized impact on morale.

Oxford had seen the last cannonball hit home. *That's enough. I can't lose many more men or some may start to flee.*

He rode to the front of the lead column where he met Simon. "Lord Lang, time to get off this road. I need you to double your speed and break left around this marsh. We can't afford many more strikes like that last one."

"Well, it won't be an issue for those of us on horses, but the men in armor and on foot will be exhausted if I run them. We'll be hard pressed if we're attacked when we get around the swamp."

"You will have to use the cavalry to skirmish until your infantry can catch its breath."

"Quick pace, follow me," Simon ordered to the men around him, including Duncan's Carmarthen archers who had already taken a head start. He spurred his Andalusian stallion into a trot, and the infantry followed him northward into the field west of the marsh. Iron cannonballs from the Yorkist gunners continued to take their toll, but the Lancastrians did not falter.

Simon looked to his left as English, French, and Welsh knights, resplendent in their armor, rode past. Pennants of all colors snapped in a newly risen morning breeze as they cantered northward past the infantry. He knew what would happen if the infantry had no time to rest after their double-time march around the marsh; they would be exhausted and slaughtered, much like the fate his father's troops suffered at Towton. Simon put Duncan in charge and ordered Kojiro and Neno to stay to protect the archers.

Then, he rode off to join the cavalry.

0815
Redmor Plain
King Richard's Army

"So he didn't cross the bridge." Richard took a moment to consider the situation. His trap hadn't worked, and now Northumberland sat wastefully on his own far left flank. "Perhaps Henry is not as green as I had assumed."

The Duke of Norfolk, who had rejoined the king after deploying his troops, said, "He has good advisors and he may just have enough sense to listen to them."

"Well, he is distantly related to me, so I suppose he can't be a complete dullard."

"But he is not a warrior like you, my king. We shall see how he reacts when his mettle is tested."

"Right you are, dear friend, right you are. But enough blathering, he's trying to skirt the swamp to the north so that's where we'll hit him. Take the vanguard, Norfolk, and smash him there. I will end this rebellion today."

"Yes, my king," Norfolk answered, and galloped off once again to direct his troops.

As soon as Norfolk was gone, Richard called for a herald. "Messenger!"

"Yes, Majesty?"

"Take a message to Lord Stanley. Tell him that if he does not attack Henry, I will send him his son's head. And when this battle is over, I will have his."

"Yes, Majesty."

0820

Behind a ridge, one half-mile east of the marsh
Lord Northumberland's lines

"Should we advance, my lord?" one of Lord Northumberland's retainers asked.

"Have we received any word on whether Lord Stanley has declared yet?"

"No, my lord."

"Then if we march west or turn to march north, that leaves him on our flank or to our rear. I don't like having a Stanley on my flank or my rear. Furthermore, we've received no direct orders from Richard. We stay put."

0830

Redmor Plain, King Henry's heavy cavalry

That's interesting, John Savage thought as he observed the Duke of Norfolk's infantry stream towards the northern end of the marsh.

They're out of formation. I don't know if it's overconfidence or a case of being hasty, but I'll make them pay for that mistake.

"Single battle line! Forward!" The commands echoed through the ranks as the column of cavalry fanned out into a single horizontal line, Simon Lang at its center.

Next to Simon rode Welsh cavalrymen, trained personally by Rhys Ap Thomas. Their horses all bore the proud red, green, and white of Wales. To the left of the Welshmen, English knights rode under the standards of many different Lancastrian families. To Simon's right, the French were universally clad in blue and gold. *As odd a charge as I'll ever take part in,* he thought.

At a hundred yards, Simon lowered his visor and coaxed his horse into a canter.

At fifty yards, Simon and the men surrounding him spurred their horses into a gallop, and at thirty yards they lowered their lances.

The results were predictable. Well-aimed lances skewered Yorkist archers, hand cannoneers, and unbraced billmen. The plate-armored horses smashed through Norfolk's front line and wrought havoc. The initial impact of the cavalry charge had its desired effect. In addition to killing many, the charge halted all forward progress of Norfolk's vanguard, giving the Lancastrian infantry time to move into formation north of the marsh. But cavalry was not well suited to battling billmen and halberdiers, and when Norfolk's second line came on in formation, men on horseback began to die.

Simon dropped his lance and drew his sword. He parried and hacked at the advancing Yorkists, but he and the cavalrymen quickly became islands in a sea of halberds and billhooks. The Yorkist hand cannoneers returned and began to shoot the knights' horses out from under them. Simon looked around and saw fewer and fewer islands.

"Withdraw! Withdraw!" he heard above the melee from John Savage. Simon wheeled his horse and fought clear. As he galloped back towards the Lancastrian lines, he looked to his right and left to see only half the men he had started his charge with still standing.

Chapter 41

0845

Behind Henry's Lines

THE GALLANT BUT costly cavalry charge had given Oxford time to form his lines north of the marsh, but as he suspected, Norfolk's line stretched hundreds of yards further than his own. And behind Norfolk, Richard's men formed a second line deeper and longer than Norfolk's.

"Messenger!"

"Yes, lord."

"Tell Savage, Philibert, Rhys, and Talbot to form wedge columns and drive straight through the enemy."

"Yes, lord."

Redmor Plain

Lord Oxford's vanguard

Under Duncan's direction, the Carmarthen archers kept a constant stream of armor-piercing bodkin arrows raining down on the advancing wall of billmen. Norfolk's archers were not as skilled as the

Welsh, but the Yorkists had a lot more men to spare, and the missile duel was about even.

If the Yorkist cannons were given enough time to shift north, Simon knew things could turn ugly in a hurry. *We need to engage quickly. I don't like standing around, just hoping I don't get shot.* He looked at Kojiro who was as still as a statue in spite of his antsy horse. *Wait until the enemy gets a taste of this one,* he thought.

A messenger on horseback called out to Simon. "Lord Savage orders you to set a wedge column formation and advance."

"Tell Savage it's about bloody time," Simon replied then turned to his men. "Spears forward!"

At Simon's command, all the halberds, poleaxes, billhooks, pikes, and spears moved to the front of the line while Duncan and the longbows moved to the rear.

Simon looked at Kojiro. "The horses won't survive for very long against the enemy billhooks."

"Yes, it is time to leave them," Kojiro agreed, knowing Kuro would protest strongly.

"There are enough grooms who lost their lords in the cavalry charge. They'll be well taken care of," Simon reassured Kojiro. Despite Kojiro's impassive face, Simon knew he was concerned for Kuro's well-being.

Kuro did not like how things were shaping up at all. He'd seen other horses charging by earlier, and now his master had dismounted and his reins were being given to a boy.

If I'm not allowed to fight soon, I will drag this boy into battle behind me, Kuro stewed in his misery.

Neno needed no further prodding to get rid of his horse. Although the Percheron had caused him no problems, he felt much safer with both feet planted firmly on the ground. He gave his reins to a dejected-looking twelve-year-old boy who had just lost his master in the cavalry charge. The boy perked up at being given a new battlefield task and took a firm grip of the horse's bridle.

"If you please, what is your name, milord?" the boy inquired.

Neno laughed so loudly the groom feared he'd taken responsibility for a madman's horse.

"I'm not a lord, I'm a sailor." Neno looked the boy in the eye as he removed his *naginata* from its sheath tied to the horse.

"Yes, milord, whatever you say," the groom answered.

Now I've been called a lord, Neno thought to himself as he walked back to Simon and Kojiro. *What's next? A duke?*

When Neno returned, Simon thought he saw a grin that appeared more stupid than usual, but he couldn't tell for sure because he'd seen Neno with many stupid grins.

"Advance!" Simon ordered.

The Lancastrians charged forward.

Neno used his light, exquisitely balanced *naginata* against the enemy with the speed of a man wielding a sword. He batted away billhook tips, broke enemy halberd shafts, and carved out a ten-foot hole in the Yorkist front line. Taking advantage of the gap in the

Yorkist spear line, Kojiro moved straight into close combat with both swords flashing. Simon watched in awe as the black-armored samurai replicated the swordplay Simon had first seen demonstrated on a ship on the far side of the world.

Before engaging, Simon watched to make sure that his cousin Duncan and his archers had made it safely to the rear. He needn't have worried, though; his cousin was swift and smooth as he maneuvered his men through the lines and had them begin firing angled volleys over the heads of the frontline troops.

"Wrrrraaaaaggggggghhhhhhhh!" Simon roared as he ran forward into battle.

Kojiro blocked an overhead axe swing towards his own head with his right sword and parried a sword thrust aimed at Neno's torso with his left as he moved to the Venetian's right. He ran his blade down the shaft of the axe where it cut through the attacker's leather glove and sliced off four of his fingers. Kojiro then swept the screaming man's legs out from under him, stepped over him, and with sword blades whirling, went to work on another slow, clumsy opponent.

Simon stepped to Neno's left, bashed a Yorkist swordsman on the head with his shield, and stabbed forward at a mace-wielding attacker to his front. With his reach advantage, he was able to keep his mace-wielding opponent at bay with regular sword thrusts, while he continued to rain down blows on the head of the dazed swordsman to his left. After the fifth blow from Simon's shield, Neno sidestepped and struck upwards into the man's groin area with his *naginata*, cutting straight up through his genitals and into his abdomen.

When Simon turned all of his attention to the mace wielder, the man knew he was outclassed. He desperately lunged forward, bringing his mace down towards Simon's head. Simon blocked the blow with his shield, stepped forward, and placed his right leg directly in the middle of his opponent's legs. Then, as if drawing a semicircle with his toe, he swept his opponent's left leg forward and out from underneath him with a swift reaping motion. It was a trick he had learned from Kojiro in the sweltering heat of Venice. The man fell squarely on his back, and Simon ended his life with a stab down through the visor of his sallet.

Kojiro, on Simon's right, both swords moving so quickly they were barely visible, was cutting the less experienced and less skillful Yorkist men-at-arms down like wheat. Although a knight wore twenty kilograms of armor, most of the rank-and-file soldiers wore much less, and Kojiro's Arai-forged blades were cutting leather, cloth, and flesh like butter.

The hand-to-hand combat was ugly, bloody, and quick: it was especially quick for the dim-witted, of which there were plenty. A dim-witted peasant, with little in the way of armor except an ill-fitting iron breastplate, doubtless acquired from a fallen friend or foe, poked his sword at Simon while shouting vile profanities.

For his temerity, Simon chopped down at the hardened leather codpiece the man was wearing. The cut was so quick, the peasant did not feel a thing, but he did notice that his codpiece was now lying in the muddy grass. Regrettably, it was still full of its contents. Then the blood began to flow, and in total shock, the peasant made another bad decision; he turned and ran headlong into a poleaxe: one wielded by a fellow Yorkist.

Simon used the opportunity to strike under the armpit of the knight wielding the poleaxe. In order to provide mobility, this knight had neglected to use mail underneath his armpit, and Simon's Arai blade cut straight through to the bone. The poleaxe, as a heavy, two-handed weapon, was effective in crushing armor, but with only one usable arm now, the knight had no hope of dislodging it from the dim-witted peasant and bringing it to bear on Simon.

Simon moved to the knight's right, and in a mighty swing, brought his sword around squarely into the lightly protected area behind his knee. The knight collapsed, losing more blood than he could ever hope to recover as Simon moved on to his next opponent.

The Lancastrians fighting beside Simon, Neno, and Kojiro fought with the same zeal; they had lived on the run for most of their lives. Now that they were back in their native England, they were not going to go away quietly. As Simon's column punched through the first rank of Norfolk's vanguard, the cries echoed up and down the line, "For Henry and St. George!"

"Henry and St. George!"

0845
Dadlington Hill
Lord Stanley's position

The messenger from Richard arrived on an exhausted horse that was covered in sweat and foaming at the mouth. The rider reined in from a gallop just short of Lord Stanley. It was impolite at the least and a maneuver that could have gotten him killed by one of Lord

Stanley's bodyguard at worst, but Lord Thomas Stanley showed no concern. His men left their weapons sheathed.

"The King orders you to enter the fight immediately or he will behead your son," the messenger panted. "Furthermore, your own head will be forfeit when this day is over."

"Thank you for the news, dear messenger. Please inform the King that I have other sons." And with Lord Stanley showing no desire to speak further, the messenger yanked his exhausted horse's head around and spurred it back towards King Richard.

0900

Behind Henry's lines

"Any thoughts, Jasper?" Henry asked.

"Oxford's vanguard is doing well," his uncle allowed. "The Lancastrians are advancing on the left, the French are holding the center although they are hard-pressed, and the Welsh are holding firm on the right, anchored by the marsh. So far we're lucky, but only Norfolk's men are committed. Richard's men are still being held back, and they're more than double Norfolk's number. I doubt they'll be held for much longer."

"What about Northumberland?"

"He has not budged from his position. It appears Lord Oxford's assessment of his character was accurate."

"And the Stanleys?"

"God knows. Both of the messengers that we've sent came back with answers that couldn't possibly be any more noncommittal."

"But we are going to need the Stanleys."

"At least one of them, yes," Jasper admitted.

"Then I will go personally to Sir William. Richard has already declared him a traitor, and he did help get us through to England."

"Not your stepfather?"

Henry pulled a face. "Lord Stanley has yet to provide us with any overt assistance, so he has less to lose by waiting it out."

"We can't pull any troops from the front lines to escort us across the battlefield, Harry. If we bring men to the rear, it will look like we're running away and surely cause a rout."

"I won't need them," the king hopeful countered. "I'll be passing behind our lines, with the marsh between me and Richard's army."

"Well, I don't like it, but it may be a gamble we can't afford *not* to take. Without at least one of the Stanleys, we will most likely succumb to sheer numbers in the long run."

"William Brandon," Henry addressed his standard-bearer, "we're riding for the hills to the south."

"Yes, my lord."

Chapter 42

0910
Left flank of Duke Oxford's Vanguard
The Lancastrian Column

SIMON WAS PROUD of his fellow Lancastrians. The long years of war had whittled their numbers down to only the heartiest and most loyal, and they fought like it. Unfortunately, the French column on their right had stalled and looked to soon be overwhelmed. The cavalry protecting their left flank were making a good showing, but they were becoming fewer and fewer in number. Regardless of how bravely the Lancastrians fought, it would not be long before the enemy would be on both flanks and to their rear.

A shouted question from Kojiro cut short Simon's visions of a heroic death and living on forever in song.

"What is that damn awful noise?"

Hmm, Kojiro just used the word damn. I must be more careful with my choice of language around him, Simon thought. *After all, Aldo may be right about hell, and there's no need to drag anyone else down with me.*

Then he heard the noise, too.

0910
Center of Duke Oxford's Vanguard
Philibert de Chandee's position

Philibert's lines were cracking. He had perhaps minutes left before the skilled Yorkist billmen would be through his lines and attacking his standard. Then he heard the most beautiful sound in the world: bagpipes. The Scots Guards had come.

The bagpipes were a musical instrument of war. The haunting and eerie sound resonated from the goat skins and reed pipes and lent encouragement to a breed of people who needed little encouragement to fight. They also struck fear into the hearts of enemies who knew the fury of the men who fought to their tune.

In front of the men playing these instruments marched Sir Walter Scott. As Sir Walter passed Philibert he raised the visor of his armet in salute, and his standard bearer planted the cross of St. Andrew next to Philibert's blue and gold fleur-de-lis standard.

"*Bonjour*," Sir Walter Scott yelled out in greeting.

"*Bonjour*," Philibert returned the greeting casually, revealing none of the anxiety he was feeling, anxiety caused by the knowledge that being taken prisoner fighting against the English in England was an experience he wholly wished to avoid.

Sir Walter Scott's booming voice rang out over the sounds of the bagpipers. "For Scotland and St. Andrew!"

"For Scotland and St. Andrew!" The refrain came back at him in one voice from the mouths of the elite Scottish Guards. Born and bred to war in the fierce Scottish Highlands and drilled until only the best remained, they had an impact on any battlefield far larger than their actual numbers.

Sir Walter Scott did not lead from behind. He raised his sword, called out again in Gaelic, and charged forward into the Yorkist line with the rest of his silver- and blue-armored Scots.

0915
Left flank of Duke Oxford's Vanguard
The Lancastrian Column

"That noise, Kojiro, is one I never thought I'd be happy to hear," Simon said. "It's the Scots. A race you would never want to meet for any purpose, unless they're fighting by your side."

Kojiro remembered their fierce competition with the giant Scottish captain in France. "Good," he replied as he thrust both swords at once under the neck plating of a Yorkist knight.

Simon could see a blue and silver wave rolling over the Yorkists to their right. At their front, even at this distance, there was no mistaking the hulking form of Sir Walter Scott.

0915
Behind the Duke of Norfolk's lines

"Someone has brought the damn sheep-shagging Scots to the party," Norfolk mumbled. *This battle is turning into a bad joke; Lancastrians, Welsh, French, and now the bloody Scots. And of course, that explains the infernal racket; the Scots seem incapable of fighting a battle without bringing a sodding band with them. What Englishman could possibly side with Henry and this horde of foreign invaders?* he thought bitterly.

"The right is breaking, my lord," the herald brought the bad news to the duke.

"How is that possible? We outnumber them," Norfolk said in disbelief.

"They broke through our extended line in a wedge formation, and now they're rolling our flank from behind. Our men are starting to run. The panic is contagious."

"Very well. Thomas, shall we remedy this situation?" the Duke of Norfolk asked his son, Thomas Howard, the Earl of Surrey.

"Indeed," the earl replied as he lowered the visor on his helm.

"To me!" the duke called to his mounted cavalrymen and household guard. Without further discussion, the Duke of Norfolk and his son charged straight for the crumbling right flank.

0920
Left flank of Duke Oxford's Vanguard
The Lancastrian Column

Is that the Duke himself charging at us? Simon wondered. He saw a column of horsemen carrying the Duke of Norfolk's white lion on a red and white pennant. The initial cramped melee had devolved into a more widespread brawl. This was an advantage for skilled swordsmen, but it also would make them easy prey for mounted knights on horseback.

Simon looked at Neno, about twenty feet away, carving up the Yorkists who were foolish enough to get within range of his deadly *naginata.* Simon parried a blow from a Yorkist axe, stabbed the man in the neck, and yanked his red rose and dragon standard out of the ground where he had planted it. Simon then yelled for Kojiro to follow him and sprinted towards Neno.

"Pike wall on my banner! Pike wall on my banner!" Simon screamed at the top of his lungs. As men looked up from their individual fights and saw the cavalry thundering towards them, they followed Simon's direction.

The Yorkist men-at-arms thought the enemy was running from them, and they followed on their opponents' heels until they ran into the pikes, billhooks, and halberds that had formed very quickly around Simon's standard. Simon was about to give the command to brace for cavalry, but even as the duke himself galloped into view, he could see it was no longer necessary. The Yorkist foot soldiers who had chased what they believed to be their fleeing prey formed a barrier of men that prevented the duke's cavalry from charging home into the as yet not fully formed pike wall.

"Dismount and attack!" the duke ordered as he realized they had lost the opportunity to bring a cavalry charge home. The duke himself remained mounted, but his son, the Earl of Surrey, dismounted and led the household guard forward into the Lancastrian line. With the duke's cavalry dismounted and the pike wall no longer necessary, Simon, Kojiro, and the Lancastrian swordsmen once again struck out into the enemy.

Kojiro had watched one knight dismount from the head of the cavalry column, and he could see that the others followed him. Kojiro thrust, cut, and slashed his way towards the person he knew to be their leader.

As Neno was bypassed by the surging Lancastrian swordsmen, he found himself in the unusual circumstance of not having anyone to kill immediately, so he selectively searched for targets. One stood out: the man on the horse. In the chaotic melee taking place in front of him, the horseman had no immediate bodyguards.

The Duke of Norfolk saw the huge man with what looked *kind of* like a halberd coming for him, and was not worried. He rode at the man and closed the distance quickly, but when he hacked downwards with his sword, the man did not do what peasants always did when attacked by cavalry, which is either stand still in paralyzed fear or run. Instead, his target parried his attack skillfully, moved in close to the duke's charging horse, and chopped down onto his helmet, mangling the right cheek piece.

The duke could taste blood coming off his cheek. He did not like it. He was in the process of wheeling his horse to return and teach this peasant a lesson when the arrow struck. In a case of bad luck worthy of the bards, a bodkin tipped arrow released from a two-hundred-pound draw weight Welsh bow sailed through the newly created opening in his facial armor.

The arrow did its work quickly, penetrating his head and severing his cerebral spine. As the duke's lifeless body tumbled from his horse, the Yorkist men nearby, who had seen the shot, began to run.

First it was a trickle, but fleeing was always contagious. Once the man next to you was no longer there to protect your flank, you had to run for your own safety. Eventually, Norfolk's entire vanguard collapsed.

Duncan Bevan saw that it was one of his prized Carmarthen archers that had hit the Duke of Norfolk. In fact, it was an archer from Kidwelly that Duncan knew well. "I suppose you'll want an extra ration of whisky for that shot won't you?"

"No, but I'll have his armor, of that you can be sure," his bowman replied.

Kojiro had almost reached his target when a cry echoed up and down the Yorkist ranks: the Duke of Norfolk was dead. But even as enemy soldiers broke and ran all around Kojiro, the man he was seeking did not. If anything, that man fought with greater ferocity.

Kojiro reached him just as he was removing his sword from a Lancastrian knight. The man screamed in rage and thrust his sword at Kojiro who knocked away the blow with his left sword, thrusting forward with his right. They battled for five minutes, circling each other and exchanging stabs, thrusts, hacks, and slices.

The man was a good swordsman, just not quite as good as Kojiro. When the Earl of Surrey thrust, he *always* stepped forward with his right foot. Kojiro took advantage of this. On the next thrust, Kojiro parried the blow to his right and stepped forward to the knight's left. Once parallel to his opponent, Kojiro grabbed the knight's right arm, thrust his own right leg forward, then swept it backwards. This reaping motion caught the knight's right leg in mid-sweep, pulling it forward and out from under him. The knight tumbled onto his back. As he lay helplessly on the ground, a Lancastrian with a poleaxe smashed the side of his helmet, rendering the newly fatherless Earl of Surrey unconscious.

Although they had broken the right flank of the enemy's vanguard, Simon knew the battle was far from over. And almost as if the enemy could read his thoughts, rank after rank of King Richard's troops began to move. To the left, newly arrived enemy cavalry took up position to charge the tattered remnants of the Lancastrian cavalry.

0930

King Richard's lines

"Norfolk is dead, Majesty, and some of his men are fleeing the field."

"What of his son?"

"We've gotten no word, Majesty."

King Richard was raging. "I want an attack across their entire front right now. And cut off Lord Strange's head and take it to his father. He will learn the price of treason."

A relay of messengers carried forward the orders to attack while a single rider carried the order back to execute Lord Strange.

Chapter 43

Behind King Richard's lines

Lord Strange did not think his chances for surviving the day were good, perhaps fifty fifty at best. He knew his father had made plans to support Henry, but he also knew that if the battle turned convincingly for Richard, his father would likely switch his support to the king. It was a tradition after all, and one that had served their family well. They had not become one of the richest families in England by happenstance.

Lord Strange sat astride a horse given to him by Richard, surrounded by two noblemen loyal to Richard and their retainers. *God, help me,* he thought as the rider approached. The messenger did not look at Lord Strange as he reined in and spoke with the noblemen.

"The king orders you to behead Lord Strange. Then take the head to Lord Stanley," the messenger said before abruptly riding off.

It was as he suspected, but he thought he had one more play. Lord Strange looked hard at his captors and spoke forcefully. "My head isn't going anywhere." He paused. "It will be here half an hour from now, and it will be here two hours from now. If you remove it—and clearly you've been ordered to do so because the battle goes poorly for the king—and the king loses, you will have all forfeit your heads."

"We don't need..."

"As I'm sure you're aware," Lord Strange quickly interrupted, "no one in England controls a personal army larger than my family. They will doubtless revenge themselves upon you." He looked around with an air of confidence. "I'm not trying to scare you, I'm simply pointing to the most logical path. If Richard wins, you can remove my head at any time, and you will have fulfilled your orders. He will not know at what time you removed it, so there is no harm in waiting." Lord Strange watched the nobles conversing, and after a minute he got one statement out of them.

"We will wait," his captor said with a wicked sneer, "for as you say, we can remove your head at any time."

King Richard's lines

As King Richard rode forward into battle with his men, he saw something curious. "That's Henry's standard, is it not?" He pointed to a small group of men west of the swamp, well south of the Tudor lines.

Sir Percival Thirwell, the royal standard-bearer, had vision almost as sharp as the king's.

"It is indeed, Majesty, and there can't be more than twenty men with him."

"The treacherous bastard is headed for William Stanley to plead for his support," Sir Robert Brackenbury guessed.

"And if he gets it?" the king replied.

"Well, it could make this a close fight. Especially since you've had Lord Strange's head cut off, making it likely Lord Stanley will join his brother," Brackenbury answered honestly.

"He's practically alone. This foolishness can end right now if I can get to him. Is there any way across that swamp without being seen?"

"Yes, Majesty," Brackenbury answered. "There is a sandy but solid path across the marsh. The only thing is, it will leave us dangerously exposed to the Stanleys if they decide to join the fight."

"Ifs and buts, Sir Robert. I would give my left testicle for a battle with no ifs and buts. Kindly arrange one of those for me next time. Meanwhile, I plan to teach this usurper how a king does battle." Richard looked at his closest knights. "Bring your retainers; we ride."

"Yes, Majesty," they answered without question. Most of them had done battle with their king before, and they knew there wasn't a braver or more skillful knight on the battlefield.

"Bring me my crown. Every man on this field must know that if they fight against me, they attack the rightful King of England."

0940

West of the swamp

King Henry's retinue

Henry's party walked their horses carefully over the soft, uneven ground. It was John Cheyne, with his incredible height, who first saw the banner, but by the time he saw it, it was too late. Somehow, King Richard had managed to cross the swamp and cut off their route to the Stanleys.

"Brave Englishmen, fight with me now, and your loyalty will be rewarded!" King Richard cried out as two hundred and thirty of his bravest knights spread out to form a line of charge; lance tips gleaming as the early morning sun burned through the cloud cover.

"For God, your King, and St. George!" Richard yelled as he kicked his horse forward.

"For God, King Richard, and St. George!" came the response as visors were dropped into place, lances leveled, and horses spurred forward.

After spotting King Richard and his men, Jasper Tudor, riding with his nephew, reacted quickly. "Messenger, get to the pikemen at the bridge and bring them here immediately. Henry, get to the rear. Prepare to receive the charge!"

King Richard's lance struck home, piercing the breastplate of William Brandon, who had moved his horse to shield Henry at the last moment. William fell off his horse dead, but he succeeded in saving Henry's life and in breaking Richard's lance.

As John Cheyne maneuvered his horse forward to take William Brandon's place and shield his king, Richard brought the broken end of his lance about in a vicious roundhouse swing that connected squarely on the giant man's jaw, knocking him off his horse, unconscious.

Seeing his two best knights fall to Richard's lance within seconds had Henry unnerved. He looked behind him, then over towards the right flank of his lines. He considered making a run for it, but he steeled his nerves. If he ran now, his men would be slaughtered. He would win or die right here. And seconds later, he no longer had the option. Richard's men had his small party surrounded.

0950
The Roman Bridge Across the Marsh

Dai Evans had been unhappy with his company's assignment, but he had a sharp mind and could see the point in it. He did not know that the idea for their posting had come from a warrior who hailed from the other side of the world.

Lord Fellowes, in an attempt to keep morale up, had shared the purpose of their mission with the men. His levy had been assigned to hold the bridge on the Roman road. The Fellowes levy being made up almost entirely of pikemen meant that, although they numbered barely more than a hundred, they could hold the bridge against ten times their number while they waited for reinforcements. Lord Fellowes had also told them that the Earl of Northumberland was on King Richard's distant left flank, and they were needed at the bridge to secure against a possible flanking maneuver from him.

Nonetheless, Dai groused with Howel about their bad luck in being removed from all the action. "From the sound of it, it's a fight that will go down in history, and we'll have to tell our grandchildren that we guarded a bridge."

"Oh, you can be sure I won't tell my grandchildren that. I'll be telling my grandchildren that I killed King Richard myself. You can tell yours what you like."

Dai was about to respond when a herald wearing Henry's livery was spotted riding towards them like the devil himself was giving chase. The herald reined in next to Lord Fellowes, spoke a few words, and immediately afterwards Lord Fellowes barked at his men. "If we don't move swiftly, Henry will fall, and we'll all have our heads on the chopping block. Now follow me, you bastards!"

Dai and Howel shouldered their twelve-foot-long pikes and ran after Lord Fellowes. The tough Welsh villagers in oak tree livery were the only men close to Henry and his dwindling bodyguard.

Chapter 44

Left flank of Duke Oxford's Vanguard
The Lancastrian Column

RICHARD'S FOOT SOLDIERS were being held on Lord Oxford's front by the Scottish Guard and valiant Lancastrians. Richard's cavalry press on the left, however, was starting to turn the tide for the king.

Simon could see that Henry's allied cavalry was diminished to the point that they would soon be ineffectual. He could also see that despite their success in defeating Norfolk's vanguard, the main body of Richard's army far outnumbered them. If their flank fell, it would be a massacre.

"Kojiro, Neno, go to the horses!"

"*Hai*," Kojiro answered quickly, recognizing just as Simon did that the cavalry holding their flank would soon be beaten.

"No," Neno answered, not wanting to disobey his employer, but also not desiring to die on the back of an untrustworthy animal. "I will follow you on foot."

In a stressful situation, Simon had no ego. He recognized that Neno would likely be more useful on the ground than from horseback. "Okay, my mountainous friend, but make sure you run your ass off to keep up. And rally as many pikes as you can to come with you."

Neno pulled Simon's standard from the ground and roared like he was first mate on the deck of a ship again. All the Lancastrians left standing who held pikes, halberds, spears, bills, poleaxes, and other long-shafted weapons came running to him. Simon sprinted towards his Andalusian.

This was it. If one more horse bearing a rider ran past him towards the sound of battle, Kuro was going to drag his boy into the fight. Then he saw him. His master in the dark black armor was running towards him. Kuro reared up onto his hind legs, ripping his bridle free of the startled groom's grasp. As he pawed the air with his front legs, he let out a whinny so long and thunderous it more closely resembled a lion's roar than any sound a horse ever made.

Just as his front feet found the earth again, his master was on his back, needlessly spurring him towards the fighting. The arrogant gray Andalusian stallion was trying to keep pace with him, but that was not going to happen. Kuro's hooves churned the turf below him, sending clumps of moist black earth spewing like a geyser in his wake. Kuro saw that his master's blades were level to the ground and pointed forward on either side of him. It wasn't the lance he was used to, but it would do.

Simon wished to lead the charge himself, yet swift as his mount was, he could not keep up with the Japanese horse in the grips of demonic possession. As they reached the ragtag remnants of John

Savage's cavalry, Simon spied Savage's standard, slowed briefly to lift his empty hand in salute, then drew his sword and continued in pursuit of the horse from hell.

John Savage had worked like a master throughout the morning, maneuvering his outnumbered cavalrymen to just the right positions at just the right times to stall the Yorkist flanking attempts. Now, as he prepared to receive what would probably be the attack that would end him, he watched the impetuous noble from Exeter gallop through his lines and on towards the enemy. More curious, however, was the black tempest he trailed after.

"Charge!" Savage howled at his exhausted men; and charge they did.

0950

South of the Marsh

Sir William Stanley's hilltop position

"I hate to point out the obvious, my lord, but I don't think Henry Tudor has long for this world," one of William Stanley's retainers said.

"Which, unfortunately, means I may not have much longer? Is that what you were going to mention next?" Sir William smiled at his old friend.

"If that's how you choose to interpret it, my lord."

From their high ground position south of the battle that would likely determine the course of English history, Sir William and his men watched the whole scene unfold. Richard's charge had been magnificent; Henry's small group was getting smaller by the second.

"Shall we join them?" Sir William asked.

"I believe that would be wise, my lord. Just one question: ahem, who are we joining?"

"Well, Northumberland has yet to show his face, and there's no chance the rest of Richard's army can reach him, so based on the precarious status of my head should Richard win, I'm going to say Henry. Pass the word, we attack the white boar."

"Yes, my lord." The retainer carefully picked a wrapped standard from between the two tied to his horse.

Sir William Stanley's men were used to these last-minute decisions. That being the case, no small amount of money would change hands at the end of the day for correct and incorrect guesses in this contest. When the red dragon banner was hoisted aloft next to the Stanleys' three-hart banner, there were both whoops and curses amongst the men.

1000

Dadlington Hill, Lord Stanley's position

"My lord, look."

Lord Stanley looked in the direction that his retainer pointed and saw that his younger brother's army was on the move. "Prepare to move. Any word yet on who he's attacking?"

"I think I make out a red dragon next to the family standard."

"We'll verify en route. Order the men forward and be prepared to unfurl Henry's standard."

"Yes, my lord."

1000

The Lancastrian Left Flank

At a full gallop, Kojiro twirled both swords at his side, and as he reached the regrouping enemy cavalry, he struck blows at neck height to riders on both his left and right. One head fell off immediately, and the other knight's head dropped to his shoulder, still clinging to the torso by ligaments and muscle.

Though all alone amongst enemy horses, Kuro could smell their fear of him. Eyes wide and nostrils flaring, Kuro built on that fear with another very unhorse-like roar. He moved as his master directed him, stomping whenever possible on the bodies that his master felled.

Then there was that damned gray horse again sidling in next to him. The gray horse's master made a lot of bodies drop, too, and he knew they were on the 'same side,' but Kuro didn't like the competition to be top horse.

What if my master wants the other horse? Kuro thought. As that thought took root, Kuro's mind filled with an unstoppable rage. In spite of his training, Kuro reared up and lashed out with his front legs; with a resounding crash, one of his hooves unhorsed an armored knight and his second hoof battered the same knight's horse.

Kojiro had known his mount was spirited, but still, that was no excuse for failing to obey his commands in combat. Kojiro rarely used his spurs with Kuro, but now he dug them hard into his sides to let him know that unexpected behavior was not acceptable. Sufficiently chastened, Kuro dropped back down to earth, where Kojiro sliced the arm off a Yorkist knight with an upward cut through his armpit.

As John Savage and his tired knights landed their charge, they slammed into an unprepared enemy who had thought them already defeated. Savage slashed his way forward to fight next to the exile from Exeter and the mysterious foreigner on the black horse from hell.

1010
West of the Swamp

Dai was nearly breathless by the time they came upon Richard and Henry. The sound of steel rang out from the center of the melee, but Henry was so outnumbered, most of Richard's men were unoccupied.

They would change that. Without wasting the precious breath that he had little left of to begin with, Dai stopped thirty yards from the enemy and presented his pike. Howel moved in next to him, and in short order, a three-level hedgehog of pikes had been formed. At Lord Fellowes' command, the hedgehog moved forward and engaged King Richard's elite knights.

It was a fair fight until the knights dismounted. While on horseback, the knights couldn't break through the wall of pikes to reach the lightly armored peasants, but once they dismounted, their superior martial training began to open holes in the pike wall. Dai watched his neighbors falling, and before long, Dai became hard-pressed to hold his ground, but hold he did.

Richard was annoyed by the Welsh pikes. They had given Henry a temporary reprieve as he was forced to redirect resources to meet the threat, but they were not Richard's main concern.

He saw both the Stanleys coming off their hills and did not want to find out whose side they had chosen. With his most trusted knights next to him, he redoubled his efforts to break through the wall of bodyguards surrounding Henry. "You're mine!" he screamed as he plunged his dagger through the opening in a bodyguard's visor and lunged forward at Henry with his sword. Henry blocked Richard's thrust and moved to attack his more experienced relative, but Thomas Brandon, who had seen his brother die at the point of Richard's lance, stepped in front of him.

"I'll kill you, Henry, you traitorous pig shite!" Richard screamed, but Thomas Brandon skillfully parried all of Richard's strikes and pushed him back away from the would-be king. As ferociously as Richard fought, he could not break through Thomas Brandon's guard. Then it was too late.

The Stanley brothers and their thousands of riders washed over Richard and Henry's parties like a tidal wave. In a matter of minutes the king's retinue was reduced to none but his inner circle.

"Traitors! Traitors!" Sir Percival Thirwell, holding King Richard's standard high, screamed as it quickly became apparent that the Stanleys were fighting for Henry.

"Take my horse and withdraw, Your Majesty," Sir Robert Percy urged his childhood friend. "We are too far outnumbered."

"The King of England does not withdraw from the battlefield. Go and save yourself."

"I go nowhere, Majesty," Sir Robert Percy answered as King Richard and his remaining knights moved to Sir Percival and Richard's proud white boar standard.

Upon seeing Henry secure, Dai called to his neighbors. Once again they formed a wall of pikes and marched forward. Stanleys' knights hurriedly cleared a path as the pikes pressed on towards the king.

Sir Percival Thirwell still stood, but barely. His helmet was battered, and blood dripped from openings in his armor. Next to him stood King Richard himself, surrounded but still fighting. All around Richard lay the bodies of his knights who had fought to the last. Sir Robert Brackenbury, Sir Richard Ratcliffe, and Sir Robert Percy all lay nearby, bodies cut to pieces. Then the pikes descended on them.

"Traitors and foreigners," Thirwell managed to sputter out, coughing up blood with every syllable. Then, knocked over backwards by a pike, Thirwell was struck time and again from all sides, eventually falling to the ground legless, but still holding onto King Richard's flag.

Dai reacted on instinct when he saw a sword fall towards Lord Fellowes. He didn't stop to consider that the sword was held by the King of England, he just thrust forward in a well-practiced motion. The tip of his pike found an opening in Richard's battered armor near the collarbone, and Dai Evans, peasant of Wales, skewered the King of England. Richard snarled and swung wildly with his sword, but Dai pushed forward and his pike thrust up and through the king's skull.

The king fell to the ground and lived a few moments longer as numerous instruments of war battered his skull. He did not grimace from the pain or cry out for mercy. He stared up at his tormentors with fury until he drew his last breath.

1030

Lord Oxford's Left Flank

The cheering traveled like a cresting wave up Lord Oxford's lines, finally reaching the battered but steadfast Lancastrians on the left flank. Word passed: the Stanleys had joined the fight for Henry, and King Richard was dead.

As this news reached the left flank, Neno and the Lancastrian spears joined in the attack on the Yorkist cavalry. Tired though he was from the long run after Simon, Neno swung his *naginata* effortlessly, unhorsing riders and dispatching them one after the other. The Yorkist cavalry fought on briefly, but when no help came from the Yorkist foot soldiers, their will failed them. They sped back towards the dead king's lines with vengeful Lancastrians and a very large Venetian in hot pursuit.

Chapter 45

ONCE THE RUNNING started, there was no stopping it. Richard's forces were broken. There was a mad dash for the horses at the rear with no regard for whose was whose. The Lancastrian cavalry on Oxford's left flank poured into the fleeing Yorkists, spitting men on their lances and cleaving them down from behind with swords and axes. With their retreat towards Ambion Hill cut off by the Lancastrian cavalry, most of the Yorkists opted to run towards Lord Stanley's recently vacated position on Dadlington Hill.

Lord Strange was, to put it mildly, extremely relieved to see Richard's men come streaming towards them. He looked in his captors' eyes to gauge if they intended to take a measure of revenge for their reversal in fortune, but he saw neither malice nor mischief there.

One of the noblemen spoke. "We preserved your head against direct orders from a king. I hope that when the reckoning comes, you will remember that."

Lord Strange dipped his head as a measure of respect. He had no personal animosity towards his captors, but when the throne changed hands, it rarely did so without one side avenging itself upon the other. He could not speak for his new king.

"I will mention you favorably should the occasion arise." And with that, his captors fled. Lord Strange rode to find his father and his new king.

--≻═◉ ◉═≺--

Lord Northumberland saw the lone riders galloping towards his position and wondered if Richard was coming for him, but as the riders drew closer, he knew what was happening. The riders were indeed Richard's men, but they were not bringing messages nor the wrath of Richard; they were fleeing for their lives. Northumberland rode forward to meet one of the riders.

"What news?"

"Richard is dead. The traitorous Stanleys have sided with Henry. All is lost."

It was not news that Northumberland had hoped to hear, but it was not news that he was unprepared to hear either. He had been right to hold where he was and spare his troops from being slaughtered. His future prospects were not bright under a Lancastrian king, but it was better than being dead.

"Prepare to withdraw, column formation! We return north." Northumberland ordered his men into an orderly retreat, and soon they were on the road back to his lands in the north of England, unbloodied and ungloried, but alive.

--≻═◉ ◉═≺--

It had not taken long for Richard III's dead corpse to be stripped naked by peasants eager to find something of value, but there was one item they did not dare take.

William Stanley noticed a golden flicker in the midst of the deep green leaves and red berries of a hawthorn bush. Leaning over to investigate, he emerged with the crown that Richard had worn into battle. "Your Majesty, I believe this is yours."

"Thank you, William. I appreciate the support you and your brother have given me." Henry meant this, but also prayed that his fate would never again be decided by the whim of the Stanley family. "You will be well rewarded, but for now, let us leave this interminable marsh to the flies and gnats so I may be crowned properly." Henry then gestured at Richard's broken, naked body. "Throw that on a horse and take it back to Leicester for display. Any man in England who doubts his death may be allowed to view the body."

On the top of a hill outside the village of Stoke Golding, Simon could see Henry's standard waving in the light breeze. Having left Neno at an inn to recover from his herculean efforts and marathon runs across the battlefield, Simon had walked with Kojiro up the hill to observe the proceedings.

As Kojiro and Simon neared the outer circle of men, they observed Lord Stanley placing the crown on Henry's head.

"Long live the King!"

The shout sprang as one from all assembled and spread down the hill like wildfire. Soon the cry echoed back from across the bloody fields of combat. Everywhere the victorious Lancastrians raised swords and pikes to the sky and reveled in their long awaited triumph. The reign of Henry VII and the House of Tudor had begun.

Dai Evans had helped kill a king, and for that Lord Fellowes and Rhys Ap Thomas had allowed him to take the king's armor. Dai would never wear it, of course. Not only was it custom fit for King Richard, a man smaller than Dai himself, but it was worth a small fortune. In spite of the damage done to it, it was possibly the finest armor in the country, and Dai would be able to purchase his own land because of it. Dai was going home to his wife to tell her they would be landowners. He looked over at Howell straining to carry a large sack filled with battlefield loot. "You'll never make it back to Wales carrying all of that."

Howel merely smirked. "Watch me."

Chapter 46

One Day Later

Jasper entered the elaborately carved Norman door of St. Mary de Castro, attached to Leicester Castle. He looked down the magnificent south aisle and saw the decomposing body of Richard lying naked on a soiled white cloth in a pig trough. Richard looked powerless and feeble, which was the point.

Feeble, Jasper thought. He smiled at the ironies and synchronicities of life. *Feebleness was the cause of this damn war in the first place,* he thought. *Henry VI with his mental illness and feeble leadership caused the collapse of the House of Lancaster and the rise of the House of York. And it was in this church, St. Mary de Castro, where Henry VI was knighted as a child.*

Jasper approached the body and studied Richard's face carefully. He didn't care that Richard had died bravely nor that Richard had a better claim to the throne than Henry. Richard was a child-murdering bastard, and the Yorkists had hounded Jasper from his beloved Wales. Jasper spat on the corpse.

"May you rot in hell."

Jasper pivoted on his heel and walked out of the church.

Chapter 47

THOUGH KOJIRO'S IDEA to place Welsh pikes at the bridge had simply been a prudent tactical suggestion, the end result that those pikes had likely saved his life was not lost on the newly crowned King Henry VII. And if that was not enough, he had also heard from John Savage and Gilbert Talbot that the heroic actions of Simon and his comrades at arms may have saved the left flank. Before leaving for London, Henry demanded an audience with Simon and his retinue.

Simon got word that the king wished to meet him just after he lost a mead chugging contest to a Glaswegian in the Cock Inn Tavern. Established in the year 1250, the Cock Inn in the tiny village of Sibson had been over serving the English and Welsh for over two hundred years. This, of course, was the first occasion for the Cock Inn to serve Scots, but much to the tavern-keeper's delight, they proved to be a profitable clientele.

"Pay up!" Sir Walter Scott demanded.

"Your man is not human," Simon protested as he pushed a handful of coins across the table.

"Of course he's not human," Sir Walter replied. "He's Scottish."

As Simon reached for another tankard, Kojiro stopped his arm and pointed at the door. A herald in King Henry's livery strode purposefully across the tavern and stopped at Simon.

"The king requests your company and that of your two men."

Before Simon could say something drunk and stupid, Kojiro spoke. "When does the king wish us to meet?"

"Now."

Kuro carried his master proudly along the roads and through the banner-swamped small towns. He knew he had fought well, and he expected that other horses and humans would recognize this. Kuro noticed that the gray horse's rider, slumped in the saddle, did not make any effort to overtake him, and this satisfied Kuro.

Kuro's master, as ever, sat upright in the saddle and rode with dignity. Kuro thought that the gray horse was jealous, but he was not completely certain. The plodding Percheron with its ungainly rider trailed behind. *At least that horse knows its place.*

They met the new king at his camp in Leicester. The three warriors from across the globe entered the King's tent and bowed dutifully.

King Henry, who had been signing documents as fast as they were thrust before him stood up when they entered. Many of the documents he was signing were arrest warrants for Yorkists who had stood against him, including warrants for the Earl of Northumberland and an order to imprison the wounded Earl of Surrey. Behind the King stood Jasper Tudor and Thomas Brandon. John Cheyne, still recovering from his wounds but refusing to be apart from his king, struggled to stand, but managed to do so. He raised his open sword hand in salute, before he collapsed backed onto a cot.

Jasper smiled at the Paris tournament heroes. "So we've been told you were instrumental in breaking Norfolk's right flank. I wish I could have seen it."

"As do I," Henry chimed in, "but I found myself otherwise occupied, shall we say? And your man's reminder to keep pikes at the bridge was quite lucky for me." Henry winked at Kojiro.

Though Henry had not slain anyone in personal combat during the melee, his refusal to turn and run, even in the face of overwhelming odds and Richard's vicious charge, had earned him the respect he needed from his troops. The stories that flowed through the army like an old woman's gossip were filled with praise for the 'fearless' king.

"So, you have clearly fulfilled your end of the bargain, Lord Lang. I have already signed papers nullifying Edward IV's gift of your family estates to Percy Blythe and returned them to you."

"You are generous, Majesty."

"Well, and I've gone one better. You are now the honorable Marquess of Exeter, Sir Lang. I trust that with your new title, I will be able to count on your maintaining my influence in the southwest?"

"You have it with or without the title, Majesty, but I'm honored."

"Now the bad news: unfortunately, you must evict the current tenant of Rougemont Castle yourself. I must go to London and let the people see me. The throne is mine for the moment, but there are a number of steps I must take to secure it."

"I understand, Majesty."

"As for your friends, I am bequeathing them land as well, including the colossal Venetian, even though I understand he is a commoner."

"He is a commoner, Your Majesty."

"When a battle as full of stories as this occurs, and yet I hear about the exploits of your men in every third story, I'm willing to take some unusual steps. I further believe that with the three of you holding lands near to each other, there is one part of the country whose loyalty I will never have to doubt."

When Kojiro heard that the King had given him land, he tried to give it back. He owed his life to Simon and Simon served Henry, so Kojiro had just done his duty. He did not want a reward. "I wish to give the land back."

"Well, I can honestly say, that's the first time I've ever had anybody try to return a gift of land. In fact, I think that's the first time I've ever heard of such a thing."

Simon chimed in before Kojiro could speak again. "I'll sort things out with him, Your Majesty. Sometimes he doesn't understand English all that well." Simon glared at Kojiro.

Kojiro still didn't want the gift, but he knew that you did not argue with your lord in front of a king, so he let it go for the moment. "Thank you, Majesty." He bowed in the Japanese way as he managed to say this with fairly good pronunciation. He really had no idea what he was going to do with land in England, but he supposed he could always give it away to someone else.

"There are still a number of Yorkists out there, albeit none with a decent claim to the throne," Henry stated.

Simon wondered if Henry saw any irony in that statement, seeing as how Henry's own claim was through his mother's father's father's mother's marriage. "Your services may be required in the future, and I expect to see a full host from Exeter."

"As you shall, Majesty."

After a few more pleasantries were exchanged and further details of their exploits were discussed, the three warriors left the tent and rode back to the Cock Inn.

Chapter 48

SIMON STAYED IN Sibson for two weeks as he worked on his strategy for retaking his lands, and while he waited for word to reach Aldo that he was, in fact, still alive and well. Unfortunately, too many victorious soldiers in too small an area had severely taxed the local supplies of ale, beer, mead, whisky, and wine, so when Aldo finally joined him, Simon had naught to offer but warm, flat beer.

"I knew that English culinary skills were dreadful, but I had hope you had more talent with alcohol. Sadly, I see that this is not the case," Aldo remarked dejectedly as he quaffed a pint of beer.

Simon, mindful that Aldo had introduced him to so many wonderful tasting wines, was embarrassed that he had nothing better to offer his friend.

"I'm afraid the cupboards in this area are bare, old friend. There is an ale brewer of no small renown in Exeter that I shall introduce you to if we do not lose our heads en route to the reunion."

"I'll believe it when I taste it," Aldo declared haughtily after choking down his tankard.

Now that Aldo had arrived, Simon had the only assets he was going to get for his attempt at reclaiming Rougemont Castle. Those assets consisted of: Aldo and the *Triarii*, Kojiro, Neno, and his cousin Duncan with a hundred Carmarthen archers.

Duncan had not only survived Bosworth, it was one of his longbowmen who was being credited with killing the Duke of Norfolk. As it turns out, Duncan's archers had only been too eager to join Simon, complaining bitterly that the battle had ended too quickly and they hadn't gotten a chance to kill enough Englishmen.

Before setting out, however, Simon, in a rare, unhasty manner, decided he should *plan* how to retake his castle. He sat down with Kojiro, Duncan, and Aldo over some very foul-smelling, rough-tasting, locally distilled liquor: the only thing left available.

Aldo gasped at his first taste of the liquor.

"Really? Really?" he inquired as he continued to drink and gasp.

"Please draw your castle," Kojiro told Simon.

"And include the thickness of the walls and nearby land features," Duncan added.

As a skilled navigator, Simon possessed reasonable cartographical skill, and in short order they were all looking at a workable map.

"How many cannon can we acquire?" Aldo asked.

"Let's go with none."

"Does the castle have water and food?" Kojiro asked.

"There's a well inside the inner walls, and if they hear of our coming, the rich lands of Devon are capable of providing enough food to withstand a siege for a year."

"How big and how loyal is the garrison?" Duncan asked.

"I've sent out inquiries these past two weeks, but I still don't know how many soldiers Lord Percy Blythe keeps within the walls full time. I would guess no more than a hundred. I should be able to find sources on the docks still loyal to my family who could give me an accurate count.

"Unfortunately, if Lord Blythe hears about our approach too soon, he'll be able to call the men who owe him fealty from the surrounding countryside and the garrison could quickly swell to ten times that size. As for loyalty, I'm going to assume he brought Yorkists with him to the castle, and they're going to be well aware that slaughter has followed nearly every battle in this 'feud of the roses.' I, of course, have no intention of slaughtering anyone, but if he has any veterans from the Battle of Towton where they butchered Lancastrians by the bushel, I would say they are highly unlikely to surrender."

Aldo spoke. "We won't be able to break down the walls without cannon, and I would think that the less collateral damage you cause to the castle and surrounding village, the more popular you will be with your subjects, if ever they become such."

"No argument there."

"And based on the fortifications as you describe them, they could be held by a hundred men against a thousand, whereas we propose to attack possibly a thousand loyal, desperate, and determined soldiers with a little over a hundred."

"So far, it seems you've gotten the gist of my plan," Simon grinned.

"How do you think the population will react to your return?" Kojiro asked.

"You mean, did my family rule like complete imbeciles?"

"Yes."

"Well, no one tells the lord's son what they truly feel, but I got on well with the men at the docks, we put on brilliant harvest feasts if I do say so myself, and we didn't go around executing people willy-nilly."

"Okay, so you wouldn't expect a full scale uprising at the sight of your standard raised above the castle," Duncan remarked.

"I wouldn't expect so, no."

"That's one thing at least," Aldo said.

"You have three advantages that I see," Kojiro offered. "If your assessment can be trusted."

"That's a big if," Simon admitted.

"Yes, so I understand, may I continue?"

Aldo did a double-take at Kojiro. *Did he just tell big-mouthed Simon to shut up?*

"Please do," Aldo said with a smile.

"If your assessment can be trusted, first, you have a friendly local population. Second, Exeter Castle is not on a towering hill with all approaches visible from the castle. Without the third advantage, however, the other three are useless."

"Surprise," Duncan threw in.

"Yes, surprise. We need to get inside the castle before they know it and before they receive reinforcements from the countryside, or we will not be able to take it."

"Huh, well, it's starting to sound an awful lot like skullduggery of some sort may be necessary," Simon stated delightedly.

"I'd think that would put an Englishman like you right in your element," Duncan said.

"And it would at that. We've been duping you poor Welsh dullards for centuries now, and you've yet to catch on."

"So," Kojiro continued, "any thoughts on getting us in the gate?"

"Well, the most likely place for me to get help will be down by the docks on the coast. I started off cleaning decks and scrubbing hulls like a common sailor, and if I had to guess, I'd say some of them still remember me. One of my old teachers was the dock master at the mouth of the River Exe. The river leads inland to the City of Exeter and goods from the coast are taken to the castle all the time."

"So it may be possible to get a few of us inside the castle with a delivery from the dock," Duncan stated the obvious.

"Yes, I believe it's possible. There is a bridge that crosses the castle ditch on the north side that can be approached without going through the city proper. There is less chance of being noticed if we avoid the town and can hide men behind the hill north of the ditch. If we could take the tower through subterfuge and hold it until we get Duncan's archers inside, it could work.

"Of course the other issue is, I'm not going to be able to march across the countryside with my dear cousin and one hundred of his Welsh sheep fanciers without word getting to Lord Blythe."

"So you will require a seagoing vessel of some sort," Aldo added helpfully.

"Yes, and my chances of finding one on short notice that is not owned by an annoying, rotund Venetian are remote."

Chapter 49

The Mouth of the River Exe

IT HAD TAKEN a week to plan and outfit the expedition.

The advantage of time was that everyone had largely recovered from their cuts, stabs, bumps, and bruises. The disadvantage was that word had now spread across the countryside of Richard's demise so that Yorkists everywhere tread cautiously.

The new king had ordered no retribution to be carried out against the common soldiers who had fought against him, but the same was not true for nobles. Richard's loyal retainer William Castesby, who fought gallantly at Bosworth, had been caught and beheaded. The Earl of Surrey and Duke of Northumberland were both stewing in the Tower of London, anticipating similar fates. Some of Richard's loyal backers had escaped, and the rumor was that they planned a Yorkist counterstrike. In the immediate aftermath of Bosworth it seemed that very little had changed, other than the fact that the Yorkists no longer had any viable claimants to the throne.

In fact, Lord Percy Blythe had ordered his lands to mobilize, notably late to make it to Bosworth, however. Since the county of Devon, in which Exeter was located, was a longstanding bastion of Lancastrian support, Lord Blythe did not expect an enthusiastic turnout from its residents, but he knew he could count on the Yorkist knights that he had bequeathed land to, and slowly, those who had not fought at Bosworth, or had survived the battle, had trickled into the castle, answering his call to arms.

Each knight brought with him as few as three or as many as twenty loyal servants, either squires or men-at-arms. Lord Blythe estimated that he had two hundred loyal men with him in the castle, but he expected that number to increase dramatically by the end of the week as his outer lands and nearby Yorkists flocked to the safety of Rougemont Castle. He did not know what threat he faced or even if he faced a threat, but he thought as long as his castle would be costly to take, he could bargain with the new king to maintain his lands.

Lord Blythe's most trusted knight was Sir George Penn. Sir Penn was not big or strong, although he fancied himself so, nor was he overly gifted with intelligence, although he personally saw himself as quite a thinker, but he was loyal to a fault and he had brought twenty fanatical men-at-arms with him. Lord Blythe also took comfort in the fact that Sir Penn, not being blessed with any original thoughts himself, strongly believed that all of Lord Blythe's thoughts were brilliant, ignoring all evidence to the contrary when necessary. But Lord Blythe didn't need Penn to be smart or strong, he needed him to obey, and he needed him to bring men, both of which he accomplished admirably. With a few more shipments of food and drink from both the port and his lands and a few more men, he would be able to withstand a siege long enough to draw terms from even King Henry himself.

"So, George, I trust your accommodations are satisfactory?"

"Indeed they are, my lord. I trust we will have sufficient food and wine?"

"With another big trade ship and the fall harvest, we will have both. I've instructed the traders at the dock to bring me all the wine that stops at my wharf, whether the owners like it or not. It's a new tax that I've come up with until further notice."

"That sounds like a wonderful way to do business, my lord. Do you need me to send men to enforce your taxes?"

"No, the brutes that offload cargo down at the docks have the muscle to strike fear into the heart of the devil himself. And I've already had a few of them executed for pilfering from my cargoes so I think I can count on them to do their job. But thank you for your offer."

Chapter 50

Aldo was skilled at sailing by the stars, thanks to his interactions with Arab traders, and Simon knew the local tides and ocean depths around the mouth of the River Exe. Using their combined expertise, Simon was able to pilot the *Triarii* at night to a safe mooring two hundred yards off the wharf.

"Did Simon tell you that bad things usually happen when we set forth on dinghies?" Aldo asked Duncan as they rowed towards the wharf.

"No, he never mentioned it."

"I wasn't asked," Simon helpfully pitched in.

He peered into the blackness of the wharf as the gunwale of the boat nudged up against the wood of the dock. The black of the night was lighter than the black of the ocean, and the boat's occupants could see roughly twenty forms outlined against the faintly starlit sky. Simon, unhelmeted and with a cloak covering his armor and the coat of arms on his tabard, stepped onto the dock and evaluated his welcoming party to the best of his ability.

Their outlines ranged in height, but they were all big in the shoulders. Their biceps bulged around crude weapons. Simon remembered the cudgels, clubs, and staffs well from his childhood. He'd learned most of the dirty tricks he used in combat from the fighting he'd done on these docks. One man stood out as being older than all the others, and Simon fixed his gaze on that man.

"Jesus, you've gotten old, Maurice. And although I wouldn't have thought it possible, you're uglier than the last time I saw you. I sure hope the night is playing tricks on my vision, and in the morning you will no longer look like a wizened old shrew."

"You spoiled, impudent, little maggot," Maurice replied. "I wouldn't have recognized you but for that bitchy, whiney, little woman's voice of yours."

"I see you've brought a bodyguard with you. Did the lord of the manor send you to greet me?"

"That officious piece of sheep dung? No." Maurice spat on the ground. "I've got spotters on the coast, and they told me there was a juicy Venetian trading ship in the vicinity. If you hadn't stopped here, we would have gone looking for you."

"So you're reduced to piracy these days, is it? I have to say, with your low moral character, inferior breeding, and poor sense of judgment, I'm not in the least bit surprised."

"And you've done well with yourself from what I hear. International idler, friend to the French and Welsh, no wife, no children, and no prospects. Your father would be proud."

With such a heartfelt welcome, Simon could not contain himself any longer; he walked swiftly towards his old mentor from the docks and embraced him with a strong hug that nearly squeezed the wind out of the old man.

"What do you want from me this time, young Master Lang?" Maurice Browning, former master of the docks and current proprietor of the Pig and Whistle asked in a voice that he meant to be harsh, but the intonation came across as caring.

"I need you to let me assist your sons with a delivery tomorrow morning."

Chapter 51

0500 Hours,
Bear Street, Exeter

THE RICKETY CART trundled up the gentle slope. Despite having nine men to guide it, the cart made painfully slow progress. The road was narrow and it was a quagmire of mud, animal excrement, fish heads, pig guts, beer, and piss. On occasion, a stray pig or dog, foraging for food among the filth, would ground the cart to a halt. The heavy load wasn't helping much either.

The cart was loaded with mead, cider, and beer. The oak casks that were being transported came in various sizes. There were a couple of kegs, half a dozen firkins, eight barrels, and two hogsheads. Squatting in one of the hogsheads was Kojiro. The space inside was cramped and pitch-black, and the ride was bumpy. Kojiro wasn't enjoying his first visit to Exeter.

"Not much further," Simon said to the large cask.

The men could have used the wider and straighter High Street, but Bear Street was much more discreet.

"Rougemont Castle?" Neno asked in hushed tones, looking at a red brick building in front of them.

"No, that's the Bishop's Palace," Simon said.

The palace looked like a stronghold and could easily have been mistaken for a castle. Simon, Neno, Maurice, and Maurice's three sons all studied the building.

"Tricky Dicky lodged there in November 1483 while he was gallivanting around Devon, executing people for treason and sorcery," Maurice hissed.

"Tricky Dicky," one of Maurice's sons was repeating to himself aloud, over and over again. He couldn't stop grinning at the witticism.

The group headed north again until they came upon a large knoll. They carried on up a slight slope and finally saw the back entrance to Rougemont Castle. The barbican was three stories high, and the iron portcullis was raised.

"We are nearly there. Stay still," Simon said to the cask.

"*Hai*," Kojiro replied.

"Halt, who goes there?" a guard shouted from a distance through the light mist.

"It is I, Maurice. I am delivering the ale."

"Advance one to be recognized," the guard yelled.

The man at the portcullis recognized Maurice and his three sons, and his eyes widened at the sight of the barrels. He paid little attention to the other dock workers that he did not recognize.

"Maurice! You're a sight for sore eyes; I assume you have a toll to pass the gate?"

"We do, we do," Maurice grinned widely as he rolled a firkin of mead off the cart for the guards. The other two guards pulled their halberds back to port arms and allowed Maurice to lead the cart into the castle. The cart slowly wheeled forward.

"I see about twenty soldiers," Simon said under his breath as his eyes searched the ramparts.

Far more than a normal morning guard watch, he thought.

The cart came to an abrupt stop just after it went under the portcullis.

Simon started to reach underneath his robe to remove his sword and dispatch the gatekeepers, but Maurice put his hand on Simon's and smiled. Simon watched as Maurice's three tree-stump-shaped sons walked hurriedly up behind the guards they had just passed, swiftly removed the guards' helmets, and cracked their skulls with their cudgels. The attacks were swift and brutal. None of the guards let out a sound.

Simon tapped hard three times, and Kojiro leaped out of the oak container. He put his left hand on his chin and pushed violently. *Crack*. His neck felt much better.

"Sorry, I guess we didn't need to have you in the cask after all," Simon apologized. "I didn't think they'd let us all in the gate." He then pointed at the gatehouse, and Kojiro walked briskly to the door leading into it. He opened the door and came upon a guard fast asleep on a chair leaning backwards against the wall. Kojiro sliced him diagonally from the top of his right shoulder across to his left waist. The man woke up in time only to look at Kojiro in wide-eyed bewilderment as his entrails spilled out.

"Maurice, take your sons and get Duncan and his archers from behind the hill. We will try to hold the gatehouse until they arrive. Neno, stay here with me."

Kojiro quickly and silently climbed the steps to the next level of the gatehouse where an unaware guard turned away from the arrow slit he had been gazing out of. The hot confines of the gatehouse had caused the man to remove his helmet, as well as the abrasive mail that surrounded his neck. Kojiro, with one conservative forward stroke, sliced open the guard's jugular vein.

Kojiro continued up another flight of stairs to the last level where doors on either side of the tower opened out onto the ramparts. Sentries stood just outside both doors on the rampart catwalk. Kojiro moved to the man on the left first, but while he was slicing that guard's throat from behind, the guard outside the right door just happened to glance over.

"Enemy inside the gates!" he screamed out in warning before rushing Kojiro with his battle axe.

Kojiro ducked a roundhouse swing from the guard's axe so that the edge flew just over his skull. He sprang back up and stabbed both swords forward into the man's face. The sharpness of the blades pierced the man's ocular cavities like butter, and he flopped to the ground.

Simon moved inside the gatehouse where they stepped over the mess of the dead guard. "Neno, stay here and don't let anybody through the doorway."

"*Si, mi pilot.*"

Simon carried the standard that he had taken from the cart and rushed up the stairs to the third level of the gatehouse, where Kojiro stood next to the bodies of two guards. Simon crossed the weakly lit, straw-colored floor and climbed up a wooden ladder through a door in the ceiling until he stood at the top of the gatehouse. There he once again raised his family standard over Rougemont Castle.

Duncan saw the rose and dragon banner being hoisted just as Maurice and his sons reached him. "*Twll din pop saes*!" he screamed.

His men screamed out in return, "*Twll din pop saes*!"

Simon stood at the tower eyeing the Carmarthen archers swarming over the hill. He only knew a smattering of Welsh, but he understood the war cry coming from their mouths. 'Arseholes to all English' probably wasn't the most appropriate battle cry at the moment. He would have to have a word with Duncan.

Chapter 52

The guard's shout had been heard, and men-at-arms quickly began to assault the gatehouse doorway. Although there were experienced Yorkist soldiers involved in this assault, none were getting through alive. Neno whipped his *naginata* around in the doorway. Any man who stepped into his funnel of death came out with fewer limbs than he started. Soldiers were also attacking the gatehouse from the ledges on the rampart. Kojiro held one entrance and Simon the other.

Duncan screamed a guttural cry in Welsh as he led his men through the open gate, filleting a half-dressed man-at-arms who had just come freshly to the fight from the barracks. His men swarmed over the small crowd of fifteen or so Yorkists trying to force their way through the door to the gatehouse, and Duncan took a quick survey of the castle interior. The enemy garrison soldiers were emerging from the barracks within the grounds, funneling into the three towers that they still held and bunching up as they made their way around the ramparts towards the gatehouse held by Simon and Kojiro.

"Archers on me!" Duncan shouted.

"*Cymru*!" the Welsh archers shouted as one.

The archers trusted Duncan implicitly after his skillful command at Bosworth. He first directed his men to shoot at the bottlenecks of men grouped on the ledges around the third floor entrances to the gatehouse. Within a minute, the archers from Carmarthen had loosed six flights of arrows, and the men on the ledges who were not skewered by arrows died at the blades of Kojiro and Simon. Duncan then directed them to shoot at the men exiting the barracks, and soon the deadly arrows caused the flow of men coming out to slow to a trickle.

Lord Blythe stepped outside the main residence and into the castle courtyard to a scene he was not expecting. Sir Penn, still adjusting his skirt armor, stepped out of the cool castle residence and into the bright sunlit courtyard behind him. He too was baffled by what he saw. How did the enemy get into the castle? Who was the enemy? What was his lord going to do about it? How was he going to protect his own ass? These were some of the preeminent thoughts in his mind.

Lord Blythe made a very quick, very insightful review of the situation. The enemy didn't seem to number more than a hundred. They'd taken one of the two gatehouses, and their archers had his troops pinned down.

"Dog's bollocks, it's the troublesome Langs," Lord Blythe mumbled as he looked atop the gatehouse. The dragon standard fluttered unmistakably above the gatehouse. *I need more men*, he thought as he surveyed the havoc wrought by Lang's archers.

His men still held three of the four towers, and it appeared that the enemy did not have his numbers, but their archers were deadly. His men could not get out of their barracks because of the damn longbows, but he had peasants to spare in the village. He needed fodder for the archers, so his trained men could advance behind them.

"Light the cauldrons," Blythe shouted.

Guards ran to the large iron pots on the ramparts. The barrels, holding a mixture of oil, quicklime, and sulfur, were lit. Black smoke billowed up from the pots and out above the castle walls. The signal was to summon the troops quartered in town.

With the Yorkists hiding from the archers and Simon's men not having the numbers to storm the barracks, the courtyard fell silent. From a distance, the noise of shouting men could be heard.

Hundreds of men came up the castle's slope and poured into the gatehouse that faced the town. Peasants entered the courtyard like a levee had broken, carrying knives, pitchforks, axes, spears, and sticks. Simon's archers could no longer cover the garrison doors without shooting the peasants, so the Yorkist knights and men-at-arms spilled out of the building and moved amongst them. Realizing that Simon's men were not firing on the peasants, the Yorkist men at arms advanced on the gatehouse within the mob.

Simon had to think fast. If he killed men from Exeter, he would be sunk. He climbed to the top of the gatehouse and yanked his family's dragon pennant from its perch. He held it aloft over the uneasy, packed courtyard, swallowed hard, and in his best West Country accent—one that he'd actually lost years ago— he shouted, "Men of Exeter, my family's banner has flown above this castle for a century."

As he started speaking, Duncan's outnumbered Welshmen listened intently, hoping to hear some words that would not require them to face five hundred angry English peasants along with some clearly professional Yorkist soldiers. Killing the English, stealing their livestock, and pillaging their villages was fun. Facing their revenge was not.

"It is time for the Langs to return to their rightful place." Simon's West Country accent got thicker by the second. He was pandering to the crowd, and they were eating it up.

Sneaky bastard, Blythe thought. Lord Blythe, fully aware that his life and property hung in the balance, also brought his full faculties of claptrap to bear. "Citizens of Exeter," he interrupted Simon, bestowing all the trappings of a republican Rome or democratic Athens on his impoverished, indentured listeners. "You are faced with a decision to uphold your vows and defend your liege lord for the good of England. Or you can surrender your land to a foreign invasion!"

Simon, realizing he had met a politician almost equally adept in the arts of bullshit as himself, decided that he had better raise his game. Not necessarily his bullshit game, because that could go on forever, and with all the Yorkist men-at-arms slowly making their way forward among the peasants, they might tire of the crap flowing from his mouth and do something drastic.

"Lord Blythe," Simon shouted down from the gate, "this castle is my birthright. It is you who are the invader here. I grew up scrubbing decks with some of the people I see here in this crowd." Simon didn't really recognize anyone in the crowd in particular, but he thought it could be true. Regardless, it had the desired effect: some nods from the peasants. "You were illegally bequeathed this land by a murderer of children who is now lying dead among the worms in

Leicester. What will become of these people and their lands if King Henry decides to punish you for your support of Richard?"

The crowd murmured loudly, and Lord Blythe looked around uneasily.

Now was about as good a chance as Simon was going to get. "I challenge you to a duel, Lord Blythe. The winner takes all, and the loser meets his maker. And by the looks of it, your maker was a four-assed sheep." Sheep jokes were always popular with the English.

Without waiting for an answer, Simon walked quickly down and out of the gatehouse, out into the courtyard, and right into the middle of the peasant mob. Maurice and his sons moved into the mob with him to show that Simon had the support of at least some of the locals.

Simon clapped Maurice's shoulder. "This man next to me used to be the master of the docks. He would whip my backside when he didn't think I was working hard enough. I am a man of Exeter, like these men around me, and I'm willing to show that a man of Exeter does not need to cower behind his men or ask them to die for him when he himself is too cowardly to do the same. I also promise you this: none of your men will be harmed after I fillet you." Simon drew his sword. "What say you?"

The peasants were now enjoying themselves and getting into the spirit of things. Audience participation started off with a couple of peasants shouting 'hear, hear.' But soon, a crescendo of likeminded mutterings echoed across the courtyard.

Lord Blythe knew he had no choice. *That bastard is clever.* The crowd had either turned against him, or at best, were willing to watch him fight a duel.

"Of course, I'll fight you, you little prick, and when I'm done, I'm going to hang *your* men from the walls for crow sport."

The crowd separated between the two combatants.

Simon strode purposefully forward. He didn't circle or feint to judge Lord Blythe's strengths and weaknesses. In two motions, Simon batted away Lord Blythe's low guard and ran his exquisitely sharp Arai steel blade straight through Lord Blythe's mouth. Blood gurgled out of Lord Blythe's mouth, and he slowly collapsed to his knees.

While the crowd absorbed what had turned out to be a very anticlimactic fight, some Yorkist soldiers climbed aboard the nearest horses and rode out the south gate.

Simon watched the horsemen fleeing and turned to the crowd. "Men of Lord Blythe, leave my land and go back to your homes in the north." The Yorkist soldiers did not wait to hear any more of the speech, choosing instead to leave with their heads intact before someone changed their minds or before the villagers got ideas of their own.

"Men of Exeter, I thank you for your hospitable welcome." The weapon-laden crowd laughed at Simon's joke. "I'm sorry to have awakened you so early. As a token of my gratitude I invite you all to feast, but not tonight. Pardon the delay, but I need to get the Yorkist smell out of my castle first. Now please go back to your homes and put away your weapons."

Simon looked around, and the peasants stood firm, no one budged.

"You have to tell the people an exact date," Maurice said in a whisper.

"On the Twelfth Night, on the eve of Epiphany, come to the castle for festivities," Simon told the assembled audience. A decidedly unsatisfied murmur emanated from the crowd, surprising Simon.

"You don't want to be doing that, sir. The town folk want another festival to enjoy, and that one's already a big one," Maurice said quietly.

Simon stood thinking a little longer.

"St. Fillan's Day," Maurice mumbled.

"They don't already celebrate that one?" Simon whispered the question out of the corner of his mouth. *Whoever the hell St. Fillan is,* he thought.

"I doubt they've bloody heard of that random Scottish saint, but it gives you until January nineteenth to try and scrape the coin together for a proper feast."

"We shall celebrate on the day of the feast of St. Fillan!" Simon announced with gusto.

The crowd erupted with a large roar and then ambled back to their hovels, each one questioning the other about who St. Fillan was and when his "day" would be.

Simon stood gazing at the red stone castle. He was back home, at last. It hadn't changed much.

"So who the devil is this St. Fillan anyway?" Simon asked Maurice curiously. "And would a feast involving beer be proper to honor him?"

"I don't really know who he was, but he was born in bleedin' Ireland and buried in Scotland. I should think if we don't have alcohol, he'd be apt to climb out of his grave and give you a good talking to."

Exeter, January 19, 1486

There was big news from London that Simon decided to save for the feast. He invited his cousin and his men to stay for the feast, and being too polite to turn down free food and drink, they all complied.

Neno couldn't believe that he was now a landowner. Being a member of the landowning class seemed to calm his notorious temper considerably. He hadn't gotten into a single fight in the Exeter taverns all month.

Aldo couldn't believe Neno was a landowner either. he'd had to promote Seaman Aversa to first mate temporarily, though he was sure Neno would find a way to bankrupt himself soon enough.

Kojiro thought the countryside of England was beautiful. He enjoyed riding Kuro down to the coast and fishing in the streams that meandered across the rich farmlands. He caught salmon and trout from the rivers and for the most part prepared his own meals. He prepared his own meals because he could not get used to the English standards of cleanliness. Of course, he was too polite to tell them that; after all, he liked the English. To keep busy, he had started teaching sword and hand-to-hand combat in the castle during the day and at night he advised Simon on governing matters. Simon even appeared to be maturing.

Simon, with Kojiro's counsel, proved to be an able administrator, and in less than a month, the town was functioning smoothly. Trade income nearly doubled, so when it came time for the feast, which he hosted in the expansive castle courtyard, the local population came in high spirits. Simon hired musicians, minstrels, jesters, and jugglers. He had oval pavilion tents erected in the courtyard to shield everyone from the constant light, cold drizzle that came with living near the English coast. Simon had casks of English ale, unhopped, and beer, hopped, from the best brewers in the country brought in.

Aldo returned to Exeter for the occasion and brought a magnificent variety of wines from across the globe, including the champagne that he was becoming very fond of. By the time food started to come from the kitchens, the entire courtyard was in good spirits and headed quickly towards inebriation.

Simon figured he'd better give his toast while people could still remember what he said. "Aldo, do you have any more of that champagne?"

"I'm afraid not, my friend. We just finished the last bottle, but I have a wonderful white wine from the Chablis region just south of Champagne."

Aldo produced a glass and handed it to Simon. "I think you will appreciate the taste of this. It is delightfully frisky with a grassy aroma. You will notice that chardonnay grapes from this region give it a magnificent deep yellow color with green hues."

Simon took the glass. "That will do nicely, thank you."

"My pleasure."

Simon stood and ordered the musicians to be silent. "People of Exeter, thank you for coming to my humble party."

The crowd roared and clapped. Simon waited for the appreciation to die down.

"In fact, I am truly honored by your presence and awed to be back in my home once again." More cheers. "I have been too long in exile and too long away from the people who raised me." And with that he turned and looked at Maurice, who sat beside him in a place of honor at the head of the table. The crowd was on its feet now.

"I ask you all to raise your cups with me," Simon continued, "as I drink to you, the people of Exeter." He raised his glass and drained it, as did the entire feasting population.

"Interesting," Simon said looking at his wine glass. "An acquired taste, perhaps."

"Absolutely, but the taste grows on you," Aldo said as he filled another glass for Simon.

The lord of Rougemont Castle looked around at his guests. "And one more toast before I leave you to enjoy your cups freely."

The crowd pounded on their tables for more alcohol as servants quickly refilled their cups.

"I received the news yesterday that our King, Henry VII, was wed to Elizabeth of York on January 18." The crowd gasped, and the courtyard became utterly silent except for the tapping drizzle on the roof of the tents. "The houses of York and Lancaster are now one. You will no longer be asked to send your sons and husbands to slaughter fellow Englishmen because their family coat of arms bears a different color rose."

And with that statement, Simon looked to the village seamstress. He'd paid her a handsome amount of silver to work overnight with her daughters on his project. Proudly, the seamstress, a woman of Irish extract, widowed when her husband died fighting for the Lancastrians at Tewkesbury, unfurled her embroidered cloth from a six-foot pole.

The crowd stared in sober appreciation of what they were viewing: a white rose embedded within a red rose, a symbol that would have been heresy less than a year before.

"People of Exeter, this is King Henry's new standard. Raise your cups to the Tudor rose."

The crowd, now solemn as they contemplated an end to the English civil war, a war that had taken the lives of so many they knew, raised their beer, ale, wine, and mead cups more slowly than they had the time before, but at the same time more earnestly; hands clenched mugs so tightly fingertips turned white and tears dripped from all but the most stoic of men. Simon drained his cup, and the crowd followed with him.

As the revelers erupted into conversation about the unprecedented joining of the houses of York and Lancaster, Simon turned to Aldo. "That wine doesn't get any better; in fact, it gets horribly worse and leaves a rather salty aftertaste."

"Well, it would. It *is* horse piss."

Simon stared in shock. "You said it was Chablis."

"No, my dear friend, I said, I *have* a wonderful French wine from Chablis. I didn't say that I was giving you the Chablis."

"Bastard!" Simon said as he looked around frantically for anything to wash his mouth out with, while Maurice, Duncan, Neno, and Kojiro practically fell out of their seats in laughter.

"If you recall, you served me a live grasshopper at dinner once."

"That was over two years ago!"

"We Venetians are known for our *vendetta*."

"I could just as likely have died before you got your revenge."

"And yet, you did not."

Simon grabbed a flagon of beer from a servant and guzzled the whole thing. "Christ in a whorehouse, remind me not to play jokes on you again." Simon grinned in appreciation at the fine revenge even as he searched for another flagon.

Aldo grasped a rosary bead and began his familiar routine of praying for Simon's soul.

The night carried on, and Exeter woke up with probably the most widespread hangover since the Vandals sacked Rome. Aldo returned to Venice, but made Exeter a major stop for his substantial trading fleet.

Soon the docks of Topsham, at the mouth of the River Exe, managed by an old goat named Maurice, became one of the busiest ports of entry into England for goods from around the world. Maurice, earning a more than comfortable living as trade manager at the docks, bequeathed the Pig and Whistle Pub to Maureen.

Maureen turned the Pig and Whistle into a warm and welcoming rest stop, famous throughout the West Country. Maureen stopped having sex for money and started having sex with Neno, who proved to be nearly as experienced in bed as she was.

Neno needed the iron-fisted rule of Maureen, and since she did not allow him to gamble, he still had the lands that King Henry bequeathed him. Maureen did not, however, place any limitations on his other two vices: alcohol and sex with her.

Simon's cousin Duncan returned to Wales with Simon's thanks and a nice chunk of Simon's nutmeg money.

Simon rode to the coast nearly every day, and nearly every day wished he could once again pilot a boat to foreign lands, but the responsibilities of governance did not allow it. He had to act like an actual adult. Of course, maintaining this adulthood required a stern lecture from Kojiro every month about responsibility, loyalty, honor, and blah, blah, blah, but Simon put a brave face on it and listened to his mentor.

Kojiro had his good and bad days. It was not always easy to live in a country that was not one's own. Some days the mannerisms and customs of the English made him desire to pull his hair out, and some days he just longed to see the *sakura* in bloom once again. On these bad days, however, he had discovered that fishing the streams of his property did wonders for soothing his soul. Initially, he had accepted the property with reluctance, but he gradually warmed to it as it became clear that the method of his service to Simon was different from that he had given to his daimyo in what seemed a lifetime ago. His daimyo had required his sword and his obedience and little else. Simon required his counsel and friendship more than he had ever had need of his sword. The political intrigues of England had proven to be every bit as complicated and deadly as those of Kyoto. The fact that Simon still had the attention span of a gnat annoyed him at times, but Simon had integrity and courage, and Kojiro did not regret his decision to follow the *gaijin* to this far-off land.

Kuro wondered when the next war would come.

27502686R10227

Made in the USA
Middletown, DE
19 December 2018